PAST
CONTINUOUS

YAAKOV

SHABTAI

PAST
CONTINUOUS

TRANSLATED BY DALYA BILU

SCHOCKEN BOOKS NEW YORK

Library of Congress Cataloging-in-Publication Data
Shabtai, Yaakov.
Past continuous.
Translation of: Zikhron devarim.
I. Title.
PJ5054.S2643Z3313   1989   892.4'36   88-42651
ISBN 0-8052-0868-2

Manufactured in the United States of America

PAST
CONTINUOUS

PAST
CONTINUOUS

Goldman's father died on the first of April, whereas Goldman himself committed suicide on the first of January—just when it seemed to him that finally, thanks to the cultivation of detachment and withdrawal, he was about to enter a new era and rehabilitate himself by means of the "Bullworker" and a disciplined way of life, and especially by means of astronomy and the translation of the *Somnium.*

The only one to notice the peculiar connection between the date of Goldman's death and that of his father's was Caesar, who even remarked on it a few days after Goldman's funeral while standing in the kitchen with Israel, who was making them both a cup of tea—but he mentioned it only as an anecdote without any significance, because by then he had thrown in the towel and was no longer prepared to make the slightest effort not connected with his own immediate needs.

In the desperate process of his decline, as he continued dressing in fashionable, flamboyant clothes, cultivating his moustache, smoking the most expensive brand of cigarettes, eating voraciously, and pursuing every woman who crossed his path—while the burden of his thoughts and vestiges of his will power were concentrated on his eldest son, who had fallen hopelessly ill with an incurable disease, Caesar could only see life as a crushing, meaningless defeat or as a freakish joke to be enjoyed as much as possible—a view he would refer to painfully in the moments of soberness and remorse which occasionally descended on him as "swinging suicide."

The only person who would undoubtedly have tried to decipher the hidden meanings behind this curious combination of dates was Goldman himself, but he was already dead.

The truth is, of course, that there were no hidden meanings—except for the kind which Ruhama, Caesar's stepsister, would mockingly have referred to as "literary": i.e., that at the beginning of the new year, as at the beginning of every new year and in fact at the beginning of almost every day, Goldman, who could not endure the experience of "being-in-the-world," had decided to turn over a new leaf in his life—which in this particular instance meant the absolute liberation from it and the transition to a new way of life, or to use his own expression: "a different mode of being" possessing absolute freedom and complete certainty, in which he tried to believe despite his skepticism and the devotion to rationalism from which he had never swerved, except for a certain period when he had made unsuccessful attempts to become religious, denying both his rationalist creed and his socialist theories. In the case of Goldman's father, Ephraim, on the other hand, the fact that he had died on the first of April might perhaps

be seen as a kind of practical joke, since practical jokes were the only type of humor it was possible to associate with him, except for the crude but amusing conjuring tricks which he had once, in rare moments of high spirits, enjoyed performing but which had long ago been forgotten.

As for Ephraim's wife Regina, who began calling herself Stefana a few days after the funeral, she saw his death as an act of malice and vindictiveness, not because he had chosen to die on the first of April, which was no longer the first of April anyway as far as she was concerned, but because on this particular first of April a terrible heat wave had descended, giving her advance notice of the summer she hated, and it continued without abating the next day too, the day of the funeral, and even grew worse, until it seemed that the whole shimmering town was about to disintegrate in the scorching air and turn into a cloud of fine dust which would float slowly away on the burning wind and disperse in the empty silver sky from whose center the blazing sun spread its terrible heat—a heat which did not let up all night long, so that Israel, who had succeeded in falling asleep only after taking a shower and standing for hours on the balcony looking at the dark deserted streets, woke before dawn and spent most of the day lying flat on his back in his room in Caesar's studio, on the narrow couch covered in a coarse, thick material made of woven brown wool.

When dawn turned swiftly to morning he rose and sat down at the piano intending to continue work on the "Goldberg Variations," but he started playing Prokofiev's *Sarcasms* carelessly from memory instead until, overcome by the heat and his own weakness, he gave up in despair and went back to bed, where his thoughts drifting aimlessly through his head of their own accord somehow seized on Count Kaiserling of Dresden, who had suffered from insomnia, and his harpsichord player Johann Gottlieb Goldberg, and he began playing with these names in his head without thinking about what he was doing, and they joined together in various combinations in one monotonous stream Johann Goldberg Gottlieb Dresden Kaiserling Goldberg Golden Johann Kaiserling Gottlieb Dresden Gottlieb Johann Kaiser Johann Gottberg Gottling Liberg Johann Dresden Golden while his eyes crept like a spider's over the mirrors in which he saw his own reflection, and over the ceiling with its dusty neon light, and over the colored photographs—of snow-covered mountains and lakes and green trees and fancy cars and sexy tanned girls in bathing suits or naked—which were stuck to the dirty white walls and the wide door separating his room from the one next to it.

Some of these photographs had been taken by Caesar himself, and it was Caesar who had stuck them all up with drawing pins or bits of Scotch tape: They refreshed his spirits and at the same time provided frank and boastful evidence of his lusts and the lack of inhibitions which he had in some measure inherited from his father, Erwin, and in some measure cultivated deliberately as part of the way of life he was proud of leading so tirelessly and demonstratively.

The only exception was a picture-postcard which Ella had brought for Israel and had taped to the top front corner of the piano: a reproduction of a section of El Greco's *St. Francis* all in shades of green, portraying a tall thin man whose elongated and black-bearded face was very serious, perhaps even solemn, kneeling on the ground in a heavy kind of monk's habit and holding a skull which he was showing to the boy kneeling in front of him, very close but lower down, also wearing a monk's habit and with his head, like that of the grown man, hooded in a cowl, and his hands clasped before his chest as if he were praying and his eyes gazing up at the skull in wonder and awe, while the older monk looked at him with an expression which was calm, sober, and above all, resigned.

A white sunbeam, penetrating the slats of the southern blind facing the street, fell onto the postcard, and Israel, waking, bathed in perspiration from a deep sleep, looked blankly at the boy and the man and the skull and listened to Caesar's footsteps as he ran up the steps and flung open the door of the studio and came into the room dressed in purple pants and a shiny orange shirt, with his big face flushed and shining and dripping with sweat and his spirits high and his little eyes under his thick eyebrows darting behind the dirty lenses of his glasses like two happy mice.

After removing the heavy camera from his neck he asked Israel if there had been any calls for him, and Israel said that Tehilla had called and said she would call again in the evening, and Caesar said, "And Eliezra?" and looked expectantly at Israel, who went on lying on his side and said without moving, "No, she didn't call." Caesar said, "Bitch," and took a packet of Rothman's out of his pocket and lit himself a cigarette and announced, almost triumphantly, the news which Israel had already heard the day before and which Caesar himself had already called to tell him earlier that morning—that Goldman's father was dead and the funeral procession was leaving the Municipal Funeral Parlor at two o'clock.

Israel said nothing, and for a moment there was a silence which Caesar, who kept wiping the sweat from his face and neck with a wet handkerchief and irritating Israel by dropping his cigarette ash on the floor, broke by asking Israel what he thought of the old man's death. Without waiting for a reply from Israel, who could not stop himself from glancing at the little heap of ashes beginning to drift over the floor, he added that it was already half past one and they had better get a move on, and Israel, sitting on the edge of the couch, asked whether they couldn't possibly skip the funeral and make do with a condolence call at Goldman's house instead—especially since both of them were well aware of the nature of Goldman's relations with his father, as well as the fact that Goldman set no store by, and even detested, religious ceremonies, and would have been only too happy to stay away from his own father's funeral if he possibly could, never mind the funeral of one of his friends' fathers.

But Caesar, who liked all kinds of gatherings and celebrations and calamities and dramatic events, insisted that it was their duty to attend the funeral, since the nature of Goldman's relations with his father was irrelevant, especially now that his father was already dead, and despite Goldman's negative attitude toward religious ceremonies and his rationalism he, Caesar, had no doubt at all that in his heart of hearts he would never forgive them if they stayed away and left him alone with his mother at his father's funeral. In this connection he also remarked that there were limits to the reason and logic of the most logical person in the world, and that life often forced us to do things that were not only illogical but also unpleasant, and in the end he said that at any rate he was going to the funeral no matter what, alone if need be, and urged Israel to get up and go with him.

Israel got up and went poker-faced to the bathroom to wash, cursing Caesar and himself and Goldman's father, whose death had caused him no sorrow or pity or even surprise, since he had been lying in a hospital in a coma for nearly two weeks after a sudden brain hemorrhage, and the doctors had predicted his death.

From time to time he would regain consciousness and make some demand or mutter something angrily, and once he had even proclaimed painfully to Goldman, slurring the ends of his words in a very hoarse and hollow voice which was no longer his own and sounded as if it was coming out of dark, empty clay pipes: "I think I've done something in my life." Goldman had nodded slightly at his father who, now that he was lying helplessly on his deathbed, gave rise in him to feelings of compassion, but above all to a feeling of uneasiness, partly because of his appearance but mainly because in the depths of his heart, even now, he bore him a grudge.

The doctors attached no importance to these brief spells of consciousness on the part of Goldman's father and advised the family to "prepare for the worst," and Regina, whom Goldman's father in one such moment of consciousness demanded be kept away from his bedside, did indeed "prepare for the worst" until it came and she breathed a sigh of relief—he was dead and no power on earth could bring him back to life again.

Twice Israel had accompanied Goldman when he went to visit his father in the hospital, and once he had even gone into the room where the old man lay stiff as a corpse, wrapped in a white blanket and attached to all kinds of tubes, with his wide-open eyes, which were always pinkish like those of a rabbit, now white and clouded and expressionless and his face, which had turned a bluish-gray, swollen and distorted.

Goldman sat down on the edge of the bed and placed his hand near his father's shoulder, and for a moment he even touched him lightly, stroking him without love, while Israel remained standing a little distance away looking at him with indifference and even revulsion, but later on, when he and Goldman had left the hospital and were walking in the street, and on the following days too, and after the old man died, the memory of the sight depressed him profoundly because of the impotence and estrangement he sensed everywhere and because of the ugly, unavoidable extinction awaiting Goldman's father—a depression which, despite Israel's powers of alienation, came back to haunt him in the wake of some chance sight, sound, smell, item of news, or bar of music, and lately especially because of Ella, for whom he had been filled with longing ever since morning, a longing he could not shake off in the emptiness of the time flowing slowly through the stifling heat of the room.

They had met by chance at a movie, and although in the jeans and black sweater she wore underneath her dark green woolen coat she was no different from any other girl, she aroused in him from the first a feeling that she came from some unknown, perhaps even non-existent place—not exactly homeless, but as if she had materialized out of thin air and would disappear into it again one day and no one would ever be able to bring her back, but he didn't tell anyone about this feeling—certainly not Caesar, who went into the second room (which served him as an office and photography studio and was full of chairs, screens, projectors, photography equipment, journals, boxes, rags, and all kinds of junk) humming "Ob-La-Di, Ob-La-Da, Life goes on" to himself, changed the film in his camera, poured himself a glass of whiskey, and went to stand in the doorway to the bathroom where he once again asked Israel, who was washing his face and brushing his hair, if there hadn't been any other calls for him.

Israel said, "No," and Caesar sipped his whiskey and said, "That Goldman deserved to die a long time ago. He earned his death down to the last crumb." Then he added, "Dying at his age is OK. Nobody could ask for more," and looked at Israel, who said nothing but replaced the towel on the rack and went back into his room to get dressed, followed by Caesar, who put the whiskey glass down on the piano, leaned against it, and pulled a white envelope from his shirt pocket, saying, "Look what I've got," and displaying a packet of pornographic photographs of two men and two women—one blonde and one brunette, both with big breasts—fornicating in all kinds of positions, in pairs and all four together.

A gratified expression spread over Caesar's flushed face as he examined the photographs one after the other, sniggering from time to time and commenting briefly or exclaiming admiringly to himself, and occasionally passing one of them to Israel with the remark, "How do you like this little dish?" or, "Take a look at him, the bastard!" When he was finished he let his eyes rest on the last photograph for a moment before returning it to the envelope together with the others, and then he took a sip of whiskey and said, "I like firm legs and big tits, that's what I like," and put the envelope back in his shirt pocket and went into the "darkroom" for a minute and came out again and called to Israel, who was in the bathroom, "Let's get out of here before Goldman's father escapes."

Israel emerged from the bathroom and put on his sandals and Caesar finished the whiskey in his glass and they both went down to the street, which was flooded with white sunlight tearing at their eyes and baking the stifling air, which now smelled of melting asphalt and dust and exhaust fumes mingled with the heavy, sweetish scent of the lilac bushes and oleanders which seemed to have bloomed overnight. The heat and the glare coming from the white-hot sky and the pavements and the walls were so terrible that it seemed as if giant bonfires were blazing underneath the thin skin of the earth and that even the tiniest birds had been smitten and died on the branches of the motionless trees, and Israel, momentarily dazzled, said, "What a hell," and went on walking next to Caesar, who was carrying his camera around his neck and singing, "Ob-La-Di, Ob-La-Da" to himself, repeating the same words over and over again and singing out of tune without any consideration at all.

They were going to the bus stop because Caesar's car had broken down and had been standing in the garage for two days already, but on the way Caesar asked if they could stop for a minute because he wanted to call Vicky, so they went into a cafe and Caesar dialed three times without getting a reply and banged the receiver down, saying, "Bitch," but later on, when they left the cafe, he smiled and said, "She's fantastic, that little Vicky, only it's a pity she's getting married." He said this in a mildly complaining tone but without any real anxiety, because on the one hand he felt that Vicky belonged to him, in the same way that anything that gave him pleasure and that he wanted belonged to him and thus could not possibly suddenly belong to anyone else, and on the other hand because he was convinced that even after she got married they would go on entertaining each other in secret with quick and enjoyable encounters in bed, since in the last analysis Caesar was unwilling to imagine, and also incapable of imagining, that good things could ever come to an end.

The only thing that had given him any cause for anxiety lately was the fact that he was going bald, a condition from which he had begun to suffer seriously and which he fought with the help of all kinds of soaps and cosmetic preparations and massages. Although his hair kept on falling out, he refused to give up and even now, when they were already standing at the bus stop, he ran into the drugstore across the street and bought two bottles of Jochem's Hormoon, a preparation he had begun using about two weeks before containing an active hormonal ingredient against premature baldness.

In the meantime the bus arrived and Caesar ran out and jumped on, with Israel behind him, and paid for both of them. He was very animated, but it was precisely this animation which gave rise to Israel's growing irritation—an irritation which Caesar failed to notice, both because Israel's face remained expressionless and because Caesar could think of nothing but himself and his own affairs, and the moment they sat down he began talking enthusiastically about Jochem's Hormoon, which according to the prospectus attached to the bottle had been discovered after fourteen years of experimentation and research and was capable of preventing baldness absolutely at any stage, even the most advanced, as had been proved in the case of the famous Dutch boxer Bef van Cleeveren, the back view of whose prematurely balding head was prominently displayed in two pictures—before and after the treatment with Jochem's Hormoon—in the middle of the prospectus, and after that he talked about the photographs he had taken that morning in a canning factory, and after that he said that he couldn't understand why Eliezra hadn't called.

Preoccupied by this question, and also by the fact that Tehilla had said she might call again in the evening, he fell silent and lit a cigarette and sunk into thought, but after a moment he turned to Israel and said, "When Tehilla calls tell her I've gone to Jerusalem and I'll be back tomorrow," and Israel said, "All right," and looked out of the dusty window of the bus at the shops and the passersby and at the movie theater standing in the place where he had once, when he was a child and it was still a big empty lot, seen Goldman's father in a cloth cap and sweaty overalls pushing a wheelbarrow and laying the foundations of the building together with the other workers.

Then too the air was full of the scent of lilac and oleander flowers and the sky was cloudless, only then it was a rich blue and the air was fresh and mild, even a little cool, like it was on the autumn day at twilight when Goldman's father had dragged Kaminskaya's black dog by the leash and tied it to the water pipe in the big yard of the house where they lived. In everything that had happened then there was a dark violence and a boundless terror, and in the mild air there was a gentle, velvety calm and the birds which had made their nests in the branches of the lilac trees and the cypresses and the jacaranda, and in the branches of the giant ficus tree and the poinsettia regia, which had already begun to shed its leaves and its red flowers, and in the corners of the water pipes, in the shelter of the bougainvillea, warbled full-throatedly as if they were celebrating a holiday, filling the courtyard with a loud, cheerful din, and Kaminskaya herself— God knows what she was up to!—blonde, tall, striking, wild and drunk, with her frightened green eyes and thick sensual lips— maybe she was making love to her retired balletmaster, whom everyone called Diaghelev, or to the young painter often seen in her company, or to someone else, even the plumber or someone she hardly knew, and maybe she was reading or sleeping, since her timetable was confused and haphazard, and her days were indistinguishable from her nights—a fact which infuriated Goldman's father, who believed fanatically in a world order with good and bad and no neutral ground between them, and fixed times for everything and getting up in the morning no later than seven or at the very latest eight, but that Kaminskaya was so wild and drunk that in the war she came down to the shelter on more than one occasion in her bra and panties, and so capricious and sad that sometimes she would sing in the middle of the night like a madwoman, as if she wanted to tear the darkness to shreds and sail to places beyond the limits of the sky on the waves of anguished longings that were in her and in the Russian words and tunes and for which she found an outlet in her singing. All in all she was so lost and despairing that she sometimes tried to find salvation even in viciousness or lies or obscenities, but Goldman's father refused to forgive her and he hated her and her ways and the songs she sang and the clothes she wore and her black dog, which she called Nuit Sombre and which stood quietly tied to the water pipe looking at Goldman's father, whose face was white as a sheet and tense with fright and wickedness.

Nuit Sombre even wagged his tail, because of course he couldn't have guessed that Goldman's father was going to kill him in a couple of seconds, but Goldman's father approached him and suddenly pulled a builder's hammer out of his shirt and brought it down swiftly and furiously on his head, and Nuit Sombre made a queer moaning sound and swayed, and Goldman's father yelled at the top of his voice, "Let him die! Let him die! He has to die!" and went on hitting the dog like a madman until he sank to the ground with his head all shattered and crushed. Nuit Sombre went on twitching for a little longer, making a feeble rattling sound in his throat, until he lay still, and the earth and leaves of the verbena and hibiscus bushes which were still in flower and the water pipe and walls of the house were spattered with splinters of bone and blood and bits of brain, which remained there until the first rains fell and washed them away.

After he had killed Nuit Sombre, Goldman's father hurried to wash the hammer, his hands and whole body shaking, and then he put the dog's body into a sack and carried it off and threw it far away in one of the big uncultivated fields covered with thorns and brambles and weeds, stretching as far as the orange groves and sabra hedges of the Arab villages, which disappeared a few years later together with the uncultivated fields and the cultivated plots and the melon patches and vineyards and the little eucalyptus glade and the jackals which devoured Nuit Sombre's carcass— disappeared because of the new buildings going up on them one after the other, and the city streets along one of which the bus made its way toward the last stop, where Caesar and Israel got off and walked with some other people to the Municipal Funeral Parlor while Caesar, perspiring freely, spoke about Eliezra and said that he hoped she would come to the funeral, but by herself, because he had no desire to meet her husband, Gidon, especially not on such a hot day.

Israel said nothing, and Caesar remarked that heat stimulated the sexual instinct and went on talking about Eliezra, saying that she was just wasting her life with that Gidon, who was incapable of satisfying her sexually and had nothing to him apart from pretty curls and English and a little book learning and boring kind-heartedness, and he continued in this vein until they arrived at the courtyard of the Funeral Parlor, which was swarming with people who had come to pay their last respects to the dead and accompany them on their final journey.

Some of the mourners were walking up and down the courtyard as they waited, and others were huddled in little groups, discussing the deceased and their diseases, families and next of kin, the heat, politics and business. Sounds of weeping, groaning and nose-blowing rose intermittently here and there, and on one of the walls large bronze letters proclaimed: "The days of a man are as grass,/As a flower of the field so he flourisheth." Caesar and Israel, who had paused at the entrance to the courtyard to look for familiar faces in the crowd, were gradually, almost unconsciously, swept up in it and absorbed by it, and Caesar readied his camera and began taking photographs of the mourners while hidden loudspeakers blared the name of the deceased whose funeral party was about to depart, and at the same moment the crowd began to move—some drawing nearer and huddling closer together, and others stepping aside to make way for the men bearing the black stretcher with the corpse of the deceased, followed by his next of kin, relatives, friends, acquaintances, and neighbors. Caesar photographed the stretcher-bearers and the dead man and his weeping wife and family in rapid succession, and he went on taking photographs until the procession left the courtyard and the black car into which they hoisted the stretcher departed for the cemetery.

In the meantime the loudspeaker announced the name of the next dead person, but this one too was not Goldman's father, nor was the next one. Israel felt himself filling with rage as he stood sweating and sweltering in the commotion of people coming and going, and in the end he turned to Caesar, who was still taking photographs, and said, "I'm getting out of here," but Caesar said, "Wait a minute. I'll fix everything," and went to find out what had happened to Goldman's father. A few minutes later he returned with the news that the funeral had departed long before and said, "Come on," and Israel asked, "Where to?" and Caesar said, "To Kiryat Shaul," and smiled at Israel, who said nothing but wished that the earth would open and swallow the whole world, including himself and Caesar, who said again, "Come on, we're wasting time," and strode rapidly out of the courtyard toward the bus stop to wait for the bus to Kiryat Shaul.

Israel really wanted to go back home to the studio and take a shower and play the piano and wait for Ella, but he followed Caesar to the bus stop and stood next to him, his face stiff with rage, letting himself be burned by the rays of the sun beating mercilessly down from the empty silver sky where a light haze hung, while Caesar took the opportunity of glancing at the Jochem's Hormoon prospectus again and re-examining the head of the famous Dutch boxer. Suddenly he smiled and said, "Liars," and put the prospectus back in his pocket. Then he cursed the owner of the garage where he had left his car to be repaired and also the burial customs of the Jews, praising the burial customs of the Romans, who according to him had cremated their dead and preserved their ashes in beautiful urns which they displayed at the entrance to their homes, and saying that he too would leave instructions in his will to have his body cremated, only in his case he wanted his ashes to be scattered to the winds, and Israel— who had never really understood why Goldman's father had killed Nuit Sombre on that autumn day at twilight—looked at the eucalyptus tree on the other side of the street and continued to hold his tongue.

He and Hanoch Leviatan, Avinoam and Sonia's younger brother who had been in his class at school and had died two years later of pneumonia, hid behind the myrtle bushes in the shade of the big cypress trees which gave off a marvelous smell and watched the terrible thing happening a few feet away from them, Hanoch shaking like a leaf while he, Israel, stood turned to stone until Goldman's father disappeared with the dog's body, and then he vomited and vomited, and afterward he washed his mouth and face and went upstairs with all the strength drained out of him.

Some of the neighbors said that Goldman's father had killed Nuit Sombre because the dog used to bark at night and wake him up, and others said that he killed him because keeping a dog in those times, in his opinion, was not only wicked and selfish but also corrupt—and he was not alone in this opinion, because the times were hard, not long after the War of Independence, and Goldman's mother and father, like most of their neighbors and the rest of the inhabitants of the town, spent their days and nights, which were sometimes unbearably hot and sometimes cold and rainy, standing endlessly in the lines outside the grocer's and greengrocer's and butcher's and fishmonger's, only to go home after hours of waiting and shoving worn out and humilated with a wretched little piece of meat, one or two soup bones, a couple of eggs, or a few onions and potatoes, and even these things were frequently obtained only after humiliating begging or loud arguments accompanied by the exchange of insults and even, sometimes, of blows.

It was the Second World War all over again and now, as then, Goldman's father refused to exploit his connections or buy a single grain of rice on the black market, and for most of the week his family subsisted on a diet of black bread that tasted of bran and smelled of jute sacking, halves of eggs, white cheese that seemed to be made of flour, herrings, and a soup made of brown noodles boiled in milk diluted with water and sweetened with brown sugar mixed with sand—a dish which was usually served up as their main course at dinner, while Kaminskaya was said to feed Nuit Sombre on the finest salami and Swiss cheese and to give him French cognac and English beer to drink, and so did her lovers—the retired balletmaster, the young painter, an architect who lived with her for a few months, a gym teacher, and for a certain period even Caesar's father, Erwin.

In any event, there is no doubt that Goldman's father passed sentence on Nuit Sombre for what seemed to him compelling reasons and killed him only after it had become clear that he had to die, and even if it had been his own dog he wouldn't have behaved any differently, because he was a Zionist and a Socialist and believed in plain living, hard work, morality, and progress, in the most elementary sense of the words, and hated right-wing nationalists, people who got rich or wasted money on luxuries, and people who told lies about Eretz Yisrael, and all this as part of a system of clear, fixed, uncompromising principles embracing every area of life and action, which he never doubted for an instant despite all the external changes and difficulties, and from which he saw no reason to deviate in the slightest degree.

He knew what was right and good, not only for himself but also for others, and could not tolerate error or sin, and for him every error, beginning with the breaking of a cup or the ill-considered purchase of a pair of shoes and ending with stealing or adultery, was a sin, and despite his own inherent generosity and even sentimentality he could not bring himself to forgive anyone, even his own family or friends, because his integrity verged on insanity and his sense of justice was dark and murky, and above all because he had a tyrannical, uncontrollable desire to impose his principles on the whole world, which went heedlessly along its different, lawless ways, leaving Goldman's father battling between disappointment and rage. There were always people who didn't know what was good for them and people who made mistakes, never mind those who actually sinned, often consciously, and in the end everyone violated the proper order of things, everyone, that is, except him, since he was the representative of this order, and accordingly he never knew a single hour of peace of mind, and his whole life, which was full of hostility and humiliation, passed in denunciations and accusations and arguments. Because of his principles he succeeded in quarreling with almost all his friends and acquaintances, and those he did not quarrel with he ostracized and drove from the house— all except Joseph Leviatan, Avinoam and Sonia and Hanoch's father—surrounding himself with a protective wall of loneliness, but by virtue of these same principles he also succeeded in overcoming his loneliness and his disappointments and his despair when his daughter Naomi, Goldman's older sister, was killed in a traffic accident—according to one version—or committed suicide—according to another version.

He received the news with a terrible outburst of violence and rage, and buried his daughter with a stony face and dry eyes, since in the depths of his heart he had turned his back on her a long time ago, because she was having an affair with a married man, apparently an Englishman at that, and according to his principles she deserved to be punished, and she was punished. It was only at night when he switched off the light and lay down on his bed, which for some years now had been separated from Regina's bed, that he turned his face to the wall and covered his head with the blanket and wept bitterly, but then he recovered and wiped his eyes with the sheet and toward morning fell asleep with his lips tightly clamped together.

Naomi was buried in the cemetery at Nahalat Yizhak. Caesar had once visited her grave some years before, when on Goldman's request he had taken him and his mother there one winter's day to plant tamarisk saplings on it. When they got onto the bus and sat down he mentioned this visit to Israel and said, "It was awful, the mud and the rain, you can't imagine how awful it was." A moment later he said, "She was a wonderful girl, that Naomi, but love is madness, believe me," and he added, "Everyone's getting divorced," and then fell silent until they reached the cemetery at Kiryat Shaul, which was teeming with the multitudes of people who had come to attend the many funeral services taking place there at that time.

People came and went and sat on the benches, tired out by waiting, and stood in little groups and walked here and there in the sweltering heat, and the funeral processions moved past an ugly building whose façade bore the words "All who come into the world assemble here," and coiled like black snakes along the paths between the rows of white tombstones: the cantor first, then the men carrying the deceased on a black stretcher, and then the next of kin, family, and friends.

Caesar lit himself a cigarette and said, "The whole town's

here," and they mingled with the crowd and began looking for Goldman or some familiar face again, and tried to get something out of the cemetery workers, but the latter were preoccupied and hurrying about their business, sweating and impatient, and could tell them nothing about Goldman's father. In the end someone advised them to ask at the cemetery office at the far end of the ritual purification building, and they went around the one-storied building and climbed two steps and knocked on the office door and went inside.

The man in the office, a big man with thick white hands, meticulously attired, received them politely and after listening to Caesar's explanations he examined the list of the deceased lying on the desk in front of him, re-examined it, and said that to his regret no one by the name of Ephraim Goldman had been buried there that day, laying great stress on the word "regret," and Caesar said, "Perhaps yesterday?" and the man said, "Perhaps," and examined another list and said that to his regret, no one by the name of Ephraim Goldman had been buried there yesterday either.

Showing signs of anger, and especially of impatience, for the first time, Caesar said, "That's impossible," and crushed his cigarette out in the ashtray standing on the desk. The man looked at him severely, but controlled himself and said politely, but very firmly this time, that to his regret there could be no doubt whatsoever about the matter, since this was a well-run cemetery and no one could possibly be buried in it by accident, stealth, or oversight without his name appearing on the register, and in the same stern tone of voice he advised them to go to the cemetery at Nahalat Yizhak—perhaps they would find the man they were looking for there.

He concluded his speech in a way that left no room for questions or arguments, wiped his hands and high forehead with a white handkerchief, adjusted his skullcap, drew the ventilator toward him, and turned his attention to the papers lying in front of him on the desk, and Caesar, dismissed, stole a quick look at him and said, "Thank you, sir," and left the office with Israel, his downcast face expressing only resentment and exhaustion, with all the excited anticipation gone.

Altogether Caesar's face now resembled a plate of cold left-over porridge, and Israel looked at him and for a moment thought of suggesting that they return to town, but instead he walked silently behind him as he cleared a path through the crowd of mourners and rude, insistent beggars, and when they emerged from the cemetery gates and started walking down the narrow path bordered by fields and cypress trees and orange groves on one side and gravestone makers' sheds on the other, on their way to the main road to catch a bus or take a cab to Nahalat Yizhak, he decided that even if Caesar begged him on his bended knees he would not agree to go back to town. Caesar did not beg him, however—he lit himself a cigarette and said, "They're all bastards, especially those religious hypocrites," and after a short pause, "You saw that shit in the office? I bet you he's the man from Frankfurter, he looks like him anyway," and Israel said, "You may be right," and Caesar said, "Let him go to hell and take his cemetery with him," and a moment later, "Anyway, the one from Frankfurter was much more human, you can ask Goldman, only his wife fucked him up"—and in fact the man in the office did look a bit like Mr. Herbert of Frankfurter, where Goldman had for many months eaten his dinners after growing sick and tired of the milk-and-noodle soup his mother was obliged to serve him almost every day.

Goldman ate in Frankfurter alone, since at that time Naomi, who was a driver in the British army, was stationed in Alexandria and his father was working mostly in British army camps and came home only on Saturdays, and when he was working in town he made do with the meager repasts provided by his wife Regina, which he ate sullenly by himself in the kitchen when he came home in the evenings, and every day, on his way to the restaurant, Goldman's spirits would rise in anxious anticipation, and when he passed the huge loam field—where they had once played football and which the Red Austrian and his wife had transformed with their tireless labor into a blooming garden in the middle of the city, growing first vegetables and then roses and carnations and snapdragons and gladiolas and daliahs on it, until a few years after the War of Independence the price of land skyrocketed and they liquidated the garden and sold the plot to someone who built a big block of offices with shops and restaurants and a night-club and a movie theater on it—his heart would swell in the expectation of a nice surprise, but the expected surprise never came, because the menu at Frankfurter was always the same: a few slices of black bread, a thin vegetable soup or something that passed for a meat soup with two potato dumplings in it, a pair of sausages with a vegetable, or a concoction called "hoppel-pop-pel" which consisted of a few wretched pieces of gristly polony floating in a reddish liquid, and for dessert, half a glass of lemon pudding with a few sweet red spots in it which Caesar, who joined him from time to time, was crazy about and to tell the truth, it was mainly for the sake of this pudding that he would accompany Goldman and wait patiently until he finished eating.

Mr. and Mrs. Herbert, immigrants from Germany, were both tall, very clean, and imposing looking. Both of them had black eyes and smooth, swarthy skin, and Mrs. Herbert had sturdy legs, thick pretty lips, and black hair drawn back in a bun, while Mr. Herbert, who was always smoothly shaven, wore a black silk skull-cap on his head. They served their customers quietly, willingly, and courteously, and that was how they behaved to each other too, and altogether they seemed like a pair of siblings living to-gether in complete harmony, until one day this harmony was shattered and after an argument which broke out between them Mr. Herbert, his face pale with hatred, began cursing his wife in German and hitting her in the middle of the restaurant, first with his fists and afterward with a polony which he tore down from its hook in his rage. Everything happened so quickly and unex-pectedly that for a moment there was a dead silence among the customers, some of whom, feeling embarrassed and ill at ease, looked down at their plates and went on eating as if nothing had happened while others tried to intervene and calm Mr. Herbert down, but most of them, and also the people who had gathered in the street outside, watched the scene without doing anything, and one man, standing behind Goldman, repeated over and over again, "Stop it. Enough already. You're ruining the polony. There's a war on."

The next day Mrs. Herbert ran off with her lover, who was an Arab, and shortly afterward the restaurant closed down and was turned into a bookshop and stationer's, and after that into a shoe shop, which it remained for a number of years, until it was turned into a restaurant again—although different, of course, from the one owned by Mrs. Herbert, whom Goldman had discovered by chance a few years before in a shop selling glassware and crystal and silverware and all kinds of ornaments and whom he had introduced to Israel and to Caesar, who now glanced at Israel and said, "Everyone's mad. To run away with an Arab, I ask you," and he sniggered to himself and a moment later said, "I told you, love is madness," and kicked a stone lying on the road, and then took the pornographic photographs out of his pocket and stole a quick look at them and said, "Boy, I could eat the whole world," and in the same breath, although there was no obvious connection between the two, he mentioned Avigdor, his stepsister Ruhama's ex-husband, who spent his spare time weightlifting and gave rise in Caesar—whose basic attitude toward him was one of contempt—to a strange feeling of astonished sympathy, because he could never understand why Avigdor went on loving Ruhama and why he went on living with her after everything she had done to him, just as he could never understand what drove this quiet man to torture himself pointlessly and go three times a week after work to the sports club to stand alone in a sordid, stifling room and strain himself to the utmost in order to lift heavy iron weights into the air and push them toward the ceiling, and he said again, "Everyone's mad," and Israel nodded slightly, and Caesar said, "They're madder than you think. Take Avigdor for example—he's no better than Mrs. Herbert," and put the pornographic photographs back in his pocket, and ran a few steps to the main road and waved his hand and stopped a cab and both of them got into it and drove to Nahalat Yizhak, and when they arrived there the rays of the sun had already begun to slant a little and the shadows of the cypress trees were lengthening but the heat was still unbearable, perhaps even more oppressive than before, rising in dense vapors from the road and the brown earth and the well surrounding the cemetery, and from the dark green cypresses which from a distance had looked so cool and inviting.

They went in at the cemetery gates and asked about Goldman's father, but here too no one had heard of him, and Caesar, who couldn't believe his ears, ran here and there, furiously angry and on the verge of despair, buttonholing people and asking them questions until he gave up, and when he did give up his surrender was, as usual, sudden, complete, full of complaints, and pitiful to see. He wiped his face and neck with a soaking handkerchief and said, "He's not here, the shit," and spat, and Israel looked at him and said, "But he's dead and buried somewhere," and Caesar, still wiping his face, shouted, "Where? In Petach Tikvah perhaps? Or maybe they threw him into the sea? He was a horror when he was alive and he's a horror now that he's dead. Let's go home. He'll manage without us," and he started toward the gate, but Israel stood still and said, "Maybe he's in Holon." Caesar stopped and said, "In Holon?" and Israel said, "Yes. They've got something or other over there," and approached Caesar, who with a face full of fury said, "I don't want to hear. As far as I'm concerned he's finished, and I'm not running after him any more. He'll reach his destination without our help. In any case he's already under the ground." Israel said nothing but went on walking and crossed the road and made for the bus stop and Caesar, standing and watching him, shouted, "Where do you think you're going?" and Israel turned his head and said, "Come on, let's go to Holon," and Caesar said, "Are you serious?" and Israel said, "Why waste time?" and started running toward the bus which was approaching the stop. Caesar ran after him with the camera bouncing around his neck, and when they got onto the bus and sat down, still breathing heavily, he said, "He's more trouble dead than alive. He's ruined my day. I could have seen the children or had something seen to. And that bitch Eliezra couldn't even pick up the telephone to say hello," and he took off the camera and put it on his knees and lit himself a cigarette and said, "I haven't seen the kids for four days already," and a few minutes later he said, "You know what? Some days are so lousy you don't know what they're there for," and threw his burning cigarette out of the bus window and sat in a dejected silence for the rest of the journey.

When they arrived at the Holon cemetery dusk was falling: The light was turning blue and soft, and here in the open country the air too, with its subtle scents, was a little softer, and the cemetery guard, who looked exhausted and was about to lock the gates, said that someone by the name of Ephraim Goldman had indeed been buried there that day, but the funeral had taken place three or four hours ago. This information encouraged Caesar and raised his spirits again, and he suggested to Israel that they go over to the grave and stand there in silence for a few minutes as a sign of respect for the dead, but especially as a sign of participation in Goldman's grief, and without waiting for a reply he turned to the guard, who was standing and playing with a bunch of keys, and asked him where the grave was, and the guard pointed vaguely in the direction of the thousands of white gravestones stretching as far as the eye could see all over the deserted cemetery, and said that he could not take them there as it was very far and it was already time for him to lock the gates and finish work and go home. Caesar did not insist and proposed to Israel that they come back some day soon with a big wreath to put on the grave, and in the meantime he suggested that they go back to town and call on Goldman to apologize and offer him their condolences, and Israel immediately agreed, although he had no doubt that the guard would agree to guide them to the grave in return for a small payment, and in fact that was exactly what he was waiting for, as was quite clear from the tone of his voice and the expression of disappointment on his face and the coldness with which he parted from them when it became obvious that they were going to leave without visiting the grave.

They went out of the gate and walked a few yards and stood facing the cemetery and the sand dunes and relieved themselves at their leisure, and then Caesar stopped a cab to take them back to town and they got in and he said, "I'm worn out, but it was worth it," and fell into a silence which he maintained all the way to town except for three occasions on which he broke it: the first time when he returned to the subject of the superior burial customs of the Romans and at the same time made a derogatory remark about Goldman's father and cursed him, the second time when he reproached himself for not having been to see his children for four days, and the third time when he asked Israel to phone Eliezra for him the moment they reached town.

Israel said "All right," and went on looking out of the window with his head full of music from *Papa Marcelli,* which he had heard for the first time a few months before on a winter's morning in a Jerusalem church with Ella, when a French priest had played it on an organ whose deep, slow notes came welling up as if from other worlds and reverberated in the air full of awe and majestic celebration, filling the dim, empty church and enveloping him and spreading through him and filling him with a glowing sense of exaltation such as he had never felt before and arousing in him a desire to abandon himself and surrender himself, and Ella rested her fair head on his shoulder and sucked her thumb contentedly, and a yellow sunbeam filtered through a break in the stained glass windowpane and fell on one of the pillars, and when they went out into the street the sky was blue and cloudless but the smell of the rain which had fallen all night and early in the morning still hung in the cool, fresh air, mingling with the scent of the pines and the smell of the wet earth, and Ella looked at the Arab children playing football in the muddy street with a noisy can, and Israel looked at her as they walked, overcome by loving and tender and, especially, protective feelings toward her, which would suddenly and unintentionally give way to feelings of hostility and cruelty so strong that he would sometimes make up his mind to break off with her for good, and on more than one occasion in the past he had seen them in his imagination parting and never meeting again, but then he would be overcome by depression and anger and futility—the same feeling which now filled the air of the summer evening and which came from the seedy, peeling houses, from the open windows, from the crumbling balconies and the men and women sitting on them apathetically or standing at the shop entrances, from the ugly, neglected streets, from the children playing on the pavements, from the courtyards and garages and warehouses, and also from the tone of the cab driver who was trying to strike up a conversation with Caesar, and said first that he could lay any woman and then that he hated the smell of women's bodies, to which Caesar, who was withdrawn into himself, retorted that there were women and women, but the driver insisted, "They're all the same," and then said that he was suffering from sexual boredom and turned up the radio to hear the news, and in the meantime they turned into cleaner and brighter streets, and after a while Caesar asked the driver to stop and told him to keep the change, and when they got off, bone-weary, he stretched himself and suggested to Israel that they go into Portofino to have a drink and a rest and recover their strength and call Eliezra before going up to Goldman's place, and they crossed Dizengoff Street and to the ringing of the bronze bell hanging above the door they entered Portofino, which was deserted except for the proprietor, a short, skinny Greek with a haggard, greenish, irredeemably sad face, and an ugly barmaid.

The proprietor knew Caesar, who often sat there drinking with friends and all kinds of girls, and he greeted him dispiritedly, looking at him slowly with his frightened, suspicious eyes hiding underneath his bulging forehead and the same unchanging expression on his face, and Caesar said "Shalom" and ordered cheese and two Tuborg beers and sat down while Israel went unwillingly to call Eliezra. Eliezra's husband Gidon answered the phone, and Israel introduced himself and said, "How are you?" and Gidon said, "Fine, thank you," but Israel understood from the uncertain tone of his voice that he did not remember him, and so he introduced himself again and reminded Gidon that they had met a few months before at the movie *Borsalino* and a couple of weeks later they had met again, in the street next to the Cafe Vered, and Gidon said, "Yes, yes," but he was still hesitant, and then he suddenly said, "Ha ha, of course, you're Caesar's friend," and apologized for not remembering him immediately, and Israel said that it didn't matter and that it was hard to remember someone after two hurried meetings, and asked if Eliezra were at home, and Gidon said that she had just gone out but that she would be back at about nine because they were going to a movie, and he asked Israel what he wanted her for, and Israel said that he only wanted to tell her, and in fact tell them both, that Goldman's father had died, and he would have told them before but it had slipped his mind, and Gidon giggled and said that they had known since yesterday and Eliezra had even gone to the funeral, and asked Israel if he had not attended the funeral himself. Flushing slightly with embarrassment Israel said, "No, I came late," and apologized for bothering him, and Gidon said, "Nonsense. It's quite all right," and then he invited Israel and Caesar to go to the movies with them and Israel said, "Maybe," and Gidon said, "Yes, yes, do come, there are a number of good movies showing," and Israel again said, "Maybe, we'll see," and glanced at Caesar, who looked back at him full of curiosity and anticipation, and said, "In any case, we'll let you know if we decide to come. Bye for now," and replaced the receiver and went back to Caesar and repeated his conversation with Gidon, but without mentioning the invitation to the movies, and Caesar listened attentively and said, "You see, what a shame we didn't make it to that lousy funeral," and after nibbling a piece of cheese and taking a sip of beer he added, "He's a good chap, that Gidon, let's hope he doesn't go off the rails," and smiled and ordered salami and another can of Tuborg, and said, "She invented sex, that Eliezra. Believe me. And every minute she spends with that impotent husband of hers is a waste. I know him—we went to school together, and we were together in the army too for a bit. That's enough to get to know someone," and when they got up to go he said, "I'm mad about her, especially in the summer," and he smiled again, and went over to the bar and bought a packet of Rothman's and paid, and they went out into the street and mingled with the people packing the pavements until it seemed that all the inhabitants of the town had abandoned their homes and escaped to the streets, which were still smothered in the heavy, stifling heat.

Caesar strode ahead without saying much, his camera bouncing on his chest and his tired little eyes darting hither and thither. There was something about his face and his paunch, his laugh and gesticulations and voracious, lustful looks which reminded Israel of Erwin, who was bigger and broader and more cunning than his son, but just as full of charm. When they stopped at a traffic light he wiped the sweat from his neck and said, "Look at what's going on here. It can drive you crazy," and then he said, "I'm sure she went to the funeral because of me," and as they were approaching Goldman's house he said, "The summer makes me drunk, or maybe it's not the summer but all this business of dying," and after a few steps he added, "I once read somewhere that grief and tiredness and traveling on a train are as aphrodisiac as alcohol," and they went into the lobby and Israel pressed the light button and on the way upstairs Caesar paused for a moment and said, "You have no idea how sad it is to be a father." He said this with a touching simplicity and frankness, as if he were continuing another train of thought which was evidently preoccupying him, and immediately went on climbing the stairs after Israel, who said nothing but stopped outside the open door of Goldman's apartment to wait for him, and the two of them walked down the narrow passage into the yellowish living room which was full of men and women who had come after the funeral to sit with the widow and console her in her grief.

Goldman's older brother Joel was there with his wife Zipporah and two of their sons, Meir and Jeremiah, who had carried their mother upstairs because of the disease in her right leg which made it impossible for her to climb stairs and difficult for her to get about at all, and Bracha, Joel's and Goldman's father's and Uncle Lazar's younger sister, her face lifeless and her lips pale and dry, with her husband Shmuel, who despite the heat was wearing a checked suit and a blue silk tie embossed with red hearts, Chaim-Leib in a black hat and his wife Mrs. Haya, his eldest son Shlomo who had once been a member of the IZL right-wing military underground, Moishe Tzellermaier, whose eyes were red and swollen with weeping, with his huge wife who was holding a big bunch of white roses in her hand, Max Spillman, Matilda (Joseph Leviatan's widow), David Kostomolski, a pipe mender who reeked of tobacco and who had come, as usual, without Mrs. de Bouton, Sarah (the widow of Regina's brother Reuven), Ye-hudit Maizler, Avraham Shechter, Moishe Tzimmer's widow, Manfred, and Yechiel Levankopf with his wife Shoshana, who had lived in the Goldmans' apartment for the last three years of the war as sub-tenants, although Shoshana had actually lived there alone with their three-year-old son, since Yechiel, who was a mechanic, had enlisted and gone to serve in the British army.

Shoshana had lived in the little room, Naomi's room, where she slept and sewed and ironed and also cooked meals for herself and her son on a little kerosene stove, partly because the kitchen was unbearably crowded, but mainly because Grandfather Moshe David, Regina's father, who had lingered on for a few years after his wife died, terrorizing the household with his religious fanat-icism and his gloomy, irascible temper, which would flare up from time to time and erupt into passionate and vociferous scan-dals, was afraid that she would defile the food and dishes by bringing nonkosher things into the kitchen and mixing up the milk and meat dishes and the separate soaps and towels.

Yechiel Levankopf spent the first year of his military service in British army camps in Sarafand and Julis drilling and doing guard duty, and from time to time he would come home on leave bringing all kinds of groceries as well as sweets and chocolate and cigarettes from the NAAFI canteen, but after that he was transferred to Egypt as a dispatch rider, and from there to the Western Desert and then to Italy, and Shoshana went out to work to help keep herself and her son. For a time she worked as a waitress in a workers' restaurant, but the work was boring and paid badly and she switched to one of the huge beer halls on the seashore, which had been put up to cater to the allied troops and was always full of pink and white British soldiers and soldiers from New Zealand and South Africa and Australian soldiers in broad-brimmed hats and Scottish soldiers who would sometimes march down the street wearing kilts in military processions to the accompaniment of the monotonous wailing of their bagpipes, which were decorated with all kinds of tassles and colored ribbons and gave rise to the astonished admiration of the onlookers.

The soldiers would sit in the great, dim halls full of the smell of beer and cigarette smoke, sipping their beer in silence, telling jokes, reminiscing, speculating about their fate, getting drunk, fighting, cursing, crying and singing beneath the waterfalls resplendent in the sunset, the coconut trees, the green meadows, and the half-naked women with stupid faces and enormous breasts which were painted on the walls, and Shoshana would bring them beer and sometimes something to eat and take their money, and clean the tables, and in the evening she would go home to take care of her son and prepare herself for the motley crew of admirers who came to take her out to the movies or other entertainments, all of which—beginning with her job and ending with her admirers—enraged Goldman's father, while Goldman himself spent his time waiting tensely for a good opportunity to peep through the keyhole and see her taking a shower, and on a couple of occasions he succeeded and watched breathless with fear and excitement as she stroked her heavy breasts, and her vagina, and her belly, which was as smooth and white as china.

She wasn't pretty, but she was alone and had, at least on the surface, a disreputable air, as well as shining black hair, sensual lips, and a kind of wanton, provocative vitality which made her attractive to men—but nothing was left of all this now and she sat next to Regina, tired and apathetic, her face big and wrinkled like the face of an Indian squaw and her eyes full of smoke, yawning so enormously that the ugly silver butterfly pinned to her bosom rose into the air with every yawn as if it were about to take off. She looked indifferently at the people sitting on the couch and the kitchen chairs and the old, stiff-backed upholstered chairs standing by the big brown table, which was set with cups and plates and a bowl of fruit and biscuits and an excellent cheesecake, Goldman's father's favorite, which Bracha had brought and which Zipporah, despite the pains in her leg, cut carefully and divided among the company, also offering a piece to Regina, with whom her relations had always been chilly, and entreating her to eat something, but Regina refused. She sat on the heavy armchair opposite the TV, looking very tired, her long, withered face pale but her cheeks blushing very faintly and delicately, as if she had rouged them, and the mourners drank tea and coffee, ate fruit and cake, and spoke in lively but lowered tones to each other and to Regina (who said almost nothing), except for Tzimmer's widow, who talked without stopping as usual in a very loud voice, infuriating Yehudit Maizler to such an extent that finally she could bear it no longer and she got up and shook hands with Regina, saying that she would drop in tomorrow or the next day, and left. Joel and Avraham Shechter held their tongues, and so did Manfred, who sat in his elegant black suit pants and carefully pressed white shirt with his arms crossed, surveying the company with a haughty impatience which showed quite clearly on his dark and ugly but expressive face, and keeping quite still except for occasionally passing his sensitive fingers over his high, smooth forehead, or lightly touching his carefully combed black hair, or turning his head slightly to look outside through the balcony door.

In some elusive way Manfred was different from the other mourners, and he caught the attention of Israel and Caesar as soon as they came into the room. They shook hands first with Goldman, who rose to greet them with a happy smile on his face, and then with Regina, and Israel also greeted Tzimmer's widow and Matilda Leviatan, but Matilda did not respond, either because she did not notice his greeting at all or because she did not recognize him and did not realize that his pleasantries were directed at her, and Caesar shook hands with Max Spillman, and he and Israel sat down next to Goldman, who asked them how they were, and Caesar explained in a sorrowful and apologetic tone why they had not attended the funeral and told him everything that had happened to them until the moment of their arrival at his house, and Goldman, signs of his happiness at seeing them still showing on his face and in his voice, consoled them and said that the funeral had gone off quite smoothly and they hadn't missed anything or come late for anything either, since the dead man was already dead—with them or without them—and asked them if they wanted tea or coffee, and Caesar said, "Nothing, sit down, we've just had something to drink," but Goldman insisted until they gave in and he went out to make them coffee, and in the meantime they sat and listened to the conversation of the men who were discussing the political situation.

They were trying to speak softly, but the argument grew heated and tempers rose after Yechiel Levankopf, who had a deep, strong voice, said that this government wasn't really interested in peace at all, but only in the perpetuation of the status quo, and that if it were up to him he would have given back the conquered territories long ago in exchange for peace, and that included the Old City of Jerusalem, since he saw no need for the title deeds to be registered in his name rather than anyone else's, and Moishe Tzellermaier said, "Nonsense," and Chaim-Leib said in Yiddish that it was impossible to transfer property held as a pledge to another party, and Shmuel said, "Quite right," and Max Spillman, drumming on the table with his thick, hairy fingers, said that no government would give back Jerusalem or anything else, and quite rightly too, because it was a question of life and death for us and because the defeated side in a war had to pay the price, and there was no reason for us to be more moral than the rest of the world. Yechiel Levankopf said, "I'm not interested in the rest of the world, I'm interested in us, and I want peace," and Max Spillman, without losing his temper, said that holding onto the territories was the only way to achieve peace, and in fact we already had peace, and the peace would become more firmly established as time went by, because the Arabs were weak and backward and because they would never agree to exchange the economic prosperity the Jews had brought them for anything else, and Avraham Shechter, whose younger son had been killed about three years before in the Jordan Valley, made a slight movement with his hand and seemed about to say something, but Yechiel Levankopf, whose wife was trying cautiously to calm him down, said very loudly that no one but a crook or a megalomaniac would talk such disgusting rubbish, because robbing others of their land would never bring peace, and economic prosperity would never make the Arabs forget their hatred for the Jews, and nor would it make the Palestinians give up their national aspirations. Moishe Tzellermaier said, again, "Nonsense," and Shmuel said, "It's not worth shouting about. In any case it's not in our hands," but no one heard him because Shlomo, Chaim-Leib's son, who had controlled himself up to now, burst out that we didn't need peace, and if it were up to him he would make all the Arabs emigrate from the country, in return for financial compensation of course, and that in any case it was impossible to talk about the national aspirations of the Palestinians because there was no such thing as a Palestinian nation. Yechiel Levankopf went pale with rage and said that Shlomo was being both brutal and stupid, because only the Palestinians had the right to decide if there was a Palestinian nation or not, but Shlomo insisted that there was no such nation, that it was a fiction invented by Jews and communists, and that the whole of Eretz Yisrael had been promised to the Jews in the Bible, the Jews and no one else, and Yechiel Levankopf roughly pushed away his wife's hand, which was trying to restrain him, and banged his fist on the table with all his strength, and shouted, "To hell with the Bible! The Bible's not a political program or a blueprint for parceling out the country!" He wanted to go on, but his wife wouldn't let him and begged him to stop, and so did Shmuel and Chaim-Leib and Zipporah, and even Max Spillman, who said, "Enough, enough. It's not worth getting excited about," and Bracha asked him if he wanted a cup of tea or some fruit juice and Yechiel Levankopf said, "No," and in the same breath he said, "If this is redemption God help us," and rose to his feet, and Avraham Shechter, with something rather shy and hesitant in his voice, said, "Yes, this is redemption. In any case, there isn't any other," and Yechiel Levankopf, who apparently hadn't even heard him, turned to his wife and said, "Come on, I'm going," and left the room without waiting for her, and Shoshana said goodbye hurriedly to everyone and went out after him.

For a moment there was complete silence, and Moishe Tzimmer's widow said, "He's got a terrible temper," and Shmuel said, "The whole argument was completely superfluous," and Chaim-Leib said, "A man should have a bit of sense, too," and there was another short silence, and then people gradually started talking again about the heat and the price of apartments and children and illnesses, and in the meantime a couple of neighbors came in and shook Regina's hand and sat down, and David Kostomolski got up to take his leave of her and the rest of the mourners and left, and a discussion sprang up about business affairs in which the leading participants were Max Spillman and Shmuel, who was referred to by his friends and relations as "the tycoon" or "Uncle Sam" and by Goldman's father as "that bluffer."

From the beginning Goldman's father's attitude toward Shmuel had been reserved, and later it became openly impatient and irritable, and he had always regretted the fact that Bracha, with whom his relationship was uniquely close and loving, had married him—because Shmuel, who had started off respectably enough as a carpenter, had suddenly turned himself into a barber and even opened a barber shop, and then had gone in for commerce and all kinds of business deals, and because in his opinion he was a frivolous person, and because he had a reckless inclination for adventure and change—not to mention his extravagance—and spent all his life trying to get rich in the quickest and most slippery ways possible—which as far as Goldman's father could see were nothing but fraud and parasitism in the last analysis—because Shmuel wanted to enjoy life and actually did enjoy it, in the same carefree, natural, easygoing way that he ran his business affairs.

When he was still a barber, before he shut down the barber shop and turned it into an unsuccessful liquor store, Shmuel had engaged in various kinds of brokerage, even marriage brokerage, and later, after shutting down the liquor store, he started trading in hardware and electrical supplies, bought a partnership in a movie theater, and started all kinds of investment companies as well as a company for importing beef, which had brought in good profits for a while until it got into trouble and had to be liquidated. In recent years he had been making a lot of money from a big restaurant, in which he had a half share, and from dealing in second-hand cars and hiring them out, but on the other hand he had lost a lot of money on the AOS shares he had acquired from Bernie Cornfeld, despite a number of warnings from people who knew what they were talking about, in the hope of becoming a millionaire quickly, and he wasn't far off either, since by means of these shares he had become a partner in Lockheed, General Motors, Telefunken, Fiat, Phillips, Mitsubishi, IBM, the giant gold and diamond mining concern De Beers, and dozens of other thriving industrial plants, oil refineries, shipping firms, banks, and real estate firms all over the world, as well as manganese and copper and iron and uranium mines and the richest oil wells in the world, which were about to be discovered under the frozen ground of Alaska. The fact that his hopes had been dashed, and in so humiliating a fashion, did not lead him to blame Bernie Cornfeld, or to sink into anger and despair, since even when he lost large sums of money or was very hard up he always felt like a millionaire and spent with a liberal hand and without calculations because he was blessed with a sunny, generous nature and a soaring imagination and a boundless optimism and, despite Goldman's father's coldness toward him, Shmuel did not resent him, but on the contrary, he felt not only esteem but also a brotherly warmth and sympathy and was very saddened by his death, and at the funeral he decided that on the coming Saturday night he would cancel the traditional Saturday night rummy game held at their house for more than twenty friends and acquaintances and relations and compatriots from the old country, who would sit around the card tables in the large living room and the balcony, men and women separately as a rule, playing cards and laughing and drinking tea and coffee and eating the delicious cakes which Bracha baked every week in honor of the game.

When the conversation now took a financial turn Shmuel argued that in view of the economic situation Regina should immediately sell the stamp collection left by Goldman's father, and that with the money she got for it she should buy a jewelry shop which also sold souvenirs for tourists, or a fur shop, because that type of thing brought in excellent profits today, although if it were up to him he would invest most of the money in gold coins and especially medals, whose value was skyrocketing, and Moishe Tzellermaier said, "That's not for her. The only thing for her is index-linked bonds," and Chaim-Leib remarked that the will hadn't been opened yet and there was no knowing what the wishes of the deceased were concerning his stamp collection, while Max Spillman, who was waiting for the appropriate moment to take his leave and glancing at his watch every now and then, said that he would advise the widow to invest in land or apartments, which were a safer investment than a shop and no less profitable in the end, or else he would advise her to invest in heavy mechanical equipment, a tractor or a truck, and rent it out to one of the contractors who were making fortunes nowadays in development projects and fortification works, and as far as speculative investments were concerned he himself would not invest in coins or medals but in shares, especially bank shares or real estate or investment company shares, which brought in dividends, and in the end he remarked, by the way, that he estimated the value of Goldman's father's stamp collection at at least two hundred thousand lira.

Goldman's father had indeed possessed a magnificent stamp collection, which he had been adding to for years, lovingly and in covert but tireless rivalry with his two brothers—with Uncle Lazar and especially with Joel, a tall, slightly stooping man whose big, sunburnt face was covered with a network of wrinkles which almost always seemed to be hiding an elusive, subtle smile, but who had recently aged badly, almost overnight, and who now looked very tired. At the funeral he stood next to Zipporah and Uncle Lazar and Yehudit Tanfuss, dry-eyed and quiet and reserved as usual, but after they had filled in the grave and everyone was leaving he placed his hand for a moment on Bracha's shoulder, Bracha who was crushed with sorrow and weeping, and when they got onto the bus he turned to Chaim-Leib and said, "In spite of everything he deserved to be loved," and afterward for almost the entire evening he did not say a word but drank his tea and looked at the people and listened, because unlike Goldman's father and unlike Bracha too, Joel was taciturn and reserved, but the intelligence and skepticism behind his silences were evident, and he would sometimes, completely unexpectedly, surprise everybody with a sarcastic remark dropped quite casually and pleasantly, like the remark he now made to Meir during the discussion being held around the dining room table about the money from the stamp collection. "They're already dividing up the interest from the capital which God has not yet given them," he said, and smiled.

Joel too was a Zionist and socialist and he too had clear principles, although not as firm and comprehensive as his brother's, but he carried them out privately and modestly as part of his whole way of life, and he never persecuted anyone because of them or tried to impose them on anyone else, not even on his children or his wife Zipporah, a small, clever woman with abundant energy and pink cheeks and faded chestnut hair and lively eyes who inspired universal respect and even reverence, and who for over fifty years of quiet love and devotion had helped him shoulder their common burdens and had kept the family fed and clothed by hard work, economy, and enormous resourcefulness with her husband's wages, which were meager despite the fact that he was a first-rate scaffolder. She made clothes and sheets and pillowcases and knitted and laundered and cleaned the house, which was always spotless and shining, and as long as she was able she also whitewashed the walls herself, and she bought the cheapest food and made the tastiest dishes from it, and she brought up and educated their five children—Meir, Jeremiah, Esther, Ruth, and Aviezer, who was Goldman's friend when they were children—and in addition to this all her life she offered a helping hand to relatives and friends and aquaintances without sparing herself or expecting any thanks, although she herself was always suffering from all kinds of illnesses: She had something wrong with her liver and something wrong with her circulation, and her skin was very sensitive to the sun, and when she passed the age of fifty her doctors warned her that she would die if she didn't start looking after herself and eating the right foods and resting, but she refused to listen to them and went on living the way she always had, because there was always work to be done and no one else to do it and there were always people who needed help, and because death held no fears for her—she had seen a lot of suffering in her life but a lot of joy too, and she had never wished or hoped for immortality, and all she wanted was to die before Joel or at the same time as him. Zipporah herself had once told Aviezer that she had kissed her father when he died and she was thirteen years old, and that kiss had cured her of the fear of death, or maybe it wasn't the kiss itself but the appearance of the dead man, and another time she said that she wasn't afraid of death because all her life, ever since she was a child, she had been so busy with the troubles and problems of keeping her own family and others alive that she had no time to worry about it and in the end she forgot that it existed. Joel, who loved and cherished her, did not interfere with the running of the house, and Zipporah did not expect him to; he would come home weary and dirty from work and remove his heavy boots and after showering and changing his clothes and eating the late midday meal which Zipporah served him he would occupy himself with the things he loved—the potted plants on the balcony, making wine, taking his brown mongrel dog Mussolini for walks, reading books about historical subjects and biographies and sometimes a good novel, studying construction blueprints, and looking after the stamp collection which, for a number of years, had disrupted his relations with Goldman's father.

Goldman's father's stamp collection, which was kept in thick albums and in special tins, was arranged according to subjects, whereas those of his rivals, Uncle Lazar and Joel, were arranged according to countries, and this was the root of the problem, at least from Goldman's father's point of view, and it went on poisoning their relations even after the rivalry had ended in total victory for Goldman's father as a result of the abandonment of Uncle Lazar's stamp collection when he went off to Spain to fight in the civil war in the ranks of the International Brigade, and the destruction of Joel's stamp collection many years later when a paraffin stove overturned and burned the whole room down together with the stamps one evening while he was out walking his dog Mussolini. When he came back the flames had turned the stamps to ashes, covering the floor and drifting through the window and lying scattered all over the garden, and Zipporah was waiting in the street in front of the house to tell him the news of his loss, which went on torturing him for weeks and months and gave him no rest, although he hardly spoke about it, and it was only very gradually and almost imperceptibly that he recovered, until suddenly one day he felt that he was free and that he had been relieved of a heavy burden which had been oppressing him for years and which somehow continued to cloud his relations with his brother, Goldman's father, even after they had, for all intents and purposes, been reconciled.

Relations between them had reached the breaking point some seven or eight years before this reconciliation, and for a certain period they had been so bad that Goldman's father intended not to invite Joel to Goldman's wedding to the beautiful Jemimah Chernov, and changed his mind only under pressure from Bracha, who was the only person in the world he loved without any reservations—except for the time when she refused to hate Uncle Lazar, let alone join in Goldman's father's ostracizing of him, which angered Goldman's father and spoiled his love for her, since his anger had to be everybody's anger, just as his hate, sorrow or love had to be everybody's hate, sorrow or love—and she kept on at him until he agreed to invite Joel, who had first aroused his animosity in a disagreement about the value of a certain stamp from Italy which developed into an unpleasant argument about the relative value of the two collections and ended up, on the initiative of Goldman's father, who refused to give up, by turning into an endless controversy about the principle according to which stamp collections in general should be arranged. Goldman's father, who in the course of these arguments also succeeded in offending Zipporah, for whom he felt a secret admiration and deep regard, not only refused to budge from the "principle of subjects" himself but also, not prepared to let matters rest there, was determined to impose this principle on Joel too, who tried his best to evade all these arguments and showed no inclination whatsoever to change the arrangement of his stamp collection, thereby enraging Goldman's father and offending him to such an extent that he broke off relations with his brother and for a number of years refused to exchange a single word with him.

All Joel's attempts at reconciliation, and all the efforts of Chaim-Leib and Avraham Shechter and Meir and Shmuel and all kinds of other friends and relations to intercede on his behalf did not help, and neither did Zipporah's harsh words shortly after Goldman's wedding, and even the entreaties of Bracha—who could not bear this new quarrel in addition to the old quarrel with Uncle Lazar—were in vain: Goldman's father clung to his grievance, which grew more bitter from year to year, and oscillated between feelings of anger and unforgiving resentment, the horror of his own loneliness and his love for his brother, which sought an outlet. The truth is that he was only waiting for one more overture from Joel, however slight, which would save his face and give him a chance to repair the damage which he himself had done, but Joel had despaired of him and nothing of the kind took place, and the years passed, until one day Joel suddenly succumbed to a heart attack and Goldman's father, horrified by the news, rushed to the hospital resolved to ask his brother's forgiveness and make up with him, but as soon as he entered the ward and approached the bed, around which Zipporah and Meir and Aviezer and Ruth and Jonah Kotchinski and Bracha were seated, he realized how difficult this would be for him, especially since so much time had passed, and he shook Joel's hand emotionally and asked him how he was and said, "What can you do, we're not getting any younger," and conversed with him and the others, and even tried to make a few jokes with the unshed tears stinging his eyelids and his face pale as a sheet, but he could not bring himself to say that he was sorry, and kept putting it off from one minute to the next until in the end he gave up the idea and decided to see the visit itself as an act of reconciliation, and so in fact it was, but nevertheless a certain strain remained in the relations between them and it vanished only months, or maybe even years, after Joel's stamp collection went up in flames.

Goldman's father never admitted that the whole quarrel had originated in the senseless argument he had conducted about the stamp collections, and in fact he ignored the entire affair, and only once, many years later, he said to Avraham Shechter that he could never forgive a man who tried to cheat at cards, and he said this, as usual, in all innocence and perfect sincerity—only it wasn't Joel who played cards but Goldman's father himself, who played rummy and regarded it as his great, albeit only, weakness, and it embittered his life because on the one hand he considered playing cards as an aberration bordering on depravity, while on the other hand he was addicted to it and played so passionately and overbearingly that in recent years it had become almost impossible to sit down at the card table with him because he was always laying down the law so irately and despotically that he spoiled the game for everyone else and often precipitated angry outbursts and offended scenes, and all the attempts of Shmuel and others to restrain him led nowhere: He stuck to his guns, usually without even realizing what he was doing, but sometimes in spite of himself, and went on telling everyone else how to play, with absolute objectivity and without backing down even when the moves he tried to impose on his opponents were likely to make him lose the game, because higher principles were at stake and he did not care if he was spoiling the game and taking all the fun out of it, and things grew worse from week to week until Moishe Tzellermaier—who was sitting next to his wife with a somber expression on his face—stopped coming to the card games altogether, and he wasn't the only one either, but he never said why he had stopped coming because he loved Goldman's father and felt great respect for him and boundless gratitude, and nevertheless he vowed to himself that he would never again sit down with him at the same card table, or even in the same room, and he stuck to this vow in spite of the sadness it caused him and the embarrassment, and of course the loss of pleasure, and despite the repeated invitations of Shmuel and Bracha—who now were saying goodbye to Max Spillman as he left the room after parting from Regina with a handshake and a word in her ear, nodding to Caesar, and gripping Goldman by the arm on his way to the door, as the latter entered the room bringing coffee for Israel and Caesar in two china cups (one of them with a broken handle) on china saucers decorated with a very delicate colored pattern.

Goldman offered them their coffee with a flourish and a smile, saying, "Please gentlemen, the Czechoslovakian tea set," and turned to Meir and Jeremiah and exchanged a few pointless words with them and asked them if they wanted anything, because he loved them and Aviezer and Ruth and Esther but had lost contact with them over the years until all that was left was the awareness of this love, and of course the awareness of the kinship between them, as well as an oppressive feeling of some kind of debt which had not been paid, and then he turned with the same question to Joel and Zipporah, whom he revered more than anyone in the world, as well as feeling indebted to her for taking him in and looking after him when Regina was suffering from a kidney disease, and Zipporah said, "Please don't bother, we're perfectly all right," and Goldman said, "Are you sure, Auntie Zipporah?" and she said, "Yes, yes, there's no need for anything," and Goldman nodded and sat down next to Caesar and Israel. Goldman seemed in high spirits and he talked without stopping, albeit with a certain abstraction, and made jokes, but he could not conceal the sadness and weariness at the corners of his mouth and in his green eyes, and thus, smiling from time to time, he spoke ironically about his father's successful funeral, about the will which he had been writing for the past four years, about the reunion of family and friends "just like the good old days," and about the fact that it was now possible to use the Czechoslovakian tea service without any fears, since his father was dead and "everything is permitted," and so saying he turned his head slightly in Manfred's direction and said, "That's Manfred, my mother's lover," and sniggered, and Caesar said, "Good for them," and smiled in surprise and embarrassment, but also with enjoyment, while Israel said nothing and his face remained expressionless, although he too was surprised and embarrassed, not only by the fact that Goldman had said what he had just said, but mainly, of course, by the fact that Regina had a lover, for he could on no account picture her as a woman subject to feelings of that kind or capable of becoming involved in an affair of that nature. Caesar said again, "Good for them," shifting his eyes from Manfred to Regina, who sat withdrawn and indifferent without so much as a glance at Manfred, and went on smiling and Goldman, who had not noticed Caesar's smile, said, "He's one of the only people here who's really sad, but not about my father's death," and picked up a biscuit and turned it around in his fingers and said, "As far as I'm concerned—thinking of the dead makes me happy," and without specifying which dead he was referring to he took a bite from the biscuit and stole a glance at Moishe Tzimmer's widow, who kept fidgeting and talking at the top of her voice, and said that he always meditated on death and the dead and tried to contemplate them joyfully and serenely, since death, after all, was the real substantiation of life and he knew that there was nothing to fear from it, and Caesar said, "Right," although it was obvious that he wasn't listening to Goldman and his mind was on other things, but Goldman didn't care and continued with the exposition of his theme and said that his favorite literature, apart from menus, consisted of the death notices in the newspapers, which he read every day, especially the ones which told a story, sometimes in the form of an acrostic based on the letters of the deceased's name, and described the virtues of the departed and the sorrow of his family, and suddenly he fell silent and his smile faded and a shadow crossed his dry face, and Israel glanced at him and thought that he looked as if he had shriveled up inside.

Caesar sipped his coffee and said, "Everything's idiotic," and Goldman smiled again and glanced at his mother and the people sitting in the room and Joel and Moishe Tzimmer's widow and said, "I can't stand that woman," and took another biscuit and said that he had once read about a Chinese artist who had painted a picture of a monk sitting in a tree and looking down, and on the picture he had written the following words, more or less: "The problem is how to find tranquillity in this world of suffering and disorder. You ask me why I came here. Well, I do not know the answer. Here in this tree I can be free of care, like a bird in its nest. People say that I am a dangerous man, but I answer them—you are devils!" and Caesar said, "I can't understand that stuff. I'm not a Chinaman," and Goldman said, "In that sense we are all Chinamen," and he wanted to say something else but at that moment Eliezra entered the room and Caesar suddenly grew tense and alert, and the other mourners too turned to look at her, and Goldman rose and went up to her and she shook hands with him, and then she shook hands with Regina and greeted Israel and in response to a signal from Caesar she went and sat down next to him, and Goldman asked her what she would have to drink, and she said, "Not for me thank you, I've just had something," and Caesar smiled at her and stroked her thigh and said, "I called you just now, but there was no answer," and Eliezra gently removed his hand and said, "I must have been on my way here," and Caesar said, "Probably." He lied effortlessly and guiltlessly, even when the lie was so obvious that it hit you in the eye, and even when it was completely unnecessary, and sometimes even when it was against his own interests, because he had become so accustomed to lying that the lies jumped out of his mouth as quickly and lightly as grasshoppers, and because he told so many lies that he often couldn't distinguish them from the truth, but all this didn't trouble him in the least, because after lying at first for reasons of convenience or moral cowardice he had ended up by making falsehood into a principle and teaching himself to believe that there was no such thing as morality and that lies were more powerful than the truth and only they were capable of guiding human life toward harmonious and pleasurable destinations, whereas the truth, which was so universally extolled, had in his opinion brought little benefit to humanity and a great deal of sorrow and unnecessary difficulties and conflicts, and he, Caesar, couldn't see any point in wasting his life on it, and he placed his hand on Eliezra's thigh again and she drew it decorously away and said, "Not now," and Caesar removed his hand and said, "Nonsense," and smiled at her and lit himself a cigarette.

Eliezra was wearing a flimsy turquoise dress with a big round décolleté which showed off her beautiful proud neck, and her fair hair was tied back with a purple silk scarf and her breasts stuck out provocatively like two big pears, and altogether she was a beautiful woman, and she knew it. In fact, she was so preoccupied with her beauty that on the one hand she managed to convince herself that it was imperishable, like some kind of spiritual quality, but on the other hand she did not really believe this and lived in constant fear of its ruin and destruction, and this double feeling made her into a vain and capricious woman, full of fears and bitterness which in the course of time distorted her innate honesty and natural generosity and corrupted them, and she was insatiable in her demands for attention and praise, as if they were her due, but in reality she was only looking for a little security and the feeling that she was worth something, which she could not find inside herself, and in this desperate search she slipped and fell again and again.

Caesar played with the ends of her silk scarf and then placed his hand on her shoulder, and Eliezra said, "Why weren't you at the funeral?" and Caesar said, "We couldn't make it," and stroked the nape of her neck, and Eliezra, without removing his hand, said, "I hate weddings and funerals because they're so phony," and Caesar nodded and said, "Mm," without paying any attention to what she was saying, but even if she would have said that the sun was a sacrificial chicken and the table was a butterfly—even then he would have agreed without a murmur because what was important to him was that she was devoted to him and gave herself to him full of lust and love whenever she had an hour to spare.

Israel turned his head away from Caesar and Eliezra and looked at Goldman's mother's necklace, and then at Manfred and Matilda Leviatan, who had aged so greatly, and at the picture of Naomi in its brown wooden frame standing on one of the shelves of the bookcase, which was crowded with books by Berl Katznelson and Ben Gurion and Bialik and Brenner and Shalom Aleichem and other old and new books (which Goldman's father had devoted great efforts to acquiring and which he had guarded jealously, although he hardly ever looked inside them), and at the same time he felt a rising impatience at the thought that Ella might come to the studio in his absence, and this thought made him increasingly restless and would not let him be and in the end it also filled him with such rage that suddenly he wanted her to leave him alone and never to come again, and he was on the point of getting up and taking his leave of everyone and going back to the studio and having a shower and sitting down to play the piano, but while he was waiting for the right moment Eliezra turned to him and asked him how he was progressing on the organ and he said, "OK," and Goldman, drawing up a plate of biscuits, started telling them about a new diet he had discovered in an American aviation magazine, which was capable of prolonging your life by seven to ten years—on condition, of course, that you kept to it strictly. In the framework of this diet, which was based on a strict selection and coordination of carbohydrates and proteins, you had to fast for fourteen to twenty-one consecutive days a year, according to your natural capacities, in order to clear your body of accumulated waste matter, and in the same article they also recommended emphotherapy (in other words, grape-therapy), a system of medical treatment based on the consumption of two and a half kilos of grapes a day, and nothing else, for a period of a number of weeks, which reduced the acidity of the blood besides benefiting the heart, lungs, liver, blood vessels, and kidneys, and when he had concluded these explanations he said that he intended taking up the diet as well as the emphotherapy and advised Israel and especially Caesar to do the same, and Caesar said, "Maybe one day, I'm in no hurry," and Goldman said, "You're ruining your life for nothing," and later he started talking about motorcycles, but before he had time to enlarge on the subject he rose to say goodbye to Sarah, Regina's resentful sister-in-law, who got up to leave after feeling that she had done her duty to these people whom she had hardly seen since the death of her husband, and although she was a stranger to him and he felt a certain antipathy toward her, Goldman made an effort to be affable and saw her to the front door, and when he came back he approached Meir and Jeremiah and Joel and Zipporah once more and asked them if they wanted anything, and he also asked Chaim-Leib and Mrs. Haya and then he sat down again next to Israel and resumed his discourse on motorcycles, the new dream revitalizing his life and serving as a focal point for his aspirations. He had already saved up the money to buy a motorcycle and for a number of weeks now he had been studying the motorcycle columns in the classified advertisements in the newspapers, visiting shops and garages, making inquiries of friends and reading all kinds of prospectuses. At first, he had thought of buying a BSA or a Norton, and then he had decided on a Honda, and all because the Harley Davidson which he really wanted was too expensive for him, but in the end he had discovered a five-horsepower secondhand Triumph and decided to buy it when his father's sudden illness had ruined all his plans, and now he was afraid that it would be sold to someone else and he would be back again where he started before discovering the Triumph.

Goldman went on discussing the complicated history of his motorcycle problems, addressing himself mainly to Caesar, who knew something about cars and a bit of mechanics, while Caesar, whose mind was on other matters and who had heard the whole story before, more than once, pretended to be listening to Goldman's doubts and hesitations and to the descriptions of the virtues of the various motorcycles available, and from time to time he even made some comment, until Eliezra suddenly interrupted with the words, "I cannot understand, Goldman, why you need a motorcycle in the first place," and Goldman, embarrassed, said that the motorcycle was a very convenient form of transportation in town, much more convenient than the automobile and much cheaper too, and then he smiled and added, as if he weren't being completely serious, that he was fascinated by the speed of the motorcycle and that he had a kind of urge, which he supposed existed in everybody, to challenge death, but Eliezra, who was listening to all this with ill-concealed impatience, interrupted him again with the words, "If you want to be some kind of James Dean then you've woken up a bit late in the day, and if all you want is to kill yourself then you may as well jump off the roof. In any case, the American diet is quite superfluous," and she laughed, and Goldman laughed too, in an attempt to disguise the embarrassment and humiliation he had brought on himself by quite unnecessarily trying to be open and succeeding only in making himself ridiculous, for he was a man of over forty and only too well aware of his impotence and the narrowing range of possibilities available to him, and he knew how absurd and unrealistic the whole motorcycle business was and how right Eliezra was to despise him, and Eliezra took a sip of Caesar's coffee and looked unsympathetically at Goldman and said, "And don't expect anyone to feel sorry for you or to beg you to go on living," and Goldman said, "I don't expect anything," and smiled again and turned to Caesar and said, "I think I'll buy the Triumph," and Caesar said, "Yes, you buy it," and took the coffee cup from Eliezra's hand and said, "Let's go, Eliezra," and they both got up and said goodbye to Regina and to Goldman, who accompanied them to the front door and came back and said to Israel, "He's going to lay her," and added immediately, "She's a good-looking girl but I wouldn't want to fall into her hands. She's a real Brunhilde, and there isn't a drop of love or humility or anything else in her. She's rotten to the core, and all she can think about is herself, just like Caesar," and then he excused himself for a moment and went to the bathroom.

Israel decided to wait for Goldman's return in order to say goodbye to him before leaving, and in the meantime he listened apathetically to the boring conversation going on around the table and watched Moishe Tzimmer's widow as she rose to her feet and said goodbye to Regina and the rest of the company, and Zipporah, who had barely responded to her greeting, gave her a hard look as she left and said to Joel, "You can't keep your mouth shut forever, but you can't go on yapping all the time, either. There are other people in the world," and after a moment she added, "Such a lot of noise. It doesn't say much for her brains," and then she turned to Regina again and pressed her to take a glass of fruit juice and a piece of cake with the words, "Eat something. You haven't got anyone to punish any more," and Regina said, "I'm not hungry," and a few minutes later she said goodbye to Matilda Leviatan, who also rose to take her leave, and when she passed Israel he nodded slightly and said, "Shalom," and Matilda, her dull, dough-colored face drained of almost all its vitality by the years and their disasters, paused for a moment and looked at him hesitantly and said, "Shalom," but from the look she gave him and the hesitant way she returned his greeting it was obvious that she didn't remember who he was, and indeed it was already twenty years since the time when he used to go to their house to visit Hanoch, who had died in the space of forty-eight hours one summer's day when he was twelve years old due to a severe case of pneumonia which he had caught, according to the neighbors and their teachers, because he had spent half the day running after the ice cart, flushed and sweating, and had eaten what amounted to almost an entire block of ice by picking up the chips which fell to the road.

This had happened a few years after the War of Independence, when Hanoch's brother Avinoam, who had been wounded in the war, was still studying agriculture in the United States, where he had been sent for medical treatment and had not yet returned to Israel with his American wife to settle in a moshav and start a farm, whereas their sister Sonia had already separated from the French engineer with whom she had lived in Nice for four years and to whom she had borne a son. Rumor had it that she had left France and was living in London or Amsterdam, working in all kinds of bars and nightclubs as a pianist and dancer and waiting for someone to discover her and give her a part in a movie or a play—a hope which was not entirely groundless, since she was undeniably talented and attracted a certain amount of attention, and although nothing had come of her dreams up to now but disappointment she had nevertheless been on the verge of realizing them on a number of occasions, and she had been men-

tioned two or three times in the local press as an actress, and
once they had even written that she was about to be given a part
in a movie, but to her father, Joseph Leviatan, all this brought
nothing but sorrow and shame, which he bore silently, whereas
Goldman's father said contemptuously, "She's nothing but a whore."

A photograph of Sonia stood next to a cheap, bronze-colored
plaster bust of Beethoven on the piano standing in a corner of
the Leviatans' big room, the center of which was taken up by a
heavy black table which was opened up to its full length every
single day, except for Saturdays and holidays, to accommodate
about twenty-five people who ate their midday meal there, a meal
cooked and served by Matilda Leviatan in big, deep china plates
whose rims were decorated with little flowers or with gold or
dark blue stripes. The food was simple but tasty and nourishing
and plentiful, and the prices were low, and in addition the place
had a pleasant family atmosphere because Matilda, who was a
bustling, motherly woman, put people at their ease with her comfortable, unpretentious ways and because the customers were
regulars who all knew each other—they were civil servants, a
doctor, a painter, a few shopkeepers, two teachers, a construction
engineer, and a man called Joshua, who was a vegetarian and
reminded people of Ghandi because he was ascetically thin and
very agile and sunburned almost to blackness and totally bald,
and he wore peculiar-looking canvas shoes and short pants and
linen or cotton shirts throughout the year and swam in the sea
and did exercises every day, and spent most of his spare time on
the beach or in the fields and orange groves and woods on the
outskirts of the city, and he knew how to imitate the murmur of
the sea and the sound of the wind and the rustle of the leaves
and the voices of the animals and birds, and was astonishingly
gifted at making silhouettes of geese and swans and foxes and
giant butterflies and all kinds of marvelous imaginary creatures
which he would create with his hands as his fancy took him—
fishes with wings, two-headed birds, and animals never seen on
the face of the earth—and throw gleefully onto the wall and in-

spire with life while the children, who sat hypnotized, watching in wonder and suspense and sometimes a trace of anxiety as well, exclaimed admiringly, and occasionally the adults did too.

There was something very captivating about Joshua, but also something upsetting and even frightening, not only because of the severity of his ascetic appearance—since he was in fact a high-spirited, life-loving man—but also because of the mystery and strangeness in his eccentricity, his total rejection of all conventional goals and pursuits and aspirations and mores, and his absolute certainty that he lived in harmony with nature and was close to the knowledge of her deepest secrets and wishes—a knowledge hinted at in the imaginary shadow-images moving on the wall, which he himself resembled, and which for all their sometimes upsetting strangeness looked completely natural and as if they had always existed in the forests and caves or in the depths of the sea, and had only been momentarily extracted from their customary haunts in order that he might reveal them, in a spirit of playfulness, to the astonished eyes of the beholders; in his vegetarianism, on the other hand, there was nothing in the least playful, or provocative either: It was a faith and a vocation, and during the midday meals at the Leviatans' he would repeatedly argue that nature was pure and right and that man in all his investigations of her made no attempt to really understand her and live with her but only to rape and distort her, and that in so doing he was digging his own grave, since nature would triumph in the end, and it was only in cooperation with her that a viable civilization could be created, since nature represented harmony and the right order of things and the deep will of the universe, which could be opposed only at the cost of eventual catastrophe and total chaos, and sometimes he unfolded apocalyptic visions in which he described, not without enjoyment and a certain gleeful relish, the end of civilization after insects had taken over the world, or giant weeds, after which he would repeat to the other diners and to Joseph Leviatan, who listened to him attentively, "Whatever is out of harmony with nature is doomed to extinction!" but Joseph Leviatan was not interested in nature, which he saw as something abstract, but in the man himself as a friend and a fellow human being.

Joseph Leviatan was an accountant who worked for the General Federation of Labor, a tall, eroded man whose ears were too big and whose arms were too long, whose sad face wore a constant expression of grave concern and helpless perplexity, who always dressed, unusually for his circle, in brown suits which were too big for him and which looked old and shabby on him, and who had become increasingly convinced, on the basis of his views and experience and as a result of long observation, wide reading, and deep reflection, that the social order was bad—perhaps iredeemably so—and that man, especially in the cities, was subject to constant economic and emotional stress, which grew worse as the cities grew bigger, becoming violent and alien, and robbing his life of any possibility of freedom or dimension of spirituality or celebration, transforming it into something mean and low, lacking in hope or significance or even in ordinary well-being. He had come to the conclusion that it was necessary to take action in order to rectify this state of affairs, and under the influence of liberal and socialist books and the example of the kibbutz, he had conceived the idea that it would be possible to achieve the desired change by means of urban communes, which would give back to man what society had dispossessed him of, and once this idea had taken root in his mind Joseph Leviatan, who was hard-working and high-minded but not a man of action, expounded his views on the matter to various people, some of whom showed an active interest, and gradually a small circle came into being which set itself the goal of establishing an urban commune uniting workers, merchants, artisans, and members of the liberal professions, who would all continue to ply their previous trades but would put their earnings and incomes into the common kitty, which would provide each member with his individual needs. They would live together, eat together, celebrate together, bring up their children together, all on the basis of absolute equality, communality, and mutual aid, together with brotherly love and absolute political freedom.

The circle expanded and new people joined, including Goldman's father, who had first met Joseph Leviatan in the old days of the Young Workers' movement and later lost touch with him, but now they took up their old friendship again and spent hours talking about the affairs of the commune, whose members held frequent meetings in order to discuss problems and formulate a program and a charter capable of uniting all the different shades of opinion existing in the group, which included utopian socialists and quasi-Marxists and dreamers and liberals, and since this was no easy task, despite all their enthusiasm and goodwill, the clarifications took time and it was two years before they finished formulating the charter, which embraced all aspects of individual, family, and social life; took into account all the rights and obligations of the members and all the problems and deviations which life might confront them with; and seemed completely satisfactory from every point of view. As an appendix to the charter they had also drawn up a manifesto, which in addition to describing the background to the emergence of the commune and its principles—communality, equality, freedom, and fraternity—announced the general aims of the commune and emphasized that this commune did not regard itself as a unique or deviant phenomenon, created simply in order to solve the personal problems of its members, but as the first link in a chain and the model for many others which would follow in its footsteps and realize the dream of a world composed entirely of free communes. At the same time that the charter and manifesto were formulated, practical steps were taken to implement them. The commune was registered as a cooperative society and affiliated with the Cooperative Center of the Labor Federation, a large tract of land next to the city was purchased, and initial attempts were made to prepare the ground and put up the houses and buildings, all of which were designed in lengthy consultation with the various members of the group, and after a few years and more than a few difficulties and disappointments and delays, most of the preparations were complete and the members moved into their urban commune— but without doing anything hasty or reckless. None of them sold their apartments in town, and the majority left most of their personal effects and furniture behind and didn't even rent their town apartments.

Goldman's father left the group about a year before this, shortly after Naomi was killed, and when the first members began moving into the commune he was already out of the country, and when he returned three years later he found neither the commune nor Joseph Leviatan, since the commune had broken up and Joseph Leviatan had died of a heart attack about six months before, although the news of his death did not reach Goldman's father until a few days after his return, driving him into a terrible rage and making him go pale and bang on the kitchen table with his fists and shout hoarsely, "How could you leave me in ignorance? Why didn't you tell me?"—after which he withdrew to the kitchen, where he held his head in his hands and cried like a baby. Regina shut herself up in her room, and Goldman went out, and his father sat alone and cried until he was tired and then cried again until evening fell, and then he rose and washed his face and went to call on Matilda, who was living on a small pension left by her husband and on the dinners which she was again serving in her home to about twenty people, almost all of whom were new, since most of the old customers had dispersed and a few of them had died, and he sat with her for about two hours, during most of which he hardly uttered a word, and after the news on the radio he rose and shook her hand and took his leave, and the next day he went to visit Joseph Leviatan's grave, and with an incomprehensibly stubborn persistence he continued to visit the grave from time to time, and once he even asked Goldman to go with him, but Goldman got out of it, because he hated being alone with his father, who had never had a frank discussion with him in his life, and who only once in a while, by mistake, looked him straight in the eye, and also because he hated cemeteries and all kinds of ceremonial occasions, especially those which had to do with bereavement and mourning—and if only he could have he would have escaped from the house and the mourners now too, only courtesy and duty obliged him to stay, but when he returned from the bathroom he said to Israel, "Let's go into my room for a bit. I haven't got the strength to take these people any more, especially not my mother," and they both went into Goldman's room, which adjoined the living room, and also the little room which had for a short time belonged to Naomi, but unlike the living room, which overlooked the street, Goldman's room, like Naomi's, overlooked the large courtyard of the house.

Apart from the period of the War of Independence, when he had interrupted his high school studies to join the army, and the three weeks of his marriage to the beautiful Jemimah Chernov, Goldman had never left his room, which had hardly changed at all during the years he had lived in it: the same iron bed covered by the same coarse, beige-colored rug with its faded green pattern, and on it the same hard cushions in the floral linen slips which Regina had made for them, and in front of the window the peeling old desk with the round-backed brown chair in front of it, and in the corner the thick, clumsy armchair which could be turned into a bed when the need arose, and next to it, opposite Goldman's bed, the bookcase with its glass doors; even the three-stemmed chandelier and the curtains were the same. The main change was the deterioration which had taken place in everything and the subtle smell of decay which hung in the air (although the room was, as always, very clean), as well as a few new objects which had found their way into it, the ugliest of which was a standard lamp in the form of a gilt snake holding the light bulb in its mouth, topped by a red silk lampshade with gold tassels. This lamp was one of the few wedding presents which had remained with Goldman after the rest had been shame-facedly returned to the many friends and relations invited to the magnificent reception which Goldman's father had insisted on holding, not because of any inclination to ostentation or outward show but because he wanted to be generous, and especially because he had a tyrannical desire to achieve perfection, and without taking any notice of Goldman's objections he had commissioned a seven-piece band and ordered so much beer and so many sausages, not to mention cakes, that every day for a week after the wedding the family ate boiled and fried and baked sausages, and that was after they had already given a lot of them away to neighbors and friends, and there still seemed no end in sight until Regina, who was afraid that they would all be poisoned, threw the rest of the sausages away, to the annoyance of Goldman's father, who despite the fact that together with everyone else he breathed a sigh of relief when the last of the sausages were gone, could not but regret the waste—but all this was completely insignificant compared with the disgrace of Goldman's unexpected divorce, an act which his father saw as directed first and foremost against himself and which he never forgave, for Goldman's father considered divorce as shameful as prostitution and he did everything in his power to prevent it from taking place and to hide it from his neighbors and friends, but all his efforts were in vain. The lamp was the gift of a distant cousin of Regina's, a tourist from America, and had arrived by special delivery after she had already gone home, with the result that there was no one to whom to return it and it remained in Goldman's room standing by the bed next to the wall, which had once many years before been covered by photographs of bulls and bullfighters, and later by photographs of racing drivers and racing cars, but in recent years it was bare save for a gloomy landscape painting and an enlarged photograph of his sister Naomi.

In this room Goldman struggled with his own problems and the problems of the world, and in his wonder and despair he created in his imagination the life of liberation, boldness, and vitality on which he was about to embark, dwelling lovingly and happily on all its details, but in this room too he learned to renounce this new life, sorrowfully and with an oppressive feeling of failure, only to throw himself desperately again, full of longing and envy and hope, into the creation of an even wilder and better and bolder life than before, a life transcending all ordinary laws and possibilities, and between one life and another he trained himself to live his slow and certain death in perfect resignation, and even willingness, even though he longed to live for a thousand years—but the results produced by his diligent and cunning exercises were unimpressive, and he did not succeed in resigning himself to the fact that one day he would cease to exist forever, while death itself, although its existence was real and close enough to him, and although he made a habit of visualizing it to himself in all kinds of different ways, remained in the end mysterious and elusive, and therefore frightening and depressing, since despite all his efforts it did not turn into something which could be experienced or compared with anything else he had experienced, except perhaps for the sudden death of Naomi, which had been a heavy blow to him and shocked him badly, besides causing an almost total breakdown of the family.

Immediately after her death the iron hoops holding the family together had burst asunder, and the hell of hatred and cruelty which had been seething for years beneath the surface of habit and politeness and social conventions erupted and started to boil until it seemed about to sweep the family away and dash it to pieces, but the threat proved short-lived in the end, since the strong and bitter bonds of hatred and cruelty, and of course the fears, which had tied his parents to each other and enabled them to present the appearance of a normal couple in the past, triumphed now too and preserved the family framework, with the difference that the hatred which had broken loose and become virulent went on bubbling openly, poisoning what remained of their lives together without any pity at all.

All this, of course, may have happened even if Naomi had not been killed in a car accident—an accident which, although she had not been in the driver's seat when it happened, gave rise to dark mutterings about Naomi's driving on the part of Goldman's father, who had opposed it from the start and predicted, on numerous occasions, that it would end badly, because he saw in her driving, as well as in almost everything else she did, an act of perversity whose sole purpose was to provoke him and rebel against his ideas, but Naomi, who was very self-sufficient and independent, went her own way stubbornly and openly, and despite the fact that her feelings toward her father were basically ones of respect and understanding and even love, she took no notice of his anger about her attitude toward money and clothes, or his anger when she stopped playing the violin, or when she decided in opposition to all his plans for her that she was going to be a gym teacher when she left school, or when she announced one fine day that she was leaving school to join the British army—not to mention the whole affair with the Englishman, about which they learned only later—and after a month of arguments and entreaties and bitter quarrels she had her way and left home to join the army.

On her last day at home Regina, who despite her reserved and matter-of-fact attitude toward Naomi was very attached to her, cooked a festive farewell meal with fish and meat soup and dumplings and roast veal and her favorite potato pancakes and stewed dried fruit and poppyseed cake, and the four of them—Goldman's father and Regina and Naomi and Goldman, who was then about twelve years old—having not eaten together for years, sat in the big room, the guest room, around the table covered with a white cloth and ate the meal which Regina had prepared for them in silence, and when it was over Naomi stood up and took the little suitcase and the rucksack standing in the passage and came back into the room and shook hands with Goldman and kissed him and her father, who went on sitting as if he had been turned to stone and only stopped pretending to read the newspaper for a moment, and then she kissed Regina, who accompanied her to the front door and stood waiting there until she could no longer hear the sound of her footsteps on the stairs. When Naomi died Goldman, who was very grieved, went into his room and lay on the bed and turned his face to the wall, but not long afterward, while still acutely aware of his loss, he submitted to the knowledge that nothing could bring her back again and gradually accepted her death, which became a permanent fixture in his life, whereas Goldman's father, who never visited her grave, not even once, saw her death as a punishment for her relations with the Englishman while at the same time resenting it as somehow directed against himself, and he blamed Regina for her death and set sail for America, where he remained for two years, after which he spent another year in Canada.

They never found out what he did during his absence or what he lived on, or whether he was helped by his relatives or by others, because during all those years they did not receive a single letter from him except for three New Year cards whose postmarks informed them of his whereabouts, and Goldman and Regina, who were as indifferent to him and his doings as a snail in its shell, did not trouble themselves to make any inquiries. Ever since Naomi's death Regina had, in fact, retired from the world— she stopped eating almost altogether, she stopped going to the theater or the movies or family celebrations, and she hardly left the house at all except for once a week on Wednesdays when she visited Naomi's grave, summer and winter, and hoed the ground, pulled out the weeds, and watered the flowers and shrubs which she had planted on it. Apart from this, she met Yehudit Maizler, her best and only friend who visited her from time to time, and Shmuel and Bracha who also came to the house occasionally, as did Joel and Zipporah, David Kostomolski, Moishe Tzimmer's widow—who got on her nerves—and Moishe Tzellermaier, the only one who came regularly. He had never forgotten how good Regina and Goldman's father had been to him when he arrived in the country as a refugee after the war and stayed in their house, and whenever he came he brought a box of chocolates and a bottle of wine, or an expensive salami, or coffee, or flowers, and Regina, who did not like him, accepted these gifts coldly but Moishe Tzellermaier did not notice and was glad of the opportunity to bring her a little pleasure and do something to express his gratitude and his love.

From time to time, Regina would also receive a letter from Manfred, or she would write to him, and these two things—the weekly visits to the cemetery and Manfred's letters—came to constitute the main content of her life and was the only calendar marking time for her and charging her days with a little interest and suspense; in any case, she was conscious of no other time, just as she had no other life or expectations save those that were connected in one way or another with Naomi or with Manfred, who lived with his family in Holland and came to Israel in the summer, and sometimes at the end of winter too, to stay with his brother in Haifa, and Regina would announce that she was going to the cemetery and would go to visit him there, or he would come to Tel Aviv and they would meet at Yehudit Maizler's house, where he also sent his letters to Regina, which had not been the case fifteen or twenty years before, when he used to visit the Goldmans at home and, although Goldman's father did not like him, was received as a guest of the family, but ever since he had decided to put an end to these family visits all the contact between them had been clandestine and indirect, and they continued in this way even during the period of Goldman's father's absence from the country, because by then it had become a habit which both of them found convenient. Their meetings were brief and they grew inexorably shorter, until in recent years they lasted no more than an hour or two and were really more in the nature of oppressive partings, full of anger and bitterness and pervaded by a feeling of disappointment and resentment, since despite great obstinacy and the will to overcome reality and fantastic hopes which knew no bounds, time and age and the conditions of life eroded their love until in the end all that was left was the dwindling memory of love and shared desires and the wonderful opportunities they had missed and the knowledge, which neither of them dared communicate, that they had both been defeated and that no power on earth could turn the clock back or rekindle the dying flame, and they would part at the end of these meetings determined never to meet again and go their separate ways, only to begin longing for each other again almost immediately and cherishing fond hopes and looking forward impatiently to their next meeting—they loved the memory of their love, and felt committed to it, and went on hoping without hope, and this made their hopes immortal and turned their lives into the eternal swinging of a pendulum which was no longer dependent on them or their wills because they themselves had become the thing in which it was embodied.

Manfred was born in a large country town at the foot of the Carpathian mountains to a wealthy Jewish family which had made money in the kerosene business. His name was Meshulem, but at school he went by the name of Manfred, which is what he was called in Eretz Yisrael too, although Goldman's father called him "the intellectual," and later on—together with many others of their circle—"the factionist," and in the end, after Manfred had already left the country, he referred to him as "the Latin lover" but of course he never called him by any of these names to his face, for Manfred was a very sharp-witted and highly educated man, and underneath his façade of shyness and refinement there was something hard and resolute and sometimes despotic. He spoke little, although when he did say anything his words were listened to attentively, and mixed with other people and made contact with them only with great difficulty, as if he were under some kind of constraint, while they, for the most part, respected him and were even in awe of him, although there were some who resented him because they considered him conceited, and he was, in fact, an arrogant man with a high opinion of his own worth and also a sense of vocation, intolerant of human follies and weakness, ignorance and errors, and sometimes even human diversity, and he quite often treated people with contemptuous coldness and judged them harshly, but at the same time he forced himself to make overtures to them and tried to be like one of them because he believed in communal living and comradeship and simplicity and open, sincere relations between one man and another, all as part of a more comprehensive world view, and it was only many years later, in a conversation with his eldest son Raphael, who became a doctor of physics and was closer to him than any other member of his family, that he said: "I thought it was genuineness and simplicity and the behavior of a new society which would give birth to a better world, but for the most part it was nothing but boorishness which led to barbarism," and Raphael asked him if he would have lived his life differently if he had had the chance, and he meant his family life too, and Manfred said, "I don't want to think about it," but once upon a time after his student days—which he himself later referred to as his "salon period"—he had deliberately suppressed his personal wishes, feelings, and talents, and apparently also his pride, and put them at the service of his logic, which was so penetrating and uncompromising that it was sometimes frightening, giving rise to the suspicion that beyond this resolute logic striving so consistently to negate everything human—fear, love, sentiment, pity, and in the end his own self too—there yawned a dark abyss, and thanks to this same logic he became a Zionist and despite the pleas and threats of his parents, who saw themselves first and foremost as citizens of the Hapsburg Empire and aspired to be as German as possible and to bring their children up in this spirit too—not to mention the great hopes they had for him personally—he turned his back on all the possibilities open to him and renounced his share of the family inheritance and emigrated to Eretz Yisrael as a Zionist pioneer, overcoming his bodily weakness by sheer willpower and devoting himself to back-breaking physical labor, but in the course of his work as a pioneer he adopted left-wing views and became a communist, and in the spirit of communism he denied the existence of the Jewish people and rejected Zionism. He did this quietly but firmly and conclusively, and at the beginning of the thirties he left Palestine and spent a few years in Strasbourg, where his disillusionment with communism increased until only two years after he had justified the Moscow trials he abandoned it entirely and left Strasbourg for Paris, where he continued his studies of medieval, and especially ecclesiastical, history and literature, and became absorbed in an investigation into Christian demonology—the development of the concept of the devil and his various incarnations, the changes which took place in the relationship between God and the devil and their significance for Christian thought in general, the demons and their different roles, their place in the demonological hierarchy and the changes taking place in their religious status and functions, and in connection with this research he spent a long time mapping hell as it was described in lay and ecclesiastical literature and surveying its various spheres and beasts and other features, and he even published a rather slim volume dealing with these matters, which was well received, but Manfred himself was not satisfied with the book, for he was very conscious of all its faults and limitations and in fact he regarded it as a first, rough draft of a more comprehensive and sophisticated book he intended writing on the same subject—a book which was never written, partly because of a chance meeting with a Polish friend of his youth, who had since become a lecturer in philosophy, which shifted the focus of his interest so that he began to devote himself to a study of Spinoza, and intended writing a monograph on him, and in the meantime, while he was doing research and collecting material for it, he published two articles on historical-philosophical problems connected with Christianity, and years later he published another article on Lenin's personality and the revolution, and that was all he ever published, because from year to year he grew more skeptical, and instead of seeing what he had achieved in his writing he saw only what he had not achieved and what was flawed and lacking, and he was full of reservations about his articles, which were almost impossible to read because his writing was so complicated, made up of a labyrinth of complex sentences contradicting and qualifying each other and expressing a Herculean effort on the part of the writer to present the problem engaging his attention in all its intricacies and contradictions, while at the same time revealing the roots of the unity underlying all this complexity. Despite all his brilliance and persistence Manfred failed in this effort, as he was bound to fail, and he threw up his hands in despair and returned to his monograph on Spinoza, which seemed to him a less complicated matter. He decided to concentrate exclusively on the facts of the philosopher's life and system of thought, and he stuck to this project in spite of the war—which was already raging around him—because he saw it as his contribution to the victory over madness and irrationality, but not long afterward he gave up his writing and research and did not resume it even after the war was over, because he had lost all interest in the humanities, especially philosophy, which in light of the war with all its horrors, barbarities, and madness he had come to see as groundless, pointless, and even shocking. This also applied to literature and poetry, and research into historical and religious phenomena, and the whole of European culture, and Manfred accordingly gave way completely to skepticism, which was the product of his critical intelligence and education and experience, while at the same time, after a period of inner nihilism and a renewed belief in force as the only way to impose order on the world, he returned to his former conviction that only reason and logic were capable of providing the basis for the creation of a new, good, and harmonious world—a world in which Manfred himself no longer believed because he no longer believed in reason and logic as forces capable of defeating irrationality and acting on history in order to mold it in a positive way, and in his despair and anger at the world and at history, which had failed and were doomed to go on failing forever, as well as a feeling of guilt, he gave everything up and went to work as a builder and a gardener, and then as a junior assistant in a research project on bird migration, in which capacity he spent a whole winter in a little hut on the Alps, and after that he took up optics, and in his spare time he began playing the violin again after a lapse of many years, and although he played it badly it made him more serene, while his experience of life and his skepticism, without detracting from his self-esteem, gave him a new sense of humility and the ability to forgive human foolishness, error, weakness, and unpleasantness, and this in turn enabled him to understand and accept his relationship with his second wife and his love affair with Regina, who was about his age and whom he had first met in the town of his birth when he was a boy.

But for the fact that Regina had fallen ill with an obscure respiratory disease they would probably have married and emigrated together to Eretz Yisrael, but as things were she was sent off to various sanitariums and spent a long time recuperating in all kinds of mountain resorts, while Manfred emigrated alone, and although they tried to keep in touch the ties between them weakened, and by the time they met again many years later in Eretz Yisrael Regina was already married to Goldman's father, and Manfred too was married to a woman who deserted him two years later and went to live with another man, and despite all the unpleasantness and confusion accompanying this event it was the happiest day of Manfred's life, because he had hated her from the first day of their married life together. Once he was separated from his wife, Manfred expected Regina to leave Goldman's father and marry him, but she hesitated and held back, and in the meantime Naomi was born and Manfred got married again to a distant relative a few years older than he was, a rich and well-educated woman, by which time he was already in Strasbourg, where his two sons were born, Raphael and Claude—who was a very gifted boy but couldn't settle down to any field of study and in the end went into business, without too much success, and of whom his father said that he devoted so much time and effort to trying to be happy that in the end it made him unhappy—whereas his daughter, Elinore, was born shortly after they arrived in London, where they spent most of the war years. Elinore was tall and fragile as a delicate piece of china, her skin was pale and transparent—as if she had spent her whole life in a closed room behind heavy curtains—she had thick, lifeless lips and cold blue eyes, and she fascinated Goldman by her appearance the first and only time that they met—a meeting which took place when she was seventeen, about ten years younger than Goldman, and which left a profound impression on him.

There was something at once attractive and repellent about Elinore and her frozen beauty, causing a morbid, uncanny fascination—but in any case she was remote and out of reach, because Elinore was doomed to live all her life in a visionary world of her own, somewhere on the borderline between reality and imagination and the dark depths of the soul, in a place where knowledge and will disintegrated and gave way to dread, or the enjoyable sensation of ceasing to be, and Goldman, who did not dare to ask about her explicitly, hoped every year that she would come back with Manfred, and indeed the year that his father left home and went to America she was supposed to come, but for some reason her trip was cancelled and she never arrived, and Goldman went on waiting for her the next year, and the one after that too, when one fine day in the afternoon the key turned in the door and his father, who had returned from America without a word of warning, came in and walked down the passage with two suitcases which he put down in the big room, next to the sofa, and then he went to the bathroom, where he washed his face and hands, and then he went into the kitchen and said, "Shalom," and Regina said, "Shalom," and Goldman, who was sitting and eating, stood up and shook hands with him and said, "Shalom" and asked how he was, and Goldman's father said, "Fine," and Regina asked him if he wanted anything to eat, and Goldman's father said, "No. I'm going soon," and took off his hat and said, "I only came to take a few things and go," and he glanced at Regina, and Regina said, "Everyone must do as he pleases," and offered him a cup of tea and some biscuits, and Goldman's father said, "I'm going as soon as I've had my tea," and Regina repeated, "Everyone must do as he pleases," and Goldman's father said, "Right" and gave her a hostile look, and then he exchanged a few words with Goldman and asked him how he was and what he was doing and drank his tea and removed some documents and other little things from his wardrobe and put them into one of his suitcases, but he did not leave the house, although every week he threatened to do so, and even took various steps toward carrying out his threats: He asked a real estate agent to find him a suitable apartment, and in the meantime he gathered all his belongings and clothes together and even packed some of them in suitcases in readiness for the move. He took care of all his own needs, bought his own food, and prepared all his own meals— except for dinner, which he ate in a restaurant—eating them apart from Regina, whom he ignored exaggeratedly, and at the same time he began drawing up his will. But none of these threats or ploys frightened anyone, especially not Regina, who had settled all her accounts with him, and since she had nothing more to lose, and was free of the fear he had once inspired in her, went on obstinately living her bitter, ascetic life as if nothing had happened and found her own ways of defending herself against his insults and also of hurting him in return—she withdrew even further into herself and when he ignored her she ignored him right back, which drove him wild and made his blood boil, and she stopped asking him if he wanted her to make him something to eat, or send his clothes to the laundry, or iron them, and she took to spending a lot of time with Yehudit Maizler, dressed in a way she knew that he hated, bought unnecessary things, and resolutely refused to accept a cup of tea from him, or even her medicine when she was sick, since she would rather have died than been beholden to him for anything, and she made no attempt to hide this from him or from others either.

They became deadly enemies waging a cruel, ruthless, and ugly war by means of small but hurtful acts of revenge, insults and humiliations, exploiting their knowledge of each other's most hidden weaknesses to this end, and even exploiting their dead daughter Naomi, with each of them trying in his own way to dominate her life and affections and each trying to blame the other for her estrangement and death, and in this posthumous battle for Naomi's soul Goldman's father was particularly active: He fired the first shots in the campaign and he pursued it mercilessly, arguing repeatedly that from the moment she was born Naomi had been attached to him and him only, because from beginning to end he had given her love and attention and profound understanding, as opposed to Regina, who had never wanted her because she was in love with Manfred, and who had spoiled and suffocated her with anxious care on the one hand, and subjected her to harsh, unreasonable demands on the other, as well as all kinds of insane prohibitions, which had made her rebellious and impatient—and in fact she had made her daughter's life such a misery, both with her kindness and with her strictness, that in the end she had driven her out of the house. As for his own role in Naomi's upbringing, he never tired of repeating how he had taken her for walks when she was a little girl, how he had told her stories and taken her to the beach and the movies, how he had bought her a bicycle when she turned twelve and a watch when she turned fifteen, and how he had spoken to her from time to time as she grew older and was confronted with new problems—and these were not lies but the pathetic imaginings of a man seeking a way to repair his life and to win, at all costs, a victory in which he himself no longer really believed. The truth was that he had paid very little attention to Naomi, that he had been impatient with her, that when he did occasionally exchange a few sentences with her these exchanges were usually meaningless and undertaken out of a sense of obligation, and that the only time he ever devoted to her was what was left over in between his back-breaking work and the rest of his public and private activities—except for a short but stormy period when he tried to force her to learn to play the violin, using flattery and persuasion, all kinds of threats, the promise of dreary rewards, and unrestrained yelling—but it was hard to blame him for this, because his hard physical labor on the one hand and his own ambitions, perfectionism, honesty, and pride on the other drained his strength and ruined his nerves, and he would come home in the late afternoon exhausted and irritable, gobble down the meal which Regina had prepared for him, and sprawl out with the Labor Party newspaper on the couch, where he would soon fall into a heavy sleep with the paper spread over his face and lie there sleeping, sometimes still in his working clothes, until evening.

Regina hardly ever reacted to his tales about Naomi, and she didn't react even when he blamed her for Naomi's death because it was her fault that Naomi had fallen in love with a married Englishman in Alexandria, and she had known all about the affair and done nothing to interfere and put a stop to it—and, in fact, Goldman's father had always believed, even before he went off to America, that Naomi's death was a punishment for this illicit relationship, and it made no difference to him that the affair had taken place a number of years before her death, and the more often he repeated this argument—each time with greater pain and more anger—the more convinced he became of its truth, until it was transformed into an established fact, impossible to deny, just as there was no denying Regina's guilt either, but he never said this to Regina directly, because shortly after his return from America they had stopped addressing each other directly, and even in each other's presence they would speak to Goldman, or the door, the wall, the kettle, the chair, the newspaper, or any other available object, referring to each other as "he" or "she." When he got onto the subject of Naomi's death and her guilt, Regina would usually retire to another room or leave the house, but once she suddenly turned to Goldman and said, "It all began the day he decided to teach her to play the violin, or even long before that," and Goldman's father said, "That's a lie. She's lying," and Goldman, who refrained from interfering in these battles and made no attempt to pour oil on troubled waters or to reconcile his parents, said, "Enough already!" and Regina said, "He destroyed everything with his pride," and shut herself up in the bathroom, and Goldman shut himself up in his room, full of anger, because his mother's nagging anxieties and self-abnegation in addition to the accumulation of weariness and disappointments which were gradually turning into a bitter, grinding nihilism, and the wild, wrong-headed tyranny of his father, had tried Goldman's patience beyond bearing and made him detest them both and long to leave home, especially now with their spiteful and pitiless battles raging around his head, but he did not move and went on living between them despite the fact that he could not bear the sight of their faces or the sound of their voices or say one friendly word to them, and although both of them were desperately in need of attention and a little affection and pity he shut his eyes and stopped his ears as best he could and let them go on poisoning each other's lives, and only occasionally did he have an attack of conscience and feel sorry for them, but it was a detached, impersonal sorrow which did not stop him from concentrating on his own affairs.

At the beginning Goldman had intended to study zoology, and later, with Naomi's encouragement, he thought of taking up Oriental studies. His father wanted him to become an engineer but, to his disappointment, in the end Goldman took up law, and completed his studies successfully, and went to work in a lawyer's office as an expert on company and contract law, but his interests ranged far beyond the confines of his profession, which became a nuisance to him and filled him with a feeling of waste and failure, and he read widely and unsystematically in all kinds of scientific fields, as well as literature and current affairs, sociology and psychology, travel diaries, biographies, books about religion and geology and history—and the books piled up on his shelves and lay scattered about the room, and when he came into his room with Israel he cleared a few books off the armchair and put them on the bed, and then he took a bottle of brandy and two glasses out of his desk and asked Israel, who sat down in the chair, if he would have a drink with him, and Israel said, "Yes, but don't fill the glass," and Goldman poured them each a drink and they raised their glasses and drank and Goldman said again, "I haven't got the strength to take these people any more, especially not my mother," and he slid his finger around the rim of the glass and added, "I'm very fond of some of them, don't think I'm not." He spoke in a gray, tired voice and took another sip of brandy, and Israel stole a glance at the dumbbells standing in the corner next to the desk with the "Bullworker" and Goldman, who had seen him looking at them, said, "You have to take care of your body. It gives you an altogether different attitude toward life," and then there was a silence in which they could hear the voices of the crickets rising from the yard, together with a distant roar which resembled the sound of the sea, whose smell hung faintly in the air and mingled with the smell of the Persian lilac and the frangippani and the pittosporum, and the almost imperceptible movement of the air bore these scents, which were now purer and clearer than before, into the room through the open window.

Israel sipped his drink and looked involuntarily at Goldman, who looked back at him and smiled, but underneath the thin cover of this dry smile his lean face was haggard and drained and lifeless and his green eyes, surrounded by crinkles and folds of skin, were full of sadness, and he poured himself another drink and said, "You know that I didn't love him, but when I saw him helpless and sinking I felt sorry for him. Anyway, it was awful. And in any case it's hard to accept that someone's dead and gone forever. Because if that's the way things are, what's it all for?" and he fell silent for a moment and then said, "You see, I'm talking about myself again." Goldman spoke very simply, and he thus succeeded in transferring his sadness to Israel, together with a sense of the hopelessness and pointlessness of everything, as well as his great weariness, and the persistent, monotonous chirping of the crickets, which sounded as if it would go on forever, went on rising from the empty courtyard, together with the summer scents so familiar to Israel from the days of his childhood which he had spent in this same courtyard, on the lawn and under the tall-topped poinsettia regia and the Persian lilac and the jacaranda trees and in the secret recesses of the giant, evergreen ficus, and the shade of the dense fir trees, in games of hide-and-seek and catch, and ball games, and all kinds of entertaining and impudent exploits and mischief, and in the soft, dewy summer nights he had been initiated here into the pleasurable secrets of sex by means of stories and rude jokes and rumors and the mutual masturbation in which the boys would sometimes secretly indulge and which gave rise to excitement and unendurable pleasure mixed with fear and feelings of guilt, and the calm voices of people and the sound of music would come floating down from the windows and balconies, and black bats would emerge from the darkness in sudden, aimless flights, diving like stones and rising again, and they all kept on warning each other to be careful not to let the bats get into their hair, because if they did they would never let go, and Israel felt himself growing old as he sat in this room, and again he stole an involuntary glance at Goldman and said nothing. For what could he say to him? If he tried to console him Goldman would dismiss his consolations scornfully, because his sorrow at his father's death was not the kind which seeks consolation, and it was quite possible that if his father could have been brought back to life Goldman would not have been too happy about it, and he might even have opposed it explicitly, whereas the other sorrow which cast a shadow over his life could not be wiped out with words, and Israel played with his brandy glass and maintained a resolute, but not ill-humored, silence, and Goldman looked at the picture of his sister on the wall and said, "She had beautiful eyes," and Israel said, "Yes, she did," and he too looked at the picture, and then he turned his head and looked outside through the open window, and Goldman said that love and hate, together with the force of habit and family ties, chained people to each other in a way over which logic and will had no control, and that even death could not sever these bonds, except through the stubborn strength of time, which wore everything away, and even then something of the other person remained behind as part of your being forever, and for years afterward the surface of the great ocean of oblivion would be disturbed by various troublesome memories which, while they were no longer the things themselves, somehow conjured them up like ghosts from the spirit world.

Outside the darkness was already complete, but not so black or dense as to obliterate the dark treetops of the poinsettia regia and the ficus, at the foot of which they had discovered the body of Kaminskaya after she had thrown herself drunkenly from the balcony of her third-floor apartment one summer sometime after the end of the war, and in the apartment full of plants and fine tapestries hanging on the walls, with the lights on in the big room and in the kitchen, they had found ashtrays and glasses full of cigarette butts, empty brandy bottles, newspapers and books and clothes, and a kettle with all its water boiled away standing red-hot on the stove. She had thrown herself off the balcony in the early hours of the morning, which for her were perhaps twilight or the middle of the night, and the residents of the house, full of agitation, stood in the courtyard in little groups, in their working clothes or their pajamas, and tried to get at the motives for her act by way of all kinds of gossip and rumors, most of which of course were true, and Moishe Tzimmer wandered from group to group shouting that what she had done was wrong from the moral point of view since no one had the right to take his own life any more than he had the right to steal or rob because his life did not belong to him, and Goldman's father, who agreed with him, said that suicide was forbidden by criminal law too, and that it showed nothing but cowardice and egotism, but one of the neighbors interrupted him with the words, "Why don't you take her to court, then?" and he laughed ironically and pointed to Kaminskaya, and then he went on to argue that there was nothing wrong with suicide, and everyone had the right to do what he liked with his own body, and the act itself showed nothing but that someone who had been alive had decided to die, and had died, and the rest of the neighbors were also divided in their opinions, although most of them agreed in one way or another with Goldman's father and Moishe Tzimmer, and Israel, who was standing there and had managed to get a glimpse of Kaminskaya lying sprawled in her dressing gown on the damp grass before Moishe Tzimmer's widow covered her body with a sheet, withdrew his eyes from the window and asked Goldman what he was going to do now, and Goldman looked at him in astonishment, and Israel, who had realized how superfluous his question was before it was out of his mouth, tried somehow to erase it and to get up and go, but Goldman forestalled him and said that for the time being, of course, he would not be able to leave home as he had intended doing, but he was definitely going to change his profession, and as for leaving home he would do that before the end of the year, certainly no longer than that, and Israel nodded slightly and said nothing, because during the course of the years he had heard Goldman, whose forehead was deeply lined and who was already going bald, say almost exactly the same thing over and over again, and the only difference was that from year to year his tone grew flatter and more exhausted, although in spite of everything it still retained some degree of conviction and faith in the future.

Goldman was about five years older than Caesar and more than nine years older than Israel, but long friendship and intimacy had closed this gap, and after a short pause for reflection, during which he finished what was left of the brandy in his glass and poured himself another, he turned to Israel once again and said that he was sorry that right after his discharge from the army he had not gone to sea as a sailor, as he had thought of doing, and that later on he had not realized his ambition of being a farmer, but he knew that these possibilities had been missed forever, because he was now too old for them, whereas if he had at least studied zoology, as he had once wanted to, he would certainly be happy, but that too was a lost cause, and so he would probably take up mechanics, or carpentry, in order to find the kind of serenity and peace of mind which Avinoam had found on the moshav. The truth was that more than he longed for serenity and peace of mind, Goldman yearned for something exciting, and even catastrophic, to happen, something which would lift him up and sweep him away and transform his life utterly and instantly into the kind of liberated and carefree life which he pictured in his imagination and which was actually in complete contradiction to both his principles and his possibilities, and he fell silent for a moment and looked at Israel expectantly, waiting for him to approve his plans, or to contradict them in the name of greater things, and there was something so lost and lonely in his look that Israel said, "Yes, that sounds like a good idea," and then he said, "Tomorrow's going to be very hot again," and Goldman took a little sip of brandy and roused himself and said that it was a pity that his mother wasn't some kind of Italian countess from an impoverished family who had fled to Paris and there met and married his father, who should have been some kind of Russian émigré, maybe an anarchist, or perhaps a drunken Irishman, half a poet and half a rogue and half a pimp, living from hand to mouth, because a geneaology like that gave a man a head start of at least a hundred years of happiness, and in any case a person with a start like that would never turn into someone who spent all his life in a lawyer's office shuffling papers and trying to behave nicely and obey the rules and be responsible. At the very least, that man would be some kind of lively gypsy and really live.

This was not the first time that Israel had heard these things either, and he said, "Maybe you're right," and smiled, and Goldman too smiled and said, "I envy Caesar. He lives as if life was a game that goes on forever. He's got no problems. He's a real butterfly." A butterfly was what the boys used to call Sonia Leviatan, Avinoam and Hanoch's sister, who was the first member of the opposite sex to arouse Goldman and who, as a woman— albeit still a girl too—had allowed him to taste the thrilling pleasures that were in the power of the body to bestow, and not without enjoying herself either, although her enjoyment was different from his, because she was a few years older than he was and she felt nothing for him, but she let him see her sometimes through the open door in her panties and bra when he was visiting Avinoam, who was in his class at school, and later on she occasionally let him touch the hair under her armpits and her firm little breasts, and once he even dared to put his hand carefully under her skirt and slide his frightened fingers slowly up her thigh and slip them into her panties and touch her belly and her pubic hair. The pleasure was so great, he felt as if he were in a trance, swooning with excitement and dazzled by delight, until suddenly he couldn't hold it in anymore and everything burst out at once, and afterward, emptied out and sobered up, he pulled out his hand ashamed and embarrassed and above all afraid, and half turned his back on her and stealthily pulled his shirt out of his trousers to cover the cursed stain spreading there and thus, without looking at her, he left hastily on trembling legs and stole through the courtyard and went home, and after he had quickly washed himself and changed his clothes, cursing himself and her, he sat down in a gloomy and repentent mood to do his homework, and although he was too miserable and confused to think a single coherent thought he went on sitting there, withdrawn into himself, in front of the exercise books and the textbooks, trying to do his homework and forget about everything, and afterward, for quite a long time, he avoided going over to Avinoam's and meeting Sonia, who was now playing the piano and dancing with all kinds of strange men, who unlike Goldman presumably enjoyed her body without any inhibitions—and he went on slowly sipping his brandy and stroked his lips with his fingers and looked at Israel and said that in the end everybody was going to die anyway, and ten years more or less didn't really change anything, and nor did the amount of sex and wild times, but what he would like was to understand death and make friends with it (if you could put it like that), like Elinore, and receive it like an expected and not unfamiliar guest, and not be afraid of it, and also not to think about the fact that the world would go on without him for hundreds and thousands of years, and while he was lying in the ground in the dark people would be walking around outside in the sun, going to the beach, talking, eating, falling in love, looking forward to things, seeing trees and cars and movies and reading newspapers.

Israel said nothing, and Goldman played with the cork of the brandy bottle and said, "No, you can't live twice. Even Dostoevski only lived once," and giggled, and after a moment he said, "But you can commit suicide. In other words, you can beat death at its own game. The only trouble is that once you've done it you can never take it back again, and the victory might prove rather a hollow one in the end," and he giggled again and nodded enigmatically at Israel, who decided that Caesar and Eliezra must have finished with the studio by now, and he stood up and put his glass down on the table and said that he was very tired and wanted to go back to the studio to take a shower and a rest and wait for Ella. Goldman made no attempt to detain him but rose to his feet and accompanied him to the living room to say good-bye to his mother, saying, "I'm planning to go and visit Avinoam soon. I haven't seen him for years," and he asked Israel if he would like to go with him, and Israel said, "Maybe," and went to shake hands with Regina, and as he turned to go Uncle Lazar appeared in the living room doorway dressed, as usual, with the utmost simplicity—khaki pants and a short-sleeved blue-gray shirt—and holding a black leather briefcase in his hand and looking so embarrassed that he appeared afraid not only of the people in the room but also of even the furniture and the light and the walls, and the only thing that seemed capable of inspiring him with any confidence at all was his briefcase, to which he clung for dear life as he went on standing there in an agony of embarrassment, not knowing where to turn or what to do, until Goldman, who had not realized what was happening at first, suddenly smiled broadly and cried, "Uncle Lazar!" and hurried over to him and shook his hand warmly, and immediately turned to his mother and said again, "Uncle Lazar," and Uncle Lazar tore himself away from the doorway and crossed the room with an uncertain step, and with everyone's eyes on him he went up to Regina and shook hands with her shyly and muttered something and kissed her on the cheek, and then he took a few steps backward and stood there again, as if he didn't know what to do next, and Goldman indicated an empty chair next to Chaim-Leib and he went over to sit down on it, but before that Bracha called him and he exchanged a few words with her and also with Shmuel and Joel and Zipporah and Meir, and shook hands with Moishe Tzellermaier and his wife and Mrs. Haya, and Mrs. Haya asked him where Yehudit was, and Uncle Lazar said, "I took her home, She was very tired," and turned to Chaim-Leib, who was humming softly to himself and beating time lightly with his thick hand on the table, and asked him how he was, and Chaim-Leib, withered and yellow and looking as if death had already invaded his body, stroked his gray beard and nodded slightly and said in Yiddish, "What is a man—here today and gone tomorrow. Such is the will of God," and a strained and weary but nevertheless gay smile appeared in his brown eyes and lit up his face for a moment, and he straightened the black hat on his head and broke off a piece of cake and put it in his mouth and nodded again, and Israel waited until Goldman had finished offering Uncle Lazar fruit and biscuits and urging him to eat something, and then he said, "So long," and turned to go, but Goldman accompanied him to the front door and before they parted he asked him to give him a call the next day or the day after, and Israel said, "OK," and descended the stairs with a great feeling of relief.

He went straight to the studio, but when he got there he saw that the shutter on the window of his room, which overlooked the street, was down, and so he knew that Caesar was still there with Eliezra, because this was the sign upon which he and Caesar had agreed, and all of a sudden he felt so full of rage that he would have liked to run straight upstairs and smash the door to smithereens and pack his things and leave, but he went on standing in front of the house, very still, looking up wrathfully from time to time, until in the end he gave up in despair and turned away and started walking until he reached Hayarkon Street and walked along it and then turned down to the promenade overlooking the calm sea, and leaned on the iron railing and looked into the darkness and the stripes of white foam appearing in it regularly and ceaselessly and advancing toward the shore, where they dissolved, and with the rage and resentment still seething in him he tried to guess whether Ella had called or come to the studio in his absence, and listened to the lazy, monotonous murmur of the rippling little waves which combined with the agreeable smell of the sea filling the warm air to create a very relaxed, summery feeling.

For almost a year now Israel had been living in this studio, which was really only an ordinary three-room apartment, enjoying the generosity and dependent on the favors of Caesar, who had turned the living room into a photography studio and one of the rooms into a darkroom and laboratory, while offering the use of the third, which also served as his office and archives, to Israel, and allowing him to live in it as much as he wanted to without taking a penny in rent or even asking him to pay his share of the water, electric, or telephone bills. The room was a spacious one containing a big desk, two office chairs, and two gray metal cupboards, as well as the brown couch and the piano which Israel had brought with him, and a big wooden board leaning against one of the walls, with a blowup of an old couple sitting in front of a haberdashery shop in the evening on two little stools and looking peaceful stuck to it, torn and full of holes because Caesar used it for his knife-throwing games. Caesar had offered Israel the use of this room with the utmost simplicity, without any calculations, and with the unthinking generosity which was characteristic of his nature and which would sometimes, in certain circumstances, take on the form of an ostentatious, although not ungraceful, extravagance, but he had made one condition—that Israel would have to vacate the apartment whenever he needed it, and he needed it every day from about two to four in the afternoon, when he made love to Eliezra on Israel's couch, but in addition to these more or less regular hours he also needed it at various other hours of the day or night, and although he would try to let Israel know in advance his need was sometimes so sudden and urgent that he was unable to do so, and on these occasions he would be obliged to take Israel by surprise, waking him from his sleep or interrupting him while he was playing the piano and forcing him to leave the apartment in a hurry, pretending not to have noticed the girl standing next to Caesar in the doorway. These sudden surprises were not infrequent, because Caesar chased women tirelessly and indiscriminately, and every conquest, no matter how unimpressive, filled him with satisfaction and pride while at the same time spurring him on to further triumphs, in which he often invested a lot of time and money and effort and imagination, refusing to give up or retreat before the most formidable obstacles, because he could not afford to fail and because he agreed with the point of view, which he had inherited mainly from Erwin and Besh, that a man has to lay a lot of women, and there isn't a woman who can't be laid, because they all want it, although they all want it in different ways, and Caesar wasn't squeamish about any of them.

Israel would wait for the days when Caesar was so busy at work that he couldn't possibly take time off even for the regular two hours, or even one hour, or for the days when he was ill or out of town, since the days when Eliezra couldn't go to bed with Caesar brought Israel no relief at all, because then Caesar would usually bring Vicky, even after she became engaged, or one of the women he had on the side, and it was only rarely, because of some unexpected mishap or failure, that the two hours in question remained empty and unexploited, in which case Caesar, in low spirits, with resentment and a feeling of defeat that he didn't even try to hide, would try to notify Israel, and Israel, who now moved away from the railing and started walking along the promenade, would feel no more than a fleeting satisfaction, because in any case he was at Caesar's mercy, and the occasional reprieve only stressed the fact of his dependence.

He walked slowly, still angry inside, looking at the sea and the people strolling like him along the promenade, and at those who were sitting on the benches or leaning against the railing, chatting to each other and smoking cigarettes and watching the passing scene or gazing silently at the sea. Among them were middle-aged people and old people, abandoning themselves to the summer indolence and enjoying the peaceful atmosphere and the refreshing sea breezes, and young couples, and boys with darting eyes who had come here in search of illicit pleasures, and Israel passed among them and crossed the street and walked along the row of cafes on the other side, the first of which was once the haunt of the rich of the town, contractors and business-men and landlords, who used to sit there on upholstered chairs in front of little tables covered with red cloths with fancy lamps standing on them, drinking tea and coffee and looking at the sea and at illustrated magazines in a soothing, complacent atmosphere, while the one after it used to have a band in the summer and a low platform at the edge of the dance floor where all kinds of crooners in Panama hats and singers in the style of Marlene Dietrich or Carmen Miranda and magicians and acrobats with Chinese names used to perform, but now both these cafes, which had been closed down years ago, were dark and deserted, and next to them were three big, Mediterranean cafes opening onto the pavement, full of painted women in brightly colored summer dresses sitting in the white glare of the neon lights, darting quick looks about them as they drank and talked and laughed to the sound of the music blaring out of the loudspeakers, and resembling nothing so much as a flock of cheerful sparrows perched on a telephone wire.

Goldman, who would take Israel with him from time to time for a walk along the promenade, said that all these women were prostitutes, and the men sitting with them, as well as those cir-culating from table to table or standing on the pavement with their hands in their pockets looking at them, were pimps or else men in search of prostitutes, and Israel looked at these men and women out of the corner of his eye as he passed, but he didn't stop and went on walking and crossed the road and passed a small cafe with dusty lamps spreading a murky yellow light, where Goldman had once taken a beating because of a prostitute, and then he passed a felafel kiosk and a dim bar with a few girls sitting apathetically in the entrance who beckoned him to come in, and he paused for a moment in front of a dirty, seedy, green-painted gaming alley full of young men milling about in the dirt and cigarette smoke hitting punchballs with their fists and shooting at little wooden figures that popped quickly up and down again with air guns and playing with pinball machines which made a dull, stupid, clicking sound, and spitting on the floor, elbowing each other, smoking, swearing, and laughing. Both before and after being beaten up Goldman had argued in favor of prostitution, basing his case on quotations from psychologists, sociologists, and doctors, let alone the elementary right which adult human beings possessed, or should possess in democratic societies, to do what they liked with their own bodies, but he went even further than this and argued not only that prostitution was a positive phenomenon which should be accorded a legal status but also that the state should provide prostitutes free, or for a nominal fee, just as it provided educational, health, and welfare services, and Israel, who listened to these arguments without expressing an opinion, paused again, this time next to the opera house, and looked at the photographs of *Madame Butterfly,* and then he walked up Allenby Street and turned onto Pinsker on his way back to the studio.

Ostensibly Israel made his living by copying musical scores, but actually he lived off Caesar, whereas if he had agreed to give piano lessons or taken the trouble to learn a trade he could have rented himself an apartment and been independent, but in spite of his pride and, of course, the inconvenience and unpleasantness, he had not taken this road because he was too selfish, and when it came to choosing between his humiliating and oppressive dependence on Caesar and his professional freedom and convenience he chose the former and adopted a monastic way of life without setting himself any clear aim, and deliberately ignored the claims of reality and time, and thus he was able to harden his heart, and stubbornly refuse to acknowledge all kinds of things which were disturbing and wrong, and concentrate resolutely on himself and on the main thing, and the main thing was the organ, which for almost a year now he had been playing in St. Antonio's church, toying with the idea that at some date in the not-too-distant future he would be able to earn his living by it, although in his heart of hearts he already knew that nothing would come of this idea.

He crossed a small asphalt square with a few spreading ficus trees and approached the house, but even before reaching the corner of the street he saw that the shutter was still down and he walked past the house without stopping, glancing up at the shuttered window once more and then, still walking, peeping into the ground floor apartment which had been turned into a ladies' hairdressing salon and beauty parlor, where he saw the proprietress, who called herself Janette, sitting all by herself after the other girls who worked for her had gone home, with her head inside the blue metal hood of a hair dryer and her eyes closed, and he continued up the street and at the corner of Ben Yehuda he turned right and went into a smallish cafe with a homey atmosphere where he and Goldman sat from time to time and ordered a cup of tea and picked up an evening paper lying on the next table and cast his eye over it without taking anything in because he was very tired and anger and resentment were taking control of his feelings again, together with impatience, because he was sick and tired of waiting for Caesar to vacate the apartment and especially because he did not know, now or ever, just how long he would have to go on wandering the streets.

Sometimes he was lucky and he only had to vacate the apartment for half an hour or a quarter of an hour, but on the other hand there were times when he was obliged to wander the streets like this for hours, not infrequently in the rain or in a heat wave, until at last the shutter went up, and this usually happened when the girl Caesar brought with him showed unexpected resistance and refused to take off her clothes and get into bed, whereupon Caesar, faithful to his principles and masculine vocation, would resort to a variety of techniques and tricks, which he would apply with great patience, persistence, and flexibility, and according to the circumstances, without sparing his dignity or his time, he would embark on long conversations, pay compliments, say pretty things, mouth platitudes, make jokes, stroke and caress, offer whiskey, and frequently utter obscenities of the crudest kind in order, as he said, to "lower the moral threshold," as well as displaying pornographic photographs, which according to him had an intoxicating effect and were capable of bringing the instincts of the coldest, most calculating, and most modest women to the boil, and in some cases he would make promises he had had no intention at all of carrying out, or pretend to be very depressed and try to inspire feelings of pity by speaking of his lonely life and his failures and his sense of the hopelessness and pointlessness of it all, while at the same time exerting himself to prove that there was no such thing as morality and no point in faithfulness and honesty and love, but only in quick sex without any emotions or commitments, and sometimes he would use aggression, or even force, because in his opinion there was hardly a woman alive who would not submit to force, and there were some who even expected to be raped, and in fact Caesar usually got what he wanted, although the struggle sometimes went on for hours, and Israel would return to his room, after having come and gone several times, and find the couch still warm from the bodies that had been copulating on it.

Caesar would sometimes return after a short interval, or telephone, in order to apologize to Israel, and he would often find occasion to acquaint him with the way things had gone, especially when the girl he had been to bed with was new, or if something unusual had happened or something which bore witness to his own prowess, and he did so with pride and enjoyment and without skipping any of the details, which were arousing enough in themselves and which Caesar did his best to make even more stimulating, but Israel remained indifferent, whereas Goldman, who quite often said that Caesar's stories were lies, or at least exaggerated—and even if they weren't carrying on like that couldn't make a person happy, or even give him pleasure—would listen curiously and smile, aroused and amused, but later on, after he had calmed down, he would be seized by anger and despair, because he was as sick of himself as he was envious of Caesar, despite his condemnations, for the ease with which he obtained women and the irresponsibility and lack of consideration with which he treated them, and in general for the uninhibited freedom in which he lived his life, which appeared to Goldman, for all his reservations and expressions of disbelief, like a blue summer sky in which Caesar floated at his ease wherever his fancy took him, and indeed, this was exactly the way in which Caesar, not without some measure of success, tried to live his life, but Israel—who was now approached by the cafe proprietor, a gray-haired man with a pleasant face and sunburnt, muscular arms which looked more like those of a building worker than a cafe owner, who put his tea on the table and inquired after his health and that of Goldman—continued to relate to Caesar's stories with indifference, and he put the newspaper down and said, "Everything's fine, thank you," and put some sugar and a slice of lemon into his tea and stirred it slowly, and while he was drinking it he ran his eyes over the newspaper until he was pulled up short by the headline "Who are you, 'Virgin Mary'?" above a story which said: "A young Australian woman called Brenda Iles, who has been married for some time, claims that she is the Virgin Mary, and that she suffers from Christ's wounds on the cross. Her claims have been substantiated by a Catholic priest, who is associated with her in a strange friendship. According to Brenda Iles, who prefers to be called Mary, she experienced a revelation ten years ago and received stigmata on her hands and feet and the sides of her body, which disappear from time to time and then reappear. Is she insane or simply a charlatan? Her former landlady, who believed her to be a saintly woman because of her association with the priest, claims that she is 'just a crook' who ran away after a few months without paying the rent. The landlady noticed that Iles wore bloodstained bandages on her hands and feet but she never knew why."

Israel folded the newspaper and drank his tea until there was nothing left and then he took the lemon out of the cup and chewed it and went to pay, and the proprietor said, "What do you want to read the papers for? All they do is shorten your life," and Israel paid and said, "Yes," and the proprietor said, "But it's hard to break the habit," and Israel said, "That's right, it is hard," and took his change and went and stood in the street outside the cafe for a moment, wondering which way to go, and in the end he turned back toward the studio. He walked very slowly, as calm and indifferent as if he had fallen asleep inside, and with the same indifference he looked up at the shutter, which was still down, and crossed the street and leaned against the wall of the house opposite and waited for Caesar, who at this time had three women in his life—Eliezra, Tehilla, and Vicky—with whom he was involved in more or less steady relationships, each accompanied by its own set of mutual demands, to finish his business and go.

It was four years now since Caesar had finally separated from his wife Tirza, after nine years of a marriage full of vicissitudes which had begun in a passionate love affair and a quick wedding and ended in ugly scandals, which had gone on for years and during the course of which Caesar had left home from time to time for periods of several weeks or months and gone to stay with his parents or his mistresses, and when he finally left home forever, without knowing when he did so that it was for the last time, he had left Tirza in possession of the apartment and the two children—a boy of about nine, the fruit of the first fire of their love, and a boy of about two, the fruit of the scandals and occasional moments of comfort and reconciliation, whose birth was supposed to bring them together again and tighten the bonds which had disintegrated, leaving nothing but bitterness and ill will between them. There were still flickers of regret and the fleeting wish for mutual consideration and even a little closeness between them, but the child did not perform the function which his conflict-locked parents had imposed on him, and this was mainly because of Caesar, who was not prepared for any effort involving compromise or risk to himself. He could not forgive Tirza for once having gone to bed with a strange man when relations between them were very bad, but he himself was running from woman to woman without making the least attempt to hide what he was doing, and he would not give up his masculine fantasies, or at least restrain the offensive freedom he had granted himself and his indiscriminate, exhibitionistic competitiveness as far as women were concerned, and he went to live where he was free of responsibility or sorrow—with his parents, who received him, as always, gladly and without asking too many questions— Erwin, his father, who was above all preoccupied with his own affairs, because he loved Caesar and could not see anything bad or wrong in his behavior, but on the contrary regarded him as a chip off the old block, and Zina, Caesar's mother, who suppressed the disapproval which his behavior aroused in her, despite the fact that she had never liked Tirza or felt anything for the children, partly for the sake of having him at home with her, and to some extent even under her protection, and partly because she was glad to have any guest, whoever it was, especially one who could joke and chat and laugh loudly and increase the commotion in the huge, grand apartment full of expensive furniture and carpets and lamps and original paintings and statues and china and wooden ornaments, all of which Zina would purchase enthusiastically and indiscriminately, just as she would buy the most expensive dresses and shoes and coats and handbags and jewelry, which she hardly ever wore, and which Erwin would pay for rather sourly but without complaining, because he had plenty of money and because he chose to believe that in this way he bought her agreement to his adulteries, and especially to his relationship with Chemda, and compensated her for the sadness and loneliness and desolation of her life, and made her happy, and in fact Zina almost always had a smile on her face and she laughed a lot, loudly and so hard that sometimes it nearly made her cry, but she was not happy.

And how could she be happy? Despite her age she was still

pretty and feminine with her auburn hair and big, dark eyes and high cheekbones, a native of Kiev with a family tradition on her mother's side claiming descent from the Khuzars. She longed to be an actress and believed in the great talents lying buried inside her and tried to make others share this belief and give her parts in plays, but without any success, and she blamed this lack of success on shortsighted and hardhearted producers and directors, and on stupidity, jealousy, and intrigues, as well as bad luck, and she never gave up and went on dreaming the dream of her discovery and triumphant appearance on the stage, but in spite of the bright and hopeful façade she continued to present to the world, this dream became more and more forced as the years went by and was transformed into a source of bitterness and resentment. She became the victim of her own hopes and began to drink, to a large extent under the influence of Erwin and Besh, and the air of disorientation which she at first adopted, together with cigarette smoking, as a kind of fashionable accessory suitable to a femme fatale moving in artistic circles, gradually became part of her real nature, together with a boring garrulousness and short-lived bursts of activity which were irritating and ridiculous because although they were illusory from the start they were accompanied by an impatient, nerve-racking restlessness which was real enough, as well as by a constant stream of persuasive and apparently logical words—and thus one day she volunteered to work in a hospital and the next she threw herself into welfare work on behalf of slum children. She started doing exercises according to the Alexander method and saw this as the gateway to salvation, studied history at the university for the duration of one semester, decided to go out and work in an office or a shop to earn her keep, but put it off from day to day, suddenly took up gourmet cooking and with the same passionate enthusiasm devoted herself for a while to painting, decided to adopt a child and even discussed it a couple of times with her sister Yaffa, and also with Erwin, who listened impatiently and nodded his head. She was tortured by disappointments and emptiness and the fear of loneliness and of growing old, and beyond all this lay her constant preoccupation with Erwin, her great love and her great disappointment, which oppressed her and terrified her and made her days and nights a prey to terrible pangs of jealousy and anxiety which never let up for a moment, and also to boundless expectations, and turned her life into a frantic and chaotic race toward some elusive horizon lying hidden in the depths of her agitated soul, and in the end she sank gradually into a swamp of emptiness and hopelessness without knowing what to do except wait, panic-stricken and at the end of her rope, for Erwin to come and save her before she went mad, but Erwin, for whose sake she made herself up every day and dressed in the best of taste, could think of nothing but himself and his own affairs, and he was not prepared to grant her more than a few crumbs of insincere and superficial attention.

Erwin had studied construction engineering, and he had a large office which supplied engineering services and supervision to its clients and dealt mainly in putting up complex structures, and in addition to this he had founded, in partnership with Max Spillman, a plant for casting concrete in special forms, all based on inventions which he himself had patented, and by dint of inexhaustible energy and the capacity for hard work, in addition to innate intelligence and cunning, as well as the great charm hiding his very considerable egotism and violence, he had become a successful man whose ambition it was to be even more successful. He was fond of saying, "The only cause for regret is the failure to look out for number one," and "God made the pigs too, and they also have to eat," and "Good deeds are better if they bring in a profit," and also "Give the other person a chance to like you," and sometimes "It's not necessary to be nasty, and it's certainly not a pleasure," and he often said, "Truth and falsehood don't last forever. After a couple of days all people remember is success," but because of the charming, mocking smile playing in his eyes and spreading to his big, flushed face, and because of the offhand, nonchalant way in which he delivered these maxims, you could never tell for certain if he meant what he said or if he was just joking and playing with words, which was exactly what he wanted—the only trouble was that in the end he himself became a party to the same confusion he sought to sow in others, although he never admitted this to himself because it was more convenient for him to leave things the way they were. Caesar, who loved his father and admired him without any reservations, would take in these maxims and repeat them whenever he had a chance to do so, trying to imitate his father's tone as well as his words, but Erwin, who in his youth had been a Zionist and a socialist and who had emigrated to Eretz Yisrael as a pioneer and lived for a number of years as a member of a kibbutz, continued to regard himself as a Zionist and a socialist with political, social, and moral principles, and although during the course of time these principles had been subjected to an almost imperceptible process of erosion until they were distorted beyond recognition, nevertheless Erwin, who had come to an agreement with himself that in the last analysis there was always a gap between the world of values and that of action, and that actually everything was permitted, went on believing that in some roundabout way he still stuck to his principles—principles which Besh held up to ridicule together with this belief, which Erwin refused to renounce, because he respected himself and because, in the last analysis, he affirmed the world and life, which fascinated him in all its manifestations and gave him real pleasure (unlike Besh), as did his work and his success and his relations with other people and his long-standing love for Chemda, whom Zina hated bitterly, just as she also hated Elisheva, Ruhama's mother and Erwin's first wife, from whom he had been separated many years before after about three years of marriage, but her hatred for Elisheva differed from her hatred for Chemda, and despite the fact that although she hardly knew Elisheva and hadn't seen her for years she wanted her too to die and her memory to be wiped out, nevertheless Zina managed somehow to resign herself to Elisheva's existence—although sometimes, not very often, she would comment in a patronizing tone of voice that Elisheva was a poor creature who deserved to be pitied or would make the impartial observation that she was a simple woman who had no idea of how to dress, or that she had ugly legs—because her hatred of Elisheva had undergone a long and deliberate process of attrition and repression and self-deception with the passing of time and the aid of all kinds of true and fictional facts relating to Elisheva's life with Erwin—which was not the case with regard to her hatred of Chemda, whose open and public love affair with Erwin poisoned her life and impelled her to seek revenge and consolation in her imagination, even in the arms of Besh. These dreams of revenge and consolation were humiliating and painful, because Erwin knew nothing about them and even if he had known she suspected he would not have cared, and because she knew that she would never find the courage to carry them out with anyone, and certainly not with Besh, who for all the pleasure she found in his company, and even in his presence, repelled her physically.

Besh was a friend of the family, in fact an honorary member of it, who came and went as he pleased, ate his meals with them and went out with them, and sometimes slept the night with them, and knew all their secrets, and many people, even friends and acquaintances, thought that he was Erwin's brother, and there really was a certain resemblance between them, something you couldn't quite put your finger on—maybe it was something about their appearance or something about their manner or their gestures, or maybe it wasn't a physical resemblance at all but something in their common aura, although in the case of Besh, who had discarded all refinement or pretense of refinement and all desire to be polite or civilized, the overwhelming impression was one of savage and cynical coarseness. He was a bachelor by intention and a man of deliberate and unrestrained appetites, who delighted in peppering his conversation with offensive obscenities and in bellowing with wild laughter, which sounded like the braying of a donkey and shook his whole body and sometimes even brought tears to his eyes; his sarcasm was brutal and his mockery and blasphemy were absolute and comprehended everything, including himself, and indeed he saw the world and history and all human acts and institutions as the incarnation of stupidity and viciousness which went on repeating themselves endlessly: the family and religion, the state, science, sports, politics and technology and laws, philosophy, medicine, art, love, the press, education—all these aroused his scorn and wrath, because in his eyes they were nothing but masks covering stupidity and viciousness, and he proclaimed himself the only wise man in his generation and all generations and chose to play the role of the fool, and thus he detached himself from the world and dismissed its institutions, expressing his contempt for its standards and conventions even in his crude and deliberate spelling mistakes.

During the period between the two world wars, when he was studying medicine in Germany, where he met Erwin, Besh was a communist, but toward the end of his second year he abandoned his studies and shortly after that he abandoned the party too, and ever since then he had spent most of his life as a wanderer, eating at the tables of strangers, sleeping in beds not his own, and enjoying other men's women, even if they were his patrons or his best friends. He did all this without a twinge of conscience, changing one abode for another and one occupation for another until with the help of Erwin and of his brother, who lived in Australia and sent him money to buy a tractor, he became an earth-works contractor, an occupation which should have provided him with a good living and even a lot of money, but instead he went on living from hand to mouth between one expropriation order and the next, in a filthy and almost bare apartment, because he always earned half what he could have and spent twice what he did, not to speak of the penalties he incurred and the holding up of payments and the deductions for not getting the job done in time and for doing it carelessly and negligently—but none of this gave rise to second thoughts on Besh's part or stopped him from living his life the way he chose to live it and devoting himself to the satisfaction of his appetites. He was a great glutton, and ate voraciously, despite the fact that he already weighed over 100 kilos, which made him short of breath and very tired, since his obesity affected his heart and lungs, and his legs could hardly carry him, and he walked with a slow, heavy tread, swaying slightly from side to side; and he was a heavy drinker and drank so much that his doctors considered it a miracle that he was still alive and warned him that if he went on drinking he would soon be dead, but Besh treated these warnings with contempt and went on drinking; and in addition to the above, as if out of some kind of spite, Besh also liked comics and sports magazines and gangster movies and musicals and silly Hollywood comedies, and in summer he went to matinees at air-conditioned movie theaters to rest and enjoy a catnap, and he also liked playing poker, especially in the mornings, and of course he was crazy about women, only he didn't try to seduce them like Erwin did—with charm, roguishness, and cunning—but pursued them with the utmost frankness and crudity, exactly in the same way that he ate a chicken—with all ten greedy fingers, with violence, and without a trace of ceremony or manners or consideration for anything at all. At the very most he might use some cynical bait to tempt his prey, and even then he would not go to any particular trouble to disguise his true intentions. He even tried to persuade Tirza, while she was still married to Caesar, to go to bed with him, but she refused without saying a word to Caesar, who learned of it from Besh himself, and only afterward from Tirza, and he chuckled with delight, because he loved and admired Besh almost as much as he loved and admired his father, and wanted to be like them and earn their respect, and to this end he tried to find a common language with them concerning life in general and women in particular, and they would sit together and exchange views and ideas and impressions, and sometimes discuss politics and current affairs, and entertain each other with rude jokes and stories, and from time to time Caesar would bring pornographic books and photographs, which Besh liked looking at to the accompaniment of loud witticisms and obscenities, and sometimes these sessions would develop into orgies of joking and laughter in which Zina would join, with a hilarious face but a heavy heart.

Besh fit very well into this luxurious home, which was wide open and falling apart and subject to all kinds of chance fluctuations, without any permanent standards or regular schedules, not because the members of the household were such liberated human beings that this was the way they wanted things, but because each of them was preoccupied first and foremost with himself and moved in an orbit which was convenient to him, and which sometimes, momentarily and accidentally, overlapped with or crossed the orbits of the others. There was a time when Zina had tried to maintain a shaky framework and preserve some kind of regularity in order to hold Erwin by these means, and she would sometimes buy tickets to the theater or the movies or a concert and cook their meals herself and try to see to it that they ate Friday night dinner and Saturday lunch together, but all these efforts were in vain, and by the time that Caesar came back to live with his parents, after leaving Tirza for the last time, she had given up all attempts to introduce some kind of order into the life of the house, which was as shapeless and chaotic as a party on the point of dying and disintegrating.

Caesar lived with his parents for a few months, in the palatial apartment with its clean air, which never smelled of cooking or ironing or seemed as if it contained a bathroom or beds that people slept in, and Shoshana the maid, who had played with him as he lay half-naked, covered with a sheet, one summer morning when he was about sixteen years old—an incident which had left them both feeling faintly like accomplices in a crime—looked after him again as if he were still a child, which he liked very much, until one day, after hesitations and delays, he rented himself a two-room apartment and moved into it because he couldn't stand living with his mother, who oppressed and irritated him by her presence, but not long afterward he moved in with Tehilla, who loved him, because he knew that she would take care of all his needs and not be too much of a burden on him, and thus he lived with Tehilla and went to bed with Eliezra, while Vicky, whom he had met shortly before this (after she had already become engaged to her blond officer) was the joy of his leisure hours, as he was of hers, and Vicky was a joy indeed: sunburnt and happy and shameless and, as Caesar remarked to Israel, "a compact little number with terrific drive who enlarges my blood vessels." Vicky knew how to extract the maximum pleasure from the stolen hours of lovemaking and demanded nothing save that he do his best to give her pleasure and to take his pleasure of her in the time they had together, which was very important to Caesar, especially during the period in question, when he was still tormented by the pain and jealousy of his separation from Ruhama and needed a lot of encouragement and distractions and easy consolations which didn't commit him to anything, whereas Tehilla and Eliezra, neither of whom knew about the other, burdened him constantly with their demands, and embittered his life with their stubborn pressures on him to marry them, especially Eliezra, who was jealous of every little thing and sometimes made angry scenes. Tehilla did this quietly, almost without putting it into words and, to tell the truth, mainly by virtue of her expectations and her devotion, whereas Eliezra, who at this moment emerged from the entrance and without a pause started walking up the street in the direction of the sea, presented her demands explicitly, in a manner so clear and unambiguous that it left no room for misunderstanding or evasiveness, and Israel, who had never liked her, watched her for a while and then looked up at his room again and saw the shutter going up, and after a few minutes Caesar appeared and started walking in the direction opposite the one taken by Eliezra, and Israel went on standing where he was, leaning against the wall and looking at Caesar, and with the same indifference he went back to watching the hairdresser, who was now sitting in front of a big mirror and doing her hair, and then he looked back at Caesar as he walked down the street and turned left and disappeared around the corner on his way to Tehilla.

Tehilla was tall and slender, and she had a delicate face and an indolent beauty and smooth black hair drawn back on the nape of her neck with a brown tortoiseshell clip, and a slight squint which added a peculiar charm to her appearance together with something provocative and very hidden, and at the same time made her seem afraid—and in fact she was shy and retiring, but not lacking in humor, and she did not have much to say for herself except when she was suddenly overcome by a fit of happiness which made her feel relaxed and uninhibited. When she was in a bad mood she would wash the dishes, clean the windows, launder the clothes, and mop the floors, since doing these things soothed her, but on the whole she didn't take too much trouble about the house, or over her personal appearance either, because she was absentminded and didn't particularly care and her mind was occupied by other matters—she liked going to the movies and reading and listening to music and to Caesar's conversation, and she listened to him gladly even when she came home drained and exhausted from her shifts at the airport. At first Tehilla had intended to teach French, but after two years' experience she had given up teaching and tried to turn her hand to the translation of literature and scientific works, but she encountered so many difficulties—and the pay, when she did succeed in obtaining work, was so poor—that in the end, almost against her will and without giving up her dream of becoming a translator, she went to work as a ground stewardess at the airport, which meant that she was often away from home in the evening and at night, leaving Caesar free to do as he pleased.

Tehilla's parents, who did not approve even of her decision to take up teaching as a profession, had arrived in the country on the eve of World War II, and they owned a large furniture store, and despite the many years they had lived in the country their Hebrew was broken and foreign-sounding, and between themselves and with their friends they continued to speak Polish, especially her mother, a good-looking, well-groomed woman, always dressed at the height of fashion, who had never succeeded in adapting herself to the heat and the light and the noise, and perhaps had never really tried to, and who regarded this vulgar Palestine with a proud and disdainful air. The furniture store brought in good profits, and they were able to provide their children with all the things that every parent would like to give his child in the way of food and clothes and education and schooling, including music lessons and private tutoring in foreign languages, but they did everything in a spirit of meanness, because the wealth they had acquired had not made them more generous, but at the same time they tried to run a rich, aristocratic home with silver and crystalware and a piano and family meals, and although they were not religious and played cards on Friday nights, never for high stakes, they kept up a strict observance of certain traditional ceremonies, and on Saturdays and holy days Tehilla's father attended synagogue services, and on the most important holy days her mother went with him, and neither of them saw any contradiction in this, because for both of them it was all part of a whole system of external manners and norms which had to be scrupulously observed and which complemented each other, and which also embraced the bringing up, education, and future of their children, while their carefulness and stinginess, especially as far as money was concerned—which they covered up by occasional gestures of ostentatious generosity and tried to explain by all kinds of principles—actually stemmed from the character of Tehilla's father, a mean man who had spent years dealing in secondhand furniture until he succeeded in working his way up to the big furniture shop and a life of affluence.

When Tehilla started work as a stewardess at the airport they were bitterly disappointed and ashamed, but not to the same extent as they were shamed by her affair with Caesar, which they regarded as a calamity and did everything in their power to hide even from their relatives and closest friends, and which made them so miserable and angry that they could think of nothing else, because they had never denied Tehilla anything and they expected her to marry a doctor or an engineer or economist and settle down and raise a family after completing her studies in the department of French literature and working for a while at some prestigious job in the Foreign Office or the university, because that was the goal in life which they had set for their daughter and they, for their part, were fully prepared to do everything in their power to help her attain it. Her two brothers, one of whom was a dentist and the other an electronic engineer in the professional army, agreed with her parents, especially the engineer, an ill-humored bachelor, and they took it upon themselves to persuade her to leave Caesar, since her mother had no influence over her while her father, who declared repeatedly that he did not want to see her or have anything more to do with her and that he was cutting her out of his will, was so overcome by rage whenever he started talking about it that once, when she was sitting with him and her two brothers in the salon, he lost control of himself completely and tried to hit her—but all their attempts to separate her from Caesar failed, because Tehilla loved Caesar with all his drawbacks, of which she was well aware, and because he was the first and only man to give her pleasure in bed.

The quiet and unshakable resolve with which Tehilla opposed her parents' wishes and her determination to go on living in sin with a divorced man, the father of two children and a photographer to boot, astounded her parents and her brothers, just as less than a year later she astounded Caesar when she became pregnant and refused to have an abortion, despite all his demands that she do so. First he accused her of carelessness, and then he petted her and explained and pleaded, and when she stood firm in her refusal he turned his back on her and sulked, and then he tried persuasion and sweet words again and promised her that he would marry her immediately after the abortion, and then he left town for a few days and came back and yelled and threatened and said he was sorry and explained that from the economic and emotional point of view they simply weren't ready for a child yet, and that this accidental, unwanted baby would spoil their relationship and also their chances for the future, since his divorce from Tirza was not yet final, and the birth of the child at this stage would ruin their chances of ever getting married properly, since according to Jewish law she would be forbidden to him forever, but Tehilla—whose knowledge of Jewish law was as flimsy as Caesar's—who wanted to get married to him very much but at the same time yearned for a child and was afraid of the abortion, said with a heavy heart, as she had already said a number of times before, that she was prepared to live with him without any religious ceremonies and to have his child outside any form of marriage and that she didn't care if the baby was called a bastard by Jewish law or by anyone else, as long as she had it, and Caesar, who in any case hadn't intended staying with her for more than a night or two, said, "In that case I'm off," and Tehilla said that she intended to have the baby even if he refused to stay with her and that if necessary she would bring it up all by herself, and Caesar, beside himself, accused her of blackmail and egotism, and Tehilla sat up in bed and asked him, for the first time, if he wanted to go back to his wife or if he had another woman besides her, and Caesar said, "Are you mad?" and swore that he loved her and only her and that there was no other woman in his life, and Tehilla looked at him suspiciously and said, "Good. Let's leave it at that," and Caesar said, "You don't believe me," and Tehilla took a sip of the cold coffee in the cup standing on the bedside table, and said, "Yes, I believe you," and Caesar put his hand on his heart and said again, "I swear to you," and he wouldn't leave her alone until in the early hours of the morning, pale and cold with exhaustion, she gave in to him, and three days later Caesar took her to the clinic and came to take her home again, and the next day she asked him to go away and leave her alone, but he took no notice, and for a few days he looked after her to the best of his ability until she recovered and got out of bed and then she asked him again to go away and leave her alone, and this time Caesar went without demur and with a feeling of relief, leaving most of his clothes and personal possessions behind, including his razor, which he forgot to take, but not forgetting to take the key to her apartment, and he went back to live with his parents, and less than a month later, despite all Zina's objections, he moved in with a friend, and for a few weeks he didn't see Tehilla at all and called her only once or twice, unwillingly, to ask her how she was, and she replied composedly and a little aloofly, as if she were protecting herself from him or as if her love for him had cooled, and then, on his initiative, gradually and at first hesitantly, they began meeting again, without any demands or conditions on the part of Tehilla, who showed no particular interest in meeting him and never referred to what had happened between them, and he would come and visit her, take her out to the movies and restaurants, and sometimes the theater, and make love to her with enjoyment but also with feelings of guilt and gratitude, which were quite strong at the beginning but weakened as time went by—feelings he had never known in relation to Eliezra, for whom he felt only a passionate infatuation accompanied by admiration for the qualities of mind and spirit he believed he had discovered in her, although at the bottom of all this was nothing but plain, insatiable, carnal lust: It was Eliezra's crude, obvious beauty which attracted Caesar, her wanton sexuality, which existed more as a promise than as an actuality, her arrogance, and the capricious, ambivalent games she played, fluctuating between modesty and abandonment, aggression and the plea for male protection.

Eliezra had something of Ruhama's restless and wanton spirit, but without her naturalness and coarseness, because Eliezra was afraid of being alone; she needed to be liked and at the same time to maintain a pose of superiority, and she was aware of this, just as she was aware of her strengths and her weaknesses and the dangers with which she was surrounded, so that with her everything was turned into a kind of act and lost part of its power— but Caesar did not sense this and neither did he care. They had met in the army, and later on, shortly after their demobilization, they had parted: Caesar went to America to study architecture, and Eliezra moved to Jerusalem and studied graphic design at

Bezalel, and it was only several years later, in the summer, that they met again—Eliezra was already married to Gidon Reiter, who had taken her out when she was still at school, and Caesar was married to Tirza, with whom he had had a couple of good years, more or less, before he started his affair with Ruhama, which he conducted openly and which reduced his family life to a shambles, until one day Ruhama put an end to it suddenly and roughly, without leaving any room for hope or the illusion that she might still change her mind, when Caesar asked her if she had anyone else besides him, and she said, "Yes. And now get dressed and shove off. I think we've had enough," and Caesar said, "You're not serious," and Ruhama said, "I'm perfectly serious. Bugger off and don't come back," and although Caesar had always been afraid that she would spring something like this on him, and had sensed the blow about to fall before the forbidden question was out of his mouth, he was stunned, and he got up and put on his clothes and left without another word, thus bringing to an end an affair which had lasted for a number of years and which in its wildness and boldness had brought Caesar immeasurable delight, but also pain and depression, because he was jealous of her husband Avigdor and all the other men she had had before him, most of whom he did not even know, and the others who came and went without him daring to ask about them until he asked the question which had put an end to the relationship between them, and because her attitude toward him was subject to swift and sudden fluctuations which kept him alternating between happiness and despair and forced upon him not only the realization that he was dependent on her and her favors but also the foreboding that one day she would suddenly decide to put an end to the whole affair, which is exactly what she did—just as she had put an end to her marriage to Avigdor, with whom she had had two children, a son and a daughter—but Caesar could not tear himself away from her, although he tried to do so on a number of occasions, and he remained tied to her and subject to her wishes and her moods, just like Avigdor, who was an attractive man with a kind heart and a subtle and sometimes even witty sense of humor, which was only rarely and diffidently revealed, because he was a man of few words by nature and because he was paralyzed by Ruhama's presence, since she was not only clever but also sharp-tongued and aggressive and temperamental, and you never knew what kind of mood she would be in or how she would react. There were times, sometimes even for days on end, when she would be pleasant and relaxed, full of humor and radiating the expansive charm she had inherited from Erwin, and also from her mother, but suddenly, because of some word or gesture, and sometimes for no apparent reason at all, she would be seized by a fit of rage or sink into a black depression, and then she would take her anger out on anyone who crossed her path and would seek consolation in the arms of all kinds of men, and in voracious eating, and she would sleep a lot, sometimes half the day, completely indifferent to the needs of her home and her children, and nevertheless Avigdor was devoted to her and took care of her as if she were ill, and he loved her (and perhaps pitied her, too) so much that in spite of all the pain and humiliation she caused him he put up with her crazy moods and her unfaithfulness, of which he was well aware, and bore them without complaint. For her sake he went to films and concerts, tried to learn English, wore clothes which did not suit him, and cared for the two huge Alsatians which she had reared and which accompanied her wherever she went, but he disappointed her, or at any rate was unable to appease her restlessness, and his devotion and self-abnegation, which Ruhama herself enforced on him, got on her nerves, and one day she left him with a short, firm announcement which he accepted, surprisingly enough, with almost total composure, after which she went off to Greece for three weeks at Erwin's expense. When she was married, Caesar made love to her in the daytime when Avigdor, who was a bus driver, was at work, and after the separation he made love to her at night too, in the room next door to the one where the children were asleep, on Avigdor's bed, and sometimes in the summer on the floor or in the shower, underneath the running water, where he would kiss her fleshy lips and her warm, heavy breasts and her belly and her thighs, and breathe in the odor of her perspiration, aroused and gratified, and all the time the shadow of their impending separation hovered over him, and when it came he felt his whole world collapsing and darkening around him.

There was a light rain falling, and he went outside into the wet, deserted street, still shrouded in the darkness of a cold winter's morning, and stood with his hands in his pockets looking straight ahead of him with a frozen face, and then he raised the collar of his coat and lowered his head a little against the rain, which was now coming down hard, and walked heavily over to his car and got into it and sat there without moving in the penetrating cold and watched the darkness gradually disperse and the air growing gray and white, and at the same time he felt himself filling with a great relief, maybe even happiness, and he started the car and cursed Ruhama and drove home. The children were still sleeping, but Tirza, whose face had grown hard and ugly with suffering and anger, was awake, and she looked at him and said, "Why have you come?" and Caesar said, "Because I wanted to," and Tirza said, "No, that's not true," and Caesar said, "Yes it is, really," and Tirza said, "Why don't you stay with her? Stay with her and be done with it," and Caesar said, "I don't want to," and Tirza said, "Isn't it enough already?" and Caesar said, "Yes," and placed his hand on her shoulder, not in love but in atonement and the wish for closeness, but Tirza would not be appeased, and he stroked the nape of her neck a little and said, "It's over. That whole thing is over," and afterward he peeped into the children's room and went into the kitchen and made himself a cup of coffee and returned to Tirza and asked her if she wanted anything, and Tirza said, "Yes, I want you to stop it," and Caesar said, "I have stopped it. It's all over," and when he went to work after taking a shower and changing his clothes and bringing fresh rolls and butter from the shop he was happier and more at peace than he had been for a long time, and in the evening they went to the movies and had dinner in a restaurant, and the emotion which had been with him since morning stayed with him all day long until he went to sleep, but after a couple of days it all disintegrated and disappeared and he began rushing aimlessly from place to place, in an agony of jealousy and loss, and he stopped working almost completely and ate and drank a lot and swore a lot and stayed away from home, and chased every woman who crossed his path, including Zahara, Tirza's younger sister, and Tirza, for all her wariness, believed, just as Caesar did himself, that this time it was all over, and she was happy, because his affair with Ruhama and all it involved, the humiliation and estrangement and hatred, had ground her into the dust, but at the same time she had done her best to keep the house running smoothly and give the children everything they needed, and hold her head high and keep up appearances, and despite her love for Caesar she had kept on demanding that he put an end to the affair or else leave home, and she even appealed to Goldman and asked him to speak to Caesar and use his influence with him, until in the end, scorned and humiliated, she had tried to salvage what remained of her self-respect by going to bed with a strange man, whom she had met only once before at a friend's party, and then told Caesar about it, but all in vain, since the anger and wounded pride which this act aroused in the astonished Caesar did not succeed in banishing his lust for Ruhama, which after she sent him away increased from day to day until it grew so strong that it caused him actual physical pain. Abandoning self-respect and common sense, he toyed with fantasies of revenge and at the same time was prepared to crawl to Ruhama on his knees and kiss her feet and beg her to take him back, and he even thought of approaching Erwin, whom Ruhama loved more than any man alive, and asking him to intervene on his behalf and try to persuade her to change her mind, and in the meantime he would hide behind the corner from which he could see the entrance to her house and the road in front of it, or in the yard of the house across the road, or in other places where he thought she might pass, and wait for her to appear so that he would see her and she would see him, and maybe he would do something to hurt her or something might happen and everything would change and be all right again, and when he saw her walking past with her two Alsatian dogs, almost always in the company of one of her strange men, most of whom were younger than she was—some years younger—pain and jealousy would tear at his heart, and he would decide that even if she begged him to come back to her he would refuse, and he would curse her and pray that she might die. At least if she had looked bad or seemed miserable—but no, she had not changed. She went on wearing her chunky rings and tasteless beads, long, wide dresses, which were usually made of cheap striped floral material and which looked ugly and peculiar, and her face, which was not pretty, seemed to Caesar even happier and more serene than ever, until he wanted to scream in despair. Unrequited love was destroying him, and all his rushing around and attempts to enjoy himself and all Goldman's lectures and other people's lectures could not console him, and he was convinced that he would never recover—and it was only later that he realized it was not love which had crushed his spirit but the humiliation of defeat and the feeling that something which belonged to him and gave him pleasure had been taken away from him and given to someone else, and this was already a long time after he had met Eliezra again, and in fact it was after he had parted from her too, and this knowledge, which in any case he did not take too seriously, was no longer of any use to him, not even with regard to Eliezra.

They had bumped into each other one evening in the street, and Caesar had invited her to have a cup of coffee with him, and they went into a cafe and started talking, at first in embarrassment, and Caesar made jokes and started making passes at her, and she ignored his passes, and afterward they went up to the studio and without a word of affection passing between them they took off their clothes and lay down on the couch and quickly quenched the lust and the hunger which had accumulated in them over the years and for an hour unburdened themselves of the sadness and disappointment which oppressed their lives, and Eliezra, who was in a hurry to get home, stood up without lingering and got dressed and left, and Caesar, who did not regret her leaving, went into the darkroom and developed some photographs, and three weeks later they met again, after Caesar had phoned her at work in a moment of boredom, and this time they were slower and more patient and enjoyed each other without inhibitions, and even once then they did it almost every day, except for an interval which did not last long but was depressing and full of bitterness, when Eliezra became pregnant with her second child. She waited about two weeks after she was sure before telling Caesar, who lay on his side listening expressionlessly, without taking his eyes off her face, and then said, "Are you sure?" and Eliezra said, "Yes. I've already been to the doctor," and Caesar said, "OK. So what?" and turned over onto his back, and Eliezra said, "It was an accident," and Caesar looked at the ceiling and bit the insides of his cheeks lightly, and Eliezra said, "I can still get rid of it," and Caesar glanced at her and asked if she were sure that it was Gidon's, and Eliezra, who had been feeling sick and depressed at this time, hesitated for a moment, and Caesar picked up his glasses, which were lying on the chair next to the couch, and began playing with them, and Eliezra said, "Yes, it's his," and Caesar sat up on the couch and put his glasses on and lit himself a cigarette and said, "Do whatever you want," and Eliezra said, "All I want is to be with you, you know that," and Caesar turned his face to her and said, "He must be pleased," and Eliezra said, "What does it matter?" and Caesar said, "OK," and got up and started walking around the room, and Eliezra said, "It really doesn't matter," and Caesar took a penknife and threw it again and again at the big wooden board, and suddenly he turned to her and said, "You're a filthy whore. Go and fuck whoever you like. I don't give a damn," and Eliezra repeated, "All I want is to be with you, that's all I want," and Caesar, who was seething with hatred, said, "Enough. Shut your trap, you whore," and then he controlled his voice and said,

"Get dressed. I have to go. I've got a meeting," and Eliezra said, "All right, whatever you want," and got up and dressed, and they parted without Caesar giving her as much as a look, but the next morning he called her at work and even before he had finished his opening sentence Eliezra told him that she wanted to see him and an hour later they met at the studio and Eliezra, crushed and humbled, told Caesar that she had decided to have an abortion and asked him if he could lend her some money, and Caesar said, "Of course," and Eliezra said, "It doesn't commit you to a thing," and Caesar embraced her and stroked her hair and said, "Nonsense. We'll get married and everything will be all right," and that same day he gave her almost twice as much money as she needed, even though he felt, despite what she said, that he was indeed committing himself by doing so, because from the moment he had parted from her he had been tortured by the fear that she was slipping out of his hands, and he wanted to hold onto her now more than ever, and the feeling of making a commitment only elevated his spirits, and Eliezra said, "Will you really marry me?" and Caesar said, "I told you that I would. You've got nothing to worry about," and Eliezra said, "That's all I want," and put the money in her purse, but about a week later she found all kinds of excuses for changing her mind and returned the money and Caesar, whose longing for Ruhama, which accompanied him all the time like a nagging echo, now filled him to overflowing, felt relieved and looked at her and saw how her beauty had deserted her, how her face had grown ugly and yellow and how her skin had dried up, and he said, "I think it would be better if we didn't meet again," and Eliezra said, "All right. If that's what you want," and bit her lips nervously, and for two weeks they stuck to their decision, and then they started seeing each other occasionally, and their meetings were full of resentment and gloom, but they kept on anyway, without joy, until soon before Eliezra gave birth to her son, when they parted, this time too intending never to meet again, but about two months after the baby was born they started seeing each other again, and Caesar gradually reconciled himself to the new reality and forgot his anger and resentment and the curses and accusations he had hurled at her, in his own mind and also to Goldman and Israel, and they took up again where they had left off before her pregnancy, with even more warmth and mutual desire than before, as if they wanted to free themselves and wipe away the sadness and the memory of the bad things that had happened to them.

As Eliezra's relations with Caesar grew closer, her relations with Gidon, who was a water engineer and made a good living, deteriorated and disintegrated in cold and nasty quarrels, but this was only the continuation of a process which had begun with the marriage itself, which apart from the magnificent wedding reception had contained hardly a moment of harmony or happiness, and if the family framework, full of criticism and animosity, went on existing this was only for the sake of convenience and due to deception and fear, because although Gidon loved her and cared for her and denied her nothing—despite the extreme parsimony of his nature—Eliezra had treated him right from the start with coldness and sometimes contempt, which she made no attempt to hide, and not long after the wedding, disappointed in herself as well as in him, she began to be unfaithful to him, both in order to compensate herself for the failure of a marriage into which she had drifted out of opportunism and cowardice and in order to demonstrate her superiority and confirm her image in her own eyes and the eyes of others as a daring, liberated woman, and Gidon, who was always busy working out ways of getting ahead and saving money and standing up for his rights in a nagging, niggardly way, asked her to stop it, and later on, in an attempt to save his self-respect and get her back, he started being unfaithful to her too, and these adulteries of his did, indeed, hurt and frighten her, but they did not achieve their purpose, for if in the beginning Gidon had given rise to Eliezra's impatience and contempt, ever since her affair with Caesar he had disgusted her. She hated his voice and his handsome face, which seemed to her feeble and insipid in its pallor, and she couldn't stand his eternally clean hands, whose lightest touch sickened her, and his every word annoyed her, and for the children too she had nothing but irritation, even hostility, and as soon as her relationship with Caesar was firmly re-established she started talking about marrying him again, but unlike before when her demands in this direction, for all their explicitness and even aggression, remained abstract and were somehow dispelled by vague and general promises, now she not only presented her demands clearly and adamantly but also tried to force him to talk to her about how they would do it, and when, and where they would stay, and Caesar, although he was as keen on her as ever, was evasive and invented all kinds of excuses, because after the immediate danger of separation had passed he saw no reason for committing himself to anything for the time being. To himself, and also to Israel and Goldman, he argued that there were two reasons why he could not marry Eliezra: He couldn't do it to Tehilla, whom he had promised to marry and for whom he felt sentiments of gratitude and obligation which he could not deny, and he was afraid of Gidon, who might try to kill him when he found out that Eliezra was leaving him for his, Caesar's, sake—and although there may have been a grain of truth in these contentions, at least from the point of view of Caesar's immediate feelings at the time, the real truth, which Caesar preferred to ignore, was that he couldn't decide, because any decision would be bound to involve some sort of sacrifice, and Caesar was not prepared to sacrifice anything, and this was reflected in his consciousness as an unwillingness and inability on his part to give pain to anyone else, whereas in fact he was unwilling and unable to give pain primarily to himself. Besides, Caesar was tired and sobered by the breakup of his relationship with Ruhama and his separation from his wife, and he couldn't see any point in giving up his bachelorhood and the good he was doing to two women, Tehilla and Eliezra, and the good they were doing him, in order to shoulder the frightening and burdensome yoke of married life once more—especially since he continued to regard himself, completely illogically and in flat contradiction to his whole way of life, as a married man with one family to look after already.

Things went on in this way for a number of months, until one day, after his suspicions became aroused, Eliezra informed him, without a trace of embarrassment or regret, that she had another man with whom she sometimes went to bed, and in some strange way, despite his jealousy and dejection, this announcement pleased Caesar and made him admire her even more than before, with a pained and excited kind of admiration, and he even told Goldman all about it as soon as the opportunity arose, and the very same day, while he was still questioning her about this man and when and how, exactly, she had gone to bed with him, he promised Eliezra that he would marry her in the spring, as soon as the divorce proceedings between him and his wife (which were crawling forward at a snail's pace because neither of them were interested in speeding them up) were over, but Eliezra did not wait for the spring or Caesar, and a few days later she told Gidon that she wanted a divorce.

Gidon was not surprised, but despite the hatred and endless quarrels and despite all the humiliations she had subjected him to, he asked her not to do it, because he believed in marriage and the family and even saw them as sacred, and—more compellingly—because he was afraid of the way his parents, especially his father, a well-known specialist in skin diseases, and all kinds of friends and acquaintances and colleagues, would react, and preferred the disgrace of a miserable marriage full of deceit to the disgrace of a divorce, and also because he was used to Eliezra and he still wanted her and was ready to forgive her caprices and infidelities, and he was sorry for the children, for whom he cared almost single-handedly, just as he took care of most of the domestic chores and household arrangements—once a week, on his way to work, he did the shopping at the supermarket, he saw to things that needed repairing, went over the accounts and paid the bills, called in the upholsterer and the man to put up the curtains, and went to PTA meetings at their older son's school, and the maid took care of the spacious apartment, which was always as clean and neat and tidy as if nobody lived in it, because Eliezra, who went back to work as a commercial artist soon after the baby was born, had no patience with all these things. She didn't even cook, and ever since their marriage they had lived mainly on canned or delicatessen foods or things that needed hardly any preparation, like steaks or grilled chicken and different kinds of salads, or else they ate in restaurants, except for Saturday lunch, which they always ate with Gidon's parents, who did not like her any more than she liked them—his clever, conceited, and domineering father and, especially, his mother, an irritating woman who was obsessively jealous of her husband and who spent most of her time putting herself down in order to demonstrate what a poor, put-upon creature she was.

Gidon pleaded with Eliezra and tried to persuade her that the family framework, however shaky, was important in itself and should be maintained, and that every divorce, in the last analysis, was a victory for illusions over common sense, and begged her to think of the children and realize that from the minute she gave birth to them she had lost part of her freedom and was obliged to take responsibility for them and put their happiness before her own, and he suggested that they move into a new apartment and take a trip abroad, and Eliezra said that she would think about it, but while Gidon was still busy trying to persuade her to stay at home she went to consult a lawyer about the right way to set about obtaining a divorce from her husband without losing her rights as a divorcee, and by this action she effectively opened divorce proceedings without saying a word either to Gidon or to Caesar, who could thus go on enjoying her favors with an easy mind, and she took even greater care than usual to keep her relations with Caesar and her meetings with him a secret from Gidon, because if he found out he would be able to deprive her of all her rights and see to it that she was never allowed to marry Caesar, who went on admiring her and telling Goldman and Israel that she had invented sex, and giving them accounts of her exploits in bed, but Goldman confided in Israel that as far as women were concerned he had nothing but pity for Caesar, since he, Goldman, had no doubt that Caesar derived almost no pleasure at all from his sexual relations, which had certainly undergone a process of standardization by now and become mechanical and boring, the truth of the matter being that Caesar was a compulsive fucker, suffering from a production-line "fucking complex," which, with his father fixation and castration complex, drove him to keep on proving his virility because he was really so unsure of it, whereas Eliezra was a frigid woman trying to act the part of a nymphomaniac in order to establish some kind of relationship with others, which was exactly what neither of them were capable of, according to Goldman, neither Caesar nor Eliezra, who refined their techniques of lovemaking and increased their enjoyment from day to day, using all kinds of aids and appliances, looking at pornographic pictures and reading erotic literature as they copulated, and observing themselves in the mirrors which Caesar had fixed to the ceiling and three sides of the couch so that he and Eliezra could see themselves making love to each other and also so that he could photograph them in the act from the various perspectives provided by all these mirrors, which drove Israel, who had left his place by the wall and started crossing the road, crazy, because the moment he opened his eyes he saw himself reflected and wherever he looked he was confronted by his own image, which would not let him be, but he said nothing about this to Caesar, and glancing at the hairdresser—who had finished curling her hair and making up her face, which now looked like the mask of fresh, young woman's face—entered the lobby, which was full of pleasant scents of soap and cosmetics, and went up-stairs to the studio, where he found a note hastily penned in Caesar's handwriting on the lid of the piano in which he apolo-gized for taking so long, mentioned the summer and the funeral by way of reminding Israel that weariness, heat, and sorrow in-creased the sexual urge, added that life was full of problems but everything would work out in the end, and signed off with a drawing of a camel with a flower sticking out of the end of its huge sexual organ.

After tearing this note to shreds and throwing the pieces into the wastepaper basket Israel stood still for a moment, feeling very tired, and contemplated taking a shower and sitting down to play the piano, but instead he took off his sandals and shirt and lay down on the couch and closed his eyes, abandoning himself to relaxation and the touch of the air on his skin, and when he opened his eyes he saw his hard, tired, unshaven face looking down at him from the ceiling. He turned his face sideways and looked without moving into his very pale blue eyes, bloodshot from the sun, which stared back at him from the mirror like the eyes of a stranger, and felt a longing for Ella swelling up from the depths of his weariness and indifference and flooding him, and he didn't care any more who she was or where she came from, what she had done in the past or what her thoughts were in the present, and all he wanted was for her to be here, in this room, so that he could see her and, if he wished, touch her too. On the chair standing by the couch, next to Israel's old reading lamp, were a few tattered pornographic books in gaudy paper covers which Caesar had left for Israel to pass on to Goldman, and Israel stretched out his hand and without looking picked up one of the books and leafed through it and read, "In the end I unbuttoned my fly and pulled out my shirt. After a while Germaine popped her pretty face around the door and slipped inside. I bolted the door and began kissing her. When I turned toward the bed she took off her panties and her bra. I laid her on the bed and kissed her nipples warmly, then I lifted the hem of her skirt and gently stroked her curves and her secret cave until her love juice dripped. Then I pulled out my cock and smeared it with oil. . . ." and put the book down and sat on the edge of the couch and rose to his feet and took the big, dagger-like penknife which was lying on the desk and started throwing it stubbornly at the wooden board with the photo of the old couple sitting in front of the shop, just like Caesar, who stopped on the way to

Tehilla's place and after a moment's hesitation changed direction and went to Tirza's to see the children, and Tirza, who was busy cooking, opened the door, and Caesar, smiling broadly, went in and pinched her bottom and tried to embrace her, but Tirza gently extricated herself and Caesar said, "What are you running away from?" and bent down to hug his younger son, who came running from the kitchen to cuddle up to him, and he lifted him up and kissed him on his forehead and on his cheeks, which were smeared with the remains of his meal, and put him down and went into the living room to his older son Shaul, who was sitting in an armchair reading a book, and patted him affectionately on the shoulder and asked him what he was reading, and Shaul, whose face was pale and listless, raised his eyes and told him the name of the book, and Caesar, without taking it in, said "Ho ho!" and ran his fingers affectionately and proudly through his son's curly hair and patted his shoulder again and smelled the smells of the cooking coming from the kitchen, the familiar aroma of chicken soup and something else, and Shaul asked him why he hadn't come the day before yesterday to take him to the movies as he had promised, and Caesar, who had forgotten all about it, was momentarily taken aback and said that he had been very busy at work and had had to leave suddenly on an urgent trip out of town and didn't even have the time to let him know, but the movie was still showing and he was ready to take him to see it the next afternoon if he liked, and Shaul said, "OK," and Caesar, who was not sure that his son believed him and was depressed by having forgotten him and having lied to him, wanted to banish this gloom with a joke and so he shut the book lying on Shaul's knees with a bang and said, "Done! Tomorrow at four," and asked him how the fish were getting on, and Shaul said, "The female had babies," and got up and went over with Caesar to the big aquarium, which Caesar had given him the day after Ruhama had thrown him out, and showed him the female and the little fishes she had spawned in the tangle of green seaweed, and Caesar said, "Great! Look after them, now," and went into the kitchen and asked Tirza, who was seasoning the soup, to make him a cup of coffee and asked her how she was getting on, and Tirza, moving very calmly, said, "Everything's just fine," and put the kettle on and told him that she was worried because three days before she had noticed blue marks on Shaul's body, but Caesar, who had also noticed the boy's pallor and listlessness, dismissed her anxiety and said, "He must be getting sick with the flu," and peeped into the pot, where meat was cooking in okra, and said, "Ho ho! Fantastic!" and put the lid back, and Tirza poured him a cup of coffee and he tried to embrace her again and stroked her breasts jokingly, and afterward, when he was leaning against the sink and drinking his coffee, he asked her what it was like fucking with the curly-headed man he had seen her with a couple of times about six months before, and if he fucked her better than Caesar did, and if his prick were bigger, and then he asked her if she were thinking of marrying the lawyer she had been going out with recently.

Tirza said nothing at all, and Caesar said, "He looks a bit the worse for wear, but maybe he's got money," and then he added, "You should marry the one with the curly hair," and Tirza said, "Thank you," and Caesar lit himself a cigarette and asked her if she would like to come back to him, and she said "No," and Caesar, who could never let a visit pass without bringing up these subjects, laughed unbelievingly, but Tirza did not laugh with him, and Caesar, his face suddenly serious, said, "I'm in a lousy mood," and Tirza said, "Why don't you stop behaving like a spoiled child and expecting other people to get you out of trouble?" and her face, which was still pretty and womanly, expressed the anxiety she could not share with anyone but her mother and her father, who was warm-hearted and honest to the point of naïveté and had no practical sense whatsoever, which made him unsuccessful by any kind of conventional criteria, but he himself did not take this lack of success too seriously and regarded it, as he also regarded himself, with a sense of humor which her mother found incomprehensible and to which she objected because she thought it was vulgar, although it was precisely this quality in her father which made Tirza love him more than she loved her mother, whom he loved with a tender, romantic, often touching love, which it took her years to learn to appreciate and enjoy because in contrast to her husband, who was satisfied to work all his life as a builder's carpenter, although he made a few attempts to change his occupation for her sake, she was an active, ambitious woman who had made her own active, ambitious nature into a vital principle situated at the core of a system of values according to which she ran her home, which was always neat and spotless, and brought up her daughters, Tirza and Zahara, hoping that with the help of their upbringing they would be able to achieve those things that it was necessary to achieve in life, which she saw as a kind of competition with prizes for the winners, and thus, on the one hand, she forbade them to bend over their plates at the table, or put on their socks in front of strangers, or to refer even among themselves to the fact that their father had false teeth, and on the other hand she believed that people should live in cities and visit the United States of America at least once in their lives, control their feelings, choose their friends with care, acquire a driver's license, and above all that they should be active and strive ceaselessly to get ahead in life and attain a certain status—by honest means of course, and preferably by means of study and the acquisition of academic degrees, for in her opinion the holders of academic degrees were the aristocracy of our times, and an academic degree, which in her eyes was proof not only of intelligence but also of worth, was the chief means by which a person could hack his way to the top—and so Tirza, like Zahara (who was three years younger), learned to dance and play the piano, which stood unused in the living room, and to type, and had private tutoring in French, and after finishing her army service she started studying architecture, but she never graduated because she married Caesar and gave birth to Shaul, and then lost all interest in something which had perhaps from the outset been no more than an expression of her mother's will and Tirza's feeling that she had no right to disappoint her—especially in view of the successes of her sister, who had studied economics in America and graduated with distinction and shortly after returning to Israel with her husband Phillip and their two children had started work as a senior economist in one of the government ministries.

All Tirza's aspirations centered on her child and her attempts to make a home, but Caesar would not let her, and he destroyed everything she tried to build with patience and devotion and many concessions and much goodwill, and he drained her strength and her vitality with the constant uncertainty and endless quarrels, and she felt persecuted and lost in the agonies of jealousy and humiliation to which Caesar subjected her, and which at first astonished and confused her, because she loved him and gave herself to him without calculations or reservations, and it was only very gradually, hard as she found it to despair of his love, that she realized that none of this was important, because love did not necessarily give birth to love, and—what hurt even more— it did not ensure its survival, and nor did all the devotion and fidelity and goodwill in the world, and sitting and waiting, however patiently and stubbornly, did not have the power to bring back the awaited one, as she was forced to realize in the wake of the fleeting hour of grace she had with Caesar after he broke up with Ruhama, when for a moment, full of hopes and doubts, she had believed, on that chaotic winter morning when Caesar sat down next to her on the bed and placed his hand gently on her shoulder, that her long wait had triumphed and brought him back to her.

Caesar cheated on her openly and humiliated her in front of everyone, and during the years of their married life he had succeeded in making her despise herself and in almost totally destroying her sense of her own worth, but nevertheless she still had some pride left and the need to preserve her self-respect and conceal her suffering and humiliation as far as possible from friends and relatives and her parents, especially her mother, who harbored very bitter feelings toward Caesar but never showed them and treated him with a chilly correctness, and she kept the house clean and tidy and cared for the children and dressed nicely and made herself up so that she would look pretty and attract men, which Caesar continued to hold against her even after they had parted for the final time—this time on account of Tirza, who could no longer bear his insults and infidelities—and he teased her about it and sometimes insulted her too, and Tirza, who was at first confused by this mockery and so depressed that sometimes, when she was alone, she would sit and cry, slowly adjusted herself to it until in the end she simply took no notice.

With the money she had saved in the last year of their marriage, when she had begun to suspect that Caesar would abandon her one day and leave her with nothing, and with a sum of money she obtained from her parents, she went into partnership in a shop selling fancy household goods and ornaments, where she worked during the day with her partner; in the evenings she tried to have people over or go out with friends or to the theater or concerts, none of which she found particularly interesting, but which she saw as part of her struggle for survival, and all the time she hoped very much that she would fall in love with someone and get married again, only now it was very hard for her to fall in love because she was tired and disillusioned, and the spontaneous feelings which still welled up in her and had not been buried under the mountains of pain and disappointment and the rubble of all the old *do*s and *don't*s were pushed aside by innumerable calculations of expedience, and especially of caution—the fruit of her experience with Caesar and the education she had received from her mother—and these erected a barrier of demands so exaggerated that they effectively blocked any possibility of marriage, even without love, except by acting as a warning of resignation and despair which she would not be able to heed until a great deal of time had gone by, time for the fear and humiliation to fade and for her to come to the conclusion that nothing was guaranteed and that much had to be sacrificed for something to be gained, and also for her finally to despair of Caesar—who finished his coffee and put the cup in the sink—who came and went and whom she went on wanting in the secret of her heart long after she had apparently given him up for lost, and hoping against hope that one day he would come back and live with her because even though she wasn't even sure that she still loved him she was still tied to him and jealous of him and she still believed that their marriage could be patched up, just as she believed that his return would give her back her self-esteem and the esteem of her friends and parents and sister and wipe out her humiliation and failure, and thus for nearly two years after her separation from Caesar she never went to bed with another man, and afterward, for a long time, she tried to evade it and did it unwillingly, not only because she was inhibited by principles and feelings which prevented her from doing what she sometimes longed to do with the same freedom that her sister and other women she knew did it, but also chiefly because she still felt a sense of obligation to Caesar, as if they were still married, and she still lived in the hope that in the end, after he had outgrown his illusions and wearied of his empty round of self-centered activities, he would come back to her, and it was only very slowly, thanks to the passing of time and vicissitudes of life, that she shook off these false hopes and retrieved her confidence and self-esteem and the capacity to be happy and to be satisfied with herself and her actions and stopped thinking about him all the time and waiting for him, not only because she had grown accustomed to being alone and independent (and even enjoyed it) but also because she understood and knew that their paths had parted forever and that she had come a long way on her own and would never be able to live with Caesar again, and if she still expected anything of him it was only for him to ask her to come back to him so that she could refuse, and later on she tried to rid herself of this expectation too, because she came to realize how unimportant it all really was, and in the course of time it became clear to her that she was no longer jealous of him and had no more grievances against him, and without any deliberate intention she began treating him like a friend, and thus, smilingly and with a feeling of quiet superiority, she watched Caesar, who went on pursuing his frantic round of activities and who sometimes thought of coming back to her—a thought which crossed his mind now too as he stood beside her in the kitchen and watched her cooking and peeped into the pot again and took a spoonful of okra in gravy and blew on it and threw his cigarette in the coffee cup and ate the okra, which was very tasty and had a subtle flavor of pepper and tumeric, and said, "Fantastic!" and put the spoon down on the sink board and smiled at Tirza and said, "You're wonderful" and embraced her lightly around the waist and said, "You've got a pretty waist," although her waist wasn't particularly pretty, but her face was, and she was very womanly and serene, and Caesar put out his hand to embrace her again but Tirza, who for a moment felt a spasm of desire (although outwardly she remained busy and reserved), pushed his hand away and pointed to their younger son, who had come into the kitchen with a book and who went up to Caesar and asked him to read him a story, but Caesar glanced at his watch and said he had to hurry off to an important meeting connected with his work, and he promised that he would come back and read him a story very soon, and play with him too, and he kissed him on the cheeks and then went into the living room to his older son and stroked his head affectionately and reminded him that the next day at four o'clock he was coming to take him to the movies—an appointment which he failed to keep on account of an involvement with an American tourist which took up the whole afternoon and evening, until she agreed to go to bed with him—and he went back into the kitchen and gave his younger son another kiss and said goodbye to Tirza and left the house with an agreeable sense of having done his duty.

In the street outside he ran into Zahara, who was getting out of her car after parking it, and they greeted each other very warmly, as was their wont, and Caesar asked her how she was and how

Phillip was, and Zahara said, "We're both fine," and asked him why he hadn't been to see them lately, and Caesar said that he was very busy but promised to come soon, if, of course, she promised to serve punch with nuts, and Zahara said, "As much as you like—and we have some very good cigars too, and you must see Phillip's new camera," and she waved and went into the yard of the house with a quick step while Caesar, who also waved, rapidly examined the back view of her figure and legs and as he turned the corner on his way to his parents' house, which was quite close by, he said to himself, as he said to himself almost every time he met her, that if he put enough energy into pursuing her she would certainly go to bed with him, and that she was sure to be a very good lay, and afterward he said to himself that there was very little probability that she went to bed with Phillip— maybe once in a while out of a sense of obligation or guilt, or just to do him a favor, and maybe even that little bit, if it existed at all, was too much for Phillip, who was fifteen years older than she was, and although he was still in his prime and quite hand- some too he was already finished, a man who had turned his back on life and destroyed himself deliberately, you could almost say out of a kind of spite.

Phillip was the son of a wealthy Jewish family from Vancouver. His father was a successful psychiatrist and his mother was a piano teacher, and he himself had studied architecture at McGill, but in addition to his professional skills he was a man of considerable culture and sophistication, who owed the cultivation and refine- ment of his mind largely to his family background and wealth, which relieved him of the cares of making a living and enabled him to enjoy the best that civilization had to offer in the way of music and books and art exhibitions, theaters, ballets, and trips abroad. He and Zahara had met in the home of mutual friends in New York and after knowing each other for two months had decided to get married, and a year later their first child was born and two years after that their second child was born, and when he was about a year old Zahara completed her studies and they came to Israel, where their third child was born six years after the second in the middle of a crisis in their marriage which had subsided a little but not been resolved and which had begun when Zahara had fallen in love with one of the young architects who worked for the firm in which Phillip was a partner. The affair had gone on for a long time without Phillip's knowledge, and when he did find out his reaction was confined to a few quiet, seemingly nonchalant remarks, after which he retreated into silence, and he reacted in the same way when Zahara left the big house where they lived with their children one day and moved into a rented apartment with her young architect, an act which greatly grieved her father, who without saying anything sympathized with his daughter's unhappiness and conflicts, and angered her mother, who spoke to her once, very harshly—none of which made any difference to Zahara, who went her own way, but after a few months she parted from the architect, although they loved each other, and he went back to his wife and Zahara went back to Phillip, who received her as quietly as he had let her go and behaved as if nothing had happened, because he was a gentle, reserved man by nature and his culture and refinement, together with a kind of aristocratic pride, filled him with doubts and weakness and killed his ability to react as he might have wished to, but shortly after Zahara came home, despite all her objections, he sold his share in the architects' office and stopped working.

From then on he lived a completely idle life on the income from his family fortune: In the morning he would send the children off to school (which according to him was the only useful thing he did), make himself toast and coffee, and then spend the whole day listening to music and looking at art books or books about birds, of which he possessed a large collection, or reading French and English literature and poetry, or solving chess problems and crossword puzzles. He deadened himself with deliberate and demonstrative inactivity and humiliated himself on purpose and lived his life surrounded by a depressing fog of apathy and bitter irony, directed mainly against himself, from which he occasionally gave vent, always with a pretense of nonchalance and never directly, to expressions of resentment and self-pity, and Caesar, who felt a great liking for this big, broad man who had resigned himself to impotence and despair, could not get over the strange relationship between him and Zahara, who despite her alienation from Phillip and her impatience and irritation at his behavior felt guilty and penitent and wanted to be kind to him but was neither able nor willing to break off her relations with the young architect, whom she went on meeting once or twice a week in a hotel even after their separation and return to their respective spouses, while Phillip, who was aware of these meetings, although nobody ever referred to them in so many words, fenced himself off from her as he fenced himself off from the world, and went on treating her with perfect politeness and nothing more, not so much as a smile or a word. The relationship between Zahara and Phillip seemed to Caesar like a dead bond between something alive and vibrant and something which had already died, or which was, at least, being irredeemably depleted from day to day, and he could on no account understand what had made Zahara marry Phillip in the first place, except perhaps for the money and the position, and he was puzzled by Phillip, whose reaction to Zahara's affair with the young architect was quite beyond his comprehension, and he wondered if the relationship between them had been completely different at the beginning, when they first met, and he opened the gate of his parents' house, where Zina sat alone in the huge living room wearing a blonde wig à la Doris Day holding a heavy wooden mask in her hands, and walked up the path paved with red and black tiles which curved through the garden with its shrubs and its beautiful orange tree, which was blossoming and giving off a heavy, intoxicating scent, and rang the bell, and Zina opened it immediately and when she saw him she shrieked with joy and her face took on an expression of happiness and relief.

Zina received all her guests in exactly the same way, partly because she felt the same need to please everybody, and mainly because she couldn't stand being alone and her own company depressed her and filled her with anxiety, and she was always waiting for someone to come and save her from her loneliness, but loneliness was in fact the only state she knew and it was only rarely that she succeeded in transcending its boundaries, because the only thing which really interested her was herself, and even her interest in Erwin centered mainly on the extent of his interest in her, but Erwin moved aloof and independent in his own orbit, completely detached from Zina, and she lost her bearings completely and drifted confused and rudderless, giving rise in Caesar—who kissed her on the cheek and accompanied her into the living room—to impatience and irritation at her meaningless activities, her panicky overtures, and her endless demands for attention and approval, but he tried to greet her as warmly as possible and asked her how she was, and Zina said, "Just fine, son, and how are you?" and Caesar, who in spite of himself was already feeling tense, said, "Well, very well," and Zina smiled and said, "Your father will be here soon," and asked him how the children were, and Caesar said, "Shaul's not feeling too well," and Zina said, "That's the way it goes with children," and showed him the wooden mask she was holding and told him enthusiastically that it was an African idol from the Ivory Coast which she had bought in an antique shop and she was wondering where she should display it, but her enthusiasm over Caesar and also over the African mask was nothing but an empty, artificial noise, because over the past few weeks her zeal for paintings and sculpture and antiques and all kinds of objets d'art and clothes had waned considerably, and even her ceaseless struggle for Erwin's love and attention had been pushed somewhat aside on account of her anxiety about her legs, which were still very pretty but as the result of a condition which had suddenly deteriorated had become blue and swollen, causing her such severe pain that she was quite often obliged to sit or lie down in order to rest them. Although she had been depressed and alarmed the moment she had noticed what was happening, Zina preferred to ignore it and hoped that this trouble which had appeared of its own accord would also disappear of its own accord, but after a few weeks, when the condition of her legs had deteriorated even further, she decided to wrap them in bandages soaked in vinegar, on the advice of Shoshana, and in bandages soaked in alcohol, on the advice of Besh, and after that she decided to rub them with a nasty-smelling vegetable oil which she had obtained from Erwin's brother Zvi's wife Beatrice, on whose advice she also changed her diet, and only after all these remedies, and others too, had failed, did she finally give in to her older sister Yaffa's pleas and sought medical advice, consulting no less than five doctors, all of whom, each in his own way and without knowing anything about the others, had told her that the condition from which she was suffering, which was very common and not in the least dangerous, was incurable and that she would probaby have to spend the rest of her life with blue, swollen, and painful legs. Zina cursed the doctors and refused to accept her doom, and full of fury and despair she gritted her teeth and fought to save her appearance because she wanted to die beautiful and fresh with legs as pretty as Françoise Arnoud's, and especially because the battle for her legs was connected in her mind with the battle for Erwin, since she saw her disease as a victory for Chemda and a defeat for herself, just as she saw every illness or accident which befell her, and there was thus no difficulty or expense or reason capable of deterring her from waging this lost battle to the bitter end and the desperation and sense of defeat which shaped her life and gave it whatever point and purpose it had also gave her the strength to fight against what she regarded as a conspiracy between nature and Chemda against her.

Now more than ever she found solace and support in Yaffa, whose troubles and illnesses in recent years endowed her in Zina's eyes with the status of an expert on life in general, and on medical matters and doctors in particular, although before this too—and, in fact, ever since she was a young woman—Yaffa had enjoyed the reputation of a practical woman with presence of mind and both feet firmly on the ground, as opposed to Zina and to their pretty younger sister Shalva, whom neither Zina nor Yaffa had seen for twenty-five years, ever since her husband had deserted her. He was a handsome, happy-go-lucky young man with a muscular body and a pleasant voice, a building worker, and Shalva met him one Saturday on the beach and he stood on his hands and turned somersaults and told stories and laughed with all his heart, very bronzed and exuding an agreeable smell of sweat and sea water drying on his skin, and a few days later they decided to get married. Her parents opposed the marriage, since they were a conservative couple with strict ideas about life and behavior and people, and this young fellow, so jolly and handsome, and a hasty love affair and a quick marriage, did not fit in with their ideas, but as usual they expressed their objections by silence and very quiet, restrained manifestations of disapproval and dissatisfaction, and only once, one Friday night when Shalva and her father found themselves alone on the balcony for a moment, was her father unable to control himself and felt compelled to say, "Are you sure that this is what you want?" and Shalva said, "Yes," and her father, who loved her very much, said with great restraint, "I hope to God you won't regret it," but all this got them nowhere, and Shalva married her sweetheart in the presence of a handful of friends, and for six months they lived in one long sun-filled holiday until one day he suddenly abandoned her and went off to America, and Shalva, cut down with her face still warm and glowing with happiness, shut herself up in her house and imposed a total ban on all her family and friends, especially her father, and all their attempts at conciliation bore no fruit and she deliberately humiliated herself by taking all kinds of stupid and sometimes degrading jobs, and by neglecting herself and giving herself to all kinds of men she hated who left her with a feeling of disgust and degradation, and all this in order to punish the world, and especially her family, for the insult she had suffered and for the terrible blow to her boundless pride.

Zina and Yaffa, on the other hand, who grew very close as a

result of all the disappointments and troubles they suffered in later years, kept in touch and met from time to time, although their relationship suffered from its fair share of ups and downs and even strains and tensions over the course of the years, because they were quite different and had taken different paths in life and moved in different circles, and Zina, who belonged to a higher social circle, was sometimes jealous of Yaffa, her sister, who once, long ago, before her daughter married and when her husband Neufeld was still alive, had been really happy, because although she had graduated from a Russian gymnasium and spent two years at a teachers' seminary, she had never aspired to anything beyond an ordinary life or anything outside the family circle, and she was a model housewife and when Caesar was a child he had loved to visit her house—which was always full of the smell of cooking and starched sheets and ironing and cakes baking and shoe polish—and to stand and watch her sewing on buttons, darning socks, ironing, kneading dough and rolling it out with a rolling pin and cutting it into strips for noodles, plucking chickens and dexterously braiding loaves of bread and smearing them with egg yolks before putting them into the oven, and in addition to all this, and besides looking after the two children, Tikva and Ariyeh, who was the same age as Caesar and had been his childhood friend for a few years, she also found time to help Neufeld, who relied on her and consulted her about all his business affairs. Neufeld was a simple, industrious man who had started out as a cobbler and gradually turned himself—by hard work, saving and the careful exploitation of any opportunity that came his way—into the owner of a shoe factory, which although it was not a large concern always brought in a good profit, and still they went on living modestly and circumspectly, because Neufeld, working quietly and almost in secret, invested all the profits from the factory in two trucks which he sent to work for the British army for the duration of the war, and the profits from the trucks he invested, together with other profits that came his way, in plots next to the Yarkon river and in the vicinity of the Arab villages and orchards to the east of the city, which were so far away that their purchase gave rise to the astonishment, and even the derision, of most of Neufeld's friends, who looked at him as if he had bought a plot of land in the middle of the Sahara desert, and he bought only one plot in his life which was not for profit, and that was the one he bought for himself and Yaffa in the Nahalat Yizhak cemetery, because he did not want even in death to be separated from his wife.

All the property he amassed and the economizing he continued to practice did not disrupt their domestic bliss or mar the happiness of Yaffa, who had rejected many more brilliant and charming suitors for Neufeld's sake, but when Tikva finished high school and before she started her army service Neufeld decided to marry her off to a certain young man with blond hair and blue eyes and pink cheeks, a recent arrival from Hungary who introduced himself as an electrical engineer, and although Tikva, who had gone out with him for a while and even brought him home a few times, where his silence and politeness made a very good impression, refused the match because she was no longer interested in him and had no desire to get married to anyone yet, Neufeld insisted and forced Yaffa, who was opposed to the whole idea, to join him in meeting the young man's parents, very simple people who could barely speak Hebrew, and after a few weeks of useless pleading and weeping Tikva resigned herself to her fate, and they led her to her nuptials in a white silk dress and a pearl necklace and silver shoes, and in the presence of hundreds of guests, who gathered round the laden tables to the strains of the band as soon as the ceremony was over, they married her to the engineer, but after a couple of months it transpired that he wasn't an engineer at all but a liar and a crook, who arrived on Neufeld's doorstep every week with new and outrageous demands and reacted to every refusal, or even hesitation, or any little thing that was not to his liking, by losing his temper and persecuting his wife, who in the meantime had given birth to a son, and shortly afterward became pregnant again, and to all her and her mother's pleading and Neufeld's generous urging that he join him as a partner in his businesses or open one of his own at Neufeld's expense, he replied with scorn and derision and laughed in their faces. He frightened and bullied them and once he even tried to beat up his father-in-law, and he made their lives a hell on earth until in the end they saw no way out apart from divorce, but despite all Tikva's requests and those of her parents he refused to give her a divorce, and when after much pleading he finally agreed, he demanded a sum of thousands of pounds and a new truck in return, and Neufeld, who couldn't take any more, agreed immediately, but the whole affair, which had dragged on for a number of years, crushed him and shortened his life, and about a year after Tikva's divorce he died of a heart attack and was buried in the plot of earth he had acquired, and all his property and business concerns passed into the hands of Yaffa, or rather into those of Ariyeh, who was then a young man of about twenty-four years old and already approaching the end of his life.

Ariyeh was a tall, good-looking boy who moved and spoke as if he were always half-asleep and who was indifferent to his surroundings and to conventional timetables, occupations, and goals, but at the same time, in order to please his parents, he did what was expected of him and even graduated from high school with distinction, to the joy of Neufeld, who saw him as his future partner and heir, but when he came back from the army, not long before Neufeld died, he was changed almost beyond recognition and although he still managed to complete his first year of studies in the department of business administration, at the beginning of the second year he suddenly stopped studying and began sleeping till noon, after which he would get up and silently dress himself in the loudest and most dandyish fashion imaginable and go out to loiter in the streets, smelling strongly of cologne. Yaffa, who was managing Neufeld's affairs in the meantime with the help of his accountant, asked Ariyeh to take over this job from her, or to go back to the university, or find himself some other occupation, and he said, "All right. Everything will be all right. There's nothing for you to worry about," but he did nothing because he was sick of everything and his gloomy soul filled with a venom of hatred and aimless malice and grew restless to the point of insanity underneath the skin of its own apathy, and he became addicted to playing billiards and cards and dice games and began deliberately, with a corrupt and careless heart, squandering the vast fortune which his father had amassed over many years of hard work and economizing, and this was in addition to the money he wasted on all kinds of casual acquaintances, who sponged on him ruthlessly and ate and drank and smoked at his expense as they accompanied him from one place of entertainment to another every night until morning, although once in a while he would take a break and shut himself up in his room, the room in which he had grown up and where he continued to live, and draw pictures as he lay on his back in bed, mostly in the India inks and chalks he had used in high school, and he responded to the pleadings of his mother—who continued to cook and launder and iron his clothes for him—with silence or rudeness, and when she spoke to him once about the need to have an aim in life he said, "I do have an aim in life," but she did not dare ask him what it was because she did not want to risk his anger, and only when she placed his plate of soup in front of him she said gently, without addressing him directly, that it might be a good idea to work and get married and have children and find happiness in that way, and Ariyeh, who never looked into her eyes, said, "I'm very happy. I do whatever I like and nobody can stop me, now or ever. My father made a lot of money," and he got up and left the house in silence.

Despite repeated requests from Yaffa, who was more concerned for the welfare of her son than for Neufeld's money, which was being squandered away before her eyes, Tikva refused to interfere, although she was very upset and worried by what was happening, but only insofar as the property was concerned, because she needed money and wanted to make sure she got her fair share of her father's inheritance, and she said so repeatedly to Yaffa, always rudely and often raising her voice, but beyond this she did nothing, because she was embittered by her suffering and busy with her two children, and besides this she had never loved Ariyeh or cared what happened to him, and the relations between them had always been strained and full of inhibitions, and now she simply couldn't bear the sight of him or her mother either, while Ariyeh avoided her too, except for one occasion when he knocked on her door in the early hours of the morning, drugged and disheveled, and woke her from her sleep, and after she had given him a cup of hot milk to drink he said, sitting opposite her in the kitchen, that everything was in a mess and that he loathed the world and also his mother and that every man had the right to be a god and the duty to be a god, but the only gods he knew were criminals, because they transcended convention and made their own world and their own laws to live by. Tikva listened to him in silence, and then gave him a towel and told him to wash his face and hands, and made him another cup of hot milk, and when he had recovered she took him home, where he dropped onto his bed and fell asleep in his clothes, and about a week later he came back, high on drugs again, with a drawing in blue India ink showing a bent arm with a snake's head instead of a hand, and a man leaning against the upright part of the arm wearing a hat (which the snake held in its mouth) and a smock and sandals and holding a kind of shepherd's crook in his hand and looking at the dog sitting in front of him on the horizontal part of the arm. The arm itself, like the man and the dog, was situated between a pair of open legs, one of which was horizontal while the other stuck up in the air at right angles to it. At the end of the horizontal leg, which according to Ariyeh had been created from a rib, was his mother's face, from which both the arm and the legs emerged, with a tree growing from the wrinkles on its forehead, and between the foot and the knee was a female sexual organ, breaking the man's leg—which according to Ariyeh's explanations meant that sin came from woman and caused the fall of man into the abyss, a fall which was symbolized by the leg lifted up to the sky, whose giant foot sheltered the head of the snake and the head of the man, whom Ariyeh called the "good shepherd" and who was surrounded by wicked wolves which were not seen in the picture, and who was none other than Ariyeh himself.

After he had completed his explanations Ariyeh told Tikva that only he was able to understand the picture fully, and that even though others might be able to understand something about it, it would be better for them not to understand it at all, because it might lead to a terrible catastrophe, and he asked Tikva to put it away and Tikva, in whom the picture gave rise to a feeling of oppression and a kind of fear, took it while Ariyeh watched and put it away in the bottom drawer of her wardrobe, meaning to return it to him at the first opportunity or to give it to Yaffa, who had not yet recovered from the death of her husband, and every night before she fell asleep and every morning when she woke she thought of him with helpless longing, and the sense of her loss haunted her and would not give her any peace, and the deterioration of Ariyeh, which flabbergasted her—as well, of course, as depressing her dreadfully—made everything worse and turned Neufeld's absence into a terrible distress, because she was in dire need of support and advice, or at least a little sympathy in the face of this phenomenon, which not only frightened and upset her but also perplexed and hurt her, since she could not understand what made Ariyeh behave the way he did after they had given him a good education and kindness and love and everything he needed, food and clothes and toys and pocket money, all with a relatively liberal hand, and Ariyeh's troubles overshadowed everything else, including her own emptiness and Tikva's wicked ingratitude, and she became a prey to all kinds of ailments and illnessess in addition to her depression and the guilt she felt for her part in her husband's death and her children's situation, and within a short space of time she grew old and all the womanly beauty for which she had once been famous withered away and vanished with hardly a trace, but still she had some vitality left and the strength to cling to reality, and she continued to keep the house clean and neat, do the shopping, cook and bake and take care of the things that needed taking care of, and she also continued to dress nicely and with taste and even to go to the hairdresser from time to time, and to tread circumspectly with Ariyeh, except for once when she lost control of herself and upbraided him harshly, and afterward she regretted it bitterly, because she saw herself as the one to blame for everything and her heart grieved for him, and in spite of everything she went on deluding herself that Ariyeh would settle down and get married and that everything would become right in the end, but Ariyeh, who was sick of women too, did not marry and went on cruelly squandering the family fortune, which he would have squandered to the last penny, despite Yaffa's pleas and Tikva's anger, but before he could do so he committed suicide.

He shot himself in the mouth with a pistol and was found two days later in his car on a dirt road between orange groves not far from the sea dressed in a leather suit and a floral shirt and a yellow tie, and Erwin and Caesar, who took the wooden mask of the African god from his mother and placed it on one of the shelves in the bookcase, went to identify the body in the morgue, because Yaffa and Tikva and also Zina, who looked at the mask absentmindedly and said, "Very nice," couldn't face it, and the two of them, together with Besh, told Yaffa, who fainted in the living room before they even told her, just as she had fainted when she heard that Tikva's Hungarian engineer wasn't an engineer, knocking over her cup and spilling the coffee, and Caesar made haste to pour cold water over her and the drops splashed onto Besh and Zina, who was trying to comfort her sister with a pale and frightened face but at the same time was filled with anger against her because of the whole business and because of the coffee stains spreading over the carpet and the wall, which Zina tried to clean with a wet cloth as soon as Yaffa had recovered a little, but without any success, and the stains continued to annoy her—until they repainted the whole room, which was already after Ariyeh's funeral—and his death and everything connected with it broke Yaffa's spirit and depressed her more and more as the years went by, and she kept repeating, with a petrified kind of pain, "If only he would have been killed in the army, at least," and Zina, who tried to comfort her as best she could, went on looking at the African mask and saying, "Very nice," but she was really listening to Erwin's footsteps on the garden path and his voice talking to someone, and as she said once more "Very nice," the door opened and Erwin came in, followed by his brother Zvi with his Alsatian, Henry, behind him, a big, awe-inspiring animal whose old age and inactivity made him seem half-asleep and who accompanied Zvi everywhere, together with the pipe which never left his mouth.

Zina uttered her shriek of joyful greeting for their benefit, but underneath the empty expression of happiness which froze on her face was anger and tension, because she knew that Erwin had come straight from Chemda's place, and besides she disliked Zvi and hated Henry, who exuded a disagreeable smell of old age and wandered freely over her expensive carpets and brushed the sofas and armchairs with his tail and endangered the glass and china ornaments and vases which were scattered all over the room. Zvi shook hands with Zina and said, "Surprise, surprise," while Erwin, who had hardly given her a glance, asked her to make coffee, and Zina looked at him expectantly in the hope of discovering traces of his visit to Chemda on his face and gave Zvi a big smile and said, "That's quite all right. How's Beatrice?" and Zvi said, "Fine. She's working hard," and shook Caesar's hand, and Caesar asked Erwin how he was, and Zina said, "I envy her. The coffee will be ready in a few minutes," and went into the kitchen, and the three men, Zvi, Erwin, and Caesar, went out to the living room porch, which overlooked the sea, and sat there enjoying the gentle evening breeze which was saturated with the scent of the orange blossom and the cypress trees and the newly watered lawn, and Zvi called Henry and filled his pipe slowly and carefully and asked Caesar what he'd been up to lately and then resumed his conversation with Erwin about the government's land policy, especially the release of land for building and the transformation of agricultural land into urban land.

Apart from their height and the color of their voices and an undefinable expression on their faces, Erwin and Zvi were so different that it was hard to believe that they were brothers, Zvi being a heavy man with a deeply lined face and a very high forehead who spoke slowly and deliberately—and that was the way he moved, too—and there was something very hard and unyielding, even austere, about him, and although he sometimes showed signs of warmth and softness they seemed somehow not to belong to him. He had spent four years in Utrecht working on his doctoral thesis, which dealt with certain hormonal processes and their influence on fertility and on increasing the yield in certain strains of corn, but an English scientist had outwitted him and published an article on exactly the same subject shortly before Zvi completed his own thesis, which came to more or less identical conclusions, whereupon Zvi abandoned his doctorate and came home with Beatrice, whom he had married in Holland, and they set up house in a small villa not far from town and Zvi worked on agricultural planning and applied research connected with organic and inorganic fertilizers while Beatrice taught ancient Oriental history at the university. She was a cheerful, lively woman, but they had no children because Zvi did not want them on the principle that he had no right to bring children into the world against their will because the world was evil and ruthless and would corrupt and harm them, a principle he also imposed on Beatrice, who longed to have a child, and which Besh claimed that, divested of its pretty words and fine feathers was nothing but pure, unalloyed egotism.

During the war Zvi had enlisted in the British army and served in the Balkans and the Western Desert and Europe, and after the war he had joined the militant terrorist underground organization of Lohamei Herut Yisrael, which led to a certain amount of tension between him and Erwin, but this tension, like the hidden tension over their inheritance, never led to an open quarrel between the brothers because Zvi, who was bound to Erwin by complicated feelings of love, was resolute and uncompromising in his views and actions, whereas Erwin was occupied by his own affairs and too intelligent and ironic to force the issue, and so the relations between them continued on an even keel even after the establishment of the state, whose spiritual climate became less and less to Zvi's liking, and his dissent became more and more extreme, especially after the Six Day War. He kept silent most of the time, but when he did express his views he did so directly and harshly and angrily, and although he was not left-wing in his views but a man of the center, he argued that the government was allowing all kinds of parasites to make easy profits at the public's expense and widening the social gap in a total blindness which would lead to a catastrophe, and that the country was sinking into a mindless nationalism and undergoing a process of fascisization and increasing brutalization under the cloak of religion or other irrational theories, and Erwin, whose opinions were the same as Zvi's—although he himself benefited financially from the economic and political situation—would smile and answer, half seriously and half ironically, that people were only people and that everything that was happening was part of an inevitable process in a rapidly developing country with a large immigrant population which had been subject for years to a continuous state of war, but Zvi was not prepared to accept this argument because he loved the country and compromise was foreign to his nature, just as foreign as was shutting his eyes to anything that seemed wrong to him—except in the case of the legacy left by their parents, which included an apartment and three fairly large plots of land, two in Tel Aviv and one in Natanya, of which Erwin had taken control, first as the executor of the will and rate payer, and in the end as the official owner of the property, while Zvi, who was extremely upset by the whole affair, said nothing, and neither did Erwin, and he believed that Zvi, who lit

slices of black bread on the wrought-iron table, and sat down between Erwin and Caesar and poured the coffee into the cups from a china coffee pot, and Erwin, for whose sake she had brought the black bread, took a slice and looked at Zina as if he had just noticed her presence and said, "When I went out you were still a brunette and now you're a blonde," and tittered, and immediately turned to Zvi and said, "You see how quickly people change," and tittered again, but Zvi's face remained expressionless while Erwin's mocking—but at the same time tired, strained, and wooden—smile stayed frozen on his face as if it had been forgotten there, and he broke off a piece of his favorite black bread, which tasted and smelled of bran and jute sacks, and put it in his mouth and chewed with enjoyment, and sipped his coffee, and all his movements were exactly like those of his mother, Grandma Clara, who was also the mother of Zvi and their younger brother Misha, who had emigrated with his wife to Argentina, and of four other children, two of whom, a boy and a girl, had died in infancy, and one girl who had perished in the Holocaust, while the fourth, a boy, Julius, had fought as a partisan and had risen to a position of importance in Communist Poland after the war, and as a high-ranking party member with an important job in the secret service had cut himself off from his family for years, and it was only recently, via the brother in Argentina, that they had renewed contact with him, although now, too, he continued to see himself as a Pole, just like Besh's brother, who lived in Australia, where he had fled to escape from the Nazis, continued to see himself as a German in spite of everything that had happened, arguing that neither Hitler nor Rosenberg nor anyone else could tell him what he was or wasn't or take his German-ness away from him.

Caesar sipped his coffee and looked at Erwin's face with its dry smile and uncanny resemblance to the face of Grandma Clara, who used to burst into their house like a whirlwind in her crazy, colorful clothes, shouting irately in her deep, rough voice which Caesar loved and which for some reason always filled him with joy, even when she was lying in the hospital shortly before she died, still very big—enormous—but in great agony, and the smells of old age and death, drugs and antiseptics, which she tried to banish with perfume and the scent of the flowers she asked to have placed by her bed, had already claimed her for their own. She no longer got out of bed, and even talking was difficult for her, but she still managed to greet him with a smile, as she greeted all her visitors, but unlike Erwin's smile now, her smile, for all its suffering, was still something full of life and gaiety and also mockery, but not malice, and her eyes were clear and clean, and of course she complained indignantly about the doctors and the nurses and the food and the noise, and especially about her sickness and the fact that she could not go outside for a little into the fresh air. Somewhere in her heart she believed that she wasn't going to die, and she was right, too, because death had nothing to do with her life, and only when Caesar came to visit her for the last time, a few days before she died, she turned her head—a skull with yellow skin stretched over it and a big mouth and a pair of ancient eyes sticking out of it—toward him and said in Yiddish, "Look what God makes of a human being," and smiled, but in this smile, full of effort and still preserving a shadow of warmth and irony, there was already, for the first time, knowledge and acceptance of the end, even though a day or two before she had asked Zvi and Erwin and Zina and Beatrice when they came to visit her about Misha and said that if he arrived from Argentina she would still get better and go home, or at least find the strength to get out of bed and go outside into the fresh air to see the sky again and the trees and the people walking at liberty outside the white hospital walls, and suddenly she coughed a slightly dry, hoarse cough, and there was a long, unclear silence, during which Caesar wished that someone would come and sit down next to him, and in the end Grandma Clara said, "I remember all kinds of things," and afterward she said, "There's a lovely song in Polish," and fell silent as if she were trying to remember it, and then she said, "My father used to blow the shofar on Rosh Hashana and Yom Kippur. He was the best shofar blower in town.

It's a pity you never heard him," and she put her skinny hand on Caesar's hand and her face filled for a moment with light and sweetness, and after a moment's silence she said again, "I remember all kinds of things," but she didn't say what they were, although she seemed about to do so, and just shut her eyes and lay there quietly, and Caesar, in whom the touch and look of her sick hand and the smell of her body gave rise to revulsion and the desire to get away, did not ask, but he went on sitting without saying a word by the bedside of his grandmother, whose memory filled him with sadness, because of all the people he knew his Grandma Clara, the date of whose death he had forgotten and whose grave he had never visited, was the only one he had loved peacefully and contentedly, without obligations or calculations or strain, and sometimes he felt such a sense of loss and happy longing when he thought of her that he wished she would come back to life for a while and even imagined it to himself, as he did now, sitting on the porch in the pleasant evening air, and for a moment or two he experienced their joyful meeting and her happiness so vividly that he was deaf to the quiet conversation of Zvi and Erwin and Zina, until Besh's booming voice rising in a shout from the street interrupted them, and when he came in a moment later he had a big, stupid grin all over his face and he seemed drunk—and in fact there was a strong smell of alcohol emanating from him as he approached the table, still shouting, and said, shaking his finger at Zvi and Erwin, that the world should be made illegal, and so should God, even though He didn't exist any more, according to all kinds of writers and journalists, who should also be made illegal because they didn't know what they were talking about, and he announced that life was so idiotic and false and perverted that on the one hand it mesmerized him and fascinated him to such an extent that he would never abandon it, and on the other hand he would never abandon it because he wanted to annoy it by his presence, and on the third hand he would like to tear it to pieces and set it on fire, and the upshot of everything was that a man should never lift up his head and look life right in the face because if he did he would have to tear off his ears and hang them on a line and climb the highest roof available and scream with the last ounce of strength left in his body, and when he said "tear off his ears" he grabbed hold of both his ears and pulled them as if he wanted to rip them off his head and burst out laughing, and then he said that he would sell the present and the future and the world to come and eternity for one plate of the fish soup that his mother used to make, and that she was without a doubt one of the wonders of the world and like his brother in Australia she had also regarded herself as a German, but unlike his brother she had been so convinced and so consistent in this belief that she had held to it until the Nazis finished her off and maybe even now—in the form of smoke or something, because according to the law of the conservation of matter nothing in nature was ever lost—she still believed in her Germany and she was sure that it was all some terrible mistake, and he burst out laughing again and went to the sideboard in the living room and took out a bottle of vodka and glasses and turned back toward the table, and Zina got up and tried to take it away from him and put it back in the sideboard because she was concerned about his health, but Besh pushed her away and said that his health was excellent and in any case it was every man's right to decide for himself when and how to destroy his health and die, and so saying he cursed and poured a glass of vodka for himself and for Zvi, who sat and smoked his pipe with a stiff, disapproving expression on his face, and for Erwin and Zina and Caesar, and said that Zina wasn't really worried about his health but only about her own bloody furniture and ornaments, and then he waved his glass in the air and drank and said, "I must repeat that backward steps have been taken by the metaphysical family, giving rise to a perverse reaction on the part of urban birds, including the owl, and damaging men of justice with no consideration for the rain or anything or the prime minister sitting there and thus because of too many earthworks the life that was bequeathed us has gone by while the reaction of the sender or the receiver moves on toward ever greater improvements in parks and the climate and the slope of the roofs in the green forests until happiness ripens and matures. Thank you," and he laughed again, but suddenly fell silent, and Caesar and Erwin, who had laughed with him, were silent too, and everyone drank in silence until Zina, who was disturbed by this prolonged and unexpected silence, said loudly to Caesar, so that Erwin and Besh would hear too, that the mask of the African god was utterly charming, and Besh looked at it and said, "You can wipe your ass with it and with all the other African gods too," and burst into laughter and refilled his glass and said to Caesar, "Nobody has to have children if he doesn't want them. This is a free country," and Caesar said, "Yes, you're quite right," and Zina said, "You've had too much to drink, Besh," and Besh inclined his head in her direction and said, "Good morning Mrs. Grandmother," and smiled, and Erwin said, "That's enough, Besh," and Caesar pretended not to have heard and sipped his vodka, which he disliked no less than whiskey, although he pretended to be equally enthusiastic about both, because he saw drinking as part of the way of life he tried to lead and the masculine ideal he had set himself to attain, and Besh stopped laughing and gulped his vodka and said, "You can't see the sand any more. But don't worry, one day the sand will bury this town. You can't mess around with sand." Besh's face was gloomy now, and his tone was solemn, and after taking another mouthful of vodka he said, "This town doesn't deserve to exist. It's all a misunderstanding. People think they can play games. It's all meaningless crap. It's a graveyard," and he looked at Zvi and then at Zina, who giggled pointlessly, and played with his glass, his face fallen and very ugly, and said, "You've got nothing to worry about. You're descended from the Khuzars," and after a short silence he repeated, "It's all meaningless crap," and hiccupped loudly. Zvi pretended not to have heard and waited for the moment when he could get up and go, while Caesar smiled a forced smile and laughed a little and looked at Besh, who went on playing with his glass and suddenly, out of the blue, said, "Time's up!" and filled his glass again and looked at Zvi and said, "He never opens his mouth," and Zvi said nothing and went on patting Henry and looked steadily at Besh, who stroked his chin in embarrassment and said, "All right then, have it your own way."

In recent months Besh had been seeing a very rich widow who was a few years older than he was: He ate her food and slept with her from time to time without any desire and extracted money from her, which he lost regularly, together with his own money, at poker—but these losses made no impression on him at all and did not cool his passion for the game, a passion which had nothing to do with money or even with an addiction to gambling as such, but on the one hand stemmed from Besh's wish to demonstrate his belief in idleness and purposelessness by wasting his time in the most idle and purposeless way possible, while on the other hand it was nourished by a pure curiosity which found its satisfaction when he picked up the cards and saw what they were—an act which Besh was fond of comparing with the suspense and pleasure felt by a man on stealing his hand under the skirt of a woman for the first time and slipping it between her legs, and thus instead of going to work and supervising his workers Besh spent much of his time in a barbershop owned by a friend of his, who would hang up a sign saying "Back Soon" on the door, and they would play two-handed poker or sometimes "Shikt" until lunch time, and when Besh had money or when he hit a winning streak, which happened very rarely, they would play all day long until Besh—who now took a sip of vodka—was left without a penny, and he let out a laugh which sounded more like a hoarse grunt, without a trace of irony or amusement, and said again that he would give the world for a plate of his mother's fish soup, and Erwin said, "Forget it, Besh. There's no use crying over spilled milk," and Besh said, "No, I won't forget it," and Erwin said, "That's just a lot of hot air," just like Grandma Clara, who died early one evening, a little while after Zvi and Erwin and Zina and Besh had taken leave of her, at the age of eighty-seven, of sound mind and with all her teeth in her head, and having lived, after all, to see the landing of the first man on the moon, an event which gave rise in her at first to disbelief and afterward to displeasure, as if someone had been trying to make fun of her and invade her life, but before long she treated the whole subject with scornful amusement, and even a touch of pity, since in her long life she had witnessed countless follies, appalling injustices, and catastrophes, most of which had resulted from good intentions and high hopes, as well as all kinds of mind-boggling marvels and wonders, at least some of which had turned out to be useless delusions which did nobody any good.

When she died Grandma Clara left no debts, either of money or of gratitude, behind her, and this was a source of pride to her because she always paid all her debts without delay as a matter of principle and out of the desire to be free, which guided her throughout her life, and she never bowed her head or looked up to anyone, treating even God, to whom she felt closer every year, as if He were a person with whom she was on familiar terms, even though He was older and wiser and more important than she was, and she quite often allowed herself to break His laws on the sly, although only in marginal matters, and in the end she treated His rituals like domestic ceremonies which were not in the least exalted, and perhaps not even very important, but which had to be scrupulously attended nevertheless, in a spirit of willingness and sincerity, nicely dressed and holding a prayer book, whose contents neither moved her heart nor inspired her with awe, partly because she was a simple, uneducated woman and it was only vaguely and with difficulty that she understood what was written in it, but none of this worried her or oppressed her spirits—only Misha, Misha whom she loved so dearly and in whose power to give her strength she believed, but she never saw him again because he was so involved in his business affairs in Argentina that despite Zvi's polite but urgent requests he could not get away and come back to the country in which she died and was buried forty years after she had arrived there, partly because of external stresses and strains but mainly for the love of Zion, dragging Grandpa David, who had been a successful hide dealer and a beadle in the synagogue in the Diaspora, with her, but she was very soon disillusioned because it was not the country she had imagined in her dreams and among the square white houses and glaring wastes of sand which got into her shoes, and sometimes even into her food, in the harsh light of the sun, in the dusty, fly-filled heat, she felt alien and deceived, and many years had to pass for this feeling to fade a little and lose its sharpness, but in the meantime she expressed her disappointment in a stream of Yiddish and Polish and Russian curses and a flood of abuse and angry, indignant complaints, which she flung loudly about her in all directions, often after working herself up on purpose and deliberately exaggerating them out of all proportion, because in some mysterious way they gave her satisfaction, just as they sometimes gave rise, perhaps unintentionally, to the amusement of those who heard them.

She inveighed against the heat and the people and the taste of the water and the rabbi and the prices and the shape of the houses and the streets and the flies and the dust and the howling of the jackals, which stopped her from sleeping and forced her to go to bed night after night, which she did very early, as an unbreakable law, except on Friday nights and holidays, with her ears blocked with cotton, and after Misha emigrated with his wife to Argentina to get rich there she started sitting in cafes and turning the pages of English and German magazines, of which she did not understand one single word, and going to the movies, and persecuting her husband as she had never persecuted him before, until he sought refuge from her in the street and the synagogue and the homes of his sons, especially Erwin, and in the bathroom, which became the private Garden of Eden in which he secluded himself and spent his time reflecting on various matters and indulging in pleasant fantasies and taking catnaps and reading old newspapers and conducting inner debates with himself or his wife and sons or all kinds of acquaintances and politicians, and he sometimes even risked Grandma Clara's wrath by ignoring her knocking and emphatic demands that he come out at once, because anyway all that awaited him when he did so was the nagging and persecution which had been his lot in life ever since he married Grandma Clara. Until this event Grandpa David had been a proud, self-assertive, and highly respected member of the community, but after his first wife died he decided to marry a beautiful young woman and he chose Grandma Clara, and no sooner had he married her than his position started slipping. Within the space of a few years Grandma Clara had succeeded in breaking his spirit entirely, and she had him so firmly under her thumb that he didn't dare make a move or open his mouth in her presence until he had obtained a nod of approval from her first, and in the end Grandpa David became a shadow of his former self and all that was left of his glorious past were a few old suits made of the best quality cloth and a heavy winter coat with a fur collar and a silk lining which hung uselessly in the wardrobe, a cane with a silver knob, and two weaknesses he could not suppress and which, despite the danger and disgrace, he tried to gratify by whatever means he could: a weakness for women and a weakness for snuff.

The snuff he obtained from acquaintances at the synagogue or bought with the pennies he managed to scrape together from various sources, and from time to time Erwin would buy him a can, and he went on stuffing it secretly into his nostrils, which grew quite brown, despite all Grandma Clara's scolding and the exhaustive and humiliating searches she conducted among his belongings and clothes, confiscating every pinch of snuff he had hidden between the pages of his prayer book, or in the pockets and folds of his pants, or behind the collar of his jacket, and throwing it all into the toilet and flushing it away while he stood and watched like a little boy in disgrace, whereas his weakness for women was an ancient fire which burned in him constantly as he lay in his bed or sat on the toilet or walked down the street or even, sometimes, when he prayed. In the old country he had watched the women doing their washing on the river banks, their arms and necks bare and their dresses hitched up to their thighs, and in Eretz Yisrael he went to the seashore and stood on the promenade and watched the women, especially the young girls, walking around on the beach below in their bathing suits or lying on the sand, and he prayed in his heart for the chance to lie with a woman like one of these young girls, so fresh and tanned, before he died, and at home, on fire with lust, he would try to force Grandma Clara to lie with him, and she would struggle against him and push him away and escape to Erwin or Zvi or one of her woman friends, and swear that never again would she go back to that old lecher, who at the age of seventy had still managed to satisfy the appetites of a certain woman of fifty-odd, whose husband wasn't interested in her anymore, in her little button shop, where they would shut themselves up from time to time after closing for a few minutes of hasty enjoyment, and who until the day he died at the age of eighty-one, as the result of pneumonia and kidney complications, found relief for the needs of his flesh in masturbation, which in the end, after the momentary pleasure, only increased his lust and depressed his spirits, and all this he kept locked up in his heart and only occasionally, when he couldn't bear it any longer, he would come and complain to Erwin, who now looked listlessly and wearily at Besh and broke off a piece of black bread, dropping crumbs on the floor to Zina's annoyance, and put it in his mouth and chewed slowly, and Besh said, "I'll forget it when I die," and sipped his vodka and smiled to himself and added, "If I forget my mother's fish soup what will I have left to remember?" and at that moment the doorbell rang and Zina went to open the door and Max Spillman, who had come to speak to Erwin about business matters, entered wearing the same kind of well-cut summer suit he had been wearing previously at Regina's, but now in a shade of beige, with his hair neatly combed and a delicate scent of deodorant and eau de cologne emanating from his person.

He greeted the company and shook hands with everyone,

including Besh, whom he disliked as much as Besh disliked him, and Zina asked him if he would like a cup of coffee and he said, "With pleasure," and sat down and exchanged a few words with Zvi and Erwin and Caesar, who played with his cigar and looked at Spillman's face, which was totally devoid of charm and very well preserved and full of self-confidence and an unpleasant smugness, and suddenly he remembered that he had forgotten his wallet at the studio with all his papers and his driver's license, which he would need early the next morning when he went to fetch his car from the garage, and he finished what remained of the vodka in his glass with a gulp and stood up to take his leave, and Zina accompanied him to the door, where she asked him if he would like a bar of chocolate for the children, and Caesar said, "No thanks," and kissed her and hurried away, but when he approached the studio he saw Ella crossing the road with a black fringed shawl around her shoulders, and he waited until she had disappeared into the lobby, and after a moment's hesitation he decided to collect his wallet the next morning and turned away and went to Tehilla's, and Ella climbed the stairs and rang the bell, and Israel, who could tell by the sound of her footsteps that it was Ella, lay on the couch without moving and looked at the knife sticking out of the wooden board, and Ella rang the bell again, a short, hesitant ring, and a moment or two later she rang again, and only then Israel got up to open the door and found her standing on the threshold with an embarrassed, apologetic smile on her fair, childish face, and she said, "I'm a little late," and Israel said nothing, and Ella looked at him expectantly with her innocent blue eyes and went on smiling in an attempt to appease his anger and placate him, but Israel's face remained hard and hostile, and Ella came into the room and put her big canvas bag with its paper and cardboard and bottles of India ink and pens and pencils and paintbrushes down on the table, her eyes already wet with tears.

Israel shut the door and followed her into the room and lay down on the couch and picked up the pornographic book and began paging through it, taking no notice of Ella, and the longer his stubborn silence lasted the gloomier and more full of violence it grew, until Ella, who could bear it no longer, approached him and said, "I couldn't come any sooner," and sat down beside him and waited a little and then placed her hand carefully on his shoulder and said, "Really I couldn't," but Israel went on lying on his side leafing through the book, hostile and indifferent, and it was only very gradually, with a great effort and as if against his will, that he cleared a way for the feelings of love and tenderness stirring inside him and seeking an outlet, and he moved almost imperceptibly and allowed her to cuddle up to him, and afterward, again as if against his will, he passed his lean, strong fingers hesitantly over her blonde hair, which was gathered at the nape of her neck with a blue rubber band, and then he embraced her, still not wholeheartedly, and still without raising his eyes from the book or looking at her, but his frozen face thawed a little and softened, and Ella said, "It's hot in here. I brought a packet of wafers. Would you like some?" and then she said, "Why don't you take a shower?" and Israel, who pretended not to have heard her, asked her if she wanted coffee, and Ella, with gratitude, said, "Yes. I'll make it," but Israel rose to his feet and said, "Never mind. You can get on with your work," and he went into the kitchen and put the kettle on the electric burner, and Ella took out her paper and bottles of India ink and the rest of her paraphernalia and arranged them on the table and sat down to work.

She was studying art and supporting herself by doing enlarged ink drawings of plants and insects for the natural sciences department at the university, sometimes of the entire plant or insect and sometimes of separate parts, or cross sections of different organs: their limbs, respiratory organs, feelers, stamens, stems, fruit, or seeds. Israel learned these things about her on the first evening they met, when they sat drinking coffee in the milk bar, and during the year which had passed since then he had also learned that she had a mother, which was the last important and undeniable piece of information he had learned about her. He imagined her mother, whom she hardly ever mentioned, as a woman with long black hair and burning black eyes, whose coarsely beautiful, masculine face, which had something bitter and very tired about it, had been ravaged and disfigured by the suffering and the disappointments which had caused her to neglect herself and lead a loose, disorderly life out of total indifference to her body and her fate, a way of life which had disfigured her over the course of the years and also undermined her, especially psychologically speaking, so that she had become confused and aimless and had arrived at the brink of madness.

Israel himself did not know where this picture of Ella's mother came from, since Ella herself, to the extent that she spoke of her at all, never went further than the bald statement of fact that she had a mother, and she never mentioned her father at all, and at first Israel took no notice of this omission, but afterward he began to question her about him, sometimes carefully and without any show of interest, and sometimes, especially later on, directly and insistently, but all in vain, since Ella evaded his questions or withdrew into silence and refused to say anything, and only once, after he had nagged and pestered her, did she say, "I never had a father," and Israel, out of patience, accused her of lying and hiding things from him, and Ella did not try to defend herself, but wrapped herself in silence and would not say a word, and it wasn't the silence of concealment but the silence of a person who had said everything there was to say, but Israel—who now came back from the kitchen with two cups of coffee—would not leave her alone, and from time to time he returned to the subject of her father, who took on a different shape in his imagination every time he thought about him, and Ella shot him a happy look and laid down her pen and cleared a little space, and he put the cups down on the table and sat down beside her, and while they drank their coffee she showed him the drawings of the silver spider which she had been working on for a number of days, and Israel said, "That's nice," and asked her if she would like to go to St. Antonio's with him the next day and listen to the organ, and Ella said, "Yes, of course. You know I want to," and when they finished their coffee she went on working on the spider's legs while Israel took a shower and sat down at the piano and began to play, and Ella, whose face was calm and radiant, worked a little longer and then got up and went to lie down on the couch, where she lay, as always, on her side with her legs drawn up, almost touching her chest, and her fair head resting on her arm, playing with a lock of her hair which she wrapped slowly around her finger and made into a curl, while sucking the thumb of her other, unoccupied hand with enjoyment and concentration and staring serenely at Israel and listening to him play the piano, and when he finished what he was playing a silence fell, and Israel liked this silence but he didn't want it to go on, and so he rose and went to sit on the edge of the couch next to Ella, who went on calmly sucking her thumb, very relaxed, and moved her head a little and laid it close to Israel's thigh, and he placed his hand on it and stroked it slowly and gently, and he looked at her thin hands, whose nails were always very short because she bit them, and then he looked at her face, innocent of everything, over which a very slight smile played, like a kind of brightness illuminating her pure skin.

Without taking his eyes off her face Israel slipped his hand under her blouse and stroked her firm little breasts and her smooth belly, and Ella lay without moving so that it seemed as if she felt nothing and was sunk in some kind of trance, and Israel, who passed his hand over her throat and shoulders and armpits and again over her belly, asked her who the first man she ever went to bed with was, but Ella did not reply and went on lying quietly and sucking her thumb, but Israel would not leave it alone and he asked her the same question again and again, at first gently and then rudely and aggressively, and he felt the anger welling up and flooding him, and Ella said nothing, but Israel persisted until in the end, still sucking her thumb, she said, "There wasn't anyone," an answer she had already given him many times before, and this expected reply only enraged Israel further and he told her that she was lying, because if she had never gone to bed with anyone before him how come she wasn't a virgin when she met him, and Ella took her thumb out of her mouth and with eyes which were already wet with tears she said, "I don't know. That's the way I was born," and Israel, who knew that she might be telling the truth, dismissed her words angrily because his rage and jealousy were driving him insane, and he told her to take her things and go away and never come back again, and Ella stood up and weeping soundlessly she began collecting her things, which were scattered about the room, and Israel looked at his book and at her, and suddenly, while he was sitting on the couch between the mirrors in which he and Ella and the whole room were reflected, he was moved with pity for her, because she looked so lost and in need of protection and so innocent and unjustly punished, and he himself perhaps felt a sudden fear of loneliness, and he went up to her and placed his hand on her shoulder, and this was enough for her to snuggle up to him, and without a word he embraced her and kissed her head and brow and eyes, and afterward he undressed her and she stood before him naked, her skin white and smooth, except for a brown birthmark on the right side of her belly, a little above the pelvic bone.

Ella switched off the light and embraced Israel, and he suddenly broke into smothered laughter, and they stood there in the middle of the room in the dim light coming in from the street, and then Israel spread the sheet on the couch and took off his clothes and lay down beside her in the pleasant evening air which caressed their skin and made them feel good, and they covered themselves with another sheet and slept on the narrow couch until day broke and Caesar came to take the wallet with his papers and driver's license, and when he passed Israel's room he paused for a moment and looked through the open door and saw them lying there naked because they had pushed most of the sheet off their bodies while they slept on account of the heat. The noise Caesar made in the next room and when he slammed the door behind him as he left woke them, and Israel, who always parted rapidly from sleep and was immediately wide awake, stroked Ella's body and kissed her breasts and her belly, which were cool and pleasant to the touch, and they went on lying together for a while, and then they rose and dressed and washed and had coffee, and Israel took his music and they went downstairs and walked by the sea, which was stormy that morning, to St. Antonio's, and in the evening they came back to the studio tired and sweaty after spending the whole afternoon idly watching the patient fishermen standing with their rods on the beach and the quays and the promenade, not far from the port, and the boat fishermen lazily preparing their nets and ropes and motors and oil lamps for the night's fishing, when they would set out slowly from the port close to the place where great flocks of white seagulls now stood, taking off from time to time and flying and then coming back to rest again.

The next day too they went to St. Antonio's and came home in the evening, and after they had showered and had had something to eat Israel called Goldman, as he had promised, and asked him how he was, and Goldman, who was very happy to hear Israel's voice, said, "Everything's fine. I'm glad you called," and Israel asked him if anything new had happened, and Goldman said, "What can happen already? The house is full of people," and sniggered, and Israel asked if there was anything he could do to help him, and Goldman said that if there was anything he could do to relieve him of his obligations he would be very grateful, and he asked him if he would come to see him the next day or the day after that alone or with Caesar, and Israel said, "OK," and they exchanged a few more remarks until Goldman said, "I have to stop now. There's nothing I can do about it, I'm the center of attention here. I'll be seeing you," and he put the receiver down and shook hands with Moishe Tzellermaier, who had just come in with his eldest boy Nathan, a quiet and not very bright boy, who was very like his father, in his kind-heartedness as well as in his appearance, and worked as a diamond polisher, and Moishe Tzellermaier, who had brought a big cream cake with him, was proud of his son and had high hopes for him and was always buying him new clothes or giving him money to spend, and if he hadn't been afraid of accidents he would have bought him a motorbike too, and from the day Nathan graduated from vocational school, where he studied electricity, and especially after he had completed his army service, he had tried in every possible way, despite his wife's objections, to influence his son to leave the country and emigrate to America, where he would be able to get rich and have a good life, and—even more important—where he would never have to serve in the army again, which infuriated Goldman's father, who heard about it from Moishe Tzellermaier himself, who in the innocence of his heart expounded his views on the subject frankly and freely on a number of occasions, and when Goldman's father once tried to rebuke him he said, "He's already been a soldier once. That's enough for him," and Goldman's father restrained himself and made no further comment on the subject, because in some strange way, despite his anger and indignation, he still felt a patronizing affection for Moishe Tzellermaier, the simple and uneducated man who in his youth had been a member of the right-wing nationalist Betar movement and who sometimes bad-mouthed the country in his broken Hebrew, and like his father Goldman too felt this affection and he shepherded them into the living room, which for the third straight day was full of people, and when he reached the door he saw Manfred out of the corner of his eye rising to part from Stefana, and he turned his head aside and went into his room and shut the door behind him, because he had no desire to meet Manfred again and because he did not want to be a witness to this parting, which was brief and contained something strained and chilly, even hostile, although all this was hidden under a mask of poise and convention and politeness.

Manfred said that he was leaving the next day for Haifa and that he would come back in a week's time, after visiting his brother and attending to some personal affairs, and Stefana said, "That's all right, Manfred, you go to Haifa. It's perfectly all right," and she accompanied him to the door and returned to her seat in the armchair, a little apart from the others, most of whom had not shown their faces in this house for years, after Goldman's father had succeeded in quarreling with many of them and in ostracizing a few, while others had scattered and moved away, and now, because of the mourning, they had come together again to console the widow, and in the meantime they ate and drank and conversed like on the first day, immediately after the funeral, and only Uncle Lazar, who had come the day before too and had brought Yehudit Tanfuss with him, hardly uttered a word and as on his previous visits seemed embarrassed and inhibited, as if he felt out of place, but after all the visitors had gone he asked Stefana, as he had asked her yesterday and the day before, if she needed anything and if there was anything he could do to help her, and this time she said "Yes," and asked him to take two trunks down from the shelf in the bathroom for her, and Uncle Lazar climbed a little ladder and brought down the two trunks, black wooden trunks with curved tops and heavy brass locks which had already begun to go green, and he dragged them into her room and stood them one beside the other, and Stefana thanked him. The trunks were full of old dresses made of velvet and printed silk and embroidery, silk and lace blouses, a coat with a fur collar and fur trimmings at the cuffs and the hem, all kinds of ruffled petticoats, and a number of elegant hats, and when Stefana opened them there was a strong smell of mothballs and old clothes which had been lying unused and unaired for a long time, and she stood and looked at what was before her for a moment, and then she rummaged among the clothes and took out some of them and examined them slowly, with an expressionless face, as if she weren't really interested, and the next day she sat in the heavy armchair, opposite the TV set, in a purple velvet dress with a black woolen shawl on her shoulders, and there was something proud and aloof about her. After recovering from the initial shock of her appearance Goldman could not bear to look at her, just as he could no longer bear the commotion of the guests, which penetrated his room through the walls and the door, and after placing a bowl of fruit and biscuits and what was left of the cake brought by Moishe Tzellermaier the day before, he exchanged a few remarks with one or two people and then abandoned his duties as host to Tzimmer's widow, who came in every evening for at least an hour, or to Yehudit Maizler, or to any of the other guests, and slipped out of the house without saying a word to anyone.

The evening sky was cloudy and the air was hot and motionless, heavy and muggy, and there was a kind of tension in everything, in the trees and in the bushes and in the clouds, which spread and thickened, and Goldman, who was irritable and nervous because of the ceaseless stream of guests and because he felt that he had behaved wrongly and had broken some kind of taboo, or at least a convention of politeness, by going out and leaving his mother alone in the house with the guests in the middle of the period of mourning, hesitated for a moment and in the end decided in spite of everything to go to visit Dita, whom he had not seen since his father's death, although he did not particularly miss her or want to see her, but he wanted to be somewhere clean and quiet, and besides, his regular visits to her had grown into a habit which in the course of time had become a necessary part of his life, just as they had become, if not perhaps to the same extent, a part of the life of Dita, who was a biochemist and after graduating with distinction from the university in Jerusalem and later continuing her studies in England and America, where she had obtained her Ph.D., was now engaged in research connected with the breaking of the genetic code. She was more than four years older than Goldman, very well organized and not particularly pretty, in fact rather plain but for her beautiful brown eyes, and she was clever, and sensible, and as a result of the circumstances of her life independent and hard-working, and it was only in the course of the years that a certain hardness, sometimes quite unpleasant, had become more pronounced in her character, perhaps because she had devoted so much of her time and strength for so many years to work and study, driving herself ceaselessly and imposing strict discipline on herself, and to some extent also perhaps because she lived alone, and also perhaps because she had no children. At first she avoided having children out of necessity, saying to herself that she would put off having them until she had completed her doctorate, and afterward, when she was absorbed in her work and had become used to living alone, she was afraid that children would be a nuisance, and also that she herself would not be able to give them the attention they needed, and in the end she realized that even if she wanted children she was no longer capable of having them, at any rate not without difficulties and grave risks to her health and theirs.

She and Goldman had met about five years before and had begun seeing each other three or four times a week, and sometimes every evening, always in Dita's house, but they did not often discuss the possibility of marriage or some other kind of permanent arrangement, and the frequency and seriousness of these discussions too underwent a change in the course of time, for in the beginning they discussed the subject quite often and with the intention at least of doing something about it, and if Dita had been a little more decisive and had presented Goldman with an explicit demand they would almost certainly have gotten married, but Dita vacillated between her independence and the wish to break out of the circle of her loneliness, and she waited for Goldman to do something, but Goldman, who during all these years had never once invited Dita to his home or introduced her to his parents, or even mentioned her to them, could not make up his mind either, because of the very same problems—in addition to which he wanted to fall in love and was afraid of failing again after his dissolved marriage to the beautiful Jemimah Chernov, and in the meantime their initial intentions and wish to act lost their force and vitality and the little enthusiasm they possessed was worn away by their countless careful calculations, by the long postponement, and by their routine meetings, which also made getting married to a certain extent superfluous, if not pointless,

but they went on meeting anyway despite the knowledge that they would never get married or have a family, and they also went to bed together from time to time although the act gave them no pleasure but had turned into a habit and a duty, and perhaps in spite of their disillusion and their experience they also hoped by these means to return to some hopeful and moving new point of departure, which if it had ever existed in their relationship had not survived for long, and they went on trying, and every time was more forced and more joyless than the time before, and for all their goodwill and determination they could no longer obtain even a little simple pleasure from the act, and it would all end in disappointment and bleak feelings of defeat and shame, and also of dishonesty, and on more than one occasion Goldman would descend the stairs and go home depressed and full of anger and decide to break this barren and oppressive bond forever, but he never did so, and he was jealous of Avinoam Leviatan, who lived on a moshav with his wife and his three children, and of Caesar, who was able to enjoy himself without any difficulties with any woman he fancied, and he found his consolation with prostitutes, a consolation which he regarded as contemptible and humiliating and sinful, but it was the only one available to him and for all its shamefulness he could not give it up, and when he came within sight of Dita's apartment and saw the light on in the big window overlooking the courtyard he came to a halt, and then he turned and retraced his steps, and walking slowly, as if he had not yet made up his mind, he crossed a few streets and turned nonchalantly into Yarkon Street, which in his eyes was the most despicable and also the most frightening street in town, and as always he felt ill at ease and also ashamed, since the adventure toward which his feet were leading him, and everything it involved, was incompatible with an ingrained sense of values and morality against which he rebelled and which he tried to get rid of, after having succeeded in convincing himself time and time again that while conventional morality was based on religion, humanistic morality, which was based on reason and in the possibility of whose existence he believed, and which was moreover the only morality acceptable to him as a nonbeliever, did not repudiate prostitution, nor adultery, and could not be opposed to human happiness, and if it was opposed to happiness then he, like Caesar, preferred happiness, but nothing helped, and the sense of shame and sin continued to oppress him as he walked along the street, glancing from time to time at the girls standing with their little handbags on the corners or in the doorways of the gloomy old buildings, abandoned to neglect and the indifferent process of decay, with their arched windows and doors and the rusty iron grilles with their pretty patterns embellishing the balconies, most of which were in darkness so that they looked as if nobody lived in them and all they contained were broken bits of furniture and dust and cobwebs and evil spirits.

He turned into one of the alleys leading down to the sea, paused for a moment as usual to look at the pictures of the acrobats and the magician and the stripper in the small display window of the Twenty-Nine Club, and afterward entered the lobby and nodded to the proprietor before stepping into the small, dark hall, where he approached the bar and greeted the man standing behind it, who was wearing a neatly pressed dinner jacket and whose name was Karol, and sat down and ordered a beer, all without any haste, and at the same time he looked around and saw that Paula was not there, and the dark hostess whom everyone called Topsy was sitting nearby in the company of a middle-aged gentleman in an elegant dark suit who was eating very slowly without saying a word, and every once in a while, still absorbed in eating his meal, he would lean slightly forward and plant a kiss on her forehead, or cut a bit of meat off the serving on his plate and impale it on his fork and put it into her mouth, and she submitted to everything, smiling joylessly. There were other people there too, most of them middle-aged, who had come to find a little release and a little happiness in the company of the hostesses, who drank with them and allowed them to stroke and embrace them, and who pretended to listen sympathetically to what they were saying, which for the most part was a boring combination of hard luck stories and all kinds of grievances and complaints, mixed with clumsy, and sometimes repulsive, outpourings of love, or a dreary recital of business affairs and money and apartments and the trivia of daily life. There were also a few solitary young men who came more or less regularly, like their middle-aged counterparts, and a few couples who had come to have an evening out and were waiting to see the floor show, which included a singer and a magician and a couple of acrobats and a famous stripper from the Crazy Horse, as it said in the advertisements, and in the meantime they drank and chatted and kissed in the dark, or danced to the strains of the band, which consisted of a piano, drums, and a saxophone, and Goldman, darting occasional glances around him, drank his beer and made polite conversation with Karol, who told him for perhaps the hundredth time about the little town of his birth in Bulgaria, in the valley of roses, where they grew roses which filled the entire valley and afterward cooked them in big vats, in special kitchens, and extracted the most famous oil-of-roses in the world from them, and rose water, and a sweet smell covered the whole valley, and while he was talking there was a loud commotion in the lobby and after a moment a young man burst into the hall, dressed to the nines in an elegant dark suit with a red carnation in his lapel, dragging a very thin girl in a white bridal gown behind him. The young man, who seemed well known to the proprietor and staff and hostesses, was intoxicated with elation and evidently with alcohol as well, and waved in all directions with his free hand, a smile across his face, and ordered the girl to sit down, and she immediately went and seated herself at one of the tables, while he banged on the bar laughing loudly with enjoyment or drunkenness and shouting, "I've done it! I'm a married man!" and pointed at the girl, who sat submissively at the table playing nervously with her fingers, watching him and looking frightened and wretched and hopeless in her wedding dress, which was crushed and limp, and her veil was awry above her wispy brown hair, but the man took no notice of her; he was busy straightening the red carnation in his lapel and shouting loudly, "They've tied up my balls!" and shaking hands with Karol, who congratulated him, as did the two waiters and the cook and the band and the hostesses, who also kissed him, and he shouted again, "They've tied up my balls!" and burst out laughing loudly and ordered a round of beer for everyone in the bar, and the proprietor and waiters and hostesses served the beer to the sound of clapping and laughter and cries of "Mazel tov!" and in the middle of all this Paula came in and stood for a moment wondering what was going on, and when she realized the cause of the uproar she hurried over to the groom, floating in a cloud of powder and perfume, and embraced him and kissed him on both cheeks, and he too kissed her and rumpled her hair a little, and afterward she came and sat next to Goldman, who ordered a glass of Madeira for her, and placed his hand hesitantly on her thick neck, and while she chatted to him and to Karol he slid his hand over her back and her breasts, which were firmly supported by a hard brassiere, and behind her head he saw the pale spotlight illuminating the little dance floor, which was the signal that the floor show was about to begin in a few minutes' time, and Goldman, tense with anticipation, went on slowly drinking his beer and talking to Paula, who nodded her head and smiled and kissed him on the cheek. She was fat with pink and white skin and very fair hair done in big curls and looked like a beauty from an old-fashioned movie, and she was a good woman, or at least a tolerant one, and Goldman was used to her, and when the program started he signaled to her and they both rose to their feet and went out into the little yard behind the building, which was surrounded by a rusty fence and a few straggly bushes, separating it from the yard of the building next door, which was in complete darkness but for the card club on the second floor, where they could see the heads of the people quite clearly in the windows and the big fans hanging from the ceiling and revolving slowly.

Something had broken in the air and a wind which had been

imprisoned began to blow, and the quiet murmur of the sea turned to a monotonous roar, and from the street they could hear the occasional noise of a car and isolated human voices, and from beyond the blank walls and windows of the bar the muffled sound of music reached their ears, and Goldman and Paula approached one another and did what they had come to do, briskly and efficiently with a few brief and unimportant routine embraces, and when Goldman had finished Paula kissed him as usual on the forehead and asked him if he had enjoyed himself and Goldman, standing with his back to her, said "Yes," but Paula probably did not hear him, since she wasn't even trying to listen to his answer because she had already finished tidying herself and was on her way back to the bar, and Goldman, who didn't even turn his head to look at her, finished tidying himself too, and for the first time he felt the coolness in the air and it was disagreeable to him, and he left the yard and went home empty and depressed, because after it was over he was left with nothing but the sense of shame and sin, and a feeling of disappointment, because none of it bore any resemblance to the wild sexual fantasies which he cultivated in his imagination, to a large extent in the wake of the pornographic photographs and books which Caesar brought him and Caesar's stories about his experiences with women, culminating in the description of an experience, which Goldman longed to emulate, of having two women at the same time.

The wind dropped and a slow, warm rain began to fall, and Goldman turned into the promenade with his hands in his pockets, and walked past the seedy gaming alley with its punch balls and clacking pinball machines and past the bar open to the street and the cafe in which he had once received a beating on account of a prostitute, and afterward he passed the cafe in which, frightened and excited and full of expectations, he had for the first time, after prolonged conflicts, approached a prostitute, but the whole thing, which did not last more than ten minutes, or even less, had ended in shame and disappointment, after the prostitute, who first took his money and put it away in her bag, took him up to the second floor, into a kind of dark hall, which Goldman thought must lead to a room with a bed where he would be able to lie with her, and she sat him down next to a table in the dark and without asking his permission ordered wine and a pack of American cigarettes at his expense and all she let him do was embrace her a little and touch her breasts through her dress and kiss her once or twice while she sat there drinking and smoking— and even that with the utmost care not to spoil her makeup or rumple her hairdo, and Goldman, who felt cheated and mocked, tried to protest, but without any conviction because he understood that it wouldn't do any good and because he was afraid of violence, and in the end he stood up and said, "I hope you realize that you've lost a customer" and beat a hasty retreat, and without taking any notice of the rain, which kept on falling slowly, softening the air and wetting the pavements and the road, which gave off an agreeable smell of wet dust, he walked back home, and as he walked he grew a little calmer, but when he came closer and saw the light in the living room window he was overcome by irritation again, and he went into the lobby and switched on the light and climbed up the stairs.

In the living room he found Uncle Lazar and Avraham Shechter and Yehudit Maizler and Shmuel and Bracha and Aharon, Shmuel's brother, who with cunning and cruelty, but especially cruelty, had pushed his father out of his own butcher shop until in the end he had him completely under his thumb and wouldn't even let him in the door, while Shmuel and Bracha, who for some reason was the object of Aharon's wife's undying jealousy, were away in Australia, and ever since then the two brothers, and of course their wives, had stopped speaking to each other, except for a few cold, polite sentences when the need arose, and this coldness was especially obvious in the behavior of Aharon, who in some strange way regarded himself as the injured party, persecuted and unjustly treated by Shmuel, who had long ago put the whole affair of the butcher shop out of his mind, together with the blows they had exchanged, but Aharon continued to nurse a grudge and he sat there silent and sulking and only when Goldman came in did he rouse himself and smile slightly, since he regarded Goldman as being in his camp, because his son, Avraham, who had been living in France for many years, had been in the same class as Goldman in school and for a time the boys had been friends.

Apart from Avraham Shechter, who rose to take his leave, the guests were still talking and drinking tea and eating fruit, Moishe Tzellermaier's cream cake having been eaten to the last crumb, and Goldman paused for a moment and said, "Good evening" to everyone, and Aharon asked him how he was, and Goldman said, "Fine, thank you" and asked him about Avraham, and Aharon said, "He's very busy, but he may come for a visit," and his wife said, "Of course he'll come. It's just that it's so hot here in summer and he's a very busy man," and she said this in a loud voice so that everyone would hear, because she was as proud of Avraham as Aharon was, but Avraham was ashamed of the pair of them, of his mother, who was a fat, loud, ignorant woman, and of his father, who was both ignorant and violent—when Avraham was a child his father had beaten the daylights out of him for every little thing—and Goldman said, "Good, let him come," and shook hands with Avraham Shechter, who looked at him with dead eyes and shook his hand apathetically, because ever since his son Yehuda—who had been born when Avraham was already a man in his forties—had been killed when his jeep drove over a mine, he seemed to have lost all desire to live and he had withdrawn into himself and become religious, although his vague and groping private creed bore no resemblance to the crude and naïve brand of religion professed by Moishe Tzellermaier, which contained neither a belief in God nor reflections on the nature of God, nor even the observance of daily religious duties, but only the uncomprehending perpetuation of a few rituals connected with religious holidays and rites of passage, such as his son's bar mitzvah, and Saturday synagogue attendance, and it was also unlike the crude religiosity of Max Spillman, which was not very different from the religious conversion of Moishe Tzimmer, pioneer and socialist, in that it was really nothing more than a sycophantic and hypocritical fashion, the side product of decadence and affluence, which glorified the traditions of Israel and the unity of the nation with empty phrases and expressed itself in occasional donations to the synagogue and synagogue attendance on Rosh Hashana and Yom Kippur, and occasionally on Saturdays, when he would sit in one of the more prominent pews, wrapped in a prayer shawl and glancing at the prayer book from time to time, and it was also unlike the religion which Goldman had once tried to believe in, since Avraham Shechter's groping and hesitant religion, which was the fruit of his despair and his inability to find relief for his distress and his agonized incomprehension of what had happened to him, was primarily the search of a broken man for a crutch to support himself with, although Goldman's father, whose friendship with Avraham Shechter was of many years' standing and dated from the days of their youth in Poland, could see no merit at all in it, despite his sympathy and compassion for his friend, because his own rejection of religion, which was part of his world view, was complete and fanatical and he held no truck with all kinds of attempts to return to religion and sentimentalities about tradition—not in the version adopted by Avraham Shechter, whose son's death had been a grievous shock to Goldman's father, who had stood a little apart from the other mourners at the funeral weeping bitterly, and certainly not in the version adopted by Max Spillman and Moishe Tzimmer, whose religiosity gave rise to his disgust and fury, because he could see nothing in it but unforgivable stupidity or hypocrisy—and he made no bones about his attitude and expressed his feelings freely in words and also in actions, unlike Joel and Uncle Lazar, who were also secular humanists on principle, but who both (especially Joel, whose secularity seemed on the face of things to be completely lacking in any ideological motivation) kept their ideas on the subject to themselves and did not give them any expression beyond the secular way of life which they led, a way of life impossible for

Bracha and Shmuel—who now turned to Goldman and asked him how he was and if it were raining outside—because Grandmother Hava had lived with them for years and although they were not religious they did not want to distress her, even in her last years when she was in a coma and unconscious of what was happening around her, and Goldman said, "Yes. But it's very pleasant," and Shmuel invited him to sit with them a little, but Goldman, who liked him and Bracha as much as he hated Aharon and his wife, did not respond to this invitation, in which Bracha and Aharon joined, and he apologized and said that he was tired and wished his mother and the visitors good night, and after drying his hair and face in the bathroom he shut himself up in his room and exercised with the little dumbbells and the "Bullworker" for about ten minutes, and then he put them away and undressed, and before getting into bed he glanced at the books on the table and in the bookcase to find something to read before falling asleep.

Among the many books cramming the bookcase were scattered books about Judaism and the Kabbala and rabbinical interpretations of the laws and prayer books, remnants of the period when he had made enthusiastic efforts, accompanied by great hopes, to return to the bosom of Judaism and to attain a religious frame of mind, and for about a year he even believed that he had succeeded, but his religion had nothing to sustain it and it dwindled and died because it was a religion without belief, which for all his efforts and wishes Goldman was unable to achieve, except in the external intellectual sense of an acknowledgment of the necessity for faith and the desirability of the existence of God, although in principle he may have agreed with Manfred, who a few months later, at the beginning of winter when they had a brief talk—which was also their last—told Goldman that he did not believe in the absolute autonomy of man, who created himself in a world which created itself, and that denying the existence of God was understandable only if you accepted the unlimited rule of instinct, without any values, and after a short silence he added,

"And we've already seen where that leads," and Goldman said, "Yes. Maybe you're right," but nevertheless his religious experiment ended in failure, as did his attempt to adopt Taoism as a way of seeing the world, a system of principles of thought and aspirations, and a way of life. In the course of his exhausting explorations of the Taoist way, his repeated readings of Tao texts, and all kinds of interpretations which set out to clarify things that in the end remained obscure to his understanding and remote from his soul, Goldman returned to psychology, which he had once rejected with scorn, and discovered a new interest in it, especially in the Jungian school, with which he now became acquainted chiefly through the works of Erich Neumann, which impressed him deeply, and he tried to examine himself in the light of the ideas he found in these writings with a view to re-shaping his life, and thus he began to examine his dreams, and at first he would sit up in bed the moment he woke up from a dream and with his eyes still shut would repeat its details to himself in a somewhat incoherent, monotonous mumble, in order to fix it in his mind so that it would not be forgotten by morning, but after a while, when he discovered that this method was not much use and entire dreams slipped away from him and evaporated, he began to get up and sit at his desk, where half-asleep and with a heavy hand he would write his dreams down on pieces of paper, and the next day he would try to decipher them in order to understand things which had escaped him and in order to acquire various capacities which might have been latent in him but of which he was unaware, but the results of all these efforts, which like his other efforts were intended to help him save himself from the difficulties and perplexities of life and attain the possibility of living in freedom and serenity in a world which possessed some kind of unity and coherence, were meager and lacking in practical benefits, and gradually he lost interest in psychology and even in his dreams and after a period of weariness and disinterest he renewed his interest in history and sociology and to a certain extent also in philosophy, and he also returned to his dreams of life in the country, which in fact he had never really abandoned and which were embodied in the life of Avinoam Leviatan as it had appeared to Goldman and remained engraved in his memory after a visit he had once paid him not many years before, mingled with the memories which he still retained from the distant days when he had spent his school holidays staying with Joel and Zipporah, who had lived on a moshav with their children for a number of years and kept a big farm.

In these memories, which were very selective and illuminated by a wonderful light of peace and harmony, there was always a deep blue sky, brown earth, an avenue of dark green fir trees dispersing a dusty summer smell mingled with a pungent, intoxicating scent; Zipporah, standing in the shade and cutting up greens for the geese; fruit trees with their trunks painted white (he and Jeremiah had painted them one year); proud, angry cocks crowing in the calm of the white light spreading from the East; in the deep peace, a plot of green clover with Avinoam standing in it, his shoes sopping wet, cutting it with a sickle in the fresh and still cool early-morning Sabbath air; the chicken run swarming with the warmth of the smell of feathers and chicken feed and manure and the warmth of the newly laid eggs, Esther gathering them carefully in a pail; beds of peppers and tomatoes and cucumbers in the harsh afternoon sun; Avinoam walking in a melon patch, sunburnt and handsome, all the time in front of him, his wife Audrey, from the state of Utah, dishing out food to them and the three children; and farther away, the broad virgin fields, covered with a carpet of weeds and dried flowers, merging somewhere in the distance into dark orange groves stretching all the way to the blue horizon, which he so loved gazing at in the soft but still warm light of dusk in the great silence when he returned with Meir or Jeremiah in the cart from the far field beyond the little eucalyptus grove, all limp, abandoned to the pleasant tiredness of his body, leaning against the wall not far from Avinoam, sitting on a stool in the cow shed, full of the smell of straw and hay and manure, and milking by the electric light, making the same movements over and over again, his five cows standing peacefully chewing, and the jets of milk splashing into the pail between Avinoam's legs with a monotonous swishing sound, and Goldman—who finally took up the newspaper and lay down with it—closed the full milk can and took it carefully outside and went back in and leaned against the wall and watched Avinoam, surrendering himself to the pleasant tiredness of his body, all the time in the world ahead of him, and the knowledge that his salvation lay in this rural life and that he must never despair of it, and in fact he never did agree to give up his dream of living in the country, which always, more than any other dream, seemed real and attainable to him—and after glancing at the paper he put it down and lay looking at the ceiling, and then he turned on his side and lay with open eyes looking at the wall, on the other side of which the voices of the guests in the living room were perfectly audible, but they grew fewer and fewer, and slowly he closed his eyes and curled up underneath the summer blanket, and not long afterward the only voice still to be heard was the calm voice of Yehudit Maizler, and in the end she too left, and then there was a silence broken only by the sound of Stefana's footsteps as she went into the kitchen and washed the dishes and put everything in its place, and from there she went to the bathroom and after that to her room, where she made her bed and lay down, and then there was absolute silence, and Goldman, who wanted to sleep, put his hand out without opening his eyes and switched off the light, but he couldn't fall asleep—this had been going on for months now, maybe even more than a year—and after tossing and turning and trying to concentrate on falling asleep he switched on the light again, and by this time he was already nervous and tense, and he opened the newspaper and read until he thought that he was calm and tired and at the point of falling asleep, and again he switched off the light, very slowly so as not to wake himself up, and he lay quietly with his eyes closed and felt sleepiness spreading through him and overcoming him and nevertheless he remained awake, and he began tossing and turning again, his head full of disjointed thoughts, and after that he got up and swallowed two sleeping pills and lay down again, tired and cross, and after a while he fell asleep and slept heavily until morning, which was cloudy and cool in the changeable weather of April and the beginning of May, and despite the things that nagged at him from the moment he woke, various things that demanded clarification and organization, he went on lying with his eyes shut, but in the end, perhaps because of the sound of Stefana's footsteps, he got slowly and heavily out of bed, and after washing himself and drinking a cup of coffee he took the key to his father's special cupboard from its hiding place among the books in order to put the death certificate away and remove his father's bank book (his identity card had been lying on a shelf in the kitchen all this time) so that he could pay a few bills connected with his illness and funeral and the erection of a gravestone, and at the same time he wanted to find his father's insurance policy and savings certificates and government bonds, and after telling Stefana what he intended to do Goldman opened the cupboard, which no one had dared to approach as long as his father was alive.

The cupboard was very clean and neat and tidy: Next to the stamp collection and photograph albums, in which old pictures of fresh young people and a happy family were preserved, there were empty checkbooks from Zerubavel Cooperative, Anglo-Palestine, and Barclays banks, and documents and receipts dating back thirty and forty years for all kinds of donations and payments to institutions which for the most part had ceased to exist long ago. Goldman stood looking uneasily at the open cupboard for a moment with remembered fear and at the same time a strange feeling of proprietorship—all of a sudden everything was in his hands—and then he bent down slightly and rummaged carefully among the papers and documents and found the bank book and the insurance policy and savings certificates and government bonds, and also an old photograph of his sister and his father's will.

He took the will in his hands, hesitated a moment, and then, without opening the envelope, put it back exactly where it had been before and closed the cupboard again, and the next morning, after some deliberation, he told Stefana about it and asked if she agreed that Uncle Lazar should open the will and read it to them, and Stefana nodded disinterestedly and said, "All right," and that evening when Uncle Lazar came Goldman gave him the will and asked him to open it and read it to him and Stefana, and Uncle Lazar, who was embarrassed by the request, looked at them uneasily for a moment and then put on his glasses and opened the will and read it slowly and so monotonously that it seemed to Goldman that the indifference of his voice concealed a note of reserve and criticism, which annoyed him, but he said nothing. The will itself, over which Goldman's father had labored over the last four years of his life, and which embodied all his savage honesty and tyranny and bitterness, was an esoteric composition of great intricacy and complexity, the product of innumerable rough drafts and endless hours of thought, at the end of which he had succeeded, with the help of a clever lawyer, in composing a circuitous document the whole of whose intention was to assure the deceased that his property would pass into the hands of his legal heirs, Goldman and Stefana, and at the same time oblige them to enjoy it only in a certain well-defined, limited way, desirable to him, which would in fact abolish their enjoyment, especially Stefana's, and when Uncle Lazar had finished reading his brother's will he asked Stefana if she wanted him or Goldman, who had not taken his eyes off Uncle Lazar during the entire reading, to explain any of its articles to her, but Stefana, who had listened to his reading with perfect coldness and a contemptuous expression on her face, said in Polish, "No thank you, that won't be necessary," and with that the affair was closed as far as she was concerned, and Goldman, in whom the will had reawakened all his old resentment toward his father, took it and put it back in the cupboard, and at the same time he glanced again at the picture of his sister, which had a piece missing, as if it had been cut out with a scissors or a razor blade, and after locking the door, with the same sensation of uneasiness and remembered fear which had gripped him before, he asked Uncle Lazar, whom for some reason he felt the need to appease and be nice to, if he wanted to play chess, and Uncle Lazar smiled slightly and said, "With pleasure," and Goldman brought the chess set and they went into the kitchen and sat down at the table and laid out the pieces on the old board and played. No one disturbed them, since the stream of visitors had been decreasing from day to day, with most people feeling that they had done their duty with one, or at the most two, visits, and the few who still went on coming (not every day either) to sit for a while with the silent Stefana were Shmuel and Bracha, Yehudit Maizler—the only one who treated her naturally and straightforwardly—Moishe Tzellermaier, Tzimmer's widow, and also Manfred, who had returned from Haifa after the seven-day mourning period was over and paid a visit to Stefana that same evening, and returned again the next day, this time to take his leave of her, for two days later he was about to go back to Holland before returning to Israel again three or four months later.

Stefana received him in a dark blue silk dress and an elegant felt hat, which did not go very well with the dress she was wearing, but there was still a kind of aristocratic grace about her, a little artificial but nevertheless not entirely foreign and at any rate impressive, and when Manfred came into the living room and they met both of them were a little moved, as usual, but their excitement soon died down and gave way to polite resentment and impatience. They did not speak for long, but their conversation was tortuous and strained, full of oppressive pauses, meaningless phrases, and words which had been too carefully chosen, and Manfred, playing uneasily with the wedding ring on his finger, or wiping his glasses from time to time with his handkerchief, stood up in the end and said goodbye to her and went away, and Stefana, who did not get up this time to see him to the door, although he waited for a moment for her to do so, looked after him until he left the room and said, "People should know how to say goodbye," and then she took off her hat and said, "Everything passes," and put it down on the table and switched on the TV and looked at it absentmindedly for a few minutes, and then switched it off and sat doing nothing and staring at the empty wall opposite her and the transparent white curtains, and two days later she told Yehudit Maizler about it and said, "He's gone. It's over. But it's better this way," and Yehudit Maizler, a woman with a Russian face who still worked as a nurse in the Labor Federation Sick Fund clinic, said, "You'll miss him," and Stefana said, "No, it's over," and Yehudit Maizler said, "You should have seen him to the door," and Stefana said, "No. He should have stayed a few more minutes. He was in too much of a hurry to leave," and Yehudit Maizler said, "You shouldn't think about your pride so much," and Stefana said, "It's not pride," and Yehudit Maizler said, "Yes it is pride, and it's not as important as you think it is," and in these words she expressed her deep respect for Manfred and the awe she had felt for him during all the many years in which she had known him, and it did not bother her that there was something hard and aloof about him, and she respected and justified his attitude toward Stefana and the way he treated her without any reservations, although she never expressed any of this in so many words, not to Stefana and certainly not to Manfred, with whom she had never, in all their meetings, exchanged more than a few polite words, because she felt embarrassed in his presence, although she loved listening to him talk, not only to the contents of his words but also to the sound and cadence of his voice.

Apart from Yehudit Maizler the only one who continued dropping in once every few days was Uncle Lazar, as if he had to make up for thirty-four years of estrangement and ostracism by a display of closeness and goodwill toward the dead brother who had cast him out. He spoke very little either to Stefana, who treated him with a distant formality, or to Goldman, who even before coming to know Uncle Lazar had felt deep sympathy and affection for him, especially because of the obscure but unrestrained and hate-filled accusations which his father would bring up against his brother whenever the opportunity arose without giving Uncle Lazar a chance to come to his own defense. The relations between Goldman and Uncle Lazar grew closer and warmer, and they spent a lot of time playing chess together and being silent together, although the truth is that Uncle Lazar was not a taciturn man by nature, and if he hardly ever spoke it was only because he knew the limitations of human knowledge, the invalidity of human reason, and the restrictions of human possibilities, and everything was so contradictory and ambiguous that doubt seemed the only thing which possessed any reality, and the ability to believe was possessed by only a few, and there was no use hoping for much, and he also knew just how far a person had to deceive himself in order to live through a single day, and how fate could play tricks on people, as it had on him, and that all the words in the world were incapable of moving the world a single centimeter from its course, or bringing back one single day that had passed, or filling in the gaps, or consoling a man whose eyes had been opened, and Uncle Lazar's eyes had been opened, and they remained open, although he was not at all despairing or embittered, but simply very realistic and sober, with all the calm detachment of a man who had experienced much and who saw clearly and for whom life, to which he continued to relate seriously and positively, held no more surprises, because he had already died and risen again, he had been at the ends of the world, he had traveled to places which were beyond the grasp of human imagination and which perhaps had already descended into oblivion and been wiped off the face of the earth, he had endured trials and tribulations he would never have imagined possible, he had seen wonderful visions of a brave new world and believed in them and stood on the threshold of their coming into being, and had seen them, after all the blueprints had been perfected, destroyed and shattered because of human frailty and malice and fear and selfishness which knew no bounds, and at the same time he had come to understand, in agony and rebellion, that there was no other redemption than this, and that even the terrible things against which he rebelled were no less human than those manifestations of goodness and honesty and courage which always had the power to move his heart afresh and inspire him with the belief that men and the world were not irredeemable, and in the same sense that he had once held this belief, because in spite of everything Uncle Lazar was still full of hopeful expectations, and not only that but also he had never stopped pursuing knowledge and reading books, partly out of interest and curiosity and the love of learning for its own sake, but mostly in an ever-renewed passion to understand the ever-changing world in which he lived and whose random chaos and arbitrariness had shaped his life from the days of his childhood when the village in which he had been born had changed hands from the Poles to the Russians and from the Russians to the Germans and from the Germans back to the Poles again in the endless back-and-forth of the wars and battles which were accompanied by hate and ignorant fanaticism and gratuitous acts of cruelty, side by side with patriotic pride and sycophantic stupidity, which were ardently espoused not only by the uneducated but also by men who were cultured and logical and even honest, and this arbitrariness continued to accompany him from the day he left Poland to go to Eretz Yisrael, when he was obliged to change his name from Goldman to Schwartz—a name he continued to bear—because according to the laws of the British mandatory government then ruling the country, he had to emigrate as the son of Ria and Yeruham Schwartz, a couple he had never met before and whom he saw only once or twice more after they had parted at the port.

He was about seventeen when he arrived in the country, and at first he stayed in Jerusalem with Joel and Zipporah, who had arrived about six years previously, two years before Zipporah's parents arrived and went to stay in Tel Aviv to be near their son Isaiah, who died a few years later of malaria, at the end of the summer when Sarah, Isaiah and Zipporah's younger sister, also arrived in the country after spending some time in aimless wanderings in Germany and Austria, and after living for about a year in Jerusalem Uncle Lazar went to Tiberias and from there to Zichron Ya'akov, Hadera, Haifa, Benyamina, and Rehovoth and in the end he settled in Tel Aviv, like Joel and Goldman's father, who had arrived in the country about four years before him, alone, and had spent nearly two years working as a member of a kibbutz in the colonies and quarries of the north. During his wanderings Uncle Lazar worked as an excavator and a quarrier, becoming an expert at boring the holes into which they put the dynamite, and also as a guard, a fencemaker, a porter, and an agricultural laborer, but when he reached Tel Aviv he started working as a builder, and after working hours, together with Goldman's father, who was already married to Stefana and had become the father of a daughter, he built a shack and lived in one of its rooms with his sister Bracha, who had arrived in the country with their parents—Grandfather Baruch Chaim and Grandmother Hava—and not long afterward they were joined there by Reuven, Stefana's younger brother, Yanek, their other brother having remained in Poland, and Goldman's father took an instant liking to Reuven, who was a tall boy with a bright, friendly face, and they became fast friends, but their friendship came to an end shortly after the murder of Arlosoroff* at which inopportune moment Reuven, as if possessed by some kind of madness, decided to become a Revisionist, and an abyss of hatred opened up between them and seethed and bubbled until it burst out furiously at the wedding of Rachel, Uncle Lazar's wife, to Akiva Weiner.

The shack built by Uncle Lazar and Goldman's father was adjoined to, and was in fact part of, the shack occupied by Joel and Zipporah and their three children, who now squeezed to-

*Chaim Arlosoroff, a Labor Zionist leader, was murdered in June 1933 under mysterious circumstances on the Tel Aviv beach. The police suspected members of the extreme right-wing Revisionist party, and although the charges against them were eventually dropped for lack of evidence, the affair led to much ill feeling and imposed a grave strain on relations between the different camps in the Zionist movement and the Jewish population of Palestine.

gether and made room for Grandfather Baruch Chaim and Grandmother Hava, who lived in one room together with the oldest boy, Meir, who was then about seven. Around this large shack with its surrounding yard, in which Zipporah grew vegetables for the family and a creeping loofah plant and a few flowers and kept a couple of chickens, were scattered in total disorder a few more shacks, covered in tar paper and whitewashed against the sun, and around them stretched a desert of yellow sand, and beyond that red loam fields covered with weeds and thorns and brambles and straggly bushes and here and there sycamore trees and mulberry trees and fig trees and firs, cactus patches and also a few low white houses, and in the distance Arab vineyards and melon patches and orange groves surrounded by acacia trees, which when they flowered filled the air with an intoxicating scent, and when Bracha and Shmuel got married, in haste because Bracha was already pregnant, everyone joined in and within a few weeks they had built a new shack, not far from the big one, into one of whose two rooms Grandfather Baruch Chaim and Grandmother Hava moved after Joel and Zipporah gave birth to their fourth child, and they went on living there during the years when Shmuel and Bracha wandered off to Australia because Shmuel, who had liquidated his hairdressing salon and his wine shop and other businesses, believed that in Australia, the land of sun and peace and prosperity, he would be able to get rich easily with all kinds of quick deals in wool and meat, in imports and exports, in construction, and even as a hairdresser, but to his disappointment all he succeeded in acquiring in Australia was a smattering of English and a few pounds sterling, which he had somehow managed to scrape together and which he lost soon after his return to Eretz Yisrael in all kinds of speculations and unsuccessful business deals. Shmuel's father, who was mean and tightfisted and never gave Shmuel a penny, warned him against these business deals and repeatedly offered him a job in his butcher shop, which some years later was taken away from him by his younger son, Aharon, who arrived in the country at the outbreak of the war and immediately started working with his father, and Grandfather Ba-ruch Chaim warned him too, from time to time, although only indirectly, because he detested anything which smelled even faintly of deception and exploitation, and in his opinion business and money deals fell into this category, and also because they gave rise in him, an unworldly man with no business sense, to feelings of suspicion and mistrust, and he was bitterly opposed to the voyage to Australia and had had no rest for days on end because of the worry and the sorrow, and up to the very last minute he hoped and believed that Shmuel and Bracha would change their minds, but when they left he blessed them and invoked God's protection for their safe journey, and safe return, and while they were away he looked after the shack devotedly: He whitewashed it twice a year, on Passover eve and on Rosh Hashana, and he repaired the tar paper when it tore and replaced the broken tiles, and planted a fig tree and a mulberry tree and a lemon tree and some grapevines in the yard and put up a dovecote—he loved animals: dogs and goats and horses and birds—and in addition to this he also built himself a little hut where he pursued his trade as a watchmaker and supported himself and Grandmother Hava.

He was a robust man with thick black hair, upright in his ways, who observed the laws and practices of Judaism in perfect, but not fanatical, faith; an ardent Zionist, intoxicated by Eretz Yisrael, and every new house that was built in the town, every pillar and post, every new bit of road filled him with joy, whereas Grand-mother Hava, a small, skinny woman who wore nothing but black silk dresses until she took to her bed, walked about in a daze, and every day, for no reason at all, tears welled up in her eyes and streamed down the furrows of her face, which shrank and turned into a heap of flabby wrinkles, giving off a smell of old age, and her body also shrank and dried up until it was nothing but skin and bones, and gradually her mind too became clouded, especially after her husband's death, but nevertheless she suc-ceeded by some sort of sixth sense in cooking and knitting and cleaning the shack and scrupulously observing the laws of God, and even in imposing certain customs on her sons, who came almost every day, at least one of them, to see her and Baruch Chaim, and she went on praying in a secret language whose words, which were printed in very black letters in the old prayer book, she tore to shreds and mutilated with an easy heart, in complete indifference, to the sorrow of her husband, and if she had any problems she went to consult the rabbi, who was the supreme authority on earth as far as she was concerned and the embodiment of knowledge and the certainty that the world was not a lawless, chaotic one without point or purpose, and despite the troubles and upheavals and injustice everything was happening according to a premeditated plan and everything had its own reason and purpose. She continued practicing great frugality too, as she had done all her life long—and it was on these grounds that she admired Max Spillman and had her reservations about Stefana (Shmuel and Aharon's father she hated for other reasons)—and thus she darned old socks over and over again, stuck leftover bits of soap together, peeled potatoes so thinly that the peel was transparent, cooked such quantities of barley soup that the soup, which was supposed to last for a week and more, thickened and hardened to such an extent that a cat could walk on it without leaving pawprints, and she never threw out a crumb of food or old shoes or used clothes or cans. During the war the Italians bombed the shack where she was still living with Shmuel and Bracha, but they hid her at the bottom of the wardrobe in time, and so she was saved, only to turn to stone not many years later and die at a ripe old age but without understanding anything or remembering anything, not even her husband, and without knowing what was happening around her, at the end of a gradual process which could not be stopped and during the course of which she sank into a state of unconsciousness in which she remained until she died.

Uncle Lazar, who was still a bachelor when his parents arrived in the country, devoted much of his time to them at the beginning, but about three years after he settled in Tel Aviv, Rachel, his childhood sweetheart, arrived with her mother and her brother, Max Spillman, and the three of them set up house temporarily in a large shipping crate standing abandoned in the neighborhood of the shacks, and the bond between Uncle Lazar and Rachel was renewed and tightened and not long afterward they began to speak of marriage, which gladdened the heart of Rachel's mother, who did not approve of free love without any obligations, but she tried to hide her happiness behind a mask of indifference because she was afraid of the evil eye and also because she thought it was undignified to show her feelings, whereas Max Spillman, who professed extreme left-wing opinions, was openly disapproving and scornful, both because he was in the middle of a sharp political disagreement with Uncle Lazar at the time and because he was opposed to marriage on principle, and although unable to define his views on the subject with any degree of precision he regarded the family in the light of a destructive and decadent capitalist cell rooted in economic interest and fossilized traditions and hypocrisy, and just as he believed in social radicalism so he also believed in love and freedom in relations between the sexes.

At that time, after a period of depression, there was prosperity in the building trade again as a result of the rapid expansion of the city, which began to close in on the sprawling shacks, which in the meantime had gained a synagogue and little paths and whose gardens were green with fig trees and mulberry trees and lemon and tangerine and fir trees, and creepers and loofah bushes and sweet peas, and here and there, following Zipporah's example, they added beds of radishes and lettuce and cucumbers and tomatoes, and a few chickens wandering freely about and dogs which barked at night at each other and at the jackals, whose howls seemed so close, right outside the walls, that it terrorized Grandmother Hava, who was ready to pack up and return to Poland immediately, or at any rate so she said. The city grew like a crazy creature over the sand dunes and the vineyards and the melon patches, until Baruch Chaim had difficulty in keeping up with all the new houses and roads and factories, and his pride was mixed with a feeling of distress because the city was slipping away from him and making him feel like a stranger, and now of all times, at the height of the boom, Uncle Lazar decided to abandon the building trade, which was too hard for him physically and which had never really interested him, and to go to work as a printer.

He was fluent in Hebrew as well as in Polish and Yiddish, and he had also acquired a reasonable mastery of German and English by his own efforts, as well as a wide-ranging, if not systematic, acquaintance with certain fields in the humanities and social sciences, because the world, which aroused feelings of anger and anxiety in him, also fascinated him and filled him with the desire to know the laws according to which things operated and with whose help it might also be possible to change them, and the printed page, in the form of books or newspapers, drew him like a magnet, arousing his unflagging interest and his deep respect. During this period, when he started working as a printer, and in fact almost from the day that they began building the shack together, fights would occasionally break out between Goldman's father, who belonged to Hapoel Hatzair, and Uncle Lazar, who belonged to Achduth Ha-avoda, and whose views grew progressively more left-wing and uncompromising, even more uncompromising than those of Max Spillman, who was more extreme than Uncle Lazar in his political positions, and these arguments between Goldman's father and Uncle Lazar would often grow very fierce and turn into bitter quarrels full of hatred and abuse, leading to periods of estrangement during which they would not exchange a single word, and Joel and Zipporah or their parents or Reuven would intervene and after much coaxing eventually make peace between them. They argued about the struggles and the goals of the working class, about the Soviet Union and the communist movement, about Zionism and the Arab question, about fascism and the problems of democracy and the use of force, about the right way to build the country and change the world—

and in the meantime Rachel became pregnant and they put up a bridal canopy for her in front of the synagogue, on the sand dunes among the shacks, to the displeasure of Max Spillman and of Uncle Lazar, who opposed these religious rituals with all their hearts, but whereas Uncle Lazar resigned himself to his fate and tried to behave with good grace and show a smiling face, even during the ceremony itself, Max Spillman stood by his principles and did not come to the wedding in spite of the pleas of his mother and sister and Zipporah and Reuven and Grandfather Baruch Chaim.

It was the beginning of October and the air was sharp and full of the scent of the sycamores and fig trees and eucalyptus trees and the chill of the approaching autumn, but despite the coolness in the air, which was especially pronounced in the mornings and evenings, they set up the tables outside, in the garden surrounding the big shack, beneath the open sky, and covered them with starched sheets and decorated them with jars full of geraniums and sweet peas and myrtle branches and bougainvillea and cypress and orange branches, and the guests, among them Yanek, who was on a visit to the country, sat around the tables in white shirts, drinking Zipporah's homemade fig and grape wine and eating the sweet and savory pastries and the cheese and potato pancakes and peppery chickpeas and the sweets and the onion and poppy seed and jam rolls and the iced chocolate cakes, all of which had been made in two days and two nights by Rachel's mother and Grandmother Hava, whose tears flowed without stopping and dripped into the dough and that was the reason, as Rachel's mother claimed later, that it did not rise as well as it should have and had a slightly bitter taste. Grandmother Hava went on weeping during the ceremony too, and during the banquet, and also when everyone, including Avraham Shechter—who loved Rachel and whose heart was torn to shreds by the pain—began singing and dancing, led by Reuven, who danced all night long with Sarah, Yehudit Maizler's sister, who whirled and pirouetted, dizzy with happiness, and whom Reuven married a few months later, despite Stefana's objections, by which time Yanek with his pointed shoes and silk waistcoats and pomaded hair, who was a past master of the tango and the waltz and a wizard at cards and billiards, had already returned to Poland, and they lived together very lovingly, but despite all their efforts they had no children, and this cast a dark shadow over their lives.

The dancing went on until very late at night and in the white light of morning, after all the guests had dispersed and gone home, with the remnants of the food still scattered over the deserted tables and the jars of flowers and branches still fresh and fragrant, Baruch Chaim died—he sat on the edge of his and Grandmother Hava's broad bed, loosened his belt, let out a groan, and fell to the floor, and the wedding guests came back the next day and in the white shirts in which they had seen Uncle Lazar and Rachel united in marriage they saw him to his grave, and Grandmother Hava, dissolving in tears and supported by Joel and Goldman's father and Uncle Lazar, kept repeating in Yiddish, "He was grand. He was a grand man," and there was something of the admiration and desire which had stirred her heart in her youth, and had afterward been swallowed up in the details of daily life, in her tearful voice and in the way in which she repeated these words again and again, and five months later, toward the end of winter, Rachel had a son and Uncle Lazar called him Baruch, and two years later she had a daughter and they called her Tzila, after Rachel's grandmother on her mother's side, whom neither Rachel nor Uncle Lazar had ever seen.

They set up house in the shipping crate, adding another room and enlarging the kitchen, together with Rachel's mother and Max Spillman, who not long after Tzila was born went to live in the shack which had belonged to Joel, who rented an apartment and lived in it with his family for a few years, after which they moved to the moshav where they lived until just before the end of the Second World War. When Tzila was born Uncle Lazar was no longer a member of Achduth Ha-avoda, but a communist, although unlike the opinions of Max Spillman, who had opened a little welding shop in Joel's shack, Uncle Lazar's thinking was tinged with anarchism, which grew stronger as time went by, arousing the opposition of Max Spillman, who was an orthodox communist, while at the same time his communism aroused the wrath and hostility of his former comrades, many of whom broke off relations with him, and also of his friends and relations, and led to constant tension and arguments and hostility, and one winter's evening, by the bedside of Grandmother Hava, who was suffering from influenza, after an acrimonious quarrel with Goldman's father about Zionism and the place of the Arabs in Eretz Yisrael, the final rift between them took place, and a few months later, when it became known that Uncle Lazar had decided to join the International Brigade and go to the help of the Republican government in Spain, this rift was transformed into a total excommunication on the part of Goldman's father, which he kept up fanatically and never broke until the day he died, vigorously rejecting all attempts to effect a reconciliation between them and saying that he would never under any conditions make his peace with a communist and an anti-Zionist, a man who had sold his soul to the devil, and he would never forgive a man who was capable of forsaking his wife and family, even in order to save the world.

Zipporah and Joel also tried to dissuade Uncle Lazar from carrying out his intention, as did Chaim-Leib, who had arrived in the country a few months before with Mrs. Haya, Shmuel and Bracha, and many others, including even Max Spillman, and of course Rachel implored him not to leave her alone with the two children, but he was determined to go and at the beginning of summer he set sail for France. When they parted they hardly spoke to each other and then two letters came from Paris and a little while later another one from Barcelona, and after that a few more, almost all of them for Rachel, after which there was an interval which lasted for a few months until one day his personal papers arrived together with a notification that he had been killed in the shelling around Teruel, but shortly afterward another letter came from him, only the date and address were very unclear, and rumors also reached them that he was alive and had been seen in the environs of Tarragona, in Valencia, in Madrid, in a little hospital in Ontaniette, lighting a spark of hope in Rachel's heart, but other rumors reached them too, including one that he had been murdered by Polish volunteers, and seemed to confirm the first, bad news, and this, taken together with the fact that they received no letters from him during all this time, except for the one with the blurred address and date, extinguished the spark of hope, but nevertheless Rachel waited for another three years until, after much inner conflict, she married Akiva Weiner, who had courted her with great delicacy for a long time, and she ignored Avraham Shechter's love, which was known to both of them although he never dared to declare it, because what Rachel now wanted above all was support and security for herself and her children, and this was precisely what Akiva Weiner was able to provide her with.

The ceremony was attended by a small circle of family and friends, who sat down at tables laden with delicacies, but the atmosphere of strain and gloom killed all attempts to instill a little gaiety into the proceedings, and in the middle of the reception, after Jonah Kotchinski sang songs in Yiddish and an aria from *La Traviata* in his tenor voice, to the joy of Sarah, Zipporah's sister, who was already married to him, when everyone sat down to eat and tried to laugh and joke, a terrible fight broke out between Goldman's father and Reuven, which led to the collapse of the festivities, and not long after the end of the fight the guests dispersed and went home. The fight was short and sudden and no one could stop it: It flared up because of an insulting remark made casually but loudly by Goldman's father about the Revisionist leader Jabotinsky and developed into a vociferous argument between him and Reuven which quickly degenerated into an exchange of harsh accusations, accompanied by personal abuse, about the murder of Arlosoroff, which Goldman's father concluded by rising from his chair, his face gray with rage and hatred, banging on the table with all his strength, and yelling "Dirty fascist! Murderer! Go and join Hitler!"—after which he rushed out of the room, stumbling into chairs and people and blindly pushing them out of his way, while Reuven, his lips and hands trembling with emotion because he had never abused anyone before, shouted after him, "Communist! Bastard! Devil! You murdered him! You people murder everybody!" and sank weakly into his chair—and from then on they never exchanged a single word and they hardly ever saw each other either except by accident, usually in the street, because they avoided going to places where they thought they might meet each other, and the few times they did meet they passed each other in an unforgiving silence, and the most unforgiving of the two was Goldman's father, whose hatred for Reuven, which had been boiling up in him even before it erupted at the wedding, went on seething inside him even after Reuven died, and it was so strong and vindictive that he even refused to attend the funeral when Reuven was electrocuted a few years later, although many people tried to persuade him to do so, and without any consideration for Stefana's feelings he continued to abuse and denounce him whenever the opportunity arose, even to her face, because Goldman's father's opposition to and hatred for Revisionism, in all of whose manifestations, even the more respectable, he saw the embodiment of fascism and a danger to the nation, knew no bounds, and not long before he died, while talking to Avraham Shechter about the political situation in the country, he said, "Begin puts on respectable airs now but it won't do him any good—they murdered Arlosoroff," and Goldman, who went into the kitchen and overheard by chance, was proud of his father, and Avraham Shechter said, "Artzi's brother says it's not true," and Goldman's father said, "They murdered him. That's a fact," and no proof in the world could have undermined this conviction, which went on poisoning his soul and which had erupted so violently at Rachel's wedding.

One week after the wedding Rachel took her children and

moved into Akiva Weiner's apartment, and the empty shack was purchased by Chaim-Leib, who within a few weeks had made all kinds of improvements and added a room and stationed a huge wooden mangle in it, while at the same time Uncle Lazar had already been living for months in the northern wastes of Yakut, where he had ended up after undergoing all kinds of trials and tribulations as a political exile and had been transported together with other members of the International Brigade to the Soviet Union, where he was put on trial as a Trotskyite and an anarchist and a counter-revolutionary without being given a chance to defend himself, and sentenced, with unaccountable leniency, to exile, and so he lived in Yakut on the shores of the frozen Arctic Ocean, with other political prisoners and exiles, at first in the remains of a shipwrecked ship and later on in the wretched wooden shacks the exiles built themselves from discarded herring barrels and fortified with layers of earth, and he was put to work as a fisherman and a building worker and a miner in the exhausting and fruitless attempts to exploit the fossilized strata of coal and oil which had been discovered in the ice and the eternally frozen ground of Yakut.

His hands grew calloused and his legs grew heavy as lead, and the everlasting cold and fatigue dulled his senses and filled him with despair, and the hard whiteness of the ice and the transitions from day to night which lasted forever in a movement of time to which he was not accustomed, with the northern radiance painting shifting phantom-pictures in the sky in a phantasmagoria of colors—pictures the squat Yakutians claimed were the dancing spirits of the dead—came close to driving him insane, and in the depths of his heart, beyond the terrible difficulties of his day-to-day existence, he was troubled by the obscure revolution which had taken place in his life from the day he had left Eretz Yisrael until the day he had been denounced as a counter-revolutionary and sent to Yakut, because everything had been thrown out of joint by some inexplicable and arbitrary force which had taken control of events and become a law unto itself, turning life and the world into a confused and depressing riddle, contrary to reason and the good and necessary order of things, and this thought gave him no waking or sleeping peace and haunted him like the smell of the fish and the smell of the ice, and he withdrew into himself and made tireless and constant attempts to find the answer to the riddle and resolve the contradictions so that he would be able to go on living without unbearable despair and find some peace of mind, for it was unthinkable that life should be chaos and consist of events not determined by logic or justice, and very gradually, in the course of his efforts, and still clinging to the main tenets of his beliefs, he learned things that he had not known before and that he had never intended to learn: He learned to speak little, to treat time with the utmost indifference, to endure arbitrariness and uncertainty and even to renew himself with them, to live without expectations and almost without hope, to live from one day to the next, and he also learned to deny the longings for his family which came back to torture him after a long period of forgetfulness and to bury them in his heart, just as he learned to withstand the terrible storms and to relieve himself outside in a temperature of sixty degrees below zero, and after about eighteen years, without any effort or request or change of heart on his part, he was set free and in the middle of winter on a cold, rainy day he returned to Eretz Yisrael, and the only people to meet him at the airport were Joel and Zipporah and Bracha and Shmuel, since his mother, Grandmother Hava, had already been bedridden for a number of years, and Goldman's father clung tenaciously to the vow not to see him that he had made so many years before and refused to budge an inch from it and would not go to the airport to meet him with his brother and his sister.

The meeting was moving and emotional, as was only to be expected, for after all, Uncle Lazar had long ago been despaired of and given up for dead, but at the same time there was also something oppressive about it, since they were no longer the same people who had parted from him so long ago, but different, and nevertheless still the very same people, with complicated old grudges at the backs of their minds, as well as harsh and painful things which only an hour before had been hidden, at least from Uncle Lazar, which had accumulated during the long years of his absence, and Rachel and the children were not there to meet him, and this in itself cast a heavy shadow over the occasion, and they waited for Uncle Lazar to ask about them, but Uncle Lazar asked nothing, except about Grandmother Hava, nor did he ask about them that evening when they sat talking in Joel and Zipporah's big room, and in the meantime, standing in the airport waiting room, they were all overcome by excitement and joy, and they hugged and kissed and exchanged pointless, confused remarks, and jokes, and embraced again, and Bracha, who cried and cried, couldn't stop touching Uncle Lazar, stroking his arm and patting his shoulder, all the way to Joel and Zipporah's, who just before the end of the war had sold their farm and moved to town, where they ate a festive meal with their children and grandchildren and also with Sarah, Zipporah's sister, and Jonah Kotchinski, who brought a delicious nut cake and several kinds of biscuits from their cake shop, and after eating they all sat talking around the dining table, which they had set up in the middle of the big room in honor of the occasion and opened out to its full length, like they did on Passover eve, and afterward, when it began to get dark, everyone went home and Uncle Lazar lay down in the little room to rest, since he could not sleep although he was exhausted from the journey, and in the evening they had a light meal and sat drinking coffee without the children or visitors, and spoke quietly, and Joel and Zipporah and Shmuel and Bracha told Uncle Lazar about Reuven's death and Isaiah's death and Grandmother Hava's illness, and they also told him about Rachel's marriage to Akiva Weiner after they had received from Spain decisive proof of his death and there was no longer any room left for doubt or hope. Uncle Lazar, who was still confused by the sudden change which had taken place in his life, and the meeting with his family, and who felt dazed, as if he had lost his sense of reality and gravity, and everything—time, people, sights, words—was floating in the air and happening in two worlds, both of them existing and not existing at once, received these items of information quietly and without any external signs of emotion or surprise, as if it were only what he had expected, and after a short silence he said that the following day, after visiting his mother, he would go and see Rachel and the children.

All the attempts of Joel and Zipporah and Bracha to persuade him to put the visit off for a while were to no avail, and the next day, after Zipporah had informed Rachel and obtained her consent, Uncle Lazar, giddy with the sights and the touch of the air on his skin, went to see Grandmother Hava, who had been staying with Shmuel and Bracha ever since they returned from America, when they had sold the old shack, and within a couple of weeks had bought an apartment, exchanging it not long afterward for another, more spacious one, where they now lived. Shmuel, who was much occupied with his restaurant business and his car radio import business and all kinds of other businesses, was not at home, and Bracha took Uncle Lazar in to see their mother, who was lying in a room at the end of the corridor, far from the living room, where she would not be disturbed.

The room was painted white and was spotlessly clean, and nevertheless, perhaps because of the cold which prevented them from opening the windows and airing it properly, the air was heavy and impregnated with the smell of bedclothes and medicines. His mother lay without moving underneath the huge down quilt, a shrunken little figure of indeterminate sex, with only her head and hands showing, almost lost in the vast white expanse of the bed, and although her mind had long been clouded, her hearing gone, and her sight dimmed to the extent that she could distinguish only between light and shade, the moment Uncle Lazar came into the room she turned her head, which was quite white, slightly, and said, "Lazar?" and Uncle Lazar said, "Yes, Mother," and approached her carefully and kissed her ravaged face and her hands, which were nothing but dry skin and bones and which exuded a sharp smell of old age, as also did the warm, unpleasant breath of her mouth, and afterward he sat down next to her and spoke to her and kissed her again, because he was moved and was seeking understanding and closeness, but she lay like a stone and did not react again, and after a while, when he felt a little calmer, Uncle Lazar rose and tiptoed from the room, and after drinking a cup of tea with Bracha he said goodbye to her and went to see Rachel, but on the way he decided to make a little detour and go to pay a visit to the old shacks, which were now surrounded by buildings and looked very small and wretched and run down, like a shaky temporary refuge on the point of being abandoned by its inhabitants.

In Shmuel and Bracha's old shack, where an upholsterer now lived and worked, the walls were sagging and here and there the tar paper was torn, and the courtyard which grandfather Baruch Chaim had tended so lovingly had fallen into neglect: The dovecote was lying rusted on the ground, the fig tree and vines were dead, and everything was overgrown with weeds and covered with pieces of paper and scraps of material and broken tiles and bits of wood and tangles of seaweed. Joel and Goldman's father's shack had also run to seed completely, and strangers had been living there ever since Max Spillman had sold it and moved away and gone to live with his mother and his wife Bruria, who was then pregnant with their oldest son, in a five-room apartment in one of the expensive new buildings which had been erected on the ruins of the Arab villages which had been swallowed up by the town, not because he craved all kinds of luxuries—on the contrary, he was very economical and well aware of the value of money—but because he felt that his position now demanded a certain style of life from him, and because he realized that living in such an apartment would further his business interests, and in addition to this he saw it, quite rightly, as a good investment.

He had already moved the welding shop from its room in the shack soon before the end of the Second World War, when the boom in orders had expanded his business, which went on expanding after the establishment of the state, when he began to get a lot of orders from the army, and he moved it again to spacious new premises where he employed more than twenty men, and he was still a bachelor living with his mother, to whom, unlike Rachel, he was devoted, and he may have remained single forever, since he no longer felt any need for a wife, having become accustomed over the years to his independent and unimpeded way of life, and especially since all his time and energy and will were concentrated on his business affairs, on the expansion of his plant and the accumulation of money—which led him, after a few years when he became the owner of a chain of gasoline stations, to dilute the gas with paraffin, and sell his customers short by tampering with the indicators on the gas pumps, as a result of which he had to face criminal charges in a court case, in which he argued that his employees had perpetrated the fraud without his knowledge, but the court found him guilty, together with two of his employees, and made him pay a heavy fine, but apart from this damage to his pocket the whole affair caused him no more than a temporary embarrassment, since despite the court case, which until the last moment he did not believe would take place, and despite the conviction, he continued to see himself as an honest man, and he believed this quite sincerely, while his position and connections with businessmen and government offices were too well established to suffer a serious setback, and most people did not see what he had done as an unpardonable sin, but at the very most as an unfortunate slip which should be forgotten as soon as possible and which was no reason for upsetting their relationship with him, and there were some who even defended him, but not Rachel or his father-in-law, Bruria's father, who was the owner of a factory which made water tanks and stainless steel goods, for which Max Spillman executed various commissions, as a result of which, some time before entering his gas station business, he met Bruria, who was then a woman of over thirty and regarded as a confirmed spinster.

After a short acquaintanceship he married her, not for love

but not out of calculation either, and shortly afterward he became a partner in her father's stainless steel factory and abandoned the shack and the old neighborhood, which was now almost entirely occupied by strangers, except for the old shack in which Rachel had once lived with Uncle Lazar, the abandoned shipping crate to which they had added an extra room and a porch and a yard with a few bushes and vegetables, where Chaim-Leib was still living, and Uncle Lazar, who stood in the cold wind on the wet sand looking around him in a daze, enveloped in sadness and longing, suddenly saw Mrs. Haya, who appeared at the window to shake out a tablecloth and glanced at him, but she did not recognize him and he quickly turned his head aside and pretended to be a stranger who had stumbled on the place by chance, and turned around and walked away, without hurrying, and went to see Rachel, who had intended to behave decently and even to show a certain degree of warmth, since it had been a long time, after all, since their parting, but instead she received him very coldly and aloofly: She did not shake his hand or invite him to sit down or ask him how he was, and the truth is that the moment she saw him standing in the doorway she wanted to ask him why he had come and tell him to leave, but something of his emotion infected her too, in addition to which she had to contend with her own curiosity and her sense of decency, and so she held her tongue, but she felt no sympathy for him.

Uncle Lazar felt no resentment against her. He acknowledged his blame and accepted his fate and felt nothing but sorrow and regret, but he had wanted and hoped to exchange a few sentences with her, and for years he had even formulated them to himself and rehearsed them over and over hundreds of thousands of times, and he was also eager and fully prepared to exchange a few sentences with his children, Baruch and Tzila, but both of them, like Rachel, stood on the other side of the table and looked at him coldly as if he were a stranger. It was all over in a few minutes, and in those few minutes Uncle Lazar learned that even the smallest and faintest of hopes—which to tell the truth were no longer anything more than a hesitant yearning or yielding of the heart, or perhaps even less than that—were null and void. There was no room for even a single sentence of apology or the request for forgiveness, and nevertheless when he was about to leave, after having made a couple of meaningless remarks and after Rachel had said something equally meaningless in reply, Uncle Lazar held out his hand to Tzila, but she stood without moving and Baruch turned away and went into the other room, and Uncle Lazar left the house and went outside and walked in the rain and wept; he wept until his face and his chest were full of tears, and he did not notice the rain puddles and the strong wind and the rain whipping his face as he roamed aimlessly through the streets until it began to get dark, and by the time he got back Joel and Zipporah were already worried, but they asked no questions, and Zipporah gave him dry clothes and a cup of tea, and afterward she made his bed, and Uncle Lazar lay down and fell asleep, and he woke up in the middle of the night with a temperature which lasted for over a week, and Zipporah, who looked after her eighty-year-old mother and helped her daughters and daughters-in-law, who always had their hands full with their children and all kinds of problems, and also her sister Sarah, who spent her time wandering aimlessly and hopelessly around her neglected apartment, full of grievances and complaints, now took care of Uncle Lazar too, until he recovered, and after he recovered he stayed on with them for a few more weeks, spending a lot of time with other members of the family as well, and even meeting Goldman's father on one of his visits to Grandmother Hava (but Goldman's father ignored him and refused to greet him) and all kinds of old friends and acquaintances, and getting to know Joel and Zipporah's children—Meir, Jeremiah, Esther, Ruth, and Aviezer—all of whom, but for Aviezer, were married, and meeting their wives and husbands and the grandchildren they had bestowed on Joel and Zipporah, and Illana and Uri, Shmuel and Bracha's children, whose elder brother, Amos, was in America, where he had gone a few years before to study business administration.

Uncle Lazar did not go back to work as a printer, but found

himself a job in a bakery and became a baker, an occupation which gave him quite a good living and also had a soothing effect on him, and after he had started working he rented a small apartment not far from the sea and moved into it and lived there by himself until, about a year later, he moved in with Yehudit Tanfuss, a modest, unassuming woman of medium height with brown hair, very orderly in her ways, who had worked for many years as an English teacher in a high school, leading a quiet spinster's life. They did not marry because they had no reason to do so, but they lived together as man and wife in the harmony of sober, aging people with good tempers and cultured minds, who no longer expected any stormy passions or changes in their lives, and were no longer interested in them, but on the contrary, and not many years later, in the same tranquillity that they had spent the end of their lives together, they died together in their sleep. After work, in the early hours of the evening, they would sit on the balcony talking or reading, and look at the street and the dense firs and cypresses and casuarinas and tamarisk trees growing in the courtyards of the houses, which in the summertime were full of the twittering of birds. In the wintertime they sat in the well-heated room, or they went to the movies or sometimes the theater, or went for walks arm in arm, which was the way they always liked to walk together, and they tried to make their walks as long as possible because walking was good for Uncle Lazar's health. They often visited Joel and Zipporah, because in their company and in the company of their children—one or the other of whom dropped in to see them almost every day—Uncle Lazar felt very much at ease. Once or twice a week, usually during one of their walks, they would pay a short visit to his mother, who went on living her opaque life in spite of the certainty with which the doctors kept on prophesizing her death, until it seemed that she had vanquished death, or been forgotten by it, and that she would go on living forever in spite of her illnesses and in spite of the upheavals and uprootings which had overtaken her, especially since the end of the war, about three years after it was over, at which time, while she was sinking ever deeper into her comatose state, Shmuel had become entangled in heavy debts as the result of unsuccessful investments and all kinds of speculations and loans at usurious interest rates, among them a loan from his brother. He had escaped to America with Bracha and the two children (Uri had not yet been born) after selling all the valuables and jewelry in their possession, and after announcing his intention at three o'clock in the morning, four hours before the flight, to Goldman's father, who went to fetch his mother with her two brass candlesticks but without her bed, which was too big, and locked the door of Shmuel and Bracha's shack, which he later rented to Avraham Shechter, but not before Aharon, Shmuel's brother, had come and carted off most of the furniture and household goods by force. About a year later Stefana fell ill again—not to mention the terrible overcrowding in the apartment—and they transferred Grandmother Hava temporarily to Joel and Zipporah's, and she stayed with them for a while, until Zipporah, who was busy with her children and her daughters-in-law and her grandchildren and her own mother and her sister Sarah, collapsed, and then they shifted Grandmother Hava and her two candlesticks back to Goldman's father and Stefana again, but she didn't stay there long because Stefana, who always treated her with polite impatience, never really recovered from her illness and she had less and less strength and patience to supervise the kitchen and keep the laws of *kashruth,* which were mandatory as long as Grandmother Hava was in the house, so that two weeks after Shmuel and Bracha suddenly returned from America and took up temporary residence in their old shack, which was standing empty at the time, they found themselves once more in possession of Grandmother Hava and her two brass candlesticks, and she returned to her old room and her old bed, and thus her wanderings could have come to an end, but for the fact that Shmuel and Bracha sold the old shack and bought an apartment, which they soon exchanged for another, larger one, and they took her with them, and she went on living for a few more years after the death of Goldman's father, until one day she too stopped living, like a run-down old clock which goes on ticking with a barely audible sound until suddenly, without anyone noticing, it stops, but during all these long years of living death her family went on regularly visiting her, and twice a year, on Yom Kippur and on the anniversary of Grandfather Baruch Chaim's death, they all gathered in her room and sat around her bed for an hour or so, and these were the only occasions, apart from all kinds of accidental encounters, on which Goldman's father and Uncle Lazar met, but in spite of all the attempts which were made to reconcile them they did not exchange a word or a look.

Uncle Lazar, who was glad to feel the warmth of family ties again and wanted to give pleasure to his mother, to whom no one could give pleasure any more, paid regular visits to her and to Joel and Zipporah, and after the death of Goldman's father he also paid regular visits to Stefana, who always received him indifferently, but Goldman always received him with demonstrative warmth, and before they sat down to play chess, which had become almost a ritual with them during all Uncle Lazar's visits, Goldman would make him black coffee laced with cognac and serve it to him in one of the two cups which had survived from the splendid Czechoslovakian tea set, which they had acquired during the days of the Second World War and which had momentarily brightened the life of the household, which for years had been plunged in an ugly kind of chaos and an atmosphere of gloom and anger and hopelessness, the fruit of strained relations and also of poverty, since all Goldman's father's skill and the tremendous efforts he invested in his work, which drained his strength and frayed his nerves, helped not at all, because of the inflation as well as his honesty and pride.

Goldman and Naomi lived with their parents in the big room in the middle of a lot of green furniture crowded together in front of a heavy black sideboard which had to be moved every evening to make room for Goldman and Naomi's beds, while Goldman's father and Stefana slept on a pull-out sofa, and Stefana's parents, as long as they were alive, occupied the second room, together with a lot of clumsy brown furniture, most of which they had brought with them from Poland together with their pillows and featherbeds and other household goods, and the boarders, who changed from time to time, lived in the little room which after the war became for a short time Naomi's room, and in the meantime, while the war was still raging, David Kostomolski, a distant cousin of Goldman's father, who had deserted from "Anders' army" after leaving his uniform and personal papers on the beach, arrived and he slept on a folding bed which they put up every night for him in the hall, and later on the same bed was occupied for over a year by Moishe Tzellermaier, who arrived in the country as a refugee and Holocaust survivor, without family or friends, and Goldman's father took him in and bought him clothes and gave him money and found him work and in the end also helped him find a wife, and Moishe Tzellermaier never stopped being grateful to him and to Stefana for their kindness, and neither did David Kostomolski, who served as a driver during the War of Independence and after the war was over went to stay temporarily in a little hotel, where he went on living with Mrs. de Bouton, a refined and handsome woman from a Sephardic family, a widow with a daughter, a first-rate dressmaker and also an excellent cook, who was too shy and awed to visit Goldman's father and Stefana at their home, even on the occasion of Goldman's father's death, although she too, in some mysterious way, felt a sense of respect and obligation toward Stefana and Goldman's father, who would carry planks from the building site home on his shoulders to fuel the heater in the shower, and mend the family's shoes himself and make new rubber soles for them out of old tires, and fix the paraffin cookers and the electricity and blocked drains and cracks in the walls and floors, and everything else that broke down in the house, which was almost always full of gloom and suppressed anger, and his sudden outbreaks of high spirits—when he would drape himself in a sheet and put a pillow on his head and march about the room banging pot lids together and singing at the top of his voice—did nothing to disperse the gloom, and instead of making Goldman happy they made him feel uneasy and even frightened—not to mention Stefana, who was repelled by these exhibitions—because in all Goldman's father's actions, both good and bad, there was a latent violence seeking an outlet, as well as something tyrannical and domineering, except, perhaps, for the three conjuring tricks which he would perform from time to time when Goldman and Naomi were children, because he performed these tricks with a happy heart and in a spirit of pure playfulness. The three conjuring tricks Goldman's father knew were swallowing knives and forks, laying an egg in his mouth, and making a glass disappear into the table with a bang of his fist.

The Czechoslovakian tea set was a gift from one of the boarders, a strong, good-looking, and very polite young man from Danzig who kept his room neat and tidy and paid his rent on time, and was hardly ever there, and even when he was they hardly knew it, because he spent his leisure time sleeping in his room and reading magazines, and the only thing about him which bothered the other occupants of the apartment a little was his pipe smoking, because of the strong smell of the tobacco. He worked at the port and brought the tea set, packed in a cardboard box, as a parting gift the evening before he left the room, and he held it out to Goldman's father and said, "This is for you," and Goldman's father, who had just finished eating and was sitting picking his teeth and reading the paper, said, "What's this? It's quite unnecessary," and took the box in embarrassment and disapproval, because he didn't like getting presents, although at the same time he was very pleased by and grateful for any sign of attention, and the boarder, who remained standing at the kitchen door, said, "It's just a tea set," and Goldman's father put the box on the table and said, "It's not necessary. You shouldn't have wasted your money. It's really not necessary," and the boarder said, "I enjoyed my stay here with you," and Stefana said, "Sit down, sit down," and pulled up a stool for the boarder, and Goldman's father, still disapproving, opened the box very slowly, and full of admiration and apprehension removed one of the cups, which like the other cups and saucers and the teapot and sugar bowl was nestled in a bed of white kapok, and lifted it up for everyone to see and examined it in the light and tapped it with his finger like an expert, and the cup tinkled like a little bell, and he turned it over to read what was written underneath it and read aloud, "A product of Czechoslovakia," and passed it to Stefana, who took it unwillingly in her hands and said, "Beautiful, really beautiful," and hurried to put it carefully down on the table as if she were afraid it would fall to pieces in her hands, and her mother stroked the edge of the cup with her thick fingers and said in Yiddish, "Czechoslovakian china is better than German" and nodded, smiling slightly, to the boarder, who remained standing at the kitchen door, very embarrassed, playing constantly with the broad silver ring on his finger, which was made in the shape of a snake, and Goldman's father, totally involved, said, "You shouldn't have spent so much money," and the boarder smiled absentmindedly and said, "It didn't cost so much," and then he said, "I thought the tea set would come in handy," and Stefana, who put the kettle on the paraffin ring for tea and thanked him again, said, "Yes indeed. It's quite true, we never had anything nice for visitors," and the tea set was really very nice indeed: It was made of delicate white china, almost transparent, and decorated with airy pictures in black and blue and green and red and dark blue and pale blue and orange, depicting mountains and hills in the Chinese fashion, and Chinese country houses, and a river and reeds and two women in traditional Chinese dresses looking into the distance, at the mountains or the horizon, with a sad expression on their faces. After Goldman's father had removed all the pieces from the box and Stefana had washed and dried them, they conveyed them in a solemn procession to the big room, where very carefully, almost worshipfully, Goldman's father arranged them on a shelf in the black sideboard and closed the green glass door, and from that evening on the tea set became the pride and joy of the household and the symbol of its secret hopes, and consequently also the focus of many anxieties, and thus it waited behind the green glass in the dim interior of the sideboard for a special opportunity which would call for its use, but for over twenty-five years Goldman's father found no such opportunity, except for the time when they had the beautiful Jemimah Chernov's parents over to meet the family, and the tea set got broken piece after piece without ever being used, and Stefana, who was afraid of it from the moment she set eyes on it because she knew only too well what awaited her, bore the brunt of the suffering and humiliation and ugly scandals which accompanied the process of the ruin of the tea set, which began in the days of Shoshana and Yechiel Levankopf, who came to live with them as boarders when the young man from Danzig moved out, and went on until close to the date of Goldman's father's death, when all that was left of the beautiful tea set were three saucers and two cups, in one of which, the one with the unbroken handle, Goldman gave Uncle Lazar coffee when they sat down to play their game of chess.

Uncle Lazar, who played well and won most of their games, had learned to play in Yakut, where the exiles spent a lot of time playing chess with chessmen whittled from pieces of wood, and apart from chess he also learned many other useful things which he would never have learned if he had not been exiled to Yakut, for example, to speak Yakutian Russian, to hunt and to fish even when the water was covered by a thick layer of ice, to eat fish raw, to light a fire without matches in a strong wind, to withstand bitter cold, to drive a sled harnessed to dogs, to find his bearings in the expanses of the tundra by the stars, and other important secrets about animals and nature and men, and these lessons were added to those he had already learned fighting in Spain. His game benefited from the fact that he possessed a strong will as well as a capacity for concentrated and systematic thinking, which Uncle Lazar himself attributed, with a touch of irony, to the fact that his perception of reality had become to a certain extent blunted, and his hearing impaired during his exile in Yakut, and in fact in one ear he hardly heard anything but for a constant buzzing, and when he and Goldman conversed Goldman was obliged to raise his voice a little.

Their conversations were usually short and disjointed and conducted rather casually, between one game of chess and the next or after they had finished playing and before Uncle Lazar rose and went to the living room, where he would sit silently for a while in the company of Stefana, who had taken to painting her lips in a subtle shade of violet-red, until he took his leave with a "Shalom" and "Lehitraoth" while she, as if she had not heard what he was saying at all, would reply, "Dobry wieczor" and "Dowidzania." During the course of these fragmentary discussions between Uncle Lazar and Goldman, Uncle Lazar would express his views of life and events, referring from time to time to his recollections of Spain and Yakut, where his ideas had been tried and tested and where he had accumulated the experience which had led him to adopt an attitude of skepticism toward the usefulness of all kinds of books of wisdom and philosophy, although he still continued to regard them in a positive and respectful light and read them with keen enjoyment and enthusiasm, in a never-ending quest for answers to the questions which bothered him, and he showed the same measure of skepticism with regard to social theories, whose relative importance he had never denied, especially when applied to limited and concrete problems, and he had also outgrown easy, harmful optimism and no longer believed as he once had that human nature could be changed, and made better and more rational, except by means of tremendous and gradual efforts involving painful and ambiguous personal experiences and the acceptance of the dark side of human nature as a legitimate part of the personality, and at the same time, without ignoring the obstacles or denying the uncertainties, he tried to go on believing in the possibility of improving the world and the quality of people's lives, or at least in the necessity of trying to do so, but not by communism, of which he had long ago despaired, nor yet by anarchism, for although he continued to hold the view that this was the only meaningful social theory, he now knew that it had no chance of succeeding in practice because it did not take human weaknesses into account and was built on a wildly optimistic vision of the human spirit, and in spite of this knowledge he did not regret the life which he had lived by this impractical faith, and the suffering and disappointments he had endured because of it, but on the contrary, in spite of all the disillusion and sadness after the event, Uncle Lazar spoke with warmth and pride of the naïve and reckless arrogance which had led him to sacrifice almost half his life, and on one occasion he remarked in this context, half seriously and half ironically, that in the end every man had his own predetermined life and inescapable fate, and Goldman, momentarily taken aback, said, "You can always commit suicide," and smiled, and Uncle Lazar said, "That's part of the game too," and Goldman said, "In that case you might as well say that everything's part of the game," and Uncle Lazar said, "Right," and Goldman said that that wasn't a very serious thing to say and it wasn't a view of life but a faith, something that could be proved only after the event, and Uncle Lazar smiled a very enigmatic smile, which faded as he began setting out the chessmen, and Goldman, who had fallen silent for a moment, asked him if he had ever thought of committing suicide, and Uncle Lazar said, "Yes. Once," and then he added, "Almost everybody has thought of committing suicide once," and Goldman, who had also begun arranging his chessmen on the board, asked him if he were against suicide, and Uncle Lazar said, "Yes. But you're not putting the question correctly," and Goldman said, "Why?" but Uncle Lazar did not reply and moved his king's pawn two squares forward, and Goldman, still waiting for an answer, moved his king's pawn two squares forward too, and said that he agreed with the view that suicide was the fullest and purest expression of free choice that life had to offer, which was the freedom to relinquish life itself and choose what looked like its opposite, in other words death, and also the only true freedom granted to man, who being absolutely subject to the power of death freed himself from the dominion of death by means of death itself, and Uncle Lazar, who had listened to him calmly, said, "That reminds me of that engineer in Dostoevski, you know, I've forgotten his name," and Goldman said, "Yes, I've forgotten it too," and looked away from Uncle Lazar, who moved his knight, and Goldman moved his queen's pawn one square forward, and after a few more moves he said that if a man could not achieve faith in God and immortality, suicide became an inescapable necessity for him, at least from a theoretical point of view, and Uncle Lazar looked at Goldman with his blue-gray eyes and said that he was expressing the point of view of a man who was already religious or who had a deep need for religion as a result of contemplating the suffering and injustice and chaos of life, but as far as he himself was concerned, he was free of all that, although on the face of things a sober examination of his life and its inexplicable vicissitudes might well have driven him either to complete nihilism or to the conclusion that there was, in fact, something that could be called "God" or "Providence" or "ultimate being" running the world according to mysterious laws of its own, and nevertheless he was an atheist and remained an atheist, and at the same time, to put it crudely, he had no intention of committing suicide, he felt no need or necessity to do so, not even theoretically, nor did he see any need to breach the frontiers of life and realize his freedom in an ultimate sense by liberating himself from the dominion of death by means of death, he accepted life and he accepted death as part of life—and after this there was a short silence and Goldman moved his knight and threatened Uncle Lazar's bishop and said, as if to himself, that the thing we secretly feared most always happened, and a moment later he looked at Uncle Lazar and added, again as if to himself, that when it finally came it would be much more humiliating and less convenient than we had imagined, and Uncle Lazar, who avoided Goldman's eyes and for some reason suddenly sounded a little impatient, said "I don't know, but it seems to me that a person has to endure a great deal before he can say the kind of things that you've been saying."

A few days later, after putting down the evening paper and

carefully drawing up the cup of coffee which Goldman had made him, Uncle Lazar said that it sometimes seemed as if devils had been editing the newspapers, and he smiled and took a little sip of coffee, and after a moment's reflection he said that he was not surprised that some people, in the face of the absurdities of existence, the suffering and injustice which had no meaning or purpose, and especially in the face of death, needed the mystery called God. In other words, it could be said that in some essential sense God was a function of suffering and death, and since suffering and death were eternal he too was eternal, although it was also possible to put the same idea in the opposite way and say that since suffering existed and man was in any case destined for death, the question of God's existence was irrelevant to him. Goldman waited for Uncle Lazar to finish talking and asked him if he were afraid of death, and Uncle Lazar, momentarily taken aback, said, "Like anyone else," and immediately added, "Sometimes I think about it. After all, I'm not a young man anymore. But it may be that once I used to think about it more," and Goldman, who sat down in his usual place, said that he thought it was possible to overcome the fear of death, and Uncle Lazar said, "How?" and Goldman said you could do it by training yourself for it, striving for it, and reflecting on it, and by these means accustoming yourself to it, and in this connection he mentioned Montaigne, who had claimed that he "practiced dying"—in other words, every time he slept or fainted or was sick he thought of this state as a "little death," and these exercises in the "little death" prepared him to face the "big death" successfully and fearlessly, and in addition to this, said Goldman, he agreed with the view that philosophy was essentially a preparation for death and that if it performed its function properly it could teach people how to accept the fact of death and go to meet it without fear, and perhaps even with joy, and here he mentioned the opinion of Socrates, who said that true philosophers trained themselves and strived for one thing only, which was to die and to be dead, and therefore death was far less frightening to them than it was to other people.

Uncle Lazar chuckled and said that Montaigne's ideas were extremely interesting but—and here he grew serious—in his opinion it was impossible to prepare for death in any way at all, and in any case, as far as he himself was concerned, what bothered him was the inevitable process of disintegration, of which death was the absolute and final expression, and Goldman said that he would give anything in order to live a thousand years or more, but he was afraid he didn't have much hope of doing so. Uncle Lazar smiled sympathetically and Goldman said, half serious and half joking, that he believed it was possible to prolong life by means of a proper diet which kept the blood and tissues clean and the body lean, and by means of sport, and he told Uncle Lazar about the new diet he had read about in the American aviation magazine, which he was about to embark upon, and he also told him that every morning, summer and winter, he swam in the sea and every day he exercised with the "Bullworker" for at least ten minutes, and Uncle Lazar, who had finished his coffee, asked what the "Bullworker" was, and Goldman went into his room and came back with the "Bullworker" and a page torn out of an old newspaper containing a big advertisement about the nature, virtues, and purpose of the instrument, whose appearance brought another smile to the face of Uncle Lazar, who did not smile often, and Goldman offered him the page and in the same half-jocular manner told him to read it, and Uncle Lazar first fingered the "Bullworker" and then took the newspaper and put on his reading glasses and read the advertisement, which took up about a third of the page, to himself in an audible murmur.

At the top left-hand corner of the advertisement was a picture of a very muscular man holding the "Bullworker," and next to the picture were the words: "Jean Taxier, Mr. France, demonstrates one of the easy seven-second exercises which brought him his title." At the bottom right-hand corner of the advertisement was a picture of another very muscular man, his face wreathed in smiles, and next to it were the words: "Jean Perlon shows how he enlarged his biceps by 5 centimeters, his chest by 10 centimeters, and his thighs by 3 centimeters in a few weeks' work with the 'Bullworker.' " The title heading the entire advertisement was: "When were you last really fit?" and underneath this heading, between the two pictures, was the advertisement itself, which read as follows:

Even if you are not particularly interested in developing enormous muscles, you owe it to yourself to keep fit. It is a sad and regrettable fact in the lives of many men that they suddenly find themselves old and worn out before their hair is gray. But now, thanks to modern methods of exercise, keeping fit is possible and easier than it ever was before. In less than the time it takes you to shave, the "Bullworker" will develop your body to proportions which will make you the envy of men and attract women to you like flies. Only five minutes a day, and scarecrow-thin arms are transformed into muscular ones with a vice-like grip, concave chests turn into broad, manly ones, and matchstick legs become strong, shapely foundations. Jean Taxier (Mr. France and a top consultant on physical education) tells you how:

Q: What exactly is meant by "keeping fit"?

A: Keeping fit is part of the physical culture of healthy people; in other words, the effective and systematic exercise of the muscles. The aim: to give the muscles tension and flexibility and keep them healthy and shapely.

Q: How does lack of fitness manifest itself?

A: The answer depends on your age. If you are still in your teens or early twenties, the aim is to develop your body. When you are older, the first signs are usually the accumulation of fat on your body, impotence, lack of energy. After forty your whole body tends to become limp and flabby.

Q: Are we talking only about waist measurements here?

A: No, anybody can lose a few centimeters around his waist by daily exercise. But even if you succeed in narrowing your waist you will certainly notice "spare tires" above and below it.

Q: Can't I keep fit by sports?

A: Yes, certainly, if you train constantly over a long period of time, at least three or four times a week.

Q: And that's it? Isn't there any easier way?

A: Yes, there is an easier, more convenient, and much quicker way. This is an exceptionally effective method which is guaranteed to produce results.

Q: Has it got a name, this method?

A: Yes, it has a name. "The Bullworker exercise system." It is based on isometric techniques and it has proved itself in practice to be three times quicker than any sport or conventional method of exercise employed in body-building institutes. In my opinion it is the most advanced method in existence.

Q: How long does it take?

A: The beginners' course is made up of seventeen exercises and it takes just seventy seconds a day. The advanced technique takes about five minutes.

Q: And when can one expect results?

A: From the first day. Yes, exactly so. The "Bullworker" comes fitted with a strength-meter which automatically shows you your growing power from day to day; generally speaking, up to a 4% increase in power a week.

Q: How long will I have to wait before I can see results in the mirror?

A: From ten days to three weeks, depending on your keenness and efficiency.

Q: Keenness, efficiency . . . so you have to sweat a lot?

A: No, the whole advantage of isometry is that you exercise only seven seconds at a time and avoid overexerting your muscles, as opposed to the exhausting "crash programs" which often do more harm than good. Your workouts with the "Bullworker" are adapted to your own personal capacity, and the exercises will always seem easy to you, because with every passing day your physical condition will improve.

Uncle Lazar, who never stopped smiling, finished reading the advertisement and said to Goldman that there was nothing in it about prolonging life but only about body building and keeping fit, and Goldman, who also kept smiling and never took his eyes off Uncle Lazar's face all the time he was reading, said that body building and keeping fit were not insignificant in themselves, but the important thing was that directly or indirectly they contributed to the prolonging of life.

Uncle Lazar glanced at the picture of Jean Taxier, Mr. France and the top consultant on physical education, and said, "And by how many years do they prolong it?" and took off his glasses and added, "Not by a thousand, at any rate," and the slight, shy smile hovered on his lips for another moment and dissolved and his face became serious and heavy and Goldman said, "No, not by a thousand," and then he said, "I've heard about pills you can take for dieting," and played with the "Bullworker" and went on looking at Uncle Lazar's face, which was so different from his father's face and nevertheless, as if out of a kind of stubbornness, reminded him of it, and for a moment he once again felt the desire to ask Uncle Lazar why he had quarreled with his father and why they hadn't made up, but he didn't do it, because in some vague way he already knew the reason, which merged, strangely and tortuously, in his mind with the reason for his father's killing of Nuit Sombre, and he went on playing with the "Bullworker" while Uncle Lazar glanced at the paper, and at the same time he was filled with sorrowful feelings about his harsh and unjust father and with longing for him, even though he had never loved him and all he had left behind in his son was a little pride in his devastating honesty and a very few good memories, which he had to exert himself to dredge up out of the darkness and relive for a moment in enjoyment, and there was only one memory which would sometimes come into his mind of its own accord, and that was the memory of a certain Saturday when he was still a child and his father had taken him to the beach. The sky was bright blue, the sun was yellow and warm, and the air was clear, and there was a feeling of spaciousness and festivity; it was still early when they left the house and walked down the quiet street and the birds—there must have been thousands of them—in the bougainvillea and the cypresses and the fig trees sang joyfully, and his father held his hand in his own strong one and they walked slowly by themselves along the white sands stretching out under the sky in a deep Sabbath silence, making him want to lie down and roll over and over and then lie without moving for hours and hours on end abandoned to the breeze and the sun and the time passing without a trace, and while they walked he saw the sea in all its beauty—blue and quiet and infinite—and they went down to the beach and put their clothes and towels down (Stefana never went to the beach), and they stood at the edge of the calm water which hardly made a sound, and his father, who was in a good mood, pointed with his sunburnt arm to the horizon which merged softly into the sea and said that there were fine countries over there, Italy and France and England and Holland, and if you crossed the sea you came to them, and then they stepped into the sea and walked carefully a little way into it. His father was wearing a black bathing suit, his legs were surprisingly white, and when the water reached his waist his father gripped his hand firmly and warned him again and again not to move away from him. Now he was nervous, and Goldman suddenly felt, in the midst of all that concern for his health and life, his father's helplessness and the terrible, persecuting fear that filled him at the sight of the expanse of calm water, fear of the dark, hidden forces which might break out at any moment and annihilate everything, and thus they stood until his father said, "Enough. Let's go out for a while and get dry," and they turned and began making their way back, and suddenly Goldman's father said, "It's a pity your mother didn't come with us to the beach," and they stepped onto the sand, which was still cool, and went for a run, and when they came back they met Moishe Tzimmer and his wife and his two little children, and his father and Moishe Tzimmer began talking about politics while Moishe Tzimmer's wife lay on the sand with her eyes shut taking no notice of the two children, who began digging a hole next to the water, abandoning her big body to the sun, and afterward—it was certainly that same Saturday—Kaminskaya appeared in a white summer dress with Nuit Sombre and sauntered slowly along the beach, receding further and further into the distance, and Moishe Tzimmer said, "Look at her, what an actress," and Goldman's father said, "I don't want to look at her, the whore," and Goldman, thunderstruck by the sound of the word "whore," went on standing next to his father but he averted his eyes from him, and afterward they went into the sea again with Moishe Tzimmer and lay splashing in the shallow water for a long time, and Goldman, who went on standing and looking at Uncle

Lazar, wanted to swim a little way out but his father wouldn't let him, and he said, "They say diet pills work wonders," and Uncle Lazar returned the paper to Goldman and said again that it wasn't death itself which bothered him but the terrible process of disintegration and decomposition, because for him this process embodied the very essence of life and its sadness, because it was very hard to accept the fact that what was once one and whole disintegrated and fell apart and receded into the distance and was irretrievably lost, like the galaxies moving farther and farther away from each other in space until they were lost forever somewhere in the infinite darkness beyond all horizons and forgotten. Goldman folded the paper and Uncle Lazar played with a crumb of bread lying on the table and suddenly he asked how old Naomi was when she died, and Goldman said, "About twenty-five," and Uncle Lazar said, "When did it happen?" and Goldman, who couldn't remember the exact date, said "In the summer. In a traffic accident," and Uncle Lazar paused for a moment, as if there were something else he wanted to ask, but he didn't, and they set out the chessmen on the board and played two games, and when they were finished Uncle Lazar stood up and took his briefcase and went into the living room to say a short goodbye to Stefana, because it was Friday and he intended to pay his usual visit to his mother, and Goldman offered to accompany him part of the way, and so the two of them went out together and walked most of the way to Shmuel and Bracha's, who were waiting for Uncle Lazar and who greeted him warmly as usual.

After leaving his briefcase in the hall Uncle Lazar went into the room where Grandmother Hava lay like a mummy underneath her quilt and sat with her for a while, and afterward, he went into the kitchen and Bracha asked him how he was and how Yehudit Tanfuss was and if he wanted anything to eat, and Uncle Lazar said, "No, no, nothing thanks, Yehudit's waiting for me," but in the meantime she had already placed a plate of chopped liver and a piece of gefilte fish and a saucer of homemade horseradish and a few slices of turnip and fresh challah and a glass of borscht in front of him, and afterward, for dessert, she gave him a cup of tea and a slice of one of the cakes she had baked for the rummy evening, and Shmuel, who had lost all his curls and had recently become very fat and paunchy, sat opposite him and drank a glass of brandy and played with a gold keyring with his nicotine-stained fingers, and while Uncle Lazar ate he told him about his car rental business and his plans to set up an airline company for taking small groups of tourists around the country and for investing in a chain of souvenir and antique shops. The house, which was luxuriously but tastelessly furnished, was spotlessly clean, and the pot of *cholent* was already on the stove cooking for Saturday lunch, for which they were almost always joined by Illana and her husband, who was a lawyer, and their three children, and sometimes by Uri and his wife and their daughter, and sometimes also by Shmuel's father, as long as he was still living, and two or three other relatives, friends, and compatriots from the old country, but not Aharon and his wife, whom Bracha refused to invite even once, and not because of the butcher shop affair, although that too revolted and infuriated her, but because she had never forgotten the thrashing which Aharon had given Shmuel because of the money he owed him and despite all Shmuel's pleas she refused to forgive him for it. The guests would sit in the living room around the big, broad table on which Bracha served big helpings of delicious food on expensive china and kept urging her guests to eat, even though she knew it was unhealthy to eat too much, and the guests would polish off the enormous helpings, and at the end of the feast they would get up with difficulty and drag themselves home while Shmuel, who suffered from high blood pressure and had been warned by his doctors to cut down on smoking and eat less and lose weight, and who was the only one whom Bracha unsuccessfully tried to restrain, would empty a bottle of soda water and lie down immediately on the sofa and fall into a heavy sleep even before Bracha had finished taking the plates off the table, and sometimes even before the guests had dispersed.

The living room, where Uncle Lazar retired with Shmuel to drink his tea, was already organized for the rummy game to be played there that night by about twenty more or less regular players, a company which until his death also included Goldman's father, and for a while also Moishe Tzellermaier. They played for low stakes, with the only one who tried to raise the stakes against the general consensus being Shmuel, sometimes joined by Jonah Kotchinski's Sarah, and except for the occasional tension introduced by Goldman's father with his spurious and irritating arguments, the game was conducted in a friendly and agreeable spirit and accompanied by gossip, laughter, and small talk, and it ended at one or two o'clock in the morning, when the players would work out their winnings and losses, pay each other, rise from the tables, stretch themselves, take their leave of their hosts, and go contentedly home, and Bracha, who spent most of the evening feeding her guests, would collect the leftover cakes and biscuits and fruit and put them away and empty the ashtrays and go to wash the dishes, almost always willingly and uncomplainingly despite her tiredness and the lateness of the hour, and at the same time Shmuel would collect the cards and sort them out into packs and put them away in the cupboard.

Uncle Lazar asked how Amos was getting on in America and Shmuel replied that two days before he had received a letter from him in which he wrote that he was doing well in the company for which he worked and was about to purchase a house. He had stopped talking about coming back to Israel and it was already clear that he was going to stay over there with his wife and children, a fact which saddened them both, especially Bracha, who for a number of weeks now had not been to visit Stefana with Shmuel, because Stefana made it quite plain that she was not interested in their visits, and she asked Uncle Lazar about Stefana and about Goldman—who now walked slowly down Allenby Street, which was almost empty now of traffic and people, with the shops already shut in the pleasant melancholy of the Sabbath eve twilight shadows, and a great calm descended, and he sensed the charm of the late Friday afternoon and his love for the city in which he had been born and grown up, a love which he only rarely, in moments of grace, felt in its pure, undiluted form. He walked to Rothschild Avenue with his hands folded behind his back, glancing at the shop windows as he walked, and when he reached the avenue he stopped and stood for a few minutes looking serenely at the trees, which were full of birds, and at the people on their way to the synagogue services dressed in their best and holding their prayer books under their arms, and then he turned away and began walking back, and when he passed Barclays Bank he saw his sister Naomi coming toward him. He recognized her chiefly by her height and her walk, and for a moment he was overwhelmed by emotion, and he stood staring at her until she passed him with her rucksack on her back, looking like an American tourist, and when she had passed he turned his head and gave her one more long look and went on walking down the street, which began to grow dim and dark, and of course, it had happened in July—the twelfth of July—although the news did not reach them until three days later (she had had no papers on her and it took some time until they identified the body); his father had just come home from work and he was sitting barefoot in the kitchen sullenly eating the midday meal which Stefana had prepared for him. It was already a number of years after Naomi's return from Alexandria, which Goldman could only imagine with its mosques and palm trees and mixture of Oriental and colonial architecture and its sea and smells of spices and perfumes and stench of rot and mold and sweat, and he walked without stopping past the shop which had once been owned by Avraham Shechter, and then he walked past the little cafe which had been the scene of the fight between Shmuel and Aharon, who had fallen on his brother in a fit of fury—it was morning and the street was full of people—and beaten him mercilessly until his shirt was torn and his mouth and nose were bleeding, and Shmuel did not even try to defend himself, but Aharon kept on hitting him and three people had to hold him down before he stopped, and he yelled, "Where's my money? Thief! Parasite! I'll teach you a lesson!" and rushed out, and Shmuel got up and stood there with his face full of blood and he didn't know what to do, because his shame was greater than his pain.

Goldman turned into Rashi Street, and from there into all kinds of little streets, walking at a very leisurely pace and enjoying the quiet and the walking and the sights. Naomi's death was connected in his memory with the sudden, strained silence which had fallen on the house and enveloped the people who came and went, their movements and the suppressed noises they made, and all he wanted was to lie down in bed, very close to the wall, and cover himself with his blanket and not let anyone disturb him, but this was impossible and he was obliged to go back and forth between the kitchen and the living room and his bedroom, finding momentary refuge in the bathroom or the kitchen porch, and afterward he crossed Dizengoff Square and went on walking until he came to Dita's house, and he went inside, and Dita, who was already washed and dressed in honor of the Sabbath, covered the table in the room with a cloth and set it with plates and silverware and a bottle of white wine and they sat down to eat their Friday night meal together, which had become a tradition with them over the years. After the meal was over Goldman glanced at the papers while Dita, who was in a good mood, washed the dishes, and afterward they watched television together and chatted a bit, and Goldman, whose feeling of serenity and contentment during his walk in the street had evaporated as he climbed the stairs to Dita's apartment and rang the bell, felt again that everything was over between them and all that was left were a few external rituals, like this Friday night supper, and all kinds of irritating obligations which turned almost every meeting with her into a drag, not to mention the boredom, and he knew that it was hopeless but he didn't have the guts to put an end to it, and thus, after the television programs were over, Goldman went on sitting impatiently for a while and then he rose and said good-night to Dita, who did not try to detain him, and he went home,

where he found Stefana still sitting in the living room with Yehudit Maizler, wearing one of her elegant old dresses, and for a
moment she reminded him of her tall, lean mother, who had
spoken only Yiddish and Polish and worn only silk and wool, and
like the face of her mother, who had died at the same age as
Stefana was now, Stefana's face too held something aloof and
dissatisfied, and now also haughty, and in fact day by day Stefana
was growing more and more remote: She took no notice at all
of the seventh day of mourning for Goldman's father, or the
thirtieth day either or the unveiling of the tombstone on his grave,
which she never took the trouble to visit, and she hardly ever
mentioned him, and there was nothing angry or strained about
her behavior, it was all perfectly natural, just as if she had never
been married to him at all, and with the same naturalness she
went on dressing up in the old silks and velvets, which seemed
to suit her more and more every time she put them on, and she
began reading Polish books and speaking Polish to almost everyone who came to the house, a high, aristocratic Polish, and in the
same way she took no notice when Matilda Leviatan was in an
accident and was badly hurt by a car as she was crossing the road
and lay for weeks in the hospital without Stefana taking the trouble
to visit her even once, and the truth was that she wasn't interested
in anyone any more except for Yehudit Maizler, and to a certain
extent Naomi, and recently she had also begun to take an interest
in her brother Yanek, the eternal playboy with his pointed patent
leather shoes and his lace shirts, smelling of perfume and eau de
cologne, the darling of aging women and silly young girls, kind-
hearted and foolish Yanek, who had never read a book in his life
and regarded himself as a Pole and tried to gain an entry into
high society and ape the Polish upper classes, at least in his manners and his foppish idleness, Yanek, who in that last summer
before the war—after which he was never seen again—had taken
her rowing on the river in the summer vacation resort and walked
with her in the woods, together with Goldman, who was then
about nine years old (Naomi had stayed behind in Tel Aviv), and

in the evening Yanek danced with the ladies and there was no one who danced like he did, and he was a marvel at performing card tricks too, until the war came and swept him away and he disappeared, and now he rose up again from the depths of oblivion, crowned with love, and Stefana mentioned him from time to time affectionately and longingly to Yehudit Maizler, the only person whom she was willing, and sometimes even glad, to see, and as for all the others, relatives and neighbors and people from the old country and friends, they were received with such total and undisguised indifference that they gradually stopped coming, except for Tzimmer's widow, who was so thick-skinned that she kept on dropping in nevertheless, and Uncle Lazar and Moishe Tzellermaier, always perspiring and a little nervous and apprehensive, whose gratitude and lack of self-esteem made him ignore Stefana's coolness, and sometimes even scorn, and who never forgot to bring a bottle of the best wine or a box of chocolates and a bunch of flowers with him, and who always asked her how she was although he knew that he would receive no more than a nod of the head or a curt word or two in reply, but he did not complain, not even in his heart, only looked at her respectfully, but lately also with growing concern, until one day he could contain himself no longer and worked up the courage to grab Goldman by the arm in the corridor before taking his leave and say in a whisper that it seemed to him that his mother was not in the best of health, and Goldman, who was one of the few people with whom Stefana continued to speak Hebrew, nodded his head and said, "Yes, you may be right," and indeed Moishe Tzellermaier's remarks did not surprise him, since he himself had noticed the signs of change in his mother some time before, but in the beginning he preferred to ignore them, and later on he decided to accept them as a fact which had nothing to do with him, and he taught himself to suppress the anger and revulsion which his mother aroused in him and to remain indifferent in the face of her peculiarities, and he consoled himself with the thought that in any case he would soon be leaving home.

In the beginning Uncle Lazar too pretended not to notice anything, or in any case to view the outlandish aspects of Stefana's behavior as nothing more than a question of personal taste and temperament, perhaps a little eccentric and disagreeable, but when Stefana began painting her lips and rouging her cheeks and withdrew further and further into her strangeness, he mentioned it tactfully to Goldman and suggested that it might be a good idea to consult someone. Goldman listened to him but said nothing, since he had no intention of consulting anyone at all but of letting her do whatever she wished and sinking as deep as she liked into her madness, if that was what it was, to which, for all the anger and aversion it aroused in him, he was growing more accustomed every day, until it began to seem to him almost the natural expression of her true self, and sometimes it seemed to him that this was what she had always been like, and sometimes, for a moment, she even gave rise to a certain sympathy, if not a feeling of closeness, in him, but Stefana took no notice of all this and withdrew further and further into her own world, utterly indifferent and totally disinterested in her surroundings, and in August she received a letter from Manfred, from London, and it lay on the living room sideboard for a week until she opened it and read it and afterward she put it indifferently in the kitchen cupboard and went to make a late lunch for Goldman, who was standing in the hall calling Israel, and he asked him if he would be willing to accompany him to the cemetery the following afternoon to visit his father's grave, and Israel said, "Yes, of course," and Goldman said, "I don't feel like going alone, but you don't have to come," and Israel said, "No, no, it's quite all right," and the next day they met and went to the Central Bus Station to take the bus to the cemetery. The sky of the city had been covered by a delicate haze since morning, and it grew thicker all the time, but when they reached the station, which was enveloped in hot, dirty air saturated with gasoline fumes and smoke, Goldman did not join the line waiting at the Holon bus station but elbowed his way through the crowds of sweating people milling on the pavement and the sides of the road and made his way to the bus which went to Kiryat Shmuel. Israel, walking behind him, drew his attention to his mistake, and Goldman, tense and irritable because of the crowds and the suffocating heat, said that it was perfectly all right and went on walking and joined the line, and when they got onto the bus and sat down Israel could no longer restrain himself and he told Goldman that it seemed to him that his father had been buried in the Holon cemetery and not in the Kiryat Shmuel cemetery, and Goldman wiped the perspiration from his face and said that he was right up to a point, but that owing to an administrative muddle they had mixed his father up with some other Goldman and the entire burial in Holon had been a mistake, and so they had removed him from his grave about a week ago and transferred him from the Holon cemetery to the Kiryat Shmuel cemetery, where he should have been buried in the first place, and reburied him, and that was the reason why he was going there, to see for himself that everything was in order with the grave and the tombstone. The inspection was a brief one, and when they returned, after waiting a while for the bus, it was still daytime, but the light was an eerie twilight, dull and sooty and shadowless, filtering through the dense haze which completely hid the sun and covered the summer sky in one layer of reddish-brownish-gray, like the color of desert sand, and wrapped the telephone poles and the trees and the TV antennas and the houses a little way off in wisps of shifting mist, transforming them into blurred, floating, ghostly shadows in the still, hot, dusty, hazy air, which made it hard for them to breathe, and when they reached town evening was already falling, very slowly and almost imperceptibly, as if the dimness of the day were simply darkening and deepening a little, and as they made their way on foot from the Central bus station, the full moon, rising early, was revealed for a moment through the foggy haze, looking like a murky circle of wax.

Goldman thanked Israel for accompanying him and invited him to come up and have something to drink, but Israel, who felt sticky and dirty, said goodbye and went home to the studio and took a shower and changed his clothes and sat down at the piano, but shortly afterward he heard Caesar's footsteps on the stairs, and he was immediately filled with rage, and a few seconds later Caesar came in dripping with sweat and panting because of the heat and the mugginess and climbing the stairs, and he had also put on weight recently and he was smoking a lot, and he removed the heavy camera from his neck and wiped his glasses with his wet handkerchief and his face, which was dead and downcast, and he asked Israel if there had been any calls for him, and Israel said, "When I was here there were four," and Caesar, who perhaps had never before looked so tired and depleted and hopeless, said that if they were bad calls not to tell him because he was beat and he didn't have the strength to hear bad news, and Israel said that he couldn't judge if they were good or bad calls, and he went to the kitchen and put the kettle on for coffee, and Caesar, who kept wiping his sweating face, followed him and said, "Who called? Tell me already," and Israel said that two of the calls were about work, and he had taken the names and numbers of the callers who wanted him to get back to them as soon as possible, and the third call was from his mother, who hadn't said anything but only asked him to tell Caesar that she had called and that she would try to call again, and Caesar said, "It must be about Shalva. She'll drive me crazy," and the fourth call was from Vicky, who wanted to tell him that she was going away for about a week and would contact him when she got back—ever since her marriage she had not allowed Caesar to contact her—and Caesar leaned against the door frame and seemed not to have heard Israel, although he said, "They can all go to hell," since there was no sign of anger on his face, and he went on standing there tired and despairing and lit himself a cigarette apathetically and threw the match on the floor and said, "I'm in trouble," and after a moment of silence he said "But don't worry, I'll run away, to Italy or America," and silence fell once more, and Caesar went to stand next to the sink and opened and shut the tap and blew a cloud of smoke and the ash dropped off his cigarette and fell onto his shirt and pants, but he took no notice and with the same hopeless air he went on playing with the tap, after stealing a glance at Israel, who said nothing even though he sensed how much Caesar wanted him to ask what had happened and why he was in trouble, and he poured out two cups of coffee and gave one to Caesar and they both stood drinking in silence, and when they had finished—Caesar took only one or two sips and left his cup on the marble-topped table—Caesar took his camera and went into the darkroom to develop his film, while Israel washed the cups and sat down by the piano and resumed his playing. After about an hour Caesar came out of the darkroom, sweating and limp with exhaustion, and called Israel and Israel rose and went into the other room to look at the photographs of the big textile factory hanging up to dry and expressed his admiration and Caesar, who was pleased by Israel's response, said, "They are good, aren't they?" and he looked at them with enjoyment and said that he would like to work in the movies, and Israel said, "So what's stopping you?" and Caesar said, "Nothing really," and examined the photos again with a satisfied air and said, "I wouldn't mind not being my own boss, it wouldn't bother me," and turned his back on the photos and leaned against the desk and took a new packet of pornographic pictures, which someone had sent him from Germany, out of his shirt pocket, and flipped lightly through them, saying, "Have a look at what's going on here," and "Not bad, not bad at all, but mine's bigger," and when he had finished looking at them all he said, "Maybe I should go into the porno business, it would be business and pleasure combined," and he sniggered and wiped his sweating face with his sleeve and threw the photos into one of the desk drawers and lit himself a cigarette and said, "She's getting divorced, the bitch," and Israel said, "Who?" and Caesar, the fleeting pleasure gone from his face, which was tired and serious again, looked at Israel and said, "Eliezra," and added immediately, "She only told me today, the bitch, when everything was already arranged. What do you think of her? They've already got an appointment at the rabbinate," and he threw his cigarette onto the floor and crushed it beneath his shoe.

emained obstinately silent, and although Caesar looked
Israel expectantly he continued to say nothing, and Caesar, look-
at him and depleted, poured himself half a glass of whiskey
and that she was getting divorced on the strength of a prom-
e had given her to marry her, but that she had dragged the
mise out of him by force and when he had given it he hadn't
elieved that it would ever happen, and in any case he had never
dreamed that it would happen so soon, and he would give a
million for it not to happen, at least not now, because if she really
did get divorced he would be in a terrible fix since he would
have to choose between her and Tehilla, and that was exactly
what he couldn't do and didn't want to do, because he had also
promised Tehilla to marry her, and in fact he saw them as com-
plementing one another, since Tehilla was domestic and decent
and gave him a sense of security with her uncapricious faithfulness, not to speak of the fact that he felt an obligation to her, but
at the same time he loved Eliezra and she was the only one who
unfailingly aroused him and brought him to new heights of pleasure every time, because there was complete sexual compatibility
between them, and also mental compatibility, and if they got married he had no doubt that in spite of all the difficulties and complications their lives together would be like one long holiday that
never came to an end. Caesar fell silent for a moment and Israel
said, "Which of them do you prefer?" and Caesar, who had expected something quite different, looked at him again with a
helpless and victimized expression, but also with irritation and
disappointment, and played with his cigarette lighter and said that
he preferred both of them, but if he had to prefer one of them
it would be Eliezra, but he would prefer not to give up Tehilla
either, and he wandered about the room and stopped at the door
of the balcony which overlooked the street, and Israel rolled a
piece of paper between his long hard fingers and said, "Sometimes you have to give up something," and Caesar said, "Yes, I
know," and glanced outside and added, "Yes, of course, you're
right, you have to give up something," but he was annoyed and
in the depths of his heart he simply could not understand why

he should have to give up anything, or agree that he sh.
as he could never accept the fact that when it came to his' iust
or his convenience there were situations which were hopele.
things which were unattainable or contradictions which could n.
be resolved without choices and decisions which had to be made.
In his opinion these ideas were nothing but detestable prejudices
or gratuitous cruelties which for the most part were neither justified nor necessary, since as far as he himself and his own feelings were concerned life was always just beginning and there was
no reason why he shouldn't have his own way, and why other
people shouldn't give in to him, and do it gladly too, because his
deepest feeling about life was that it was fluid and formless and
aimless, and everything was possible in it to an infinite degree,
and it could be played backward and forward like a roll of film,
just as he wished, and in accordance with this basic belief he tried
to control the world he lived in and shape it to his heart's desire,
and even if he knew it wasn't really possible he demanded, perhaps unconsciously, that it should be, and so he acknowledged
no responsibility apart from the gratification of his own desires,
and every other obligation or restriction he regarded as unwar-
ranted interference or even simple spite, and he looked at Israel
reproachfully and said, "But how can I leave her? Just say goodbye
and leave?" and Israel nodded his head, and Caesar, looking angry
and disappointed, jiggled his foot nervously and said, "She'll kill
herself," and threw the cigarette he had lit a moment before out
of the window, and said again that it would be horribly cruel to
Tehilla, to whom he owed a great deal after staying in her apartment and living with her as man and wife and after she had
quarreled with her family on his account and perhaps missed a
number of other opportunities to get married. He did not allude
to the affair of the abortion by so much as a hint, although he
himself remembered it very well, but Israel did not soften and
went on rolling the piece of paper between his fingers and said,
"She won't kill herself. But if that's what you think then leave
Eliezra and marry her," and he looked at Caesar, who looked

back at him angrily and said, "But I love Eliezra," and then there was a silence, and Caesar sipped his whiskey and started wandering around the room again and came to a stop at the desk and turned to Israel and said, "She's got something, that Tehilla, there's something about her that gets to me," and then he said, "She's a *mensch*," and he said these things solemnly, as a continuation of the thoughts that were running through his head, and then he paused for a moment and started moving around again, and after a few moments, alternately pacing about the room and stopping, he turned his thoughts into a different channel and said, "I've gotten myself into a mess with her," and he opened and shut one of the desk drawers and said frankly that the truth was that he didn't love Tehilla and the only reason he had started going to her place was to go to bed with her, and the third or fourth time he went there she had suggested that he stay the night and he had accepted her offer since it was late and he didn't want to make an issue out of it, and after he had slept over at her place another night, about two weeks later, he had stayed on, not because he was short of girls, but because being alone depressed him—at the time he was living alone in an apartment he had rented after leaving his parents' place—and because there was always something to eat in the fridge, and soap and a clean towel in the bathroom, and he always found his clothes laundered and ironed in the wardrobe. Tehilla took care of everything, and in addition to this she was often busy in the evenings and nights because of the nature of her work so that she wasn't a burden to him and he was free to do as he pleased—he said this leaning on the desk and then he fell silent, and after a moment or two he said that the truth was that in spite of all the difficulties and obstacles he would have married Eliezra but he was afraid that as a wife she wouldn't be any good and she wouldn't arouse him the way she did as a mistress, and he was even more afraid that she wouldn't be faithful to him if he married her, and in addition, he said after a short pause, he was afraid of Gidon, since if he ever found out that they had been having an affair during the time she was married to him and that she was divorcing him in order to marry Caesar he might kill him. There was real anxiety, which he made no attempt to disguise, in Caesar's voice as he finished speaking, and after a moment he added, "He's a good fellow, Gidon, but he's too ambitious, and he's got no sense of humor," and then he said "It's only natural, really. After all, he's only human," and he glanced at a picture of a girl which he had hung on the wall and then he looked at Israel and said, "I'm not joking. A few days ago he beat her up," and he didn't look at Israel but took another sip of whiskey and said, "You know what, I can't stand him. He's a creep," and he looked out at the city covered in a heavy haze—he looked at it for a long time—and said, to himself, "And besides everything else there's my son. I have to put everything off until he's better," and afterward he sat down on a stool opposite Israel and said that if she was already divorced, or if at least she wasn't getting divorced specifically because of him, everything might be different, and at the same time, he said in a sudden burst of energy, he did not intend giving her, Eliezra, up, but would try to persuade her to put off her divorce until the winter or the following spring, and he looked into Israel's face in order to find a sign of agreement or under-standing, but Israel's face remained stiff and blank and Caesar, hurt and embarrassed, played with the whiskey glass and said, "I'll marry her yet, you'll see," and Israel said, "Good," and Caesar went to stand by the balcony door again and said that the truth was that he didn't understand what was so bad about things as they were, and why Eliezra had to get divorced, just as he didn't understand why he had to get married just because those two bitches wanted him to when he himself didn't have the faintest desire to do so, and in any case he didn't believe in the institution of the family, which was clearly on its way out, an obsolete left-over from another period, which was completely fossilized and bankrupt and which was capable of performing only one function successfully, which was to kill love and abandon the husbands and wives to each other's meanness and selfishness and make their lives a hell on earth, like, for example, the lives of Phillip and Zahara or his own parents or Goldman's parents or Avigdor and Ruhama until they separated, and besides, he said, man was polygamous and would remain polygamous and there was no reason why he should deny his true nature and attach himself to one woman, not even if she were Brigitte Bardot.

A strong, hot wind suddenly blew up and burst into the room through the window and the door, ruffling Caesar's thinning hair, which he continued treating with Jochem's Hormoon, despite its uselessness, although he added other preparations as well, and he stood silently for a few moments looking at the white wall opposite and then shut the window and said, "I'm damned if I know why I got divorced in the first place. All in all it wasn't so bad and I was quite happy the way I was," and a moment later he said, "It's all because of that shit that she went and let fuck her," and in fact the one and only time that Tirza had been unfaithful to him with another man gave him no rest and he could not erase it from his memory and overcome his humiliation and jealousy, although over the years the incident had lost much of the sharp pain it possessed at first, when he had nagged at her for days on end and forced her to tell him again and again all the details of how she had met him and where they had gone and how it had all happened, and cross-examined her about why she had agreed and if she had enjoyed it and if the other man's prick was bigger than his, and at the same time, for several weeks, he had tried to find out who the man was, he wanted to see him and perhaps even exchange a few words with him, but all these efforts were doomed to failure because Tirza, who became increasingly irritated by Caesar's constant questions, to which she replied with increasing unwillingness, was adamant in her refusal to tell him the man's name or any other details which could have identified him, and all she said was that they didn't know each other and that he was a doctor, which added insult to injury as far as Caesar was concerned, and he went on interrogating her because what she had done shocked and disturbed him, and shortly after Ruhama left him and the terrible storm of distress which this parting caused him had somewhat abated, the matter of Tirza's unfaithfulness came back to persecute him, until he left her amid quarrels and insults and humiliation by which means he attempted to retrieve some of his offended honor, but in spite of his repeated claims Tirza's unfaithfulness was not, of course, the reason for their divorce, or at the most it was a marginal reason, the real reason being his selfishness and self-indulgence and unwillingness or inability to commit himself, and the films and the magazines and Erwin and Besh and his frivolous and empty expectations and the relentless need to conquer as many women as possible and prove his strength and virility over and over again—but now, as in every hour of crisis or distress, he succumbed to a mood of sentimental realism and regret and said, "It was a big mistake, that divorce, I behaved like a child," and then he said, "I'd like to go back home and finish with all the rest," and he said this quite sincerely, and even with a certain intention of actually doing it, but at the same time he knew that he would never do it and that it was a lost cause, and nevertheless he went on playing with the thought and said, "It would be the best thing for me. I'm sick of all this running around. Do you think she would take me back?" and Israel said, "Maybe," and at that moment the telephone rang and Caesar tensed and asked Israel to take the call and if it was Eliezra to tell her that he had had to leave town on a job and would be back very late, or maybe not until the following day, and in fact it was Eliezra, she was talking from a public phone booth, and Israel gave her Caesar's message, and she said, "All right. Just tell him, please, that I called," and Israel said, "Yes, I'll tell him," and put the receiver down and transmitted the message to Caesar whose gloomy and regretful mood was now interrupted by the stirring of other feelings and who said, "She's great. I'll marry her yet, and let the rest of the world go to hell, I don't give a damn," and he finished the whiskey in his glass and said that he was sure he would be able to persuade her to put the divorce off for a while, and he put the glass down on the table and grabbed Israel by the lapel of his shirt and said, "You wait and see, she's not getting divorced so quickly. For the moment it's all just talk," and his spirits soared on the whiskey, and especially on the wings of his own words, which liberated him and filled him with relief.

The haze outside dispersed and slowly the lovely summer sky and the full moon were revealed, and Caesar lit another cigarette and said that he loved the summer and that he would like to live like one of the poor people in Brazil or Mexico who lived a natural existence of idleness and sea-bathing and the Samba and women, a life without striving or cares, or like that American tourist who didn't really care who she ate with or went to bed with and what would happen tomorrow, and hitched rides with different men all the time and traveled with them for a while without any great expectations and without any obligations. Caesar said these things in a tone of longing but also of happiness, as if this dream were already being realized, or would be realized tomorrow, and at the same time he shifted his eyes to look disinterestedly at the balcony on the other side of the street where a girl was sitting and writing, and he looked at her for a long time and then suddenly turned back to Israel and said, "It's not serious. Everything will work out. Maybe we'll go to a movie tonight or visit Zahara?" and Israel said, "Maybe," and Caesar pushed his pack of cigarettes into his shirt pocket and his handkerchief into his pants pocket and said, "It's a pity that American tourist left," and took his camera and said that he had to go over to his parents' place because of the death of Shalva, whom he had seen perhaps twice in the course of his life, and Israel accompanied him to the door and when Caesar closed it behind him and went down the stairs he sat down at the piano, but the heat in the room and especially the conversation with Caesar had exhausted him and broken his concentration, and he went out onto the balcony and leaned on the railing and abandoned himself to the touch of the cool currents of air coming from the sea and dispersing the suffocating heat, and at the same time he looked

at the people coming and going and at Caesar's huge car, a battered old Plymouth covered with dust and scratches, which was
parked in front of the house, and for a moment it seemed to him
that he saw Ella approaching, and this surprised him, because for
two weeks she hadn't come and he hadn't seen her and he was
filled with happiness and the anger of resistance, the same combination of happiness and anger which had dominated their relationship from the start and transformed it into a complicated
pattern of accusations and rejections and reconciliations full of
tenderness and regret, reconciliations whose end was as sudden
as the beginning of the quarrels during which Israel, his heart
hard and bitter with hatred, would try to hurt her as cruelly as
he could, although he knew how unjustly he was treating her,
and his cruelty consisted mainly of rejection and denial and long,
stubborn silences, while Ella spoke to him and smiled at him and
tried to appease him and make him happy and embraced him
hesitantly, and also begged, but all in vain—his rejection became
more hostile and his silence grew gloomier—and he watched the
girl in the street until she passed beneath the balcony, next to
Caesar's car, which he maneuvered backward and forward until
he finally managed to extricate it from the row of cars parked
along the pavement, and Israel, who did not know how to drive,
watched the car in which Caesar charged up the street and made
a rapid right turn and disappeared from view.

A few minutes later he stopped in front of his parents' house
and parked the car and walked across the garden and rang the
bell in a dispirited way and Zina, who was standing in the kitchen
making coffee with Yaffa, opened the door and received him with
cries of joy, and he kissed her cheek as usual and asked her how
she was and she said, "Just fine," and then he went into the
kitchen and greeted Yaffa and asked her how she was and how
Tikva was, but before Yaffa could reply she was interrupted by
Zina, who had already called Caesar the evening before to tell
him the news of Shalva's death, which she now repeated with the
same excitement and astonishment as she had delivered it the

night before, and Caesar listened to her with impatience and also with loathing.

The truth was that neither Zina nor Yaffa knew how to relate to the death of their sister Shalva, whom they had not seen for so many years that the bond between them seemed forced and artificial, and who had rejected them in her death as she had rejected them in her life, and even succeeded in pointing an accusing finger at them from the grave, in their opinion at any rate, and in leaving them affronted and bewildered and upset, for she had committed suicide about four months before without leaving any kind of message for them or any other member of the family. Her mother and father, who for so many years had kept an anxious eye on her from a distance, their hearts full of anguish and hopes of reconciliation, were long dead, and she had taken such good care to conceal and deny all family connections over the years that no one imagined there was anyone to inform when they discovered her suicide, in honor of which Shalva had bathed and washed her hair and dressed herself in her best clothes and seated herself in a big armchair, opposite the mirror on the wardrobe door, after which she had swallowed sleeping pills and sunk into a deep sleep from which she never woke.

For two days and three nights the light shone in her apartment until one of the neighbors noticed and called the police, who came and broke down the door and found Shalva in all the dignity and splendor which had been lost to her in her life and returned to her in her death, and on the table in the room they found a legal document stating that she had bequeathed her body to science, and it was thanks to this bequest that Zvi accidentally discovered her death when he was going through some old newspapers in connection with his work and came across one of the standard mourning notices published by the university in honor of the deceased who had donated their bodies to science, only this time it was in honor of Shalva, and he hurried to tell the news to Erwin and to Zina and Yaffa, who since the evening before, after the inquiries they made at the police station had been substantiated at the university, had never stopped discussing it and trying to decide what they should do and how they should express their sorrow at the event, which did not give rise to any sorrow in them—Erwin was of the opinion that there was no need to do anything at all and so was Besh—because despite their lack of sorrow and despite the anger and feeling that they had been ill treated by Shalva both of them also felt an obligation and a need to respond in some way to their sister's death—Zina, because she loved tragic situations in general and because in recent years she had been searching for something to hold onto in the traditional family ties which could not be denied or subverted and which she had too long neglected, and Yaffa, who had aged greatly since the deaths of her husband and son and the deterioration of her relations with Tikva, because she had possessed a strong family sense all her life and since the deaths of her parents she had considered herself responsible for the family, and because Shalva had always aroused her guilt and her pity, but Caesar was not in the least interested in Shalva, neither alive nor dead, and after listening to them for a few minutes he asked Yaffa again about Tikva, and Yaffa said, "She's all right. Bringing up the children. She's perfectly all right,"—although the truth was that Tikva lived a life of empty and resentful wastefulness, since her father had left her enough money to squander pointlessly and her mother could not restrain her, and she waited impatiently for the love which would rescue her from her oppressive loneliness and boredom, and indeed from time to time a new lover appeared in her life and they would go to restaurants and movies, even at four o'clock in the afternoon, and to parties, and joke and laugh until he disappeared and left her alone again in her large apartment with its luxurious furniture and her two children, for whom she hardly ever had any time or patience, just as she had none for her mother, with whom she was always having hurtful, abusive arguments, which flared up quickly over every little thing, and Yaffa, whom these arguments always left speechless and very hurt, said "All she needs is a husband," and Caesar said, "I haven't seen her for ages," and Yaffa said, "I asked her to come, maybe she'll come," and Caesar said, "Great," and went out to the veranda where Erwin was sitting on a cushioned wicker chair and looking vacantly at the street and the trees and at Besh, who was sitting opposite him and talking, but Erwin did not respond at all and went on staring apathetically in front of him.

It was no longer possible to ignore his illness, which was getting worse from day to day—he had lost weight and his body hung loosely about him as if it were too big for him, his graying reddish-brown hair had grown hard and bristly, his face had shrunken and taken on a grayish hue and his ears had grown bigger, his head drooped and altogether he looked like a dry old marabou which had lost its feathers and its lust for life—but Erwin stubbornly ignored all this, and it was only after some time had passed that he began dropping an occasional, joking remark about the need for people of his age to take up some form of exercise, and later on he also began massaging his neck and arms and face, which he took to examining for a moment from time to time in the mirror, but when Zina carefully suggested a visit to the doctor he said that there was nothing wrong with him, and when she repeated her suggestion he rejected it impatiently and said, "Let other people go to the doctor if they like. We're a healthy family."

Caesar greeted them with a big hello, smiled at Besh, and slapped his father on the shoulder, and Erwin turned his head and smiled with an effort and asked him how he was, and Caesar said, "Nothing to complain about," and sat down, and Besh said that anyone who said he had nothing to complain about should be locked up in a lunatic asylum, and afterward he said that he hated happy people but luckily he didn't know any and so he hated all kinds of people for no reason at all because he was clever and embittered, and after a moment he added that if only God existed in this town he would have someone to talk to but even the devil had run away and left them in the hands of a rabble of animals like Max Spillman and all kinds of mad dogs who called themselves Jews, but the sand would teach them a lesson. Caesar

laughed, and Besh said that it was no laughing matter but a trag-
edy, because that was the sorry state of the whole miserable country from the Prime Minister down to the last of the street sweepers,
and he felt like throwing his plumed hat into the air and shouting
the Italian battle cry, "Anyone with legs take to his heels and run
for his life!" at the top of his voice, and he laughed and turned
to Zina and Yaffa, who came in from the kitchen with coffee and
sugar and cake and put them on the table, and he asked Yaffa
how she was getting on with her French, and Yaffa said, "All the
French I learned in high school is beginning to come back to
me," and Besh said, "Thank God for French," and told them about
three of four cases of French girls he had read about in the
newspaper who had been given a special dispensation by the
Church to marry their dead lovers, one of whom was a soldier
killed in an accident and another a policeman in a little town
who had been killed by a gunshot while pursuing a criminal, and
he said that he couldn't make up his mind whether they were
absolutely insane or extraordinarily wise, and then he turned to
Zina and asked her why she didn't take up French too, and Zina
said, "Maybe one day I will," and Besh said, "You're not so young
any more, Madame," and Zina said, "Yes, I know, you don't have
to remind me," and put a cup of coffee in front of Erwin, who
took it with a shaking hand and drank it slowly, and it dribbled
down his chin and stained his shirt and pants and Zina, who never
took her eyes off him, helped him discreetly, and from time to
time, also very discreetly, she wiped his lips and chin and pants
with her handkerchief—Erwin's illness had breathed new life into
her and she had almost forgotten her legs and devoted herself
zealously to his needs and she would have been delighted if it
could have gone on forever—and in the meantime the doorbell
rang and Zina got up to open the door and Ruhama, who had
returned from America a week before without letting anyone
know, walked in.

About two years before this Ruhama had given the children
to Avigdor to look after and gone to America to learn speech

therapy, but after a few months there she had abandoned her studies and gone to work as a shop assistant and a Hebrew teacher, and for a while she had also been married to an American from Philadelphia who owned a big sports equipment factory, and now that she had returned to Israel she came almost every day to visit Erwin, who greeted her with a smile full of affection, and Caesar, who had not seen her since her return, rose to his feet to greet her and they shook hands and he asked her how she was and she said, "As you see. Not too bad," and Caesar said, "It's good to see you," and he examined her stealthily and noted the great changes which had taken place in her during the years that had passed since their last meeting—she had grown fat and ugly—and said again, "It's really good to see you," and Zina, who treated her with demonstrative but flustered graciousness, went to make coffee and Ruhama sat down between Besh and Yaffa and exchanged a few remarks with Erwin and Besh and Caesar, who asked her how she was getting acclimated and examined her again and again and realized that everything there had once been between them, all the love and attraction, had vanished without a trace. She aroused no emotion or desire in him, or even memories, but only an indifference so complete that it astonished him, and the more he inspected her and listened to her the deeper this astonishment grew, and he asked himself again and again if it was really possible that only a few years before he had been so madly in love with this charmless woman, with her fat fingers and ravaged face and nicotine-stained teeth, that when she left him he had gone almost insane with jealousy and despair, and standing in the cold wet street after being banished from her bed and emerging into the grayness of the morning, still unable to believe that their relationship was really at an end, he had been sure that his whole world lay in ruins and that he would never recover again.

He listened to her conversation with Erwin, her inquiries about his health and activities, her stories about America, and her exchanges with Besh and Yaffa; no one mentioned Shalva until after

Ruhama and Besh had gone, and he asked her what she was going to do now, and she said that she hadn't made up her mind yet, and in the meantime Zina brought her coffee and Besh said that she would do exactly what she had done up to now, which was to fuck, and he laughed and offered to spike her coffee with brandy, and Ruhama laughed and said that she liked coffee by itself and brandy by itself, and Besh rose from the table and went over to the bar and came back with a bottle of brandy and two glasses and despite Zina's objections he poured a glass for himself and one for Ruhama and said, "Drink up!" and they raised their glasses and Besh said, "To your last husband, Ruhama!" and they drank, and Ruhama said that as far as she remembered he wasn't worth a toast even as a bad joke, because although he cultivated his body and had a suntan all year long and even some kind of degree in engineering, he was semi-impotent and a deadly bore, and—what was even worse—he was insanely stingy and couldn't bear to part with one lousy cent, and she licked her lips and said, "A man who doesn't know how to spend money isn't worth bothering about," and Besh was delighted and laughed happily and filled their glasses again and began flirting with her, which he did with his usual outspoken and unceremonious crudeness, in front of Erwin, who had also laughed at her remarks about her husband, and in front of Zina and Yaffa, who maintained a very disapproving silence, while Caesar drank his coffee and observed them dispassionately, and even when Ruhama responded to Besh's attentions with laughter and words and looks she did not give rise to any emotion in him, and it was Besh who began, for the first time, to get on his nerves with his tone and his behavior, and he felt irritated and disgusted and turned his head away from him and looked at the trees and the evening sky, and out of the corner of his eye he glanced at Erwin, whose smile had disappeared and who looked dull and defeated and indifferent to everything, sitting and staring in front of him with lifeless eyes which were covered with a repulsive film of moisture, and all of a sudden Caesar felt an urge to turn his back on all these people and get away, and as soon as he had finished his coffee he rose to his feet and despite the fact that Zina, and also Ruhama, urged him to stay a little longer, he turned away and left them with a hasty goodbye.

Outside in the street he saw Max Spillman coming toward him and waving at him from a distance, but he averted his face slightly and crossed the road as if he hadn't seen him and got into his big, battered car and drove off, but he couldn't decide where to go, because he had no desire to see his children, whom he had not seen for some days now, or Tehilla or Vicky or Eliezra or Israel, and in fact he didn't really want to see anyone, and he went on driving aimlessly until he emerged from the city and started speeding along the highway, which stretched between the uncultivated fields and the low loam hills and the settlements and eucalyptus groves and cultivated fields lying serenely in the warm, pleasant evening twilight, and he abandoned himself to the pleasure of speeding through the open countryside and after a while he forgot all about his parents and Besh and Ruhama and his children and Max Spillman, who had come, as usual, to consult his father about their business affairs, and who shook Ruhama, whom he too was seeing for the first time since her return from America, warmly by the hand and asked her how she was and what it was like over there, and Ruhama said, "It was great, but I've had enough," and she asked him how he was and how his eldest son, Benjamin, who had been to high school with her own son, was getting on, and Max Spillman said that Benjamin had recently left for England, as soon as he had finished his military service, to specialize in computers, and Ruhama said that she would like to see him and Max Spillman said, "You'll see him when he comes home for the holidays," and Ruhama asked him how his wife was and Max Spillman said, in a matter-of-fact tone, that she was dead, and Ruhama, said "Oh, I'm so sorry, please forgive me, I didn't know," and Max Spillman said, "Never mind, it happened a long time ago," and he put sugar in the coffee which Zina had made him, and Erwin turned to Ruhama and said, "Don't you remember?" and Ruhama said, "No, I'm sorry," and Erwin said, "It happened a few years ago," and in fact Bruria had died about five years before from a thrombosis, and Max Spillman went on living in his enormous apartment—lately he had been living there all alone—and because of the extensive business interests in which he invested most of his strength and energy and intelligence, he had begun to lead a more affluent style of life, as if he had woken up one day and decided to hurry up and make the most of what remained of his life and have a good time and make up for what he had missed during the years of austerity, and so he bought himself the finest and most fashionable clothes, drove big American cars, went to expensive restaurants, and stayed in the most luxurious hotels, and he could afford it, because in addition to the profits from his factories and gas stations Max Spillman had made a fortune in land and real estate and all kinds of financial manipulations, and nevertheless, despite his wealth, he was unable to enjoy himself as much as he would have liked to, because he was a calculating man and as far as nonessential expenses were concerned he could not rid himself of his stingy and anxious attitude toward money, just as he could not entirely free himself from his socialist past, which gave rise in him to contradictory feelings of sentimental pride, contempt, and hostility, and which not infrequently made him feel uneasy and imposed annoying restrictions on his enjoyment of his money.

Besh despised him and Erwin, who had business interests in common with him, regarded him as a coarse, ruthless, and totally unscrupulous man, and he was repelled by him, but Max Spillman, who admired Erwin, ignored all this with the same self-confident impudence with which he ran his business affairs and looked after his money and interests, because he was absolutely shameless, both in his cruelty and in his sycophancy, and he had no loyalty to anything except his own needs and interests and felt no compassion or sense of obligation to anyone except his sister Rachel, to whom he was tied by bonds of love and concern and whom he supported in every way he could, and to whom he would have been prepared to give the shirt off his back, and except his mother, with whom he had lived for most of his life and to whom he felt as attached as he did to his sister, as well as respecting her more than anyone he knew, and he listened to her advice and refused to put her into an old age home or a sanitorium and looked after her patiently and devotedly in her spacious room in his apartment until she died, and he wept heart-brokenly at her death, just as he did at Bruria's death, not because he was sentimental or cried easily, and toward her too he behaved tenderly and generously and protectively until the day she died, and he was a good father to his two sons, and Uncle Lazar respected him for this, although he was well aware of the faults in his character and of the disgusting way in which he was capable of behaving, and although on the few occasions on which they had met after Uncle Lazar's return from Yakut Max Spillman, who quickly gulped his coffee down, had treated him like a stranger and apart from a chilly greeting had barely spoken to him, and he put his cup down on the table and glanced at Erwin, and Zina asked him about his younger son, Yair, who was a year younger than Benjamin and had recently married a girl from Belgium with whom he was now living in Brussels, and Max Spillman lit himself a cigarette and said, "I got a letter from him a week ago. For the time being he seems quite satisfied to stay where he is," and he looked at Ruhama and said, "He's in Brussels, with his wife," and he glanced again at Erwin, who had also finished drinking his coffee and who after a moment rose heavily from his chair and retired to the living room with Max Spillman, where they sat down together in a corner and began talking, and a few minutes later Besh too rose and said to Ruhama, "Are you coming?" and Ruhama rose without a moment's hesitation or embarrassment and they said goodbye to Zina and to Yaffa, who responded to their farewell with a slight, disapproving nod, and to Max Spillman and Erwin, and went off together.

That night Ruhama went to bed with Besh, as she had known she would from the moment she came into the room and saw him there, or at least from the moment he had started joking with her and risen to bring the bottle of brandy for her, and Besh knew it too, and he also knew that she knew, and she went to bed with him even though he did not give rise to any feeling of attraction, or even curiosity, in her, and even though she felt no need for consolation or adventure and she did not even hope that he would give her any pleasure, and indeed he didn't, but she was willing to shut her eyes and abandon herself to the blindness of chance and let things take their course without expecting anything, and she spent the night with Besh and lay with him without the least desire or shame, in total passivity, and when she got up in the morning and went away she did not feel regretful, cheated, or deceived.

The affair continued for a couple of months in the same way that it had begun, until Ruhama accepted the hand of Max Spillman, who had begun courting her the day after their meeting at Erwin's house and showered her with expensive presents and entertainment and tried to endear himself to her by means of all kinds of gestures which struck her as completely superfluous and for the most part also as ludicrous, and he also tried to impress her with the little knowledge he had managed to acquire about wines and cheeses and different kinds of food, and before Benjamin came home on vacation from London she married him and went to live in his magnificent apartment whose five rooms were filled with antique furnishings, which aroused her scorn and disgust, and carpets and original paintings, most of which had been acquired in the recent past, and in honor of Ruhama Max Spillman, with a heavy heart, removed all traces of his first wife from the apartment, although Ruhama, who had not asked him to do it or even dropped a single hint in this direction, because it made no difference to her one way or the other, showed him very little kindness and hardly ever went to bed with him, either before or after their wedding, and tried to avoid him as much as possible because his body disgusted her, especially his lips and hands and fingers, and all she let him do was stroke her and warm her cold feet with his hands, and also take her to restaurants and sometimes the movies or the theater, and bring her fancy cigarettes and huge boxes of imported chocolates, which she devoured greedily even when she was pregnant and the doctors warned her to stop and told her to lose weight, and he did all this willingly because he was infatuated with her and also proud of her, but Ruhama, who gradually learned to be grateful to him and even to some extent to enjoy his company, went on sleeping with Besh for months after the wedding, mainly out of habit and indifference, until Max Spillman found out about it, and then she gave Besh up without any difficulty at all.

The wedding was attended by a small circle of family and friends and Rachel, who did not like Ruhama and regarded the whole thing as a big mistake, saw to it that there was plenty to eat and drink and everything was in the best of taste, but Zina pretended to be ill because she did not want to meet Elisheva, Ruhama's mother, and did not attend the wedding, and neither did Caesar, who told Israel and also Goldman that Ruhama was marrying Max Spillman for money and convenience, and because he was some fifteen years older than she was and she hoped that he would die before her and leave her in possession of a fortune—the last he said half in earnest and half as a joke, but the truth was that Ruhama married Max Spillman not because he had won her heart with his expensive gifts and clumsy gestures and not because she coveted his wealth, but because she was so tired that nothing made any difference to her and all she wanted was to find some rest from her endless wanderings, for she had had her fill of life and adventure and love affairs and sex and was no longer able to enjoy them, and if Besh had proposed marriage to her she might have accepted him, even on that first night when they left Erwin's house and dashed around the town in a taxi because Ruhama had a craving to eat *hamin* and *kishke* in a restaurant overlooking the sea, but in the end they were obliged to forgo the *hamin* and the *kishke* and they returned to Jaffa and ate a big, rich meal in a nice restaurant overlooking the sea, where a fleet of fishing boats bobbed on the waves with their lamps, but

Besh did not ask her to marry him because Besh, who loved eating, had only one thing on his mind, and that was to finish the meal as quickly as possible and take Ruhama home and get into bed with her, and that was all he could think about on the other nights too, and before Caesar had driven halfway to Haifa and back to Tel Aviv again Besh and Ruhama were already rolling about on Besh's bed in his filthy and neglected apartment, after which they turned their backs to each other and went to sleep, and a little while later Caesar drove back into town and through the dark, deserted streets, and when he passed the studio he saw a dim light in the window and for a moment he thought of going up to visit Israel, who had fallen asleep without switching off the light, but he went on driving and parked his car outside Tehilla's apartment, where she was lying in bed and reading, and when he saw her he wanted to placate her and give her a little pleasure, and there was something attractive to him in her tiredness, and he made love to her and fell asleep, and the next morning when he woke up, Israel switched off the light and got up and showered and had a cup of coffee and took his music, and just as he was about to leave the studio the phone rang and it was Goldman speaking from his office and he told him that he had been called up for reserve duty in three weeks' time and Israel advised him to try to get out of it, but Goldman said, "Why should I? It's a godsend," and Israel said, "In that case, good," and Goldman said, "Hang on, we've got to celebrate," and Israel said, "Whatever you like," and Goldman said, "Maybe you'll come over to my place this evening?" and Israel said, "Maybe, but don't wait for me," and they said goodbye and Israel put the receiver down and went outside and walked along the seashore.

There was still an early morning chill in the air and the horizon was wreathed in a delicate mist, but otherwise the sky was clear and blue and beneath it was the sea, a little choppy, and far away in the distance, opposite the entrance to the Jaffa port, where the beachfront houses and the pink church and the minarets of the mosques were already bathed in the strong light of the sun, white seagulls hovered, as always, above the water. Israel walked slowly in the cool shade which the buildings bordering the promenade still cast on the pavement and the street, looking at the sea and the bathers and the fishermen standing on the rocks and the sewage pipes and casting their rods into the sea with infinite patience in the hope of catching a fish, and afterward, the closer he came to Jaffa, the farther he strayed from the sea until in the end it disappeared entirely and he caught only an occasional glimpse of it between the houses, and he walked along the streets which were so familiar to him, at first with their ugly stone houses and shacks improvised out of tin and planks and one-story houses made of concrete blocks, whitewashed and surrounded by fences, all jumbled together and interspersed with junkyards and seedy garages, and after them came the streets of big stone houses, all grimy and dusty, full of high arched windows and little balconies with rusty iron railings, and as he walked Israel looked at the passersby and the fruit and vegetable stalls and the bakeries and fishmongers' stalls, where different kinds of fish were displayed in their crates, some of them covered with ice, and at the shoe shops and furniture shops and the welding and carpentry shops and little printing works, most of which were crowded into narrow storerooms and basements and dark warehouses, and in the end, when he passed the bend in the road along which he was walking and it widened out and opened up in front of him in several directions, from one of which the sea came into view again, he found himself face to face with the white church, and he approached the big garden surrounding it with its cypresses and tamarisk and poplar trees and loquats and bougainvillea and hibiscus and yellow sunflowers and roses and carnations and geraniums and gladiola, and he went in at the gate and confronted the bas relief on the façade depicting Jesus kneeling and holding out his hands to a small child, who was St. Antonio, and he walked along the path which was covered with a layer of gravel and broken seashells and greeted the gardener, who was standing and hoeing the ground between the flowers, and then he greeted the priest, a short, sturdy man with a white beard and suspicious, bespectacled eyes and a black skullcap on his head, who was standing in the shady hall in a dark brown habit and responded to Israel's greeting with a nod of his head and accompanied him with silent footsteps, his hands crossed behind his back, to the heavy wooden door leading to the interior of the church, and Israel thanked him and climbed the narrow stairs leading to the organ gallery opposite which, on the far side of the church, were three very big, long windows made of stained glass, depicting Jesus in a red robe with St. Claire on his left hand and St. Francis on his right. Israel sat down in front of the organ and opened his music and began to play, and his face with its refined and ascetic features and high forehead looked very serious as his long, hard fingers moved over the keys, and struck the deep, dense notes which spread out gradually until they filled the empty church, which was shrouded in darkness but for the dim light filtering through the stained glass windows and illuminating the thick marble pillars and the brown benches and the altar with its brass candlesticks and big globes, and reverberated in the cool air, heavy with the smell of incense and old furniture and cold stones.

Israel played for a couple of hours, and when he had finished he collected his music and descended the narrow stairs and thanked the old priest, who once again responded with a nod of his head, and went out through the garden, which was bathed in the harsh light of the afternoon sun, shining down from the middle of the empty, burning sky, a faded blue sky, and walked down the street, which was sweltering in the heat, keeping as close as he could to the strip of shade cast by the walls of the buildings, and passed a bakery and smelled the fresh *pitot* and the pretzels sprinkled with sesame seeds and thyme, and soon afterward he crossed the street and turned into a shady alley and entered a fish restaurant where he sometimes ate with Ella, and sat down at one of the tables among the workers who filled the place, some of them in their undershirts and some of them half naked, and after a few minutes the man who fried the fish in a big vat full of boiling oil put one in front of him with a quarter of a loaf of white bread and a few hot peppers. The restaurant, which was small and completely unadorned and resembled an old storeroom painted pale green and furnished with a few chairs and Formica-covered tables, was full of the smell of the fish frying in the oil and the people sitting near the door could also get a whiff of the pungent smells of animal hides and turpentine and varnish and stagnant water drifting in from the alley, together with the noise coming from the carpentry shops and shoemakers and mingling with the roar of the kerosene burner under the fish kettle and the loud voices of the workers, who glanced at the newspapers as they ate and spoke to each other in Hebrew and Bulgarian and Arabic to the strains of the Oriental music blaring out of the restaurant across the street, where people were sitting on little stools on the narrow pavement and the street playing dominoes and backgammon and drinking Turkish coffee in little china cups and dark tea flavored with mint, and occasionally they broke into arguments or shouted and their shouts mingled with the shouts of the man frying the fish, who was dressed like a building worker and wearing a dirty apron and standing in front of the fish kettle with his face to the alley and shouting, "Fish! Fish!" from time to time, beating his huge fork against the sides of the kettle, and Israel, indifferent to all the commotion around him, ate his fish slowly, and when he had finished he wiped his hands on an old newspaper and paid and went outside and walked in the burning sun and let the sweat pour down his face and neck, his eyes roaming over the silver-blue sea which was now very calm and covered with a shimmering haze.

Two weeks before he had still come this way with Ella, who had disappeared in the wake of another quarrel which had broken out between them, during the course of which he had again told her to go away and never come back again, and he wondered if he shouldn't go over to her place and apologize and bring her back, and this thought, which had started nagging at him a few days after Ella had stopped coming, would not let him be and came into his head when he got up in the morning and on his way to the church, and when he sat and ate his fish, and on his way home in the sweltering heat, and in the evening, which was the time when Ella usually came to him, but whenever it came into his head it was immediately followed by a sullen resistance and rage, which prevented him from doing what he would have liked to do, and so the weeks passed until it was time for Goldman to go into the army, where he served as a medical orderly attached to a unit stationed in the Sinai desert, and on the eve of his departure he invited Israel and Caesar to have dinner with him at Helfgott's, but just before they were due to meet Caesar called Israel and told him that he wouldn't be able to make it because Tehilla had bought tickets to the movies and she wanted him to spend the evening with her.

He sounded very irritable and dejected and before putting the receiver down he said, "Man, I've had it. Life's a load of shit," and after a short pause he added, "They just won't let you live," and he asked Israel to tell Goldman that he didn't feel well and wouldn't be able to come, and Israel, who listened to him silently, asked him why he couldn't call Goldman and tell him himself, and Caesar said, "I haven't got the heart. He'll be hurt," and he immediately added, "You do it for me. I'm asking you nicely," and Israel said, "OK," and when he met Goldman he gave him the message and Goldman didn't react, as if he hadn't heard what Israel was saying, although later on he said, "He's a liar, Caesar, but it doesn't matter," but at the time his only response was to suggest that instead of going to Helfgott's they should try a more intimate Romanian restaurant where the food was excellent.

Goldman wasn't stingy, but his attitude toward money was careful and full of anxiety, and this was a source of constant distress to him because he was always busy with calculations and obsessed with regrets, and this character trait seemed to him a shameful and unmanly weakness, and with all his heart he wished that he could overcome it and despise money and behave like Caesar did—with careless extravagance—and indeed from time to time he would go on a binge and squander large sums of money at once, but the feelings of pride and enjoyment he derived from these bursts of extravagance were short-lived, because he would soon emerge from his intoxication and succumb to torturing regrets and eat his heart out because of the reckless foolishness with which he had wasted his money, and he would calculate how much he had spent and think about what he had spent it on and reproach himself for it bitterly, and for some time afterward he would try to economize in order to recover even a small part of the money he had squandered, and although his attempts to economize, together with the petty and annoying calculations which accompanied them, humiliated him and distressed him far more than the extravagance they were supposed to atone for, he could not overcome this tendency in his nature and was obliged to spend much time and effort on suppressing it each time it manifested itself anew.

He now suggested to Israel that they go to Nello's place, although Mon Jardin was also a fine restaurant, and so was the one next to the tennis courts, but in his opinion the atmosphere at Nello's was more agreeable and Nello had a big selection of hors d'oeuvres and all kinds of stuffed fish and it was worth going there just for the sake of the sauerkraut, which was the best in town, but of course they could also go to Stephan's or to the *couscous* place, and Israel said it made no difference to him where they ate and it was up to Goldman, and Goldman said, "Good, let's go to Nello's," and he stopped a cab and they drove to the restaurant, which at this early hour of the evening was still empty but for Nello and his wife, who were sitting at a bare table in the corner which served them as an office and cash desk playing backgammon, and the man behind the counter, who was standing smoking a cigarette, and the waiter, who was sitting near him reading the newspaper with his legs crossed.

Goldman went in first, took two or three steps, and stopped and looked around him, and Nello's wife raised her eyes from the backgammon board and smiled at them, and Goldman nodded at her and at Nello, who had just thrown the dice, and went up to a corner table and hesitated for a moment and then went up to another table in the middle of a row on the other side of the room, but before sitting down he looked around him again and then went back to the first table and sat down at it, and Israel sat down opposite him, and Goldman, who only now allowed himself to relax, smiled a proprietary smile and picked up the menu and said, "This is the best literature I know," and started reading the list of dishes aloud, and in the background they heard the dice shaking and the backgammon counters clicking on the board and the radio playing Balkan music, whose horns and violins, sinuous and curling as the tendrils of a vine, were full of tenderness and yearning and melancholy and the sweet taste of fig trees and smoke and dry blossoming and breaking waves and suppressed desires, and while Goldman studied the menu and considered what to order, commenting from time to time on this dish or that and reminiscing sorrowfully and greedily about dishes which he had once enjoyed and which were no longer to be found on the menu—for he loved talking about food—the waiter, who had a sad and indifferent face and looked like Charles Aznavour, approached them and said, "Yes, please," and Goldman, who was now in high spirits, told Israel to order first, and he ordered brains in tomato sauce and rice cooked with spinach, and Goldman ordered stuffed eggplant and a salad of zucchini and nuts, and he also ordered a double portion of sauerkraut for both of them and a bottle of red wine.

Outside it was already dark and inside the restaurant the neon lights shone down on the many tables covered with white tablecloths and standing in rows in the big, cold hall between the light blue walls, which were very high and adorned with brightly colored tapestries depicting blue lakes and waterfalls and grapevines and palm trees with round orange suns rising between them and ruddy buxom women sitting in green meadows holding bunches of huge grapes, women whom Nello's wife resembled so closely it seemed she must have come down from one of the tapestries on the wall in order to enjoy a game of backgammon, and Goldman broke off a piece of the bread in the basket and glanced at the tapestries and at Nello and his wife and said, "How happy they are," and smiled with pleasure, and Israel, who did not know whom, precisely, he had in mind, said "Yes," and Goldman said, "People complicate their lives," and he put the piece of bread into his mouth and said that the best steak in the world came from Japanese cows, which were fed on beer, giving their meat a special taste and spots of fat as in a sausage, and in the meantime the waiter brought their orders and the bottle of wine, and Goldman filled their glasses and said, "Pity Caesar isn't here," and they raised their glasses and drank and began to eat.

Goldman tasted the eggplant and said, "The eggplant is excellent," and his face glowed, and afterward he expressed his enthusiasm for the zucchini, and especially for the sauerkraut, which he praised in the highest terms, licking his lips and urging Israel to taste it, and the sauerkraut, which really was very good, was soon finished and Goldman ordered another double portion and said, "See how good life can be," and sipped his wine and said that he was glad to be going into the army because he was dying to get away from home and his mother and the office, which he couldn't stand any more, and from the city, and to be in nature, to see sand and rocks and bushes and birds and sky, and meet new people, because in addition to the pleasure he would get out of all this he believed that it would also constitute the first step toward changing his life—at any rate, this was what he wanted to happen—and he took another sip of wine and said, "God knows why I went and studied law and Latin and all that stuff," and he wiped the plate clean with a piece of bread, sopping up the remains of the stuffing of the eggplant and the gravy, and beckoned the waiter, who was standing and talking to the man behind the counter, and said, "Pity it's finished," and afterward he said, "I could have boarded a ship and stayed on the sea. In any case, everything should have been different," and the waiter approached them and Israel ordered sea fish cooked in butter and mushrooms for his second course while Goldman decided on roast mutton and rice with okra, and he also ordered two helpings of baked vegetables, and afterward he said, "This isn't the most dietetic food in the world," and Israel said, "Never mind," and Goldman said, "I'm going to start on that American diet soon," and he refilled their glasses with wine and said that he hoped his unit would be sent to the front lines and prayed there would be shooting incidents so that he could take part in them, and then he glanced at Nello and his wife, who were talking to each other in loud voices, apparently about the game, and said that he wasn't afraid of being killed but of being wounded and losing one of his limbs, especially his penis.

He made this last remark in a jocular tone of voice and smiled at Israel, who smiled back at him and said that he could put in a request for a discharge or a transfer to a noncombat unit, but Goldman said again that he was glad to be going to the army and that he liked his unit, and a moment later, nibbling on a piece of bread, he said that the coming weeks, when he would be out of town and far away, would probably be decisive for his relationship with Dita, which had reached a turning point—they would either get married or put an end to the affair once and for all—and he sipped his wine and said again that he had a feeling his life was about to undergo a radical transformation, and he drew up the plate of mutton which the waiter had placed before him and examined it closely and glanced at Israel's fish and said, "Terrific, eh?" and tasted the baked vegetables and said, "Fantastic. Come on, help yourself," and then he examined his mutton again and started eating and said, "It's a good thing we came here," and began eating greedily to the accompaniment of sucking and grunting noises, laughing from time to time, partly for pleasure and partly because the wine had gone to his head, and he filled his glass again and also urged Israel to drink some more, and he said that he had read somewhere that the best and most expensive wine in the world was produced in Indonesia by drowning monkeys in the wine vats, and afterward he re-

turned to the subject of Dita and said that they had no alternative
but to part ways because their relationship had become burdensome and oppressive and full of bitterness, and he filled his mouth
with food and looked at Israel and waited for a moment, with
his greenish eyes glittering and his perspiring face beaming, for
him to say something, but Israel said nothing and Goldman dipped
a piece of bread in the mutton gravy and said, "For two pins I'd
go to a moshav," and paused a moment and said, "A man has to
learn to live alone," and then he said, "He's a liar, Caesar. But
never mind," and put the piece of bread into his mouth and said
pleasantly and with a twinkle in his eye that he envied him, and
also Moishe Tzellermaier, because he was such a simple man,
without any education or culture or subtlety, and in fact Moishe
Tzellermaier had indeed married and fathered children with almost the same naturalness as he ate and drank, won or lost at
cards, and helped other people, and it seemed that even his terrible memories did not bother him, and nor did his good fortune—for he should have died ten times over and he was alive
and he should have gone bankrupt a dozen times and instead
his pockets were full of money—but he accepted all this with
equanimity, without any gratitude or even surprise, and his days
went by in an endless round of busy activities and hard work,
with no goal or ambition in mind but to provide the best he
could for his children and to secure their future, and now he
was happy because his son had finally given in to his wishes and
agreed to go to America with a view to settling there, and he had
already obtained a passport for him and made all the arrangements necessary for his trip, and he would have been even happier if his son could have said goodbye to Goldman's father,
who had turned his back on Moishe Tzellermaier when he was
alive because after working for five years in a shoe factory he
had opened his own little business and began dealing in leather
and afterward also in imported footwear, and in the last year of
his life also because of Moishe Tzellermaier's attempts to persuade his son to emigrate to America, which was the worst of all

as far as he was concerned, and all this lowered Moishe Tzeller-maier in the eyes of Goldman's father, who felt cheated and in-jured, but at the same time, in some strange way, continued to feel, together with all his resentment and anger, a patronizing and proprietary affection for him, but Moishe Tzellermaier took no notice of all this and never for a single minute did he forget all the favors which Goldman's father had done him without ex-pecting anything in return and he felt all the respect and grati-tude and love for him that he would have felt for a benevolent father, and not only for him but also for Stefana and Goldman. He had been overwhelmed by Goldman's father's illness and had gone to visit him in the hospital every day, sometimes twice a day, tiptoeing silently in and out of the room, standing at a re-spectful distance without saying a word, sometimes lightly touch-ing his head and quietly retreating again, and during the funeral service and the burial, standing a little apart from the other mourners, he had wept without stopping and his broken-hearted, uncontrollable sobbing had shocked and angered Goldman, who stubbornly refused to look at him, more than anything else hap-pening around him at the time—and he now looked away from Israel and cut himself a piece of the delicious meat on his plate and smiled and said that the truth was that he didn't really envy Caesar or Moishe Tzellermaier but Avinoam, with whom he had gone to school and with whom he had served in the army dur-ing the War of Independence until Avinoam was wounded and sent to America to recover, and after his recovery he stayed there and studied agriculture and six years later he came back to Israel with his wife Audrey, the daughter of a rich industrialist in Utah, and their oldest son Jochanan, and settled on a moshav and worked hard and built up a flourishing farm.

When Goldman had visited them, about eight years before, Audrey was already exhausted, and despite her girlish body and smiling face there was little left of the fresh American beauty which Goldman had so much admired the first time he saw her at Matilda Leviatan's a few days after they arrived in the country, but both of them—she and Avinoam, who was still strong and handsome although he suffered from terrible headaches as a result of his old war wound—were very happy with their country life and farm and three children, and something of that happiness and contentment, which reminded him of the happiness of his childhood visits to Joel and Zipporah when they lived on a moshav, had infected him when he arrived at twilight and saw the moshav bathed in the tranquillity of a summer evening after the day's work was done and when he went out on the first morning of his visit to the clover patch with Avinoam and lifted the clover Avinoam cut with a pitchfork and helped Avinoam lift it onto the cart, and afterward, after breakfast, he helped him move the irrigation pipes in the common fields, and from there he went to clean out the cow shed and scattered straw on the floor and gave the cows their fodder, and the stuffiness and heat in the shed and the pungent smell of the manure distressed him, and bits of straw and dust from the fodder got into his shoes and underneath his clothes and stuck to the skin on his neck and face and made him feel unbearably itchy, and straight after lunch, his body limp with fatigue, he went back to the cotton fields, this time alone, to shift the irrigation pipes again, but now the whole area was covered with a heavy cloud of moisture rising from the irrigated ground and the cotton plants, and clouds of maddening gnats got into his nose and eyes and ears and filled the heavy, sweltering air with cobwebs, and Goldman, puffing and sweating, could hardly drag his feet through the sticky mud, and he felt very tired and irritated and impatient, as if it would never end, and only in the evening, at sunset, when the air grew light and pleasant again and everything was bathed in tranquillity, he too relaxed and after taking a shower and changing his clothes he went for a little walk with Avinoam through the moshav, and later on, after Avinoam had finished milking and tidied himself up, he sat with him and with Audrey on the veranda, where the mosquitoes gave them no peace, and they talked, a forced and uninteresting conversation, until Avinoam, who could hardly keep his eyes open, said "Bedtime," and they all got up and went to bed. Goldman had intended to spend a week with them, but on the fourth day, after hesitating for two days, he parted from them on some flimsy excuse and went back to town, and nevertheless this visit remained in his memory as something wonderful, full of freedom and freshness and contentment, and this impression did not fade with the passing of time but on the contrary, and he put into his mouth the piece of meat he had cut with some rice and okra and said, "They're happy there, Avinoam and his wife and children," and a moment later he said, "I wish I could have a farm and live on a moshav. Maybe it's not too late," and he waited for a reaction from Israel, who took a fish bone out of his mouth and put it on the edge of his plate and looked at him and asked him how his mother was, and Goldman, as if waking from a trance, said, "Very well. She's going crazy," and gave a short laugh—he was slightly drunk—and laughed again, and when he had recovered he said that lately she had begun speaking Polish almost exclusively and reading only Polish books and newspapers and behaving as if she lived in Poland, and in his opinion she really did believe that she was living there, or at any rate she tried to force herself to believe it, and Israel asked him if he was intending not to do anything about it and Goldman said, "What?" and cut himself another piece of meat and said that he should really send her to a psychiatrist, but he thought it was a waste of money and it would be better to wait for her insanity to pass of its own accord, and he drank the wine remaining in his glass and refilled it and after a moment's reflection he said that he had the feeling she was better off now than she had ever been before, and that in any case it was the most she wanted or was capable of achieving, and he had grave doubts as to whether he had the right or the duty to interfere and destroy her happiness, which others might regard as madness but which as far as she was concerned was a paradise to which she had been readmitted the day her husband died, which had, apparently, been one of the happiest days of her life, and when he said this Goldman burst out laughing, and then, with the smile still on his face, he said that he had often wondered if they went to bed together, and Israel said, "Who?" and Goldman said, "My parents," and took a sip of wine and said that in recent years this question had often engaged his attention and he had the feeling that they hadn't done it for a very long time, twenty or even thirty years, although it was a well-known fact that according to the findings of research conducted mainly in America a very high percentage of men and women, over fifty per cent, were capable of doing it at the age of seventy, and past seventy too, and of enjoying it, and many of them in fact did do it, but he didn't think that his parents were among them, and not because of their age or physiological reasons but because his mother loathed his father and she had never, or so it seemed to him, taken any interest in sex, while his father hated his mother so much that he could have lived like a monk for a hundred years if only in order to humiliate her and make both their lives a misery.

Here Goldman paused for a moment to take some baked vegetables—there was hardly anything left of the mutton—and said that he was sure that his mother had never gone to bed with another man, maybe with Manfred, and the same went for his father, but for different reasons, although looking back today he thought that he had been attracted to Tzimmer's widow, who had been unfaithful to her husband without even trying to hide it, and wanted to go to bed with her, and as he was collecting the last of the rice and okra on his fork he suddenly asked Israel if he had ever been afraid of impotence. Israel looked at Goldman for a moment with a startled expression on his face, and Goldman, who was so embarrassed by his own question that he blushed, giggled, and asked it again, but he didn't wait for an answer and said that the reason he asked the question was that it was today known that fear of impotence was very common among men of all ages, much more common than people supposed, and most researchers today agreed that if impotence in the broadest sense of the word was taken into account then forty or fifty per cent of men suffered from chronic impotence, and there wasn't a man alive who hadn't suffered from temporary impotence, whose causes were mostly psychological, stemming from insecurity and various kinds of anxiety, which in turn stemmed very often from false perceptions and exaggerated expectations regarding male virility, perceptions which came into being as a result of all kinds of rumors and boasts and tall tales told by other men, and, of course, were encouraged by the movies and television and magazines, and to a large extent also by the clothing, cigarette, food, and cosmetics industries. Goldman continued expanding on this theme as they finished their meal with a double portion of Bavarian cream pie and Turkish coffee and said that it was impossible to imagine life without sexuality, even negative sexuality, but that sex should be protected not only from puritanism but also from those who spun webs of falsehood and frenzy around it, and he wiped his face, which was perspiring, and said, "I've had too much to eat," and then he said, "It's very unhealthy," and Israel said, "You don't do it every day," and Goldman, who was drinking his coffee in little sips, said that they could always imitate the Romans and stick a finger or a feather down their throats to make themselves vomit, by which means they could both enjoy their food and protect themselves from its ill effects, and he laughed, and beckoned to the waiter, who came and presented him with the bill, and he glanced at it and then they both stood up and went over to Nello and his wife, and Goldman said, "It was fantastic," and Nello's wife said, "As long as you enjoyed it," and Goldman, who was merry with the wine and the food and the extravagance, said, "I wouldn't mind living right here in your restaurant," and he held the money out to Nello, who laughed together with his wife, who took hold of Goldman's extended hand playfully and said, "Open it for a minute," and Goldman opened his hand and showed her his palm and said, "You know about those things?" and she said, "You'll see in a minute," and Nello said, "She knows," and gave Goldman his change, and Nello's wife held Goldman's outstretched hand and moved her finger over his palm and said that the line of the heart showed he was a man of strong feelings, and his emotions were more powerful than his logic, and smiling slightly she said that he was fond of women but he remained attached to one woman, and then she said that he was sensitive to beauty and order and that he could be very lucky with money, business, or cards, but he was afraid, and she fell silent for a moment and said that his line of fate showed that something nice was going to happen to him soon, probably in connection with a woman, and his line of life was long but twisted, and if he was careful of water she predicted a long life for him, and Goldman smiled and said, "Thank you, Mrs. Nello," and he said goodbye to Nello and his wife and when he and Israel had left the restaurant he said, "It's all nonsense of course, but maybe I'd better stop going to the beach," and he laughed, and when they reached the corner he asked Israel if he didn't think that he should have left a tip for the waiter and Israel said, "No, it's all right," and Goldman said, "Yes, you're right," and a moment later he said, "After all, they get a salary," and a moment after that he said, "I must start that American diet."

It wasn't very late but the streets they passed through, commercial streets, were silent and deserted, even the cars were few and far between, and they walked in silence until Goldman, who was feeling tired and heavy from the meal, asked Israel how Ella was and Israel said, "OK," and Goldman asked him if he wasn't thinking of marrying her and Israel said, "Maybe," and Goldman, who liked this old neighborhood, which gave rise to many sentimental feelings in him, said that he really should have married Dita and had children and a home like Avinoam, because that was the accepted social norm and the accepted social norm was important, and because with all its failings and difficulties family life was still the most real and fruitful possibility, with every other way of life leading to emptiness and degeneration, but he didn't do it and his life slipped by in futility and indecision and the anticipation of some event which would sweep him away and rescue him in an instant from the dreary daily routine and fill his life with contentment and give it a clear, perhaps even thrilling, meaning, and he was even prepared for this event to appear in the guise of a catastrophe, although he hoped that it would be a great, fatal love, like in the books and the movies which he often ridiculed, a love whose object sometimes appeared in the form of Jeanne Moreau and sometimes in the form of Elinore, but nothing happened and life went on in the same dreary routine, full of the feeling of futility, and his barren expectations turned into a despairing habit of thought and feeling accompanied by a whole set of empty speculations and self-deceptions, because no Jeanne Moreau appeared and Elinore became more and more wraithlike and lost all substantiality, although both Stefana and Manfred mentioned her occasionally over the years, and Goldman too would speak of her from time to time, as he did now too, walking with Israel along King George Street beside the row of giant sycamore trees towering in the middle of the road, but as usual Goldman said nothing clear or exact about her, for her personality remained opaque to him, and veiled in the magic of their first meeting, and the only thing he was able to say about her appearance was that she was tall and had thick lips and blue eyes and a very white, almost bluish skin, and that she gave off a special smell which was hard to define—sometimes he said it was like the smell of a very good soap, perhaps a little sour, and sometimes like pine trees—but all these words came from abstract knowledge and not from living memories, for in his memory she existed only as a yearning for something vague and undefined, and he repeated them now and added, as usual, that there was something lost and in need of protection about her which he found attractive, even compelling, and he hoped that he would have a chance to meet her at least once more.

Goldman spoke about Elinore gladly and excitedly and pronounced her name lovingly, as if it were a magic spell by whose means he could bring back the past and make Elinore come back to him and do his bidding, and as he spoke they left the sycamore trees behind them and crossed Bograshov Street and when they reached the solitary sycamore tree next to the curb which had once marked the boundary of the neighborhood of the old shacks he stopped and surveyed the empty space which had once been a world full of life, to which he was bound by many threads of memory and longing, and as he stood and stared at the expanse of sand where this extinct world had once stood a group of youngsters approached, laughing loudly and pushing each other, and Goldman moved aside to let them pass, and afterward he said, "Savages. I'd like to kill them one by one," and then he said, "It's not my town any more, and it never will be. It's just a pile of shit," and as they walked on he turned his eyes again to the empty lot where two years before, at the end of a long and gradual process, most of the shacks which had once populated it had already been demolished, leaving only a few solitary survivors standing blackened and dilapidated, looking like a little flock of refugees who had lost the remnants of their will to live. One of the surviving shacks was the one which had once belonged to Uncle Lazar and Rachel, which many years ago had been purchased from Max Spillman by Chaim-Leib, who had renovated it and added the room in which he had stationed the antique wooden mangle, for Chaim-Leib had obstinately refused to move out and for years he had conducted a stubborn campaign against the municipality and the company which had bought the land from it with the intention of putting up giant buildings with offices and shops and cafes and restaurants and a movie theater, because the compensation offered him for evacuating his home amounted in his eyes to nothing but daylight robbery and brazen fraud, and thus, with all the surrounding shacks abandoned and demolished, Chaim-Leib remained where he was with Mrs. Haya, but the last time Goldman had visited him, dropping by without any advance notice as usual, it was already due to be demolished in a few months' time, Chaim-Leib having at long last come to an agreement with the municipality and the construction company.

Goldman had knocked on the door and waited happily for Chaim-Leib to open it and stand opposite him on the threshold, for there was something radiant and wise and full of life in Chaim-Leib and all his ways, and he liked eating and drinking and reading the newspapers, wandering in the streets and getting into all kinds of idle conversations and political arguments, and he also liked *pidyon ha-ben,* briss, and bar mitzvah celebrations, weddings and funerals, and altogether he lived in harmony with the world and God, and Goldman—who in his childhood and youth had spent many hours watching in fascination as Chaim-Leib turned the handle of the mangle, his hands thick and heavy as those of a building worker—felt more affection for him than for almost anyone else in his parents' circle, and nevertheless since he had grown up years would go by without their meeting, and four years, or perhaps even more, had passed since their last meeting, which was at the funeral of Shmuel and Aharon's father, who had spent his declining years in an old age home, and Chaim-Leib had walked among the mourners in his best black hat with his hands behind his back and Mrs. Haya, wearing a small beige felt hat, beside him; it had rained in the night but in the morning the weather had turned fine, and when he passed Goldman he had smiled and said in Yiddish, "You don't have to worry. God doesn't forget anybody," and Goldman smiled and wiped his face with his handkerchief and looked around him and knocked on the door again.

It was the middle of summer and the giant sycamore tree exuded a pungent smell, giving rise in Goldman to memories of the virgin fields and vineyards and Arab villages, and its crushed fruit lay on the ground and stained the pavement and the street, where cars drove swiftly by, and on the other side of the street, close to the place where the two bears had danced with the monkey, was a movie theater with a huge poster on its façade depicting a man with a mustache carrying a beautiful blonde in a white summer dress in his arms, and Goldman looked at them and while he was doing so the door opened and Chaim-Leib came out, his brown eyes sunken and his yellowing face shriveled, his body emaciated and his belly so shrunken that his pants were gathered in folds around his waist and a long piece of his belt dangled uselessly. Goldman held out his hand and said, "Shalom, Chaim-Leib," but Chaim-Leib stood staring at him with lifeless eyes and did not recognize him, and only after Goldman had told him his name and his father's and mother's names a faint smile appeared on Chaim-Leib's lips and he limply shook Goldman's hand, which had been suspended in the air all this time, and invited him in, and they went into the front room, which had once been big and high and dark—although the walls were white-washed and full of the smell of starched laundry on weekdays and of cooking and bedclothes on Saturdays—and which was now light and small, and the old furniture, which was still standing there mixed up with a few new pieces, had lost its charm and gave rise in Goldman to a feeling of disappointment, as did the white electric presser, which they had not operated now for a year and which stood in the corner instead of the old wooden mangle with all its mystery.

Mrs. Haya came in from the kitchen, flustered as usual by the arrival of a visitor, dragging her feet in slippers which were much too big and holding the skin of a turkey neck and a needle and white thread in her damp hands, and when she saw Goldman her withered face, all wrinkled like the skin on top of boiled milk, broke into a beaming smile and she uttered a joyful little shriek and hurried back into the kitchen and returned, wiping her hands on her apron, and took his hand in hers, which was still damp. Mrs. Haya was a tall and slightly stooping woman whose appearance somehow reminded Goldman of the leg of a chicken, the blue of her eyes had faded and all her glory had fallen into ruin and nothing was left of the beauty, or at least the delicacy, which she had possessed in her youth, when she had worn fine silks and wools and washed her face with Lilac Milk, and as the daughter of wealthy parents—her father was a tailor who made clothes for rich men—who had lived fashionably until they lost their money and sat at dinnertime clinking their silver spoons on almost empty Rosenthal plates, she had also learned to play a little

on the piano, which was unusual for those days, but her father—
who was a rather eccentric man and liked walking around in the
middle of the day all dressed up in fancy clothes with a silver-
knobbed cane and talking German—wanted his daughter to have
piano lessons, and altogether she had lived a pampered life until
she married Chaim-Leib, who dragged her off to Eretz Yisrael
despite the pleas of her parents, especially her mother, who begged
them to stay in Poland, and despite the efforts of his brother, who
wrote him many letters urging him to join him in America, where
he could get rich, but Chaim-Leib, who now went with Mrs. Haya
and Goldman into the other room, took no notice of any of them
because he did not want to stay in Poland until the Poles drove
him out and because his heart was full of love for Eretz Yisrael.

Mrs. Haya asked Goldman how his parents were and Goldman
replied, "They're fine, thank you, Auntie Haya," and Chaim-Leib,
who smelled strongly and disagreeably of old age, said, "Lazar
was here a few days ago with his lady friend," and they sat down
at the round table, which was covered with an old green velvet
cloth decorated with enormous orange and yellow and purple
flowers, and Mrs. Haya placed a bottle of brandy in front of them,
and red cut-glass tumblers, and slices of herring on a long cut-
glass dish, and homemade onion pretzels which she took out of
an old breakfast cereal container with a picture of a sunburnt
man wearing a broad-brimmed straw hat on it, and then she
poured them each a drink, filling Goldman's glass to the brim
and giving Chaim-Leib hardly enough to cover the bottom of the
glass, and they clinked glasses and drank, and Chaim-Leib said,
"Take a piece of Jewish herring," and gave the herring dish a
push in Goldman's direction. He himself did not touch the herring because after the operation he had undergone a few months
previously his doctors had forbidden him to eat such things, just
as they had forbidden him to drink, and Goldman took a piece
of herring and ate it by himself together with an onion pretzel,
and Chaim-Leib said, "Have you put on *tefillin* today?" and Goldman said, "Not yet," and Chaim-Leib said, "Why put on *tefillin?*

You can get on all right without it," and Mrs. Haya said, "Eat eat. I made it myself," and hurried back to the kitchen, and Chaim-Leib said, "It'll all come back to you in the end. Nothing will help you," and fell silent.

Almost nothing survived of his radiant warmth and sparkling vitality and he was sunk in weakness and apathy, as if he were full of dust, and all Goldman's efforts to stimulate him and make him talk were to no avail, and but for an isolated word or two he said nothing, only once rousing himself to say, "If Begin was in power everything would look different, but even Begin isn't Begin any more. He's become a good boy too," and chuckling, and Goldman chuckled too, but not in enjoyment or amusement, and took another piece of herring and averted his face from Chaim-Leib because he couldn't bear the smell of old age coming from him, and looked out of the window onto the street, where the low loam hills and sand dunes had once stretched out under the open sky, which in Goldman's memory was always blue, and through which he had once seen the Arab in the black *abbaya* and the *keffiyeh* making the two bears and the monkey dance on the sand of the road, although Stefana claimed that it had happened a very long time ago, perhaps even before he was born, and in any case even if he had seen it he couldn't possibly have remembered, but he did remember it all as if it had happened yesterday and this filled him with perplexity, just as he was always filled with perplexity, although a different kind of perplexity, and also uneasiness, by the fact that Chaim-Leib, the worker and pioneer who had been so close to his father and Joel and Zipporah and Uncle Lazar and all the rest of their circle, supported the Revisionists and the IZL, and a good many years had to pass before Goldman, who now turned away from the window and glanced at Chaim-Leib, succeeded in overcoming this perplexity in his heart, and suddenly, in a flash of insight, he saw himself reflected in the mirror of Chaim-Leib's old age and all at once he realized that old age was not something foreign to him and outside him but, on the contrary, it was part of his very being in this world, and it was moving toward him, and in fact already casting the tip of its shadow on him, a shadow which would grow and spread until it engulfed him completely, and he took another pretzel, and Mrs. Haya asked him again how his parents were and he said again, "They're fine," and Mrs. Haya said, "Thank God. Our Shlomo's wife has been sick for two weeks now, maybe it's the food," and Chaim-Leib, who sat without moving and looked without interest at the brandy bottle and the pretzels, said, "I saw your grandfather in a fox fur coat. He seems to have grown rich in the next world," and he chuckled again, and Mrs. Haya said, "That's enough," and pushed the dish of onion pretzels toward Goldman and said, "Eat. I've got plenty more where that came from," and Goldman said, "No thank you. I've already had," and he finished the brandy in his glass and got up to go, and Mrs. Haya said, "Leaving already?" and Goldman said, "I only came to say hello," and at the same time he looked out of the corner of his eye at the picture of the Garden of Eden which was in its usual place above the brown sideboard, and which had left such a profound impression on him in his childhood.

In the center of the picture, in the foreground, stood Adam and Eve in the form of a beautiful, healthy young boy and girl, girdles of fig leaves covering their loins, holding a pink baby in their arms, and all around them, in a kind of green meadow, animals were grazing peacefully—a lion, a tiger, a lamb, a stork, a wolf, a bear, and a peacock—and on either side, on steps which began at the bottom corners of the picture and rose to meet at the top, there stood facing each other a little girl and a little boy, a teen-aged girl and boy, a man and a woman, and at the end, at the top of the picture where the two flights of stairs met, an old man and an old woman leaning on their canes, and above them a kind of flying scroll, which Goldman knew was inscribed with the words, "This is the Law and this is its Reward," and he thanked Mrs. Haya and took his leave of her and of Chaim-Leib, who nodded his head and called after him, "Go and visit your grandmother," and chuckled again, while Mrs. Haya, who accompanied him to the door, screeched in his ear, "Give my regards to your mother and father," and Goldman said, "Yes, I will," and made his exit through the back door, the kitchen door, and went down the two stairs, reflecting again for a split second on the matter of growing old, and walked on the sand which together with the blue sky and the bright open space before him bathed in strong sunlight and silence roused him to a happy excitement, which soon clouded over at the sight of the few derelict shacks still left standing and the wreckage of the demolished shacks scattered over the expanse of sand which was at once so strange and so familiar, and at the far end of which two blocks of buildings, white as paper, thrust themselves surprisingly up into the summer sky.

Goldman plodded through the sand and passed the place where the big shack, which had disappeared without a trace, had once stood, skirted the wild mulberry tree and arrived at the place which had once been the garden in front of Shmuel and Bracha and Grandfather Baruch Chaim and Grandmother Hava's shack, which had been demolished like most of the others, but of which the concrete blocks forming the foundation had miraculously remained standing, tracing the floor plan of the shack on the sand, and Goldman paused for a moment in front of the place where the dovecote, the pride and joy of Grandfather Baruch Chaim, had once stood, and afterward he approached the place where the kitchen, a low, dark lean-to attached to the façade of the shack, had once stood, and walked past it through what had once been the entrance to the big front room—the panes of the high front door had been thick and lumpy and colored a dense yellow like honey—and he stood in the place which had once been occupied by the oval table which had always been covered by a thick, velvet cloth and surrounded by four upright, slender chairs whose backs were carved with worn patterns of stems and leaves and flowers. To the left of the table Shmuel and Bracha had placed a sofa, and above it brown-framed pictures of Grandfather Baruch Chaim and Grandmother Hava, who for years had refused to have her photograph taken for fear of the evil eye, and to the right the big, brown wardrobe where they had hidden Grandmother Hava during the Italian bombardment of Tel Aviv in the Second World War, next to which, at first in a cot and then in a folding bed, Amos had slept. The sand, which had been hidden underneath the floorboard, was now exposed, full of broken glass and china and dead leaves and stems and pieces of coal and scraps of paper borne by the wind, and Goldman bent down and picked up a piece of china and played with it as he went into the second room, which had once held the big iron bed on which Grandmother Hava had slept with Grandfather Baruch Chaim and on which they had laid his body covered with a white sheet, and also a clumsy armchair and a heavy sideboard bearing a few secular and sacred books, and two brass candlesticks. Grandfather Baruch Chaim loved fresh air and the feel of the wind on his body and apart from really rainy days he wanted the window kept open day and night, but Grandmother Hava did not like the dust and suffered from the cold and he gave in to her and so the room, which was almost unbearably stuffy and overcrowded, was always full of the smell of mattresses and down cushions and valerian drops, and although the walls and ceilings were painted a harsh white, like the front room, it was never properly lit, but now everything was wide open and dazzlingly bright—the broad summer sky stretched above Goldman's head with its yellow sun, and the castor oil plant, which used to grow up the side of the shack, penetrated the room with its large leaves, a fresh purplish green— and Goldman, who stood looking around him for one more minute, walked through the wall and went on walking until he came to Dizengoff Street, on the other side of which a giant bulldozer was busy excavating.

From one day to the next, over the space of a few years, the city was rapidly and relentlessly changing its face, and right in front of his eyes it was engulfing the sand lots and the virgin fields, the vineyards and citrus groves and little woods and Arab villages, and afterward the changes began invading the streets of the older parts of the town, which were dotted here and there with simple one-storied houses surrounded by gardens with a few shrubs and flower beds, and sometimes vegetables and strawberries, and also cypress trees and lemon and orange and mandarin trees, or buildings which attempted to imitate the architectural beauties and splendors of Europe, in the style of Paris or Vienna or Berlin, or even of castles and palaces, but all these buildings no longer had any future because they were old and ill adapted to modern tastes and lifestyles, and especially because the skyrocketing prices of land and apartments had turned their existence into a terrible waste and enabled their owners to come into fortunes by selling them, and Goldman, who was attached to these streets and houses because they, together with the sand dunes and virgin fields, were the landscape in which he had been born and grown up, knew that this process of destruction was inevitable, and perhaps even necessary, as inevitable as the change in the population of the town, which in the course of a few years had been filled with tens of thousands of new people, who in Goldman's eyes were invading outsiders who had turned him into a stranger in his own city, but this awareness was powerless to soften the hatred he felt for the new people or the helpless rage which engulfed him at the sight of the destructive plague changing his childhood world and breaking it up, but on the contrary the hatred and rage seethed in him more bitterly than ever and enflamed his longings for the streets and neighborhoods and landscapes which were being wiped out and vanishing without a trace, like the ugly neighborhood of the old shacks lying before him like an empty lot crossed by men and women who walked through it without pausing and cars which sped past without taking any notice—and he quickened his pace a little in order to catch up with Israel, who accompanied him to the entrance of his house, where they stood in the pleasant evening air, and Goldman, watching a couple walking past them, said, "Tomorrow morning before I leave for the army I'll call Dita," and then he said, "I can't believe that a woman could love me," and he smiled and looked at Israel, who plucked a leaf from the ficus tree and crushed it between his fingers without saying a word, and a moment later Goldman said, "Let's take a piss together," and they went down into the dark courtyard and stood behind the hibiscus, near the big cypress trees, and pissed, and Goldman said, "I wish Naomi would come back, even for an hour. It would be wonderful," and then he said, "If she was alive today she would have been fifty in about three years' time—funny, isn't it? She was about twenty-five when that business with the car happened," and afterward a short silence fell between them and Goldman, who could not see Israel's face because they were standing a little withdrawn from each other and so spoke to the darkness, said, "Lately I've been having difficulty falling asleep," and afterward he said, "You know what, the best things in life are those that are never realized," and he tittered softly and said, "That's a banality, but I think it's true," and when they were finished and turned back toward the street he said, "I wish I was happy," and Israel, who felt constrained to say something, said, "Yes. Like everyone else," and picked another ficus leaf, and Goldman smiled and said, "Anyway, the sauerkraut was great, wasn't it?" and Israel said, "Everything was. The fish was fantastic and so was the Bavarian cream pie," and after that they parted with a handshake and said, "So long," and Israel said, "Take care," and Goldman said, "It'll be OK. Say hello to Caesar," and waved his hand and turned into the lobby, and Israel, alone at last, started walking in the direction of the studio, but the mildness of the evening and the light, ruffling touch of the breezes blowing from several directions at once and hinting at the approach of autumn together with the slight sensation of intoxication from the wine he had drunk with his meal aroused his lust and he longed for Ella, to see her and to go to bed with her, and he roamed about in the street for a while before going unwillingly up to the studio.

Too tired to play the piano, Israel took off his shirt and washed his face and picked up a book, and as he lay down on the couch with it the doorbell rang and he got up to answer it, thinking it was Caesar and hoping it was Ella, but it was Eliezra, and when she saw Israel she was surprised and embarrassed but she did her best to hide her embarrassment and asked if Caesar were there, and Israel, who was also embarrassed, said, "No, he's not here," and Eliezra hesitated for a moment and finally said that she had arranged to meet Caesar there at half past nine, and Israel said he thought it was already past that hour but perhaps Caesar had been held up somewhere and he would come later, and he invited Eliezra to come in and wait for him a while, and Eliezra, who was as tanned and fresh as if she had just come from the beach, entered Israel's room and sat down on the edge of the couch and took off the big sunglasses she was wearing.

Israel came in behind her and for a moment there was an uneasy silence in the room, which Israel broke by saying, "He's sure to turn up," and then he said, "It's a bit stuffy in here," and Eliezra said, "Never mind," and Israel asked her if she wanted coffee and Eliezra said, "I'd love some," and Israel went into the kitchen to put the kettle on the burner, and when he came back into the room she asked him what he was playing and Israel said, "Something by Bach" and sat down on the piano stool opposite Eliezra and stole a look at her legs, which were exposed up to above her knees, and Eliezra said that she liked chamber music and pre-classical music, and Israel looked at her neck and shoulders and her sunburnt arms and said, "Goldman likes pre-classical music too," and Eliezra, who was playing with her glasses, said, "But I don't like him," and smiled, and Israel stole another look at her neck and breasts and legs—he was already familiar with them from the photographs Caesar had taken of her standing up getting undressed and lying naked on the couch, and also from the photographs he had taken, directly or by means of the mirrors, of both of them in bed together, and from time to time he showed these photographs to Israel, who was annoyed by what Eliezra had said about Goldman, and above all by the arrogance of her tone, but in spite of this and in spite of her pride and conceit, which was sometimes positively insulting, she gave rise in him, for the first time, to a feeling of sympathy because she was embarrassed and cheated and helpless, and he shrugged his shoulders and said, "What he likes best is vocal music," and went out to make the coffee, but when he came back and they sat drinking their coffee Eliezra started talking about Goldman again and said that he was hopeless and there was no point in feeling sorry for him because he didn't do anything to change his situation and she had no sympathy for people who tried to make other people feel sorry for them, and Israel said, "How about people who don't try to make other people feel sorry for them?" and Eliezra, who was confused by his question, said, "Yes, sometimes I do; anyway, Goldman gets on my nerves," and Israel said nothing and again there was an uneasy silence until Eliezra, whose face was now serious and strained, broke it by suddenly asking Israel if he thought there was any chance that Caesar would marry her, and Israel looked at her face and her brown-green eyes, which were looking at him in anxious expectation, and said, "I think there is," and then he said, "Anyway, I'm sure he loves you."

Eliezra went on looking at him for a moment and then she suddenly burst out laughing and put her coffee cup down and went up to the desk and picked up the paper knife and asked Israel if he could throw it and make it stick in the wooden board like Caesar, and Israel said he was prepared to try, and Eliezra, without waiting for his reply, threw the knife with all her strength, and it stuck in the board and she ran and pulled it out and took a few steps backward and threw it again, and ran to pull it out again, but this time Israel beat her to it and pulled the knife out of the board and went to the back of the room and threw it as hard as he could, but it didn't stick, and Eliezra laughed again and picked it up from the floor and stepped back and threw it neatly and accurately once again. The game grew more boisterous and they ran and pushed each other and threw the knife and vied with each other to see who could grab hold of it first until they both laid their hands on it together and stood next to the board, both of them hot and excited, holding the knife, and Eliezra, whose hair was a little disheveled, laughed and let her hand rest on Israel's for a moment, and the last barrier between them fell and all he had to do was put out his hand to embrace her, which is just what he did, because both of them were already standing in the heart of the circle from which they had neither the will nor the wish to retreat, and both of them were seeking release, and with his one hand still holding the knife he embraced her as if it were the most natural thing in the world, and she submitted, and afterward they kissed, and after that Israel took the receiver off the hook and locked the door, and when he lay with her, catching glimpses of their bodies from time to time in the mirrors which Caesar had installed around the couch, he treated her roughly and with no consideration at all, as if he wanted to bury all his rage and grief in her flesh and at the same time extract from it all the pleasure he could get, and Eliezra abandoned herself to him completely, and afterward she washed and dressed herself and left, and Israel, whose excitement soon died down, fell asleep feeling profoundly depressed and slept until Caesar came in the morning to fetch some photographic equipment and some film and woke him up.

Caesar was in somber spirits, and he pulled the knife out of the board, where it was still sticking, and played with it and asked Israel how things had gone the evening before and Israel said, "It was very nice. Goldman sends his regards," and Caesar nodded his head and remained silent for a moment and then said that he should never have gotten married in the first place, and at any rate he would never do it again, and Israel, his face heavy with sleep and appeased lust, asked him what had happened, and Caesar threw the knife onto the desk and said, "Everything's gone to shit," and Israel asked him how his son was, and Caesar said, "God knows, those bastards won't say anything," and he picked up the knife again and played with it a little without talking, and afterward he threw it back onto the desk and said, "Everything's a load of shit," and went away and came back late in the afternoon restless and in an even blacker mood than before, and thus he continued, with short intervals of distraction, day after day, and grew even gloomier, because of the uncertainty with regard to the state of his son's health and the obvious deterioration of Erwin's condition, and the only thing that got any better was his relationship with Eliezra, who suddenly stopped putting pressure on him and making demands and asking questions and their meetings became less frequent and more relaxed, and in fact all they did was make love and then part, and Caesar, who was very relieved, told Israel that she had apparently decided to postpone her divorce for a while because of the children, and in the meantime Israel received a brief postcard from Goldman, which was also intended for Caesar and in which he described his experiences in the army in a few amusing sentences and then ended with the words, "I've rediscovered the sky here. *Lehitraoth*— Goldman."

Israel read the postcard aloud to Caesar, who said, "He likes it there," and took it from Israel and read it to himself and said again, "He likes it there, the bastard," and put it on the piano and said, "It's a shame that Vicky got married. She was the only one who knew how to soothe me," and afterward he said "They're all whores," and lit himself a cigarette and went up to the window and glanced outside at the street—the early show had just come to an end and there was a lot of traffic—and asked Israel how things were with Ella and Israel said, "All right," and Caesar said, "She's a nice girl," and then he said, "This summer is going to drive me crazy. Let's go out for a bit," and Israel said, "Where to?" and Caesar said, "It doesn't make any difference. We can go see Phillip and Zahara, I've promised to visit them a hundred times already," and when he saw the unwillingness on Israel's face he said, "Come on, they're nice people. We won't stay long, I promise," and Israel said, "OK," and went into the bathroom and washed his face and combed his hair, and Caesar, standing next to him and examining his face in the mirror, said, "My hair's going," and took the bottle of Jochem's Hormoon from the shelf and poured a little into the palm of his hand and smeared it on his hair and massaged his scalp vigorously and then he also combed his hair and said, "We'll stay a bit and have something to drink and then take off. It'll be OK, you'll see," and while Israel was putting on his sandals Caesar phoned Zahara and told her they were coming, and he and Israel went down the street and got into Caesar's car, and Caesar started the car and said, "I'm damned if I know what to do," and a moment later, after extricating the huge car from the line of vehicles parked along the pavement and racing it up the road, he said, "I'm telling you, man, soon I'll be smoking hashish. I tasted it once, I told you about it, it had a kind of greenish taste," and afterward he said, "Who knows what these sicknesses are?" and he sank into a silence which he did not break throughout the drive except to say, "Remember that American tourist? She knew how to live. She was like a leaf blown by the wind—and she was an architect. But maybe I should have gone home and forgotten about everything else," and about half an hour later he parked his car in front of Phillip and Zahara's villa, which stood in a big garden, and they got out and went in through the gate and walked down the paved path in the clear chilly air rising from the damp lawn and shrubs and the pungent smell of the pines.

Caesar rang the bell and Zahara opened the door with a broad smile on her face and said, "I'm glad you came," and she embraced Caesar, who kissed her on the throat and said, "You smell marvelous," and introduced her to Israel, although they had already met, and afterward, when they went into the living room, he introduced him to Phillip, who was wearing a tennis shirt and moccasins, and said, "He plays the organ," and Phillip said, "The traditional organ?" and Israel, who felt ill at ease, said "Yes," and Zahara introduced both of them to Ada, a friend of about her own age who was sitting in a leather armchair wearing white jeans and stroking the cat lying next to her without any affection, and Caesar and Israel shook hands with her, and Caesar said, "We just dropped in to say hello and have a drink and then we have to go," and he and Israel sat down on the soft sofa, next to a big, low table where several glass and silver dishes containing almonds and walnuts and dried fruits and crackers were standing together with an ice bucket and some bottles of fruit juice and soda water and whiskey.

Caesar took a handful of nuts and asked Phillip how he was and Phillip, with the faint, bitter smile which hardly ever left his face, said, "Ask Zahara. She must know," and immediately added, "Not so bad considering the possible alternatives. Lately I've been looking after the cat, too," and he glanced at Zahara, who placed a tray of cheeses and a basket of thinly sliced black bread on the table and asked Caesar and Israel what they would like to drink, and Caesar cut himself a piece of cheese and said, "Whiskey and soda. And where are those cigars you promised me?" and Zahara, who wasn't looking as good as the last time he had seen her, brought the wooden box from the small chest where it was standing and said, "Here you are. Take one," and poured him a drink, and Phillip asked Israel, who was sitting withdrawn into himself, where he played the organ, and Israel said, "In Jaffa. In St. Antonio's," and Phillip, his Anglo-Saxon accent far less obvious now but still perceptible, said, "I envy you," and Caesar took a cigar and prepared it with enjoyment for smoking and said, " 'Wilhelm the Second.' Some people know how to live," and lit it and blew a puff of smoke and said, "Who said life was a drag?" and took a sip of whiskey, and Zahara said, "Your life was never a drag— that you leave to others," and laughed dryly, and asked Israel what he wanted to drink and Israel asked for grapefruit juice with soda and took a few nuts, and Caesar, who was smiling without any good humor, said, "You're being unfair to me," and Phillip said, "It's only because she likes you," and although Zahara did not react Caesar said, "Yes, I know," and recoiled from the cat, who had descended from the leather armchair and jumped onto the sofa and pressed against him until Phillip noticed his discomfort and said, "Come here, Eurydice, come here," and Eurydice let out a thin wail and arched her back a little and jumped off the sofa and slipped under the table and settled herself in Phillip's lap, and Zahara said, "Phillip's right. He knows me better than anyone," and she asked him if he wanted anything to drink, and Phillip said, "A drop of whiskey," and Zahara poured it for him and told Caesar that she was thinking of trading her Fiat sports car in for an Alfa Romeo or a BMW, and Caesar said, "I prefer the American models," and blew a puff of smoke and added, "What do you want to change it for? Your Fiat's almost new," and Phillip said, "She won't stop until she gets a white Rolls Royce," and then he added, "She's always changing things. It's almost a principle with her," and he glanced at Zahara. His heavy face with its faint, bitter smile was looking tired, his age was already beginning to show, and his slow and ironic voice sounded dull and resigned, he knew that she was still seeing her young architect, and she knew that he knew, but they both preferred to ignore it and not to talk about it, and Zahara said, "He's only joking," and Phillip said, "I never manage not to joke. Everything I say around here is a joke," and Zahara said, "That's not true," in a very firm tone and looked at him without love but with the wish to express sympathy and to spare him suffering, and Phillip turned to Caesar—but he was really addressing them all—and said, "Everyone's waiting for me to die, but for the time being I'm still alive," and he laughed softly and dryly, and Zahara said, "That's enough, Phillip," and turned to Israel, who was silently observing the people and the enormous living room with its furnishings and ornaments, and invited him to taste the cheeses, and Phillip again called Eurydice, who was pressing herself against Caesar's leg again, and Ada said, "Would anyone like to make two thousand lira with a minimum of effort?" and Caesar said, "I would, but how?" and Ada said that she had read an announcement in the paper about a competition to find a name for a big new hotel in Jerusalem, and the first prize was two thousand lira, and Caesar said, "Not bad, but where will we find a name?" and cut himself another piece of cheese, and Zahara asked if there were any special conditions, and Ada said no, but they would prefer a name that sounded good in English too, and she asked them what they thought of the name Ariel, a name which had occurred to her when she read the announcement, and Zahara said, "Ada, you're a genius," and Caesar said, "Yes, yes, that sounds great," and Phillip, who had been sitting withdrawn into himself behind a thin curtain of weariness and dejection, now came back to life and said that as far as he remembered the name Ariel appeared several times in the Bible, in the book of Isaiah and elsewhere, and if he wasn't mistaken it had originally been used to designate Jerusalem and also the altar in the Temple, and on the other hand the name Ariel sounded fine in English and also in French and, as they knew, it was the name of the airy sprite in *The Tempest* and also of the rebel angel in Milton's *Paradise Lost,* and had various meanings in the language, and of course there was also the Ariel in Pope's *The Rape of the Lock,* Belinda's Sylph, and he said something about the ambiguity of the word "rape" in the title of Pope's poem, and smiled, and suddenly he stopped short and said, "This is becoming boring," and Ada said, "No, no, go on, it's very interesting," and Caesar said, "Anyway, no hotel could possibly ask for more," and Zahara said, "Certainly not—the only question is whether they've read Milton and Pope," and Phillip told Ada to send off the form first thing in the morning and to add a few explanations if she liked, and she would win the competition hands down, although he himself had a much better name, but since he had to get the children off to school every morning and take care of Eurydice too he didn't think he would have time to send it in, and Ada asked him what the name was and he said, "The Bordel Hotel," and everyone except Israel laughed and he asked them what they thought of his name and Caesar said he thought it was the greatest, it sounded wonderful in Hebrew and English and every language in the world, and if he himself owned a hotel he wouldn't dream of calling it anything else, and Zahara said a hotel with a name like that would never be short of customers, and Phillip, basking in this favorable response, said that if he could take some time off from Eurydice he would be prepared to work there as a *bardak* man and Caesar said he would be glad to join him as the *bardak* man's assistant, even without a salary, and Zahara said, "I believe you. But why should you? That's just what you are already," and Casear said, "You don't like me," and Zahara, a faint smile still hovering on her drawn face, said, "All you want is to be liked," and Caesar said, "Yes," and laughed, and Zahara said, "You think you'll always be forgiven, that you'll always be able to indulge yourself at other people's expense. But it doesn't work that way," and Caesar, still laughing, said, "You think so?" and Zahara said, "Yes," and offered the tray of cheese to Israel again, and Israel said, "Thank you," and cut himself a piece of cheese and returned to his examination of the room, which had a ceiling paneled in wood and in the far corner, next to the French windows opening onto the garden, a black grand piano on which Phillip occasionally played.

Israel stared at the piano and the rich reddish-brown velvet curtains and then he shifted his eyes to the carved wooden cupboard and the carpets and let them rest for a moment on the antique chess table opposite with its chessmen set out in readiness for a game and the antique pistol lying next to them, and the lamp standing next to the table and casting its light on it and the magnificent bureau above which, behind Phillip's back and a little to one side from a group of etchings, hung a large, exceptionally beautiful tapestry depicting a battle scene in the forefront of which a white horse was falling to the ground with its four legs up in the air, and opposite it a chestnut horse rearing on its hind legs, and between them a blue horse, a stallion like the other two, and around them a host of warriors with armor and shields, some of them lying down and others standing up, some of them holding long spears pointing up to the sky, where an angel floated, blowing a ram's horn. Israel went on gazing at this tapestry while Ada said to Phillip, "You should send it in," and Phillip, the burst of happiness which had flared up in him for a moment already extinguished, said, "I think I'll keep it for next time. There'll be other hotels," and he put Eurydice down and rose from his chair and said that he was sorry but he was tired and thought he should go to bed, and Zahara said, "Stay with us a little longer," and Phillip said, "No, no," and apologized again and said good night to everyone and went out of the room with a heavy tread, and Zahara asked Caesar and Israel if they wanted coffee and Caesar said, "I think not, we have to be on our way soon," and Zahara said, "It won't take a minute," and Caesar said, "All right, we'll have coffee first," and Zahara went into the kitchen to put the kettle on, and when she came back they began talking about cars again, and then about Eurydice, who was dozing on Phillip's chair, and Zahara sang her praises and described her little habits, and Caesar said that he would never keep a cat or a dog and Ada said that she wouldn't either because the grief of parting from a pet was too terrible to bear, and Caesar said, "I could bear parting from them all right, I just can't be bothered to keep them," and afterward they drank their coffee and stayed a few more minutes and in the end Caesar got up with Israel, who had been waiting impatiently without saying a word or so much as hinting that he wanted to leave, and they said goodbye to Ada, and Zahara, who accompanied them to the door, asked Caesar if there was any news about his son, and Caesar said, "No, there's nothing new, but it'll be all right," and they said goodbye to her too and left.

The air outside was cool now and Israel found this fresh, nippy coolness pleasant, and they got into the car and Caesar said, "Bitch," and after that he said, "I'd like to fuck her, the bitch," and started the car, in reverse—he had parked it very close to Zahara's car—and said, "I'm sorry for Phillip, he's a beaten man," and afterward he passed Zahara's car and started speeding through the streets—the traffic was quite light by now—and dropped Israel at the studio, and for a moment he thought of going to visit his parents, but Zina's presence and his father's illness were too much for him and besides, it was too late, and so after a slight hesitation he drove to Tehilla's and parked the car outside her house and went upstairs and rang the bell and waited a moment, and then he opened the door and went into the apartment, which was empty because Tehilla hadn't come home from work yet.

Caesar switched on the light in the passage and the room and wondered whether he should stay and wait for her, and in the end he decided to wait and took off his shirt and threw it onto one of the chairs in the room, which ever since Tehilla's abortion had given rise to a mixture of feelings of belonging and not belonging in him, exactly like when he went to Tirza's, and he went into the kitchen and took a can of beer from the refrigerator and went back into the room and sat down in an armchair and turned on the radio and looked at the newspaper he found on the table and at the same time he glanced at his watch—it was almost midnight already—and he picked up a book and leafed through it and looked outside through the window overlooking the courtyard, where the summit of a tall casuarine tree was barely visible in the darkness, and looked at his watch again and turned off the radio and lay down on the bed, but the sudden silence made him feel uneasy and he turned it on again and went into the bathroom and examined his face in the mirror—if he had had anywhere to go he might have gone there, but besides the fact that he had nowhere to go he felt a sudden need to see Tehilla, whose lateness was slowly giving rise in him to impatience, together with a feeling of having been forsaken—and he went back into the room and turned down the volume of the radio, which he had bought Tehilla for a present on his way to fetch her from the clinic after the abortion. Tehilla had objected, although not very firmly, to his coming and said that she would take a cab, but Caesar had insisted on bringing her home himself, although when he was about to leave for the clinic he had felt a shadow of regret at his stubbornness in this matter, and on his way there, on a momentary impulse, he had stopped next to a shop where they sold electrical appliances and bought her the radio, and afterward he drove to the clinic to pick her up. She was pale and a little tense, and she didn't seem sad but on the contrary, she smiled and laughed, which made Caesar think that she was happy and to a large extent relieved his feeling of oppression and uneasiness, and on their way home, with Caesar driving very carefully as if he were transporting something fragile made of china, she suddenly asked him to stop at a cafe because she felt like having something good to eat, and Caesar did so gladly, he was so happy to be able to do something to please her, and Tehilla, who was still in pain and had to be supported by Caesar when she walked, ordered a big helping of ice cream with fruit and nuts, and when she had finished it she ordered a cream cake with strawberries and cappuccino, and Caesar ordered the same thing, and they ate and drank and laughed, and afterward, with both of them still in high spirits, especially Tehilla, they went home and Tehilla got into bed and lay down and her good mood lasted until evening, when she sank into a depression, and the next day she cried all day long without stopping, and Caesar, who did not know how to calm her and on the other hand did not feel free to desert her despite her repeated requests for him to go away and leave her alone, came and went and roamed around the apartment and looked after her as best he could, his face blank with suppressed anger and impatience. He couldn't stand her face, her voice, or her weakness, not to mention her tears, which made him feel positively hostile, and all he wanted to do was run away and never come back again, and indeed, a few days later, after she had recovered and gone back to work, when she asked him again to go away and leave her alone, Caesar left without any arguments, leaving most of his clothes and also his electric shaver behind him—he never asked about them afterward and behaved as if they didn't exist—but he took the key to her apartment with him, he didn't offer to give it back to her and she didn't ask for it, and he went to stay with his parents, but he couldn't stay there long and despite Zina's pleas he moved out in less than a month and went to live with a friend. This happy vacation from Tehilla lasted for a few weeks, during which he would call her up occasionally to ask her how she was, at first purely out of politeness, but later on, when it gradually became apparent to him that she was getting over him and returning to her previous independent way of life, he called her in a state of growing anxiety and jealousy, and in the end, during one of these telephone conversations, he asked if he could see her, and Tehilla, who always answered him pleasantly but slightly remotely, as if she were protecting herself or as if her love for him had cooled, hesitated for a moment and then agreed.

She greeted him warily, holding herself back a little, but she looked well and even, in spite of herself, excited, and quite soon, far sooner than he had expected, Caesar succeeded in overcoming her apprehensions and breaking the ice, and after they had had coffee and talked a while, deliberately ignoring everything that had happened between them, he went to bed with her, although he felt uneasy about it, not only because he was aroused by Tehilla's desire but also, mainly, because he himself felt an urgent need to do so, a need which had nothing to do with lust or desire, and afterward he got up and washed himself and while Tehilla lay naked on the bed, half covered by a thin blanket, very relaxed and drowsy, he got dressed and when she opened her eyes she saw him fully clothed and ready to leave, and in her surprise she asked him if he was going, and Caesar said, "Yes," and Tehilla said, "Already? We haven't seen each other for so long," and Caesar said, "It's late," and then added, "I thought you were asleep."

Tehilla looked at him for a moment and then she got up and asked him not to leave yet, and Caesar hesitated, he was standing by the door and itching to be on the other side of it already, and Tehilla asked him again, and he mumbled something but remained standing by the door, and suddenly she burst into tears, hurt, defeated tears, and only then Caesar, embarrassed and confused, came back into the room and embraced her and stroked her hair sympathetically, and also happily, and afterward he lay down beside her, still fully clothed, and went on stroking her, still sympathetically but also with well-hidden impatience, and at about midnight he got up to go, and after a period of a few days he came back, and from then on he came to see her at regular intervals, sometimes without letting her know in advance, and

Tehilla received him without any conditions or demands, and without ever questioning him about the future of their relationship, and she never referred, not by so much as a hint, to what had happened between them, much to the relief of Caesar, who promised to marry her from time to time without even being asked, and he did so mainly because of the self-sufficiency and independence which Tehilla displayed in almost everything she did, which filled him with uneasiness—the same uneasiness he felt now as he lay down on the bed again and listened absentmindedly to the music on the radio and decided not to leave until she arrived, after having made up his mind only a few minutes before to go and leave his handkerchief on the pillow as a sign that he had been there, and a few minutes later he heard her footsteps on the stairs, and then the key turned in the lock and the door opened and Tehilla, panting slightly, came into the room with a joyful smile and said, "Have you been waiting long?" and Caesar, his face expressionless, said, "Quite long, but it doesn't matter," and Tehilla said, "What a pity. If I'd known you were coming I'd have come back earlier," and Caesar said, "Where were you?" and Tehilla, whose fresh, ingenuous face infuriated him, said, "I went to the movies, to the Studio," and Caesar said, "Oh," and then, "Who with?" and Tehilla said, "With a girlfriend. The film was rather boring. Would you like something to eat?" and she took off her sandals, and Caesar said, "No, I'm not hungry," and lit a cigarette and said, "So who's this friend?" and Tehilla said, "One of the stewardesses I work with; you don't know her," and went into the bathroom, and after washing her hands and face she came back into the room and said, "Are you sure you won't change your mind about having something to eat? I'm starving," and Caesar said, "All right, I'll join you if you like," and Tehilla went into the kitchen and made a salad and heated up the soup left over from the day before and sliced some sausage and opened a can of sardines and they sat down to eat with Caesar full of gloom, and afterward he stayed the night and the next morning Tehilla, who had a morning shift, had to leave early and she slipped quietly out of the flat so as not to wake Caesar, and when he woke up the apartment was empty and full of sunlight, and this put him in a bad mood again and he cursed Tehilla for not waking him and himself for going to bed with her in the first place, and especially for waiting for her and not leaving the night before when she didn't come, and he got up and washed and had a cup of coffee and went to the studio, where he found another postcard from Goldman, who came back two weeks later, a few days after Shmuel came home from the hospital where he had been recovering from a heart attack brought on by a fight with a customer, who had returned his rented car damaged and scratched and obstinately insisted that that was the condition in which he had received it.

Goldman came home from the army dusty and sweaty and exhausted, but in high spirits and full of energy, for in some mysterious way he felt like a new man with a new, as yet unknown destiny awaiting him, and he was glad to be back in town just as he was unexpectedly glad to see Stefana, who was not expecting him because he had not notified her of his impending return, and who nevertheless greeted him without surprise and also without any signs of emotion, but with a smiling face which seemed to reflect his own happiness. She gave him a clean towel and clean clothes and made him a meal from all kinds of leftovers and even opened a can of pineapple in his honor, and after taking a shower he sat down at the kitchen table to eat and as he ate he examined her and her withered face, which was delicately made up. This little eccentricity, which usually aroused Goldman's anger and disgust, did not affect his good humor, and while she served his food he asked her how she was and what she had been doing and Stefana answered him briefly but willingly, and she even smiled, and afterward he asked her about Uncle Lazar, and she said, "He was here," and he asked about Yehudit Maizler, and Stefana said, "She's all right," and then she said, "Last week she went on a two-day excursion to Jerusalem," and she served him his meat and said, "People will go on living at any price," and then she said, "Tzimmer's widow was here too. A woman who wears red blouses..."

Stefana had never liked Tzimmer's widow or Tzimmer himself, and Goldman's father too had disliked them, her for no particular reason, perhaps simply because she was Tzimmer's wife, but Tzimmer he disliked because he regarded him as a parasite living at the public's expense, and he said so too, whenever the opportunity arose, insisting that Tzimmer's work was nothing but corruption and paid idleness, and to tell the truth it was nothing but pure and simple theft, and this was in addition to the so-called legal way in which he had been brazenly stealing from the Histadruth and the Party for years, and he had proof of this too, for example, the drawers full of pens and pencils and note paper in Tzimmer's house, all stolen from the Histadruth, and the renovations which took place in Tzimmer's apartment after all the election campaigns in which he was so active, not to mention the new furniture he was always buying and the new refrigerator, and the trip to America, all of which he could never have paid for out of his salary, not to mention the scandalous favoritism and preferential treatment he meted out to himself and his family and friends, and all kinds of irregularities and fringe benefits—free tickets to concerts and the theater, vacations at Histadruth rest homes without waiting his turn, all kinds of trips, dinners, and so on. These things angered and upset Goldman's father and made him as unhappy as if it were his own personal integrity which was being damaged and as if he himself were being cheated, and what made things even worse was that Tzimmer accompanied all these misdeeds with moralistic speeches about the decline of the state and the labor movement and perpetrated them under a cloak of hypocritical socialism, full of infuriating opportunism, which in recent years had been joined by his phony piety—all of a sudden Tzimmer began going to the synagogue on Saturdays and holidays and wrapping himself in a prayer shawl and praying and observing all kinds of other religious customs, which infuriated Goldman's father beyond bearing, and besides all this he was also disgusted by Tzimmer's bourgeois acquisitiveness and his bottomless concern for himself and his own comfort, and he despised his stinginess, which he described by saying that Tzimmer was so stingy he would throw himself off the balcony for a penny. His hatred and scorn were ruthless, and he did not soften even when Tzimmer suddenly and dramatically, almost overnight, began to age and fade away right before their eyes: He grew hard of hearing and his speech grew slow and weak, and later also garbled, and the same thing applied to his movements too, the movements of his hands and feet, which he dragged at a slow shuffle, sometimes as if he didn't even know where he was going, and his eyes grew vague and unfocused and his face looked tired and lifeless, and at the same time he began to shrink rapidly, as if he were emptying out from inside, his flushed cheeks sank into hollows and his whole body shriveled up and he spent hours lying in bed dozing among the newspapers, helpless and pitiful, but without arousing any pity, and at the same time, apparently without any desire, because there was no desire left in him, he went on mechanically accumulating possessions and attending all kinds of committee meetings, and he was very punctilious about attending these meetings although his brain had already dried up and was incapable of absorbing anything that was being said—according to Goldman's father he only went to them in order to drink the free fruit juice and eat the free sandwiches and get the bus fare and expenses— and when he came home from one of these meetings he died.

It was summer, in the afternoon of a very hot day, and Tzimmer climbed the stairs very slowly and when he reached the top he rang the doorbell—he had forgotten his key—and a moment later his wife opened the door; there was nothing unusual about his appearance, but he took one or two steps and dropped to the ground like an empty suit of clothes and died, but with such inevitability that it gave rise to no alarm or even the least surprise: He had simply reached the end and stopped. No one missed him, neither his widow nor, of course, Goldman's father or Stefana, who now added, "A woman has to be from a very small place to go out into the street in red blouses like hers," and removed the soup plate from the table, and afterward they spoke about a number of money and business matters which had come up while Goldman was away, but during the entire course of the conversation, which flowed peacefully from one topic to another, Stefana did not even mention the fact that Shumel had had a heart attack or that Zipporah had been hospitalized again as a result of the worsening condition of her leg, because she had detached herself completely from any concern in these matters, and Goldman did not hear about them until two days later from Uncle Lazar, who had continued coming once or twice a week during Goldman's absence to spend a silent hour with Stefana, who opened a can of pineapple for dessert, and as she stood by the sink with her back to Goldman he saw how much her thin body, which was still strong and erect, resembled Naomi's, and he remembered how she had almost stopped eating when Naomi died, and how for the first two years she had taken nothing but tea with milk and a little fruit and grown very thin, which had saved her life, or perhaps it would be better to say stopped her from dying, since she had suffered for many years from high blood pressure and heart attacks, one of them so severe that they had been sure she was going to die and sent for Naomi and Goldman and Goldman's father, and when she had become so thin she had recovered from these ailments, but now it seemed that she had grown even thinner than before, perhaps because of the years which had shriveled her body and withered her skin, which was now drawn dry and wrinkled over the skeleton of her bones.

After he had finished eating Goldman stretched out on the bed in his room, to which he was so glad to return, and he asked Stefana to wake him in the evening, but Stefana did not wake him and he went on sleeping very deeply and did not awaken until the next day at noon, in a very bad mood. He went on lying in bed until late in the afternoon, gloomy and empty of any desire, and in the end he rose and washed and dressed and after drinking the cup of coffee and eating the biscuits which Stefana gave him he left the house and went to visit Dita in the firm resolve, which he had reached during his military service, to put an end to the relationship between them.

The sun was about to sink and the streets were full of shade and in the air, which was still hot and humid, there were already delicate intimations of a remote chill, heralding the approaching autumn, and this pleased him, as did the walk through the familiar streets after his deep sleep, and all this almost banished his gloom and once more he felt himself free and elated, but the closer he came to Dita's apartment the gloomier he grew, and he became very tense, and when he entered the lobby and climbed the stairs he felt full of resentment and hoped that she would receive him coldly, and all he wanted was to get the whole thing over as quickly as possible without any superfluous words, but Dita, who was wearing a white summer blouse and a dark blue skirt and looked fresh and neat, greeted him gladly, and they went into the room which was so familiar to him, and after they had exchanged a few words Dita gave him a glass of iced coffee and a slice of walnut cake, which she had bought especially in honor of his homecoming, and he told her about his experiences in the army, the people and the life and the desert, and he was still aloof and hostile and waiting for the right moment to say what he had come to say, but at the same time, without his wishing it, he suddenly rediscovered in her, after a very long time, hints of tenderness and grace, and even traces of a neglected beauty, and afterward, taking him all unawares, while he was sitting and talking to her, a peacefulness descended on him and his spirit thawed, and he felt close to her, closer than to any other human being, and used to her, and he began asking himself why, in fact, he should do what he had come to do and why he shouldn't rather ask her to marry him, and he went on asking himself these questions while they ate the supper that Dita had prepared in honor of the occasion, and which included his favorite dishes, and while they watched television and saw the news and the movie after the news, but in the end, to his own surprise, all of a sudden and in fact quite involuntarily, he told her why he had come, and Dita listened to him with a serious expression on her face but without raising any objections or expressing any sorrow, as if it were all expected and even self-evident, and they spoke to each other briefly and politely and at the end of this conversation Goldman rose to his feet and parted from her and left the apartment with a feeling of relief but not of happiness, because he had a sensation of ending and emptiness, and life in its familiar, day-to-day sense too suddenly lost all direction, and this sensation accompanied him all through that night and the next day, full of discontent and doubts, and for many days afterward too, and in the morning he went on lying on his bed in his room which was already flooded with sunlight and he gradually withdrew into himself and curled up underneath the light summer blanket with his eyes shut and his face to the wall and he didn't want to see anyone or talk to anyone, and at the same time he was seized with a longing to be sick with the flu like when he was at school and to feel once more the special sweetness of lying in bed underneath starched sheets, in a room with the windows shut tight against drafts, with the sensation of fever making him sleepy and the sensation of weakness and the special influenza pains in his legs and arms and back, and hear Stefana behind his back coming and going and bringing him an apple or a glass of lemon tea and biscuits and putting them down carefully on the chair covered with a white towel, and thus he lay, without moving, for a long time, and then he rose heavily to his feet and got dressed and went about his business—there were several matters calling for his attention—and the same sensation he had felt before, the lack of any direction, overcame him again, and it was only toward evening, when he met Uncle Lazar, whom he was so happy to see again, that it left him for a while.

This time they did not play chess, just spoke a little as they sat in the kitchen drinking their coffee, and Goldman told Uncle Lazar about his military service, and afterward he told him that he had made up his mind to leave the law office and abandon his profession and get a job teaching in a school, and Uncle Lazar, who listened to him quietly, asked him what his reasons were, and Goldman said that he wanted to do something useful and that he hoped, in fact he was sure, that teaching would bring him the peace of mind that he longed for, and save him from the feeling that he was wasting his life. Uncle Lazar made no comment on this project until a few weeks later, and then only indirectly, when Goldman was telling him about the problems of astronomy which were preoccupying him at the time and said that he might try to translate the *Somnium,* an idea which aroused great, although vague, hopes in him, and Uncle Lazar passed his hand over his brow and said that people should beware of excessively high expectations, and afterward he said that although there was something in men which he called the "redemption instinct," his life experience had taught him that there was no single act in public or private life, however right or revolutionary, which was redemptive in the sense that from a certain point onward a new era would commence in which everything would be perfectly good and work out just the way people wanted it to, and at the same time, despite this awareness, it was necessary to live as if redemption were possible and to strive for it, and Goldman said, "Yes, I understand," and Uncle Lazar said that as far as he himself was concerned it was difficult for him to make this awareness a natural and integral part of his thoughts and feelings, because he had been dominated for too many years by the belief that there was one redemptive act, which in his case had been communism and anarchism—but when Goldman first mentioned his plans to change jobs Uncle Lazar just looked at him with a gaze full of affection and sympathy and nodded slightly, and when they had finished drinking their coffee they left the house together and went to visit Shmuel, who was sitting up in light summer clothing, smiling but still pale, in the rocking chair in the living room, which was unbearably stuffy because Bracha had closed all the windows to protect him from the drafts, while she herself, drained and yellow with worry and anxiety, did not take her eyes off him for a moment and hurried to fulfill his every wish, spoken or unspoken—anything to prevent him from moving and exerting himself.

Goldman shook hands with Shmuel and Bracha, and then he greeted Moishe Tzellermaier, whose son was leaving for America in less than a month's time, and Chaim-Leib and Mrs. Haya and Jonah Kotchinski, who had come without Sarah, who was already very ill, and went to sit down, glancing as he did so at a young man dressed like a foreigner who had been watching him uneasily ever since he came into the room, and suddenly he recognized Amos, who had come from America to visit his father's sickbed, and he hurried over to him and they shook hands and exchanged a few words, and Amos introduced him to his wife, who had come with him and their two children, and asked her in English to meet his cousin, the lawyer, and Goldman shook hands with her too and exchanged a few remarks with them, and also with the children; he asked them how they liked Israel and the older son said, "It's great," and Goldman smiled at them and then he went to sit on the edge of the sofa, next to someone he didn't know, and as he sat down he stole another glance at Amos and saw how much he had changed and how much older he looked than his age, and the same was true of his sister Illana, who was helping Bracha serve the tea and coffee and cake to their guests, and who was very tastefully dressed but who no longer resembled the girl he had once known—she had grown fat and of all her former charms nothing remained but the smooth, rosy face and the shining brown hair and perhaps a faint twinkle in her eye, which it seemed to Goldman that he had discerned when she bent down to serve him his tea and asked him how he was and he said "Fine, thanks," and asked her how she was and how her husband was and what she was doing with herself, and she smiled and said, "Nothing in particular, bringing up the children," and called her husband and said, "This is Ephraim and Regina's son. He's a lawyer," and her husband put out his hand and said, "I think we've already met," and Goldman shook hands with him and said "Yes, yes. A long time ago," and Illana invited him to come and visit them, and Goldman promised that he would, and Illana's husband said, "We would be very glad to see you. We're almost always at home," and Goldman nodded and Illana said, "Do come. We'll be expecting you," and turned away and went to stand next to Amos and said something to him and stroked his son's hair, and Goldman, who sat down again, saw that she had thick, short fingers.

These people were his cousins, but over the years the relationship had turned into something without any living meaning for him, embarrassing and sometimes even oppressive, because apart from the given fact of their kinship, which existed in his consciousness as a system of duties and obligations which could be avoided only by an act of explicit repudiation and by turning his back on them, they were strangers to each other, since each of them had taken a different direction and settled in a different place and lived in a different world, and most of them he saw very seldom and only by chance, and some, especially their children and spouses, he had never seen at all, or if he had it was so long ago that he wouldn't have recognized them if he saw them in the street, a state of affairs which was very different from the days of his childhood, when they had all lived close to each other, or at least they had shared a common environment, and apart from marriages and births and funerals they had met often on Saturdays and holidays and at political or professional meetings, or on ordinary weekdays to drink tea and talk and argue.

As a rule Goldman did not feel that he was missing anything because of this disintegration, but from time to time he would feel brief pangs of longing for that cosy golden age, or for what remained etched in his memory as such, and sometimes he also felt pangs of guilt, and then he would decide to go and visit his uncles and aunts, Joel and Zipporah and Shmuel and Bracha, and his cousins and various other relatives in order to renew the ties which he had neglected and to acknowledge them and to get to know them and their children again, but he never did so, and he met them only by chance or on duty calls like the present one, which were of course full of embarrassment and strain, and he sat in his corner, not far from Shmuel, and drank his tea and looked at Chaim-Leib, upon whose face death had already set its stamp, and at Mrs. Haya, and at Moishe Tzellermaier and Bracha, all of whom had changed so much and grown so ugly, and then he glanced at Amos again, and then at the color photograph of Shmuel standing on the sideboard, in which he looked so young and pleased with himself under the mane of curly blond hair of which nothing was now left but the sideburns and a few thin wisps on top, and Mrs. Haya, who looked very worried, asked Shmuel again how he was feeling, and Shmuel smiled and said again that he felt perfectly all right, and Goldman, still holding the empty cup in his hand, felt sadly and helplessly how everything was wearing out and coming to an end, bodies and people and the ties between them, and how he himself was a part of this process of deterioration, and in the meantime he heard Shmuel once more telling the story of how the customer had returned the car, an almost brand new Peugeot, completely ruined, and how they had begun arguing after the customer had insisted that that was the way he had received it, and how he went on insolently repeating this lie, which was what infuriated Shmuel more than anything, and how suddenly, in the middle of the argument, he had fallen to the ground and lost consciousness and woken up in the hospital, where the doctor told him that he had had a heart attack, and this information, besides surprising him, had given rise in him to a peculiar sensation, uncomfortable but not frightening, except for a moment, of direct contact with death, as if he had stood facing death, which appeared in his imagination like a big black spot, without any barriers between them, not at all like in illnesses such as influenza or jaundice, but like a man confronting another man who was aiming a gun at him but somehow not shooting at him, and Bracha, whose worried expression never left her face, asked him to stop talking for a while and rest, and Goldman decided that it was time to get up and go, and he wondered if he should pop in to see Grandmother Hava lying in her room before leaving, but he went on sitting on the sofa and looking at the people without really seeing them, reflecting incoherently about the theories of space which stimulated his mind, and in his imagination he saw before him a night sky full of stars, giant galaxies, thousands of times bigger than they looked in the photographs in books, whirling about in all their radiance, receding farther and farther from each other in the dark and silent vastness of space, created from nothing in the continuous process of the formation of new interstellar matter which was the birth of a new galaxy, whereas its recession to beyond the rim of the observable universe was its death, and while he was thinking about this with his empty cup in his hand Amos came up to him and said, "It's hot here. Very hot," and Goldman said, "Yes, but it'll be better soon," and Amos said, "They should have opened a window," and afterward he asked him about his work and career prospects and Goldman said, "It's OK. The salary's not bad," and Amos asked him why he didn't open a law firm of his own and Goldman said, "It's not so easy. You need money to start out, and then you have to put a lot of work into it," and Amos said, "But it's worth it, isn't it?" and Goldman said, "Yes, but not always," and he asked Amos, whose face now seemed attractive to him, what it was like in New York, and Amos said, "Oh, it's a tremendous city. If you've never been there you must come and see it," and Goldman said maybe he would, and Amos said, "We'd like to move to California, but it's complicated," and Goldman said, "Is it?" and Amos said, "But in the end we'll move, it's worth it," and Goldman said, "Yes, you have to take risks," and in the meantime he saw Joel come in and he felt great uneasiness and regretted coming and especially not having left a few moments before, and he wished he could vanish into thin air, but Joel, who looked tired and more despondent than Goldman had ever seen him, was already inside the room, nodding at Chaim-Leib and Mrs. Haya, and Goldman, who rose to greet him, shook his hand and asked him how he was and how Zipporah was and Joel said,

"She's all right," and Goldman said, "What about her leg?" and Joel said, "They don't know yet. In any case, they're doing whatever they can," and he went up to Uncle Lazar and Bracha and Shmuel, and Goldman, who sat down on the edge of the sofa again, decided to visit Zipporah in the hospital the very next afternoon and unburden himself of the feeling of guilt which had been bothering him for months, maybe even for years, and which did not stem solely from the sense of his delinquency in the performance of family duties, but first and foremost from the feeling of respect tinged with awe which, like his father, he felt toward Zipporah, and which he wanted to express, and also from the profound sense of gratitude which he still felt toward her for all the help and kindness she had offered him and his parents without ever expecting anything in return, and without getting anything either, when Stefana was suffering from a kidney problem and for a certain period of time was unable to look after him and Naomi, and Zipporah, whose relations with Stefana had been reserved from the outset, so that they hardly ever met or spoke to each other, quietly came and took him to stay with her and Joel in the shack where they were then living with their five children and her mother, Grandmother Rachel.

The shack was so overcrowded that Ruth had to sleep in the linen chest, while Meir slept in a camp bed under the sloping roof which formed a kind of veranda in front of the shack—it was summer—and Goldman slept in the same bed as Aviezer, who was a few months older than he was, and at night their hands would steal into each other's pajama pants and they would masturbate each other quietly under the thin summer blanket, but in spite of the overcrowding the shack was spotlessly clean because Zipporah, who taught her children to be neat and tidy, was always scrubbing the floors and dusting the furniture and sweeping away the cobwebs and whitewashing the walls: She would get up every morning together with Joel and while he was shaving at the kitchen sink and dressing and putting on his heavy boots she would make him a cup of tea and put some slices of bread and butter and turnip and a pinch of salt in a scrap of newspaper and a jar of pickled herring and a hardboiled egg, and sometimes a meatball or a slice of cake, in the bag which he took to work together with his sack of tools and square saw, and when he left she would start on the housework. She washed and ironed, and darned socks and patched the old clothes which were handed down from child to child, and cut the toes out of shoes grown too small for their owners, and turned old dresses into blouses and pants into jackets and tablecloths into dresses, and cooked sumptuous meals out of tomatoes and spinach and barley and eggplant, which came out tasting just like meat, and rice and noodles, which she kneaded and rolled and cut with her own hands, and used the feet and wings and necks of chickens which cost her hardly anything, and sometimes she also cooked whole new meals from the leftovers of the day before, because she refused to throw food away, and this was a matter of principle with her and one which she also taught her children, and she baked cakes from pumpkins and made delicious fruit soup from marrows which tasted just like apples, and jam from orange and grapefruit peels, and wine from the figs and mulberries which grew wild in the fields, and she saw to it that the children went to school every day and did their homework and polished their shoes themselves and fetched ice or firewood and helped in the house as much as they could and also made a little money, especially during the school holidays, working at all kinds of jobs, and she made them do all this because she thought that people should learn to be self-reliant as well as to help others to the best of their ability, and because she believed in the dignity of labor and considered laziness and idleness to be the root of all evil, leading inevitably to degeneracy and backbiting and even crime, and together with running the house she also helped her mother, who tried to take care of her own needs as long as she could, and her sister Sarah, a beautiful and gifted but lost and helpless woman, who seemed almost to enjoy her hopelessness and spent most of her time wandering aimlessly about her apartment with wild, untidy hair, as if she had just got out of bed, and constantly, as the expression of her own deep despondency, disparaged and belittled others, sometimes even Zipporah herself, and complained of various pains and about the weather, and her husband Jonah Kotchinski, a kind-hearted man who was an expert whistler and knew how to whistle whole operas and symphonies by Mozart and Haydn—usually he whistled for his own enjoyment but sometimes he did it to cheer her up—and he also had a very pleasant tenor voice and at parties and on Saturday nights he would sing sentimental songs in Polish and Yiddish even without being asked, and also arias and Neapolitan songs in fluent Italian.

He was a pastry chef and owned a cake shop and loved his wife with all his heart and soul and tried to please her and make her happy in every way he could, and so almost every night they would get dressed up and go out to dance or play cards, or sit in cafes or go to the movies, and there were always a dozen different kinds of cakes and biscuits in their house, as well as all kinds of other delicacies which Jonah would buy and bring home, and they would lie about in corners until they grew stale and attracted the ants or became moldy with age because nobody ever touched them—Jonah because he was diabetic and Sarah because she didn't particularly care for cakes—and they had no children, but all Jonah's efforts to win her heart and make her happy were to no avail and she would wander aimlessly about from morning to night, the bed unmade and the sink full of dirty dishes and the house full of crumbs and pieces of dry bread and peels and clothes, complaining about her sad fate and arguing that if only she had stayed in Poland—during and after the war Poland was replaced by America—she would have become what she had always dreamed of being, a dancer or a fashion designer or a textile engineer, and she wouldn't have wasted her life, or complaining about Jonah, accusing him of not paying her enough attention and not loving her enough and being unfaithful to her in his imagination with a certain woman who had been his sweetheart many years before, long before he even met Sarah, and all kinds of other women too, not only in his imagination, some of whom he didn't even know, but neither the facts nor his repeated denials made any difference to her and hardly a week went by without her firmly announcing that she was going to get a divorce.

Zipporah, who couldn't stand idleness or self-indulgence or grumbling, just as she couldn't bear it when anyone disparaged Eretz Yisrael in her presence or troubled her with endless talk of depression and illness and death, tried to help her sister as best she could, sometimes consoling her and sometimes denying what she said and sometimes scolding her aggressively and even rudely, and always trying to spur her into finding some kind of work which would fill her days and break the vicious circle of grumbling and backbiting and depression, and she even tried to persuade her that a person living in Eretz Yisrael needed an ideology to live by, but she never said exactly what this ideology was, and the truth is that it wasn't clear to her either, and all it amounted to was the idea, which she had built up very gradually from the details of her education and experience, that life demanded a constant effort, since its complications and difficulties were not accidental but the very stuff of life itself, and it had to be lived with responsibility and the acceptance of duties and values such as honesty, industriousness, loyalty, modesty, simplicity, and other values whose rightness and validity she never doubted and of which she never needed any proof, because they suited her own feelings and intuitions and the common sense by means of which, sometimes cautiously and sometimes even cunningly, but usually directly and frankly, she managed courageously and successfully to chart the course of her life and the lives of her family between all the obstacles and pitfalls and contradictions, and in accordance with these values, and also her own willingness to lend a hand, she made room in her house for Goldman, who went home a couple of months later, when Stefana was somewhat recovered, but a few years afterward, when Joel and Zipporah had settled on the moshav, he went to stay with them again, during the summer vacations from school, and by then he was already helping with the farm work, whose main burden fell on Zipporah, assisted by Jeremiah and Ruth, and also to a certain extent by Esther and Aviezer, who were younger, since Joel continued to work at his trade and for much of this period he was working in British army camps and came home only for the weekends, and Meir enlisted in the British army after they went to live on the moshav and after a few months' service in Eretz Yisrael he was sent to Egypt; from there he sent photographs from time to time showing himself in army uniform standing in the parks of Cairo and Alexandria and next to the Pyramids and the Nile.

Goldman would get up with everyone else before sunrise and Zipporah would give them a cup of hot milk and a saucer of honey, and afterward he would go out with Jeremiah into the tranquillity of the early morning whose blue-gray air was full of the chill rising from the damp grass and the fruit trees and the cypresses, and whose deep silence was emphasized by the sounds of animals lowing and squawking, or the trundle of a passing cart, and he would go to the barn, which was full of warmth all through the summer and the smell of bran and red loam and sacking, and he would prepare the fodder for the chickens and the geese, and collect the eggs, some of which were still warm, and afterward, depending on what was needed, he would clean out the chicken run and the stinking geese pen, fix fences, dig basins around the fruit trees and water them, or weed the vegetable beds, pick peppers and tomatoes and cucumbers when the air was already hot and humid and full of gnats, and after an afternoon nap if he felt like it he could go with Jeremiah for a ride in the little wooden cart drawn by the carthorse, whose name was Dawn, to the supply shed or the dairy in the center of the moshav, or to the distant field which the family had been given temporarily to cultivate and from which they could see only the water tower of the moshav, where they would work unhurriedly until the sun sank behind the dusty old fig trees and the low hills, and on their way home, in the pleasant calm which settled on everything toward evening, to the soothing sound of the mooing of the cows and the barking of the dogs, Jeremiah would sometimes let him take the reins and lead the horse along the broad red path which passed through vegetable beds and melon and pumpkin patches and fields covered with wildflowers and thorn trees and weeds and turned and skirted the farmyards of the moshav houses, and then, in the mellowness of that evening hour, Goldman would feel so proud and happy that he wanted to burst.

Zipporah, flushed with sun and effort and perspiring with the heat and humidity, her pale skin covered with freckles, ran the house and the farm and had her hands full from early in the morning until everyone went to bed at night, and in addition to her regular work she would sit down late at night to answer Meir's letters, and look after her mother when she was with them, and in addition to this there was Aviezer, withdrawn into himself and wrapped in a kind of cloud, who had dropped out of school and besides his work on the farm, which he did diligently and uncomplainingly, had become passionately attached to animals. He kept various insects and adopted stray dogs, and after that he bought a foal from an Arab and reared it, and the only member of the family with whom he communicated was Ruth, and he served as the main focus of Zipporah's anxieties and concern and attention, from year to year he grew handsomer and more withdrawn, and she tried to understand what it was that was bothering him and making him so remote—until one morning she woke up and discovered that Esther was having a love affair with one of the members of the moshav, a married man with children, and for a number of weeks she had no rest by day or night and she wondered what to do and said nothing, and in the end, without saying a word to Joel, when the rain started, she spoke to Esther and sent her off to join Jeremiah, who had also dropped out of school, even before Aviezer, and joined the Palmach and was living with his fellow recruits on a kibbutz, and there, on the kibbutz, Esther spent a number of unbearable months—she stopped eating almost entirely and vomited all the time until they feared for her life—but in the end, in a process which was full of suffering, she gradually and painfully recovered from her separation from her lover.

These summer holidays in the country, so full of freedom and adventure, which always merged in his mind with the visit he had paid to Avinoam, remained engraved in Goldman's memory as the best days of his life, and they went on for a few years until Joel and Zipporah were obliged to sell the farm, because she had been suffering for years from eczema and allergic symptoms in the spring and the beginning of summer which grew worse from year to year, and they were exacerbated by the weariness which accumulated in her body and grew more and more oppressive, and in spite of everything they tried by every means in their power to hang onto the farm, and it was only when they had no strength left that they closed up and went back to town, but without Meir, who was serving in the Western Desert, and afterward in Italy, where he stayed on for a short period after the war was over in order to work with the illegal immigrants to Eretz Yisrael, and without Jeremiah, who was in the Palmach, while Aviezer had joined a kibbutz and left it not long afterward and gone to work in the ports, and then as a hired tractor driver on farms and earthworks all over the country, and he came only once a week or fortnight to see Joel and Zipporah, who bought a little house in the suburbs of Tel Aviv, where they lived with Mussolini, the Arab mongrel dog they had brought with them from the moshav, and with Grandmother Rachel, who despite her age was still sharp-witted and spry and took care of her own needs and read the Yiddish newspapers, and sometimes the Hebrew ones too, and visited her friends and went to pray at the synagogue, where she was much respected, and needed little help from Zipporah, who for a few months devoted a large part of her time to Nahama, Meir's wife, a country girl whose father had a dairy herd and a few acres of irrigated crops in one of the old colonies, whom he had married when he was on leave from Italy and who gave birth to his son while he was still serving there.

This marriage was the fruit of a brief, and at the beginning also a casual, acquaintanceship, and it took place hastily and without too much thought, as if in an attempt to hold onto something and not allow time to extinguish the seeds of a closeness that was only just coming into being, but it was successful because Meir was a man of modest and uncomplicated demands and Nahama was a straightforward and hard-working girl, and apart from the first few months after having the baby she did not need Zipporah's help and Zipporah did not try to press her because she was always careful not to impose herself and because most of her time and energy was now being devoted to Temima, Jeremiah's wife, who gave birth to a son a few months after Nahama, because Temima, unlike Nahama, was scatterbrained and impractical to the point of naïveté, and being unused to working she was, for all her goodwill, helpless and even frightened when faced by the demands of the baby and the running of the house, where they were always hard pressed because Jeremiah, who had been demobilized from the Palmach and gone to work as a land surveyor, did not earn much, and despite their poverty they had another son a year later and when he was two years old they had a daughter. Zipporah was against the marriage from the start because she felt that it would bring them nothing but trouble, but she kept her peace and made no attempt to discuss her objections with Joel, nor, of course, with Jeremiah, both because she had made up her mind never to interfere in matters of this nature and because she understood that her interference would do no good because Jeremiah, who was as hard-working and pure-hearted as his father, was very much in love with Temima, who possessed a special, if somewhat childish, charm of her own and whose very impracticality had something captivating about it, not to mention the simplicity and generosity of spirit which over the course of the years revealed themselves to Zipporah, who had her hands full during the first years of their marriage because it was she who did most of the shopping for them and cooked and ironed and tidied their cupboards and kept an eye on the children, and in the meantime Meir came back from Italy with a furrowed brow and a balding head and started working as a mechanic, and after work in the evenings he did odd jobs repairing electrical units and installing blinds and locks to earn a bit of extra money, and in the next two years they had another two sons, and in the meantime a young man called Alter arrived among the refugees from Europe, a very distant relative of Zipporah's, whose parents neither she nor her mother had ever seen—they knew of them only by hearsay—and Joel and Zipporah took him in and gave him clothes and shoes and a temporary bed on the porch.

This Alter was a restless young man, very simple and uneducated, and Joel took him to work with him and began teaching him his trade, but even before he had learned to saw properly the troubles preceding the War of Independence broke out and young Alter, together with Meir and Jeremiah and Aviezer, was taken into the army, but despite the troubled nature of the times they started getting ready for Ruth's wedding to Jacob Teich, and Joel and Zipporah went to visit his parents and invited them to come for lunch one Saturday, and the date for the wedding was already set, and Zipporah, who was preoccupied with worries about her sons and young Alter and also had her hands full with Meir and Jeremiah's children and her sister Sarah, who gave her no rest, sat all night long at her sewing machine and made Ruth sheets and pillowcases from the best material she could find, but a few days before the wedding, when the sheets annd pillowcases were already starched and ironed and tied up in bundles with blue silk ribbons, they were informed that Jacob Teich had been killed on one of the convoys taking food to Jerusalem, and Zipporah put the sheets and pillowcases away in the cupboard, and less than a year later she gave them, with mixed feelings, to Esther, who from time to time remarked to Zipporah and to Ruth, and also to other people, that she would marry only for love, even if that love lasted for only a month, and otherwise she would rather remain a spinster for the rest of her life, and one day before leaving the house—she was then working as a signal woman in the army—she went up to Ruth and said, laughing, "Last night I was on my back. Spring's begun," and nine months later she had a child by Michael Kaplan, whom she married after a short acquaintanceship in a modest ceremony attended by a small number of guests—even Meir and Jeremiah and young Alter were missing because of the war—and when she stood under the bridal canopy in Temima's white wedding dress which Zipporah had altered to fit her it was obvious to everyone that she was pregnant.

About a year later Ruth got married too, to Gershon Gothelf, a precision mechanic who was about ten years older than she was and who loved her very much, and Zipporah, with an obscure feeling of uneasiness, made her new sheets and pillowcases, but in the meantime, while they were still in mourning for Jacob Teich, the war spread and raged all over the country, and Zipporah, silent and maintaining a façade of calm and keeping up all her routine duties and activities, could not tell day from night for worry over her three sons and young Alter, of whose whereabouts both she and Joel, who also kept up appearances and only asked, every day, as if by the way, whether there were any letters, were quite in the dark, not knowing if they were in the north or south or Jerusalem, and this ignorance was worse than anything, and the news that filtered through to them only increased their confusion and anxiety, because their letters were disjointed and fragmentary and arrived only after long delays, and thus, in the chaotic upheaval of the times, they heard indirectly that young Alter had been killed, and for almost a month Joel and Zipporah, who ran from office to office and person to person trying to find out if it were really true, could not console themselves and recover from the depression into which this death had cast them, until one evening the bell rang and Ruth opened the door and young Alter, who knew nothing about his death, came in tired and dirty and sweating, but alive and well, and Zipporah, who could not control herself, went into the bathroom and cried and came out a few minutes later after washing her face.

Soon after this they heard that Jeremiah had been wounded;

he had been wounded in the chest and arm and lay under a bush in the boiling sun for half a day until the orderlies got him out and transferred him to the hospital, where he lay in a ward with dozens of other wounded soldiers and Zipporah, who when she first came to visit him—Temima had been there the day before—stood gazing about her for a few minutes in the entrance to the ward before she finally spotted him, went to visit him almost every day, usually with Temima and sometimes with Joel or Ruth, and on these visits she would bring him cake or fruit or onion pretzels, which she baked especially for him because she knew how much he liked them, and onions were worth their weight in gold, and all that time, between the running of the household and the anxieties of the war, she had to keep on intervening in the endless, and also boring, quarrels between Sarah and Jonah Kotchinski, which grew more and more acrimonious and filled their lives with fury and chaos, and led them to the brink of divorce, now with the consent and even at the insistence of Jonah, who one day when Sarah was not at home packed a few articles of clothing and personal belongings in two suitcases and went out and locked the door behind him, and while he was standing there a neighbor came out and looked at him inquisitively and he picked up the two cases and said, "Mrs. Riebenfeld, I can't stand it any longer," and went off, and two days later he came back and made up with Sarah, who had nearly gone out of her mind with grief and loneliness, but the reconciliation lasted no longer than a few days and then everything was back to normal, the anger and the fights, and Jonah demanded a divorce again, and Zipporah was also in favor of it, but Sarah, who had been pushing things in this direction for years, was now in no hurry to give him a divorce.

Zipporah also sent parcels to Meir and Aviezer and young Alter with friends who came from time to time to deliver hasty messages from them, and in these parcels she carefully packed cakes and biscuits and sometimes a jar of pickled herring or a tin of canned fruit, and to these she would add clean socks and underwear and sometimes bootlaces or a scarf, and for Aviezer she also sent cigarettes, the best she could lay her hands on. The years had made Aviezer even more handsome, but also more silent and withdrawn, and when he came home on short leaves he would drop onto the bed and fall immediately into a deep sleep, and if he could have he would have gone on sleeping for a week, and when he woke and had an hour to spare before going back to his unit he would play with Mussolini, who spent most of his time sleeping in a corner of the room and had already begun losing weight and stinking of old age, or else he would sit in the kitchen and listen to Ruth, who embroidered and made decorations full of fantasy from paper cutouts and scraps of material and bits of glass and wood and woven mats from raffia in the shape of birds and fishes, and he often visited her afterward too, when she was married to Gershon Gothelf, and to Aviezer alone, after many years of silence and restraint, she poured out her heart and spoke without complaint or even longing about Jacob Teich, who sometimes appeared in her dreams, and sometimes, not often, even when she was making love to Gershon.

A few weeks after he was wounded, as the fighting died down all over the country, Jeremiah was discharged from the hospital, and although he had not completely recovered from his wound, which continued to bother him and hamper the movements of his arm, he went back to work as a land surveyor and drove all over in a dusty pickup, coming back at night to a house which had become unbearably crowded since the birth of his fourth child, but he did not have the money to buy a bigger apartment and refused to get into debt, so he was obliged to wait until the war was over and things were more or less back to normal, when his brothers and brothers-in-law and young Alter, building in the afternoons after work and on Saturdays, helped him to extend his house, which was located not far from Joel and Zipporah, adding one big room and enlarging the kitchen and the veranda and the two existing rooms. They all now went back to work at their old jobs, except that young Alter, who looked much older than his age, opened a grocery shop, and Aviezer, who did not marry and toward the end of his army service suddenly decided to become a pilot and was accepted for the pilots' training course but failed to become a combat pilot and was trained instead to fly light aircraft, specializing in reconnaisance and signals work and aerial photography. He spent three years doing this and then left the army and went to America and after spending about two years there he came back to Israel and started working as a pilot in an agricultural crop-spraying outfit. He enjoyed this work which, although it lacked the advantages of speed and height, offered danger and challenge and risk and therefore appealed to Aviezer and filled him with intoxication every time he flew over the cotton and sorghum and sugar beet fields in his Piper, swooping dangerously low to the ground, almost touching treetops and roofs, dipping under electrical wires and climbing up into the air again, and after work, in his spare time, he devoted himself to reading books, which he had never done before, and to his old love of animals and the rearing of a beautiful Alsatian dog after his boxer died of parathion poisoning.

Aviezer lived alone and on Saturday evenings and on holidays he would come with the rest of his brothers and sisters and their families to visit Joel and Zipporah, who despite the signs of old age which were creeping up on them went on living their lives as before—Joel went on working at his trade and Zipporah looked after the house and the family and never had a moment's rest because there was always something that had to be done and someone who had to be helped among her tribe of sons and daughters and sons-in-law and daughters-in-law and advice that had to be given or oil to be poured on troubled waters, or peace to be made, as in the case of the crisis that overtook Jeremiah and Temima's marriage in the wake of an unimportant love affair upon which Temima embarked, one last fling before her life finally settled down into routine, which hurt Jeremiah so much that he asked her for a divorce, but Zipporah stopped him and suggested that he wait a while before doing anything, since the affair was not really important, however much it hurt, and it would blow over as quickly as it had begun, which is exactly what happened, and it was only then, after it was all over, one day when she was alone with Temima, whose face was as open and youthfully fresh and smooth as ever, she asked her if it had all been really necessary, and Temima said, "Yes," and Zipporah slowly smoothed the oilcloth on the table with the palm of her hand and then looked up at her daughter-in-law, of whom she was still as fond as ever, and said that she shouldn't have told Jeremiah, and Temima said, "He heard about it from somebody else," and Zipporah said, "Then you should have denied it completely," and when she saw that Temima was listening to her she added that we should be careful not to hurt people unnecessarily, and then she said that life was full of imperfections and limitations and it was impossible for it to be otherwise and we had to accept this state of affairs without bitterness, and she repeated, "You have to be careful," and Temima said, "Yes, but it's not always possible," and Zipporah wanted to stroke Temima's cheek but she only looked at her with a look full of sympathy and affection and said, "Yes, I know," and went on smoothing the oilcloth with her hand and after a short pause she said that there was a kind of beauty even in the unavoidable routines of daily life, and afterward she said that there were responsibilities and obligations which in the last analysis were not necessarily opposed to freedom, and in any case there were people who could not turn their backs on them, and that this was something that had to be taken into account too, and she fell silent for a moment and then said, "All my life I've prayed never to become bitter," and a slight smile appeared on her face and again she said, "You have to be careful," and she said this as calmly and quietly as she had said everything else; there was no anger in her voice or words and she did not blame Temima, unlike Esther, who hated her, perhaps because of her youthful bloom, or perhaps because of the openness and naturalness in everything she did, and on a number of occasions she did her best to arouse Jeremiah's suspicions that Temima was being unfaithful to him again, or that at any rate she was quite capable of it, and she urged him to leave her, but Esther, who had turned into a bitter woman eaten up with envy, hated Ruth and Nahama too, and also her husband whom she nagged mercilessly, and she was always looking for excuses to feel aggrieved and provoke quarrels, which were sometimes vociferous and insulting, and usually, perhaps without intending to, she pushed these quarrels in a certain direction and turned them into arguments about money, and especially about her parents' property and how it should be divided on their death, which was extremely embarrassing for everyone, and she claimed that she had more rights than Nahama, because Nahama's father had left her his land and cows, and even more than Ruth, because she was the oldest daughter, and as for Temima she would not agree to her being left a penny on account of her love affair with another man, not to mention her wastefulness, and she spoke her mind and made no attempt to control her feelings even at the family gatherings on Saturday evenings and holidays.

These gatherings had become a family tradition and one by one they would all arrive with their clans—Meir and Nahama and their six children, Jeremiah and Temima and their four children, Michael and Esther and their three children, and Gershon and Ruth and their three children and Gershon's mother, a fine-looking woman with a Russian face who had worked for years as a laboratory assistant in a hospital and come to live with them when she retired—and they would all gather in the big room, which seemed to grow smaller from year to year, and they all sat around the table which was opened out to its full length and upon which Zipporah placed sweets and fruit and peanuts and bottles of fruit juice, and everyone ate and drank and talked about family affairs and work and the difficulties of existence, and sometimes political arguments would break out too, mainly on account of Michael Kaplan, who was a construction engineer with left-wing views and couldn't stand the way in which "they"—in other words, the leadership—were trampling justice underfoot and squandering, in their short-sightedness and avarice, the strength and goodwill of the working classes and leading the country on a slippery downward slope, but in spite of his impulsiveness, which died down over the years, he had charm and a sense of humor, and thanks to these qualities the arguments usually ended in a spirit of friendliness and mutual compromise, and toward the end of the evening Joel would distribute little presents among his grandchildren, but with the passing of time the family grew bigger and bigger, because the grandchildren began to get married and have children of their own, and they stopped meeting in full force except on rare occasions, because some of them moved away and others were in the army or busy with work or family affairs, but most of them, if they possibly could, would still show up regularly with their children, whom Joel would jog on his knee or lift onto his shoulders or sing songs to, and when Zipporah turned seventy everyone assembled, including Goldman's father and Stefana and Shmuel and Bracha and Uncle Lazar with Yehudit Tanfuss and Jonah Kotchinski and Sarah, who stayed for only a little while, and young Alter with his wife and his two sons, the oldest of whom was about to complete his military service, and also Nahama's mother and Temima's parents and even Michael Kaplan's parents, both of whom were doctors, who had never been on familiar terms with the family, and Zipporah for her part had made no overtures to them, but now that they had come she greeted them warmly and they sat with the rest of the guests in the garden and celebrated the event, which Zipporah, to tell the truth, would have preferred to pass in silence, and in the middle of the evening, when the festivity was at its height, Joel extracted from his pocket a little box wrapped in pretty paper and tied with a ribbon and presented it to Zipporah, who opened it and took out a gold watch which Joel had purchased for her in secret, because ever since coming to the country Zipporah had never had a new watch, and Zipporah, smiling broadly, looked at it with shining eyes, joyful in her gratitude, and they kissed, which made them blush, but Meir and Jeremiah and Aviezer and Esther and

Ruth had also decided to surprise their mother with a gold watch, and so she became the possessor of two gold watches at once, to the applause and laughter of the company, who went on celebrating until after midnight, and then gradually dispersed and went home, leaving Joel and Zipporah and Aviezer, who, as on most of these family gatherings, remained with his parents for a little longer after everyone else had gone home.

Zipporah wanted him to find a wife and settle down and have a family because she believed that it would save him from his isolation and be good for him, but she said nothing to him, not even by as much as a hint, and she would only look with eyes full of affection and expectation at his handsome face, which had grown lined and furrowed and sadder and more withdrawn, and at his curly hair, which was quite white now, and try to guess what was going on in his heart and head, and silently convey her wishes, in whose realization she no longer believed, to him and make him do what she wanted, but by now most of her energies and attention were being devoted to Sarah, whose body was being eaten up by cancer, and to Jonah Kotchinski, whose face had grown as skinny and wrinkled as a chicken's and whose voice had dried up, and he would weep in sorrow and helplessness— she was dying before his eyes and he could do nothing to save her or even to meet her needs and take care of her—because he didn't know what to do and he was a broken man and he couldn't bear the sight of her face and her blighted body, which gave rise in him to an uncontrollable revulsion, and also because he was afraid, and on the other hand he didn't have the means to hire a professional nurse to look after her because all his money had been spent on clothes and carpets and all kinds of luxuries and amusements, and it was Zipporah who looked after her, but Zipporah was no longer in the best of health herself, because the years and the illnesses had taken their toll, the circulatory troubles and the diabetes, and especially the disease which had infected her right leg and which caused her unbearable pain and drained her strength and energy and made it so hard for her to move about that shortly after Sarah's death she could no longer walk without support and spent most of the day in bed or sitting in a chair, and Joel, with the help of one of his sons or daughters-in-law, who never left her alone, would shift her from place to place and assist her in everything, especially Nahama, who cooked for her and Joel and cleaned the house and washed and ironed and took care of her personal hygiene as well.

Although Joel tried to keep up a front of calm and good humor in front of Zipporah, and sometimes even made jokes, he became more and more depressed at the sight of his wife's approaching end and it became harder and harder for him to hide his feelings, and so too with the rest of the family, who hoped for the best and feared the worst, from which they knew there was no escape, and only Zipporah, despite the pain which never left her and despite the fact that all her life she had been used to looking after herself and had feared above all needing the favors of others, on whose help and support she was now totally dependent, tried to cheer them up and most of the time she managed to hang onto her vitality and optimism, not because she had any illusions about her condition but because she believed that it was forbidden to lose the will to live and the affirmation of life and she felt she had no reason to despair or bemoan her fate since, after all, her mind and her hands were still perfectly sound, and so were all her senses, just as she believed, with the same instinctive certainty, that man was obliged to struggle against adversity and had no right to abandon himself and his troubles to others, and when the family gathered she would still cut the cake, which they would place next to her, with a dexterous hand, and pour out the fruit juice and ask them all what they were doing and dish out advice and reproaches and scoldings, the fruit of knowledge and experience and honesty, and only once her face fell and filled with a rage which she could not control, which was when young Alter came to say goodbye to her and Joel before leaving with his family for Australia, and Zipporah listened with Joel to his humble and respectful words of parting and then said, "What did you lack here in Israel?" and young Alter, his scanty hair rumpled by the ventilator whirring at his side and making him feel uncomfortable, rubbed his thick, ugly hands and said something about the income tax and about a man having only one life to live, and Zipporah said, "Of that I am perfectly well aware myself. You don't have to be a genius to know that," and Joel asked him if he wanted anything to drink, the day was hot and humid and his face was dripping with sweat despite the ventilator, and young Alter, whose tongue felt like a piece of dough in his mouth, shook his head and said incoherently that his brother in Australia was the only one left of his whole family, and Zipporah said, "Good. Go then and I wish you a good journey. I only hope you won't live to regret it," and then, after a short silence, she said, "No one has to stay here against his will. You can go," and young Alter said, "Yes," and went on sitting on the edge of his chair, his face gloomy and his head sunk between his shoulders and his eyes darting from the table to the chairs—he didn't look at Zipporah or meet her eyes—and from time to time he tried to smooth his ruffled hair, and Joel offered him a glass of fruit juice or cold water, and young Alter said, "No thanks," and wiped the perspiration from his face and said something about his brother again and then he got up and shook hands with Zipporah and Joel, who accompanied him to the door and said, "In any case, if you ever want to come back the door's always open," and young Alter thanked him with a movement of his head and went out of the house into the sun, and Joel, whom Shmuel and Bracha now asked about Zipporah's leg, looked after him until he disappeared behind the hedge and went back into the room and sat down in young Alter's chair and said, "People go chasing about like mice. He'll be back," and Zipporah said, "I don't need him here," and a moment later she said, "No, I don't believe it," and Joel said, "We're hoping for the best. In any event the doctors aren't making any promises," and Bracha said, "You can never tell," and Joel said, "Yes, maybe you're right," and afterward he said, "Tzalik's getting married soon," and Shmuel said, "Mazel tov. Who to?"

and Joel said, "A girl from Hadera, a teacher. They met in the army," and sat down next to Uncle Lazar and Goldman, holding his empty cup and pretending not to hear, saw in a flash, for the first time, how much they resembled each other, Joel and Uncle Lazar, and he waited until Joel had completed his visit and taken his leave and shortly afterward he too rose to his feet and said goodbye to everyone and left, and the next morning he went to St. Antonio's with Israel and sat on one of the church benches and listened to him playing the organ, and afterward they had lunch at the fish restaurant and while they were eating Goldman talked a lot about his experiences in the army and especially about his plans for the future and suddenly he said, "I envy you for your music," and Israel said, "Yes," and at that moment he knew for certain that nothing would come of him and his music, and Goldman said, "It's wonderful," and after a short pause for reflection he returned to the subject of his plans for the future, and when they had finished their fish they drank Turkish coffee with *baklava* and walked home along the seashore, where there was a sudden, surprising feeling of autumn in the air and a sharp smell of fish and seaweed, and in the evening they went to the movies together, and Goldman put the visit to Zipporah in the hospital off until some other time. The shadow of his separation from Dita hovered over him and oppressed him more than he would have thought possible and he thought of going to visit her, or at least of calling her, but he restrained himself, and thus the first days after his return from the army passed by in going to the beach and reading and all kinds of chores and he did not go back to work, or even let them know at the office that he was back, and apart from one brief meeting he did not see Caesar, who was restless and depressed and hardly listened to what he said.

Three days after this meeting, on the day that Eliezra and Gidon went to the rabbinate to finalize their divorce, Caesar took his camera and drove out of town, where he had spent the past few weeks in a state of terrible confusion, with hopes that sky-rocketed one day and evaporated the next morning, promises that changed, sometimes at the very moment of their utterance, into lies, firm resolutions which disintegrated after an hour and left him feeling helpless and confused, and also full of hostility, because he did not want this divorce, which was suddenly about to become a reality, and he did everything in his power, lying and pleading and threatening, and sometimes simply disappearing, to stop it from taking place, and until the very last evening he believed that it would not in fact take place, even though Gidon and Eliezra had already been to the rabbinate a number of times and the main stages of the divorce proceedings were already behind them, because he was sure that Eliezra would draw back at the last minute, but Eliezra did not draw back, and even if she had it would probably have been too late because Gidon had finally decided that he too wanted a divorce after trying for months to persuade her to change her mind and making her life a misery when he failed—he moved out of their bedroom and either ignored her or abused her, sometimes at the top of his voice, and threatened to take revenge on her in every way he could, and informed her that he would refuse to let her see the children and that he wouldn't give her a penny, and one day he even beat her up—but in the end, thanks largely to the influence of his parents, he accepted the situation and agreed to the divorce, even insisted on it, and all he wanted was to get the whole thing over with as quickly and quietly as possible.

The divorce took place at noon and immediately after the ceremony was over Eliezra called the studio and asked for Caesar, and Israel, who didn't have the heart to tell her that he had left town, said that he was out and would probably be back toward evening, and toward evening when she called again Israel went on lying and said that Caesar had called from Haifa and asked him to tell her that he wouldn't be able to get back until the next day, and Eliezra said, "He promised me that he would wait for me at the studio today or that he would get in touch with me," and Israel said, "I really don't know anything about it," and Eliezra said, "OK, just tell him when he gets back that I'm at my parents'

and I'm waiting to hear from him," and Israel said, "All right,"
and Eliezra said, "I'm divorced," and Israel hesitated and said
nothing, and Eliezra said, "Don't forget to tell him," and hung up
and two days later Caesar came back like a thief in the night,
sweating and disheveled, and he looked so pathetic and forlorn
that Israel wanted to burst out laughing at the sight of him but
he restrained himself and regarded him in silence as he removed
his jacket and took the heavy camera off his neck and went into
the darkroom for a moment and came back and wiped his face,
and after a short silence he asked if there had been any calls for
him and if anything had happened in his absence and Israel,
sitting on the edge of the couch, said, "Yes. Eliezra got divorced,"
and Caesar said, "What else?" and Israel said, "She called and
asked me to tell you that she was at her parents' place and that
she was waiting to hear from you," and Caesar said, "The dirty
bitch. Let her go to hell and the quicker the better," and he took
off his shirt, which was stinking with sweat, and threw it onto the
table and went into the bathroom, and after taking a shower and
changing his clothes he poured himself half a glass of whiskey
and lit a cigarette and leaned against the piano and said that he
had never asked her to divorce her husband, or even suggested
it, but on the contrary, he had been opposed to the idea and in
fact he had begged her not to do it, or at least not to do anything
in a hurry, so her divorce was nobody's business but her own
and had nothing to do with him.

Israel said nothing and Caesar, who was very confused and
upset, moved away from the piano and started pacing about the
room, cursing Gidon and Eliezra, and suddenly he stood still and
asked Israel if he should call her, and Israel said, "You haven't
got a choice," and Caesar looked at him irritably and asked him
why he didn't have a choice and what he had to call her for and
Israel said, "So that you can meet her and put an end to the
business," and Caesar hesitated for a moment and then went
unwillingly to the phone and picked up the receiver and slammed
it angrily down and a moment later he picked it up again and

began dialing, but before he had finished dialing the number he put it down and said that it wasn't urgent and nothing would happen if he waited until tomorrow since she was already divorced and in any case she didn't know that he was back in town, and then there was a silence during which Caesar stood gazing out of the window—the sun was sinking and the sky was full of little gray clouds—and afterward he sat down on the couch next to Israel and said that maybe he should marry Eliezra after all, because he really loved her, but Israel said nothing, and Caesar lit another cigarette and said that he was sick and tired of living and that he would like to grow a beard and run away to Spain or America or go and live on one of the Greek islands because he didn't have the strength left to face all the difficulties and obligations and groundless demands that were being made of him, and he didn't have the faintest desire to marry Eliezra and have another family, one was quite enough for him, and no power on earth could force him to do it, certainly not Eliezra, who was not meant for family life in the first place, and he began once more to expound his theories about the stupidity and bankruptcy of marriage and the institution of the family in a world which was fluid and striving toward amorphous situations and relationships, theories which Israel had already heard from him on innumerable previous occasions, but this time he expanded them, or introduced a certain variation, by arguing that it was precisely those people who loved each other who should never marry and that marriage was intended only for people who did not love each other, since the realization of love in marriage was also, inevitably, its death, because everything that was alive, and love was life, could not exist without movement, whereas marriage was static and therefore unable to sustain love.

Caesar pronounced these arguments very firmly, as if he really wanted to convince Israel, because now more than ever he was desperate for some magic formula which would enable him to avoid making a decision which could no longer be avoided, and allow him to go on living in a situation in which he would go on getting everything without losing anything and, when there was no longer an alternative at all, would allow him not to do whatever he did not want to do and feel that he had justice on his side. Israel listened to him patiently and when Caesar said, "Don't you think so?" he said, "I don't know. I've never thought about it," and Caesar looked at him for a moment and then went to the phone again, but this time he didn't even pick it up, and after a few moments of indecision he said he would call the next day and the next day he called Eliezra and that evening they met in the studio.

Eliezra, who was tired and tense, tried to hide this as best she could and keep up an appearance of happiness and she did, in fact, feel a certain exhilaration, and of course she also felt expectant, and after they had embraced and kissed she announced to Caesar that she was now divorced from Gidon and there was nothing to prevent them from getting married, and Caesar, who had made them coffee, said, "Yes, of course, that's wonderful," and asked her how Gidon was taking it and Eliezra said, "All right. It didn't come as a surprise to him, you know," and then she added, "I'm glad it's behind me," and she sat down on the couch next to Caesar and repeated that now there was nothing to stop them from getting married, and Caesar, who was stroking her knee, said, "Yes. But perhaps we should wait for a while, until things calm down a bit," and in the meantime he saw that her beauty was no longer what it had been, especially her face, which had something bitter about it and seemed on the point of losing its bloom, as did her neck, and he felt that he no longer loved her and wasn't even attracted to her, and the truth was that her presence burdened him and he wished that she would finish her coffee and go away and he would never have to see her again, but Eliezra went on sitting there and they discussed plans for the future and an apartment and money and a trip abroad for fun, and Caesar showered her with loving words, interspersing them with comments on his difficult situation and his troubles, and dwelling especially on the illness of his son, and he petted and pampered her as much as he could, but when she wanted to go to bed with him—at first she waited for him to understand by himself and then she asked him outright, she was so much in need of affection and encouragement—he got out of it by saying that he was tired, and Eliezra, who said she understood but at the same time made another halfhearted and indirect attempt in the same direction, resigned herself to his refusal and submitted joylessly to his empty and impatient caresses, and then Caesar took her back to her parents' place, and with his mind made up to break off with her immediately—a plan which seemed to him both necessary and easy to implement—he went over to Tehilla's place and woke her up and went to bed with her with a feeling of relief and happiness, suddenly she felt closer and more necessary to him than anyone else in the world, and thus he fell asleep, but the next day, almost from the moment he woke up in the morning, he was overtaken by gloom and restlessness, and this gloomy and irritable mood continued, with short interruptions, for a number of weeks, during which the battle was waged between him and Eliezra, with Caesar making promises and withdrawing them again on the basis of various explanations and evasions and excuses and apologies and attempts to make her feel sorry for him, once again chiefly by means of his sick son, and soon afterward he would be seized by anxiety and the feeling that he was about to lose the thing most precious to him in the world, and he would rush over to see her, moved and very much in love, and go to bed with her and promise to marry her, even going so far as to fix a date, and then he would withdraw again and evade her with feelings of impatience and irritation and sometimes also with a wave of loathing.

Eliezra gradually stopped putting pressure on him, and then she almost stopped calling him and they hardly ever met, and Caesar, tired of it all, breathed a sigh of relief—until he heard that Eliezra was dating an engineer, which roused him from his serenity and galvanized him into action and he began rushing about, eaten up with regrets and a terrible feeling of loss, as if everything were slipping away from him never to return, making desperate attempts to get her back again, but all in vain, because now for the first time Eliezra had realized that Caesar was leading her astray and in spite of his pleas she refused to meet him and told him to stop calling her, but Caesar, despite the certain knowledge that it was too late, did not stop until Eliezra married her engineer and then his lust for her turned into a venomous hatred. He disparaged and besmirched her whenever he could to anyone who would listen, and cursed her and her parents and her engineer, about whom he had been making inquiries and whom he had been trying to meet, or at least see, ever since the day he heard about the relationship between them, and at long last, one evening a few days before the wedding, he succeeded quite by chance in seeing him with Eliezra, when he stopped his car in front of a traffic light—they were crossing the street—and he sat watching them until they disappeared, it was all over in a moment, and afterward, later that evening, he said to Israel, "I saw her with her old man. Let her have him. He could be her father. I'm damned if I can understand how she can go to bed with that impotent old man. I bet he's got a prick like a pea," and then he said, "Let her marry him if she likes. I don't care," and then he said, "It won't come to anything, it's all nonsense," and he looked at Israel, who was sitting by the piano, which he had been playing when Caesar came in, and who said nothing. For the first time it had now become clear to Caesar that all this was not a bad dream or a story Eliezra had invented to make him jealous, or a passing whim on her part, and all that remained to him was thus to cling to fantastic hopes that time would stop, or that there would be a catastrophe, and he really did pray that Eliezra would die in an accident or from an illness or drown in the sea, or that her engineer would be badly hurt, lose a leg, or be paralyzed, but there was no catastrophe and time did not stop and the day of Eliezra's wedding to the engineer arrived.

It was a pleasant, sunny day, a few days after the first rains had fallen, and Caesar came to the studio early in the morning, his face gray, and did something in the darkroom and then he had a cup of coffee and looked distractedly at some photographs and threw them down—he couldn't take in what he was seeing and he didn't have any patience—and he talked to Israel for a bit, a desultory and distracted conversation (he seemed to be moving about in a fog), and then he took his car to the garage and after that he went to see a morning movie at the Paris theater, but he left in the middle of the film and went to do all kinds of unnecessary chores in town, hoping that he would meet someone he knew, but he was really waiting for Tehilla to come back from work, he needed her so much, and she was late, and in the meantime he went to see his parents and he sat there for a few minutes and then left, it was more than he could stand, and he went back to the studio, and afterward he went to visit Tirza and the children, but Tirza's parents were there and he hardly had a chance to speak to her, and when Tehilla finally came back—by then the wedding ceremony must have been over and the guests were sitting at the tables and eating—Caesar was grateful to her and took her to a restaurant and tried to hold onto her for as long as possible and suggested that they go out dancing or to a movie, but Tehilla, who knew nothing at all about what had happened, was exhausted, and at a rather early hour he took her home, very disappointed because he didn't want to be left alone, and he went downstairs and got into his car and drove along the road to Jerusalem and came back early in the morning, exhausted and miserable, and cuddled up to her and Tehilla, half asleep, let him have his way, and less than a month later, one Saturday afternoon a few days after the ceremony itself had taken place in a small family circle, they had a party to celebrate their wedding at Tehilla's parents' apartment.

Apart from an evasive hint or two Caesar said nothing about this party—about the wedding ceremony itself he said absolutely nothing, either before or after it took place—but at about four o'clock on Saturday afternoon he suddenly called Israel and asked him to get dressed and come to the party, he literally begged him as if he were begging for his life, and Israel said, "OK, I'll come. Don't worry, it'll be all right," and Caesar said, "You have to come. And the quicker you get here the better. And try to bring Goldman too," and Israel said again, "It'll be all right, don't worry," and without delay, albeit unwillingly, he called Goldman, who was surprised because it was the first he had heard about the wedding, apart perhaps from vague hints to which he had paid no attention because by this time he was already absorbed in other matters, but he agreed to go, and Israel showered and dressed and went to fetch him and the two of them went to Tehilla's parents' apartment, which was very large, but shrouded in a kind of gloom which seemed to emanate from the thick walls covered with dark wallpaper and the heavy wooden furniture and which clung to the silverware and the crystalware and the men and women in their elegant suits and dresses who were standing in little groups in the big rooms or moving about with glasses of wine and little sandwiches in their hands, talking to each other for the most part in Polish.

Israel and Goldman, who were overcome with a feeling of strangeness as soon as they stepped into the apartment, hesitated for a moment in the lobby and then slowly made their way through the people looking for Caesar, and in the meantime they bumped into Tehilla, who was looking very pretty in a dark blue batiste dress and whose face glowed with happiness when she saw them, and they shook hands with her, and Goldman also kissed her on the cheek, and they congratulated her and also her parents, to whom Tehilla introduced them before leading them to Caesar, who was sitting by himself in a corner, on the edge of a sofa, trying to pretend that it all had nothing to do with him, and that he wasn't even there, but as soon as he saw them he roused himself and hurried forward to greet them, as if it were only for them that he had been waiting all this time, and they embraced him and afterward they sat down with him on the sofa, where they remained for the duration of the party because Caesar, who was doing his best to demonstrate by his behavior that the entire affair had been imposed on him against his will, which hurt Tehilla, who did her best to placate him, would not let them move from their places or leave him alone for a moment, because he felt as out of place there as they did, and also very isolated, since none of his family or friends had come, apart from Yaffa, who put in an appearance for about half an hour and then left, and Besh, who although he never showed his face at wedding receptions or other festivities of the kind, because they aroused his scorn and fury, appeared all of a sudden, taking them all by surprise, full of smiles, and embraced Tehilla and kissed her and shook hands with her parents and wished them "Mazel tov" and slapped Caesar heartily on the shoulder and said, "Stop behaving like a spoiled child, Caesar. Smile. Nobody's done you any harm," and kissed Tehilla again as she offered him a glass of brandy and smiled affectionately at her, and raised the glass and said, "L'chaim!" and drank the brandy and said, "There's no point in crying over spilled milk. It's a waste of tears. Believe me," and Caesar said, "Yes," and Besh said, "You say yes, but that's not what you think," and although the doctors had repeatedly forbidden him to drink and recently he had even made some attempt to obey them, he poured himself another glass of brandy and emptied it and said, "Sometimes I think that I should have gotten married myself, but I'm a lost cause. I've got too many bad habits and besides, I can already see the gate in the fence, and I don't have to stand on tiptoe to see it. So what for?" and once again he slapped Caesar on the shoulder and gently stroked Tehilla's hair as she stood beside him looking at him affectionately, and then he took his leave of them all and went to visit Erwin and Zina, who had excused themselves from attending the wedding party on the grounds of Erwin's illness, which was, in fact, getting worse from week to week.

Erwin's body had grown very gaunt, his skin was dry and wrinkled and lately it had become increasingly difficult for him to walk, as if his bones and flesh had hardened, and he would spend most of the day sitting in an armchair in the living room or on the veranda—he had stopped going to the office—and staring with lifeless eyes at the street or the sky or the wall, repeatedly asking Zina or Besh or anyone else who happened to be there what the time was, and they would hasten to reply and soon afterward, sometimes only a few minutes later, he would ask them again, without turning his head and in the same dry and demanding tone. It seemed that he had developed a fear or deep suspicion of time and watches and clocks, and from time to time he would gaze at a clock with a strained expression, as if he were trying to decipher what the hands and numbers were really saying, in a kind of code which had to be interpreted by him in his own special way, and despite his disbelief and his repeated lack of success in this venture he could not leave the clocks and watches alone or stop asking people what the time was.

His doctors did not hold out much hope, but it was precisely this which injected Zina with new life and underneath her skin, in the shadow of her fears and her knowledge of the approaching end, she felt a current of joy, since Erwin's helplessness—he was sometimes seized by uncontrollable fits of trembling and sometimes he dirtied his pants, out of indifference or because he couldn't control his muscles—and his general debilitation and occasional hallucinations cut him off finally and completely from Chemda and made him for the first time since their marriage dependent on Zina and gave him up entirely into her hands, and her life, which had already dried up and lost its point and purpose, suddenly became revitalized and received a new vocation, and almost all her wishes were fulfilled after she had already lost hope, and unexpected efforts and sacrifices beyond the satisfaction of her own needs were suddenly demanded of her, and despite the pleas of Zvi and Yaffa and Max Spillman that she hire a nurse to look after Erwin or put him into a nursing home, she looked after him herself and spared no effort in doing so: She bathed him and shaved him and changed his clothes and sheets and put his shoes on for him and took him to the bathroom and sometimes she also fed him like a child, and she did all this willingly and with a profound feeling of satisfaction, but not without the hope of receiving a reward—she hoped that now, before his death, Erwin would express his gratitude and appreciation and that he would love her again, even if only for a short time, as he had once loved her, at the beginning, when they first met in Vienna, when Erwin was on a study tour and she was on her way to Eretz Yisrael, and thus, day after day, irredeemably romantic and endlessly disappointed, she followed his every movement and his every word, but to her sorrow she sometimes found it difficult to decide if he even remembered her name, or maybe he remembered it very well and was only pretending not to out of spite, for quite often, and almost every time that he became delirious and started hallucinating, he would call her by a different name, sometimes even by the name of a man, and among all the dozens of names that escaped his lips—the names of towns and women and foods and business competitors and hotels and medicines and politicians and movie stars—her name was hardly ever mentioned, and if it was she was never sure that she was the one he meant, and then again, in the throes of the same confusion, he would sometimes unexpectedly burst out with accusations that she was being unfaithful to him with Besh or with someone else, and this pleased but also frightened her, and in any case she denied it vehemently, but Erwin kept on because he believed in what he was saying, and then he would dwell lovingly on Chemda, and once he even asked her to invite Chemda to the house, and this hurt her very much, but she overlooked it and went on taking care of him as if nothing had happened and listening to him as he continued conversations which had taken place years ago with people who were no longer alive or described the hallucinations in which he visited all kinds of countries he had once traveled or countries of the mind which had never existed except in books or movies or his own fantastic visions, and saw complex structures which no one had ever seen before—huge barns and buildings composed of changing parts, camels with five humps, wonderful flowers, young girls with sturdy hips and many beautiful breasts, marvelous roads and bridges, or himself gliding in a rocking chair above a great lake—although there were also hours in which Erwin was in full possession of his senses and he would read the newspapers and listen to the radio or to the television, converse with Zina or the guests who came to the house, and even meet the manager of his office or Max Spillman and discuss money and business matters with them, but in the midst of his sobriety, in some mysterious shift of emphasis, he would sometimes be seized by a sudden fit of rage and pour out his wrath on his business competitors or partners or the members of his staff, and also on Zvi, whom he accused of behaving toward him in a calculating way and of waiting for his death in order to get his hands on the family inheritance, or else he would reminisce about faraway days in a spirit of yearning and the refusal to accept the fact that these things, which were past, would never return again, not even a little part of them, because the shadow of the end was already hanging over him, and he spoke often of the ugliness of the way in which death was approaching him, which hurt and insulted him, in addition to the fact that he would have liked to have lived forever, and in his despair, in the emptiness gaping all around him, he would repeatedly announce, usually to Besh but also to Ruhama, who together with Caesar was perhaps the only person whom he now loved without any suspicions or reservations, and he would say so quite frankly: "I have seen many wonderful lands in my life, eaten my fill of good food, made a lot of money, slept with many beautiful women, some of whom I was so madly in love with that I was sure I couldn't go on living for a single hour without them. And now I don't even remember their names. I hardly know that they once existed. And the same goes for everything else. So what's the point of anything?" and afterward, without rhyme or reason or any warning in advance, he would start weeping softly, with tears so detached that they seemed to fall from his eyes alone, an old man's weeping which shocked even Besh, in whom something seemed to have broken and disintegrated at the sight of Erwin's condition, and Zina, for all her love and hopes, would say to herself that perhaps it would be better if he died and was saved from his sorrow and pointless suffering, and especially from his terrible humiliation.

During one of his sober interludes, when he was already very close to death, Erwin said to Caesar—they were sitting in the living room and Erwin was clear-headed and cheerful—that he had only one wish left in life and that was to go to bed with an eighteen-year-old girl, since apart from the pleasure it would give him he was sure that it would also, at least for an hour, give him back his youth, but he would be happy even if it brought about his death. Caesar, with a smile on his face, listened silently and waited for his father to finish so that he could go, but Erwin, whose spirits suddenly sank, started pleading with him to arrange the meeting for him, without Zina's knowledge of course, and he took hold of his hand, and Caesar suddenly felt such profound revulsion and hostility toward his father, who kept urging him insistently and without a thought for his own dignity, that he felt a fierce desire to push him away and make him fall to the ground and hit him again and again in a fury of loathing until he died, and he tried to pull his hand away, Erwin's touch horrified him so that he wanted to scream, but Erwin would not let him go, and in the end Caesar promised him that he would arrange it and Erwin said, "But do it soon. My funeral procession has already come into the street," and he let him go and fell back into his chair, limp with exhaustion.

This conversation took place a few days after Caesar's wedding party and Erwin died about a week afterward on a cold, clear day, when Zina went out for an hour and left him alone, which was something she always did her best to avoid, and when she came back she found him lying lifeless on the floor, although his body still held a little warmth, which soon evaporated, and without having to think about it—everything was ready—she called the doctor and sent for Yaffa and Caesar and Besh and Zvi (Ruhama turned up quite by chance to visit Erwin), and when the initial alarm and confusion were over and the doctor had confirmed the fact of his death, Zina felt, in the midst of her distress, relief and a profound sense of exaltation, which was still in the process of coming to fruition but intimations of which she had already begun to feel when she imagined his death and afterward, for a split second, when she opened the door and knew that he was dead, and only the fact that he had died when she wasn't there disturbed her, but not as a feeling of guilt or even as the thought that there might have been any possibility of saving his life.

The funeral took place the next day and Zina, celebrating her final victory, walked behind the stretcher bearing Erwin's corpse in a black dress and a black coat, elegant and beautiful, and with every step she took she felt important and full of life and as if she were marrying him for the second time, or even for the first time, only this time everything would be perfect and just like in her dreams, and even while she grieved for Erwin, who for all her love had belonged more to death than life for a number of months now, she was glad of her own triumph and the defeat of Chemda, toward whom she had considered making some kind of magnanimous gesture, perhaps even offering to let her walk beside her behind the stretcher, but in the end, in spite of the temptation, she did nothing and she ignored her demonstratively, and Chemda, trying not to be conspicuous, walked at the end of the funeral procession. Yaffa and Zvi and Beatrice walked next to Zina, while Caesar and Tehilla walked a little way behind them, and not far from them Max Spillman and Ruhama, who was very obviously pregnant and whose face, pale and yellowish as a result of her condition, bore an expression of sorrow which made it beautiful and touching. Besh walked at the back, next to Chemda, and talked to her—it was he who had informed her of Erwin's death—and although he did not try to console her, for he was not capable of it, he concentrated his attention on her and tried in this and other ways to stress that she was a part of everything and that the grief was her grief too, and belonged to her no less than to Erwin's kith and kin, and every now and then he let out a curse and spat on the ground.

He did not approach the pit, but stood a little way off, apart from the rest, and when they started praying and lowered Erwin into the grave and covered him with earth he turned his head and looked indifferently into the distance, and afterward, when the funeral was over, he escorted Chemda to the bus and parted from her with a handshake and joined Zina and Caesar and the rest of the family, and when they returned to the house, which was clean and neat and solemnly festive, Zina, still wrapped in an aura of exaltation, felt for the first time a sense of anxiety and loss and the oppression of the approaching emptiness, and Besh opened a bottle of vodka, and after a few weeks of almost total abstinence he poured himself a drink and despite the pleas of Zina and also Caesar and Ruhama he emptied it in one gulp, and afterward he polished off the rest of the bottle and as he did so he swore and cursed the doctors and death and religion and women and the whole world, and suddenly he cursed the city and said that if it were up to him he would tear it all down and leave only one wall standing for the dogs to piss against, and he mocked Caesar and Max Spillman, who was sitting poker-faced next to Zvi without saying a word, and also derided himself as a liar and a coward, an insect who had never done one good or useful thing in his life, never married a wife or given birth to a child or built a house or anything else, because all his life had been spent in exploitation and cowardice, especially cowardice, and lies, and thus he had chosen to play the role of the buffoon and one who humiliated himself in humiliating others, and he began banging his fist on the table and laughing bitterly, gusts of ugly, drunken laughter, until Ruhama managed to calm him down.

For the next few weeks Besh continued drinking heavily, almost without a pause, and in spite of this, or perhaps because of it, he seemed on and off in better shape than he had been for years and he even offered a certain amount of support to Zina, whose life soon succumbed to emptiness and aimlessness again, but now without any hope at all, after the short but joyous period of looking after Erwin, and in the emptiness and dreariness which greeted her wherever she looked and stretched out endlessly before her she thought of beginning to paint or sculpt or of studying something like Yaffa, who was taking evening classes in English and attending lectures at the university in Bible and Hebrew literature, which gave her pleasure chiefly in the sense that it gave her the feeling she was doing something with herself, something spiritual and intellectual, and not wasting her life, but after three days, when Besh suddenly failed to show up or to call her, Zina was overcome with anxiety and she asked Caesar to go over to his place and find out what had happened to him, and Caesar went there and found him sitting dead on the toilet seat with a newspaper.

Besh's death depressed Caesar more than his father's, and in the feeling of impotence and loss which surrounded him on all sides he remembered Besh gratefully, first of all simply for being there, and of all that bundle of existence so suddenly transformed into memories he remembered his gaiety and his generosity and his brief appearance at the wedding party, after which he and Tehilla, who did all she could to comfort him about Erwin's death, and especially about Besh's death, went to visit Erwin, and Israel accompanied them for some of the way and then parted from them and walked by the sea, which was covered with clouds and very stormy, while Goldman went home, where he found Stefana sitting alone in the living room.

With the onset of the cold weather and the occasional rains Yehudit Maizler came less frequently to see her friend, preferring to spend her time reading and watching television, which had begun to some extent to take the place of the movies in her life— next to reading what she liked best was going to the movies, especially American ones—with the result that Stefana, who now spent most of her time alone, had stopped speaking almost entirely, and it was only rarely, when she needed something specific, or when someone came to pay what was usually a short and formal call, that she would utter a few, necessary sentences, usually in Polish, and sometimes when no one was there she would also sing to herself one of the Polish songs she used to sing to Naomi and Goldman when they were children. She was in good spirits and appeared to have detached herself from the stream of time and to be living in the place of her heart's desire, calm and contented, and no longer bothered by anything, not even the absence of Manfred, whom she had loved for so many years, in fact for all her life. Her love for Manfred was not the kind of love that she had felt for her brother Reuven, or for her brother Yanek, with his lace shirts and pointed patent leather shoes, who had believed with all his heart in the charm and eternity of his own youth. She would never forget the joyful summer she had spent with him in the pleasure resort in the shady forests by the river-side, which was soon followed by the outbreak of World War II, which had long been hanging over their heads and which consumed everything when it came and brought five years, or almost five years, of anxiety and hardship and anger and overcrowding—how she had hated the overcrowded house with the boarders and David Kostomolski, who never brushed his teeth, and afterward Moishe Tzellermaier. She had not seen Manfred, who was living in London, and she thought she would never see him again, just as she was never to see Yanek again, although she did not yet know this, but as soon as the war was over they met again, still in her house and in the presence of Goldman's father. Manfred as usual said little and she was afraid to look at his face or even his hands and fingers, they were so sensitive, and thus they sat, the three of them, Manfred and she and Goldman's father, whom she no longer loved although she was obliged to do so, but whom she still respected, and she clung to this, and admired his strength and integrity, and she was afraid of him, most of all she was afraid, even before he beat Goldman viciously with a belt for breaking one of the china teacups belonging to the Czechoslovakian tea set, the tea set she had hated from the moment she set eyes on it, but nevertheless she felt obliged to admire it and to go on admiring it, and even before he killed Nuit Sombre—she saw him take the hammer and afterward she heard the screams—and at about this time, or shortly after, Manfred stopped coming to the house, because he could no longer stand the lie, which was so blatant and obvious, and everything it involved, and she was glad, because she too could no longer bear it, nor could she bear the hateful and insulting attitude, which he sometimes did not even trouble to conceal beneath a veneer of politeness, of Goldman's father, who had never forgiven Manfred for his communist views, and especially for his having left the country, but in spite of his absence from the house, and without ever asking, Goldman's father knew that Stefana was still in touch with Manfred, to whom she had never made love, although she wanted to—she wanted to very much—and two or three times they had been on the point of doing it, once in Yehudit Maizler's apartment, but there were too many prohibitions weighing them down, too many obligations and fears, it was a different world from Naomi's, and thus she never went to bed with anyone but Goldman's father, and not for pleasure, except perhaps once or twice, during a certain period, but as the fulfillment of a duty; she saw nothing demeaning or wrong in this, it was her duty as a wife and besides she wanted to please him, and sometimes she was afraid of him too, and this fear had nothing to do with Nuit Sombre or any other incident, and afterward, even before Naomi's death, they almost never slept together because the estrangement between them had grown very great, and when Naomi died they stopped altogether, and they stopped sleeping in the same room too, they hadn't slept in the same bed for years, they pretended it was more comfortable to sleep apart, and she was still afraid of him, in fact she was afraid of him until the day he died, but the hatred was already stronger than the fear, and it could no longer be kept in, nor did she have any reason for trying, since he blamed her not only for Naomi's joining the British army and falling in love with the Englishman, but also for Naomi's death, and it was no longer possible for her to hold back the flood of hatred and the rebellion, he simply left her no alternative, and everything burst out and fell apart, which had never happened before in the regime of austerity and self-restraint which he imposed on her, in which everything had to be done in accordance with his tastes and ideas and almost everything might turn out to be sinful, and often did, her clothes and the way she did her hair or a brooch she pinned on her dress or a dish which lacked salt or sugar or a word out of place or a broken glass or cup, like the cup from the Czechoslovakian tea set, not to speak of Goldman's divorce from the beautiful Jemimah Chernov, and in the atmosphere of bitterness and violence, always on the point of exploding, which he generated everywhere he went and which seethed in everything he did, in the way he came into the house tired after work and the way he took off his shoes and the way he sat at the table and ate his chicken, with his head slightly lowered and his face stiff with hate, tearing the flesh from the bone and afterward gnawing and breaking it with his teeth and sucking out the marrow and spitting the splinters onto his plate, and even in his playfulness, in which he usually indulged on Saturdays, when he would march about the room with a cushion on his head making faces and singing at the top of his voice and banging the lids of pots together, and she hated these performances of his more than anything else, even more than the violence with which he supervised Naomi's piano practicing, but she smiled and pretended to be amused, and thus, unamused but submissive, she suffered too the terrible quarrel with her brother Reuven at Rachel's wedding to Akiva Weiner—he hated Reuven and he hated Yanek and he did not trouble to hide his hatred and she did not protest; sometimes, however weakly, she even agreed with some of the accusations he made against them—and still she had seen him taking the hammer, and she knew where he was going with it because he did not hide his intention from her, but she was so frightened that she didn't say a word and she shut herself in her room, and nevertheless, through the windows and the doors, and even through the walls, she heard Nuit Sombre moaning, and then, crazed with horror, she ran to the window, but everything was already over, and she stood for a moment in front of the window through which she saw Kaminskaya's body sloppily draped in a dressing gown lying in front of the ficus tree. After waking from her sleep to the sound of a dull thud, as if a sack full of flour or sand had fallen from a height and landed heavily on the ground, she hurried to the window and saw the scene, confused by her sudden awakening—she would never have gone out of the house in a dressing gown like that—but not surprised, as if she knew what she would find, or at least what she was likely to find, and afterward she turned her face calmly, even indifferently away, because Kaminskaya's death aroused no feelings of compassion in her and she would not allow herself to show any other kind of feelings, whereas Goldman's father hurried down to the courtyard and came back full of anger with Joseph Leviatan and they sat in the kitchen drinking tea. It was late already but the events of the night had thrown everything out of balance, and Joseph Leviatan, who was sitting with his legs crossed, said, "She was a special kind of woman," and Goldman's father said, "She was corrupt, it's better not to talk about her," and Joseph Leviatan said, "In any case, what she did was wrong," and Stefana asked, "Why?" although she didn't really disagree with him, or agree with him either, in fact she had no opinions on the matter one way or the other, but she didn't like Joseph Leviatan, that ascetic and tortured man who had enslaved himself to one idea, and she didn't like his friendship with Goldman's father because she didn't have the least desire to go and live in a commune in the country, even as things were their way of life was too crowded and exposed for her, but she accepted these and other difficulties because she had no alternative, and sometimes even willingly, and she laundered and ironed and cleaned the apartment herself and did the shopping and the cooking—Goldman's father liked her cooking although it was plain and monotonous—and she tried to feel part of his family and to love them and Eretz Yisrael, and even the Histadruth and the party and the political discussions and arguments and the plain living and graceless manners, after all they were her life and her world, and for many years she even succeeded, but perhaps she grew weary, and perhaps it was only an illusion in which she herself believed, and the truth was that she did not love either the country or the people, not even the closest of them, Shmuel and Bracha and Chaim-Leib and Mrs. Haya and Uncle Lazar, although she admired the way he went to Spain, or even Joel, for in the last analysis she was remote from them, or at any rate she aspired to be, and she did not want their simplicity or their goodness, and especially she disliked Zipporah, although she respected her and stood in awe of her, and she was afraid of her too, but she saw herself as above her, and also the rest of the family, perhaps because she had come from a wealthier and more enlightened part of the world and was better educated than they were—she knew German and a little French and Latin—and when she needed Zipporah's help when she fell ill with a kidney disease, in one way or another she blamed Goldman's father, who was annoyed by her illness and helplessness, she felt very bitter about it, and she did not like Grandmother Hava, a simple and ignorant woman, either, and she felt no compassion for her although she took care of her as best she could, not to mention her attitude toward Moishe Tzellermaier and David Kostomolski—Kaminskaya was in a category of hatred all her own—and the hostility tinged with contempt which she felt for Tzimmer's widow, with her big, floppy bosom, a woman who laughed out loud with her mouth open and went to the theater in a yellow blouse or in pants (Tzimmer himself she regarded as no better than a worm), but even toward her children her attitude was reserved, especially her attitude toward Goldman; with Naomi she had still sometimes been capable of real affection, and somehow at the core of her exaggerated anxiety and concern for them, suffocating in its goodwill, there was something chilling, something dutiful, and she knew it too, but this wasn't the reason that she wasn't sorry when Naomi joined the British army and went to Egypt, and she never felt that she had anything to reproach herself for in Naomi's love affair with the Englishman, she had known about it long before Goldman's father but she had kept it to herself, and the truth was that she had never loved anyone but Manfred, with his ugly, haggard face which had never bothered her—and neither had his views—and his sensitive fingers and vein-roped hands. She was attracted to him and she trusted him, and in a completely different way she also loved her brother Reuven, his good looks and his open-heartedness—Goldman's father would not even go to the funeral and she did not protest although her heart was torn in pieces—and later in life she loved Yanek, her feather-brained brother who had granted her that dream-like summer before the world went mad, and for Yehudit Maizler she felt friendship and also admiration, since she had remained a spinster by choice because the man she wanted to marry had married someone else, and because she repeatedly advised her, not condescendingly but forcefully, to leave Goldman's father, or at least not to let him subjugate her, and to hang onto her freedom with all her strength, only she wasn't capable of it, until Naomi died and without her intending it everything came apart and she rebelled, he simply left her no alternative, and she wanted him to die so badly, and without feeling any guilt, that she wanted to die herself, and even before he went off to America they moved into separate rooms and they each took their own letters out of the mailbox, which made no difference to her because she didn't get any letters anyway, except from Manfred, which were addressed to Yehudit Maizler and which were long and complicated, and she read them over and over, and from time to time she looked in the mirror, for his sake, naturally, and saw the network of wrinkles under her eyes and the flabbiness of her face, and how old it looked, and her hands and body too, which had grown so white and dry, she examined it in the shower and before she went to bed, and she lamented her lost beauty and felt how every part of her was growing more and more deformed and losing its vitality from day to day, but Manfred too was growing old, although in a different way, and so was Goldman's father, and when he came back from America their hatred was so savage and unshakable that it no longer occurred to them to restrain it, and the truth was that she didn't even have to rebel but only to shut her ears and avert her eyes, or at the most get out of the house, which she frequently did, because all of a sudden he had turned into an old man and everything had died and disintegrated, his ideology and his loyalty to the party and his aspirations and his circle of acquaintances—some of the people had died and some of them had moved away—and all that was left of him was obduracy and bitter but helpless rage, and he would come and go aimlessly or wander about the house dragging his old feet in slippers, whose endless shuffle on the floor nearly drove her out of her mind, like the endless bickering and vicious quarrels of former times, only then she had been young and sure that it was her duty to meet her obligations to him and accustom herself to the rages and humiliations, just as she had to accustom herself to the heat and glare of the sun and the pushing and crowding, not to mention the fact that she always felt guilty about something, and in between there were always a few hours, sometimes a whole day or even two, which always ended wretchedly, when full of regret and sometimes even with a breaking heart he would try to stop himself and appease her and find his way to some kind of contact with her again, and cast out the anger and the hatred so that he could be with her in closeness and peace—once he even put his head down on the table and wept bitterly so that his whole body shook—and she too wanted to be reconciled and sought for a way to reach him and pinpoint the crisis in their relationship, if indeed there had been anything that could be called a crisis point, and these efforts, isolated but repeated, continued even after Reuven's death and even after he killed Nuit Sombre—he himself washed his blood-spattered clothes—and even during the period of her heart attacks, which filled him with anxiety and he would go white and lose all self-control in his panic and his anger, until Naomi's death cured her of them, she never knew exactly how Naomi died and she didn't want to know either, and now there was the terrible shuffling of his old and lifeless feet, and of course the heat, to which she had never grown accustomed, and the weariness, only the shuffling stopped too, as soon as he fell ill and died, not for one single hour did she miss him, not a single drop of pity entered her heart, and she was left with Goldman, who in spite of all her anxious care did not love her, or his father either, nor did Naomi, and she knew this and it hurt her but she never spoke to him about it, just as she never spoke to him about Nuit Sombre or Kaminskaya or Naomi, or his divorce from the beautiful Jemimah Chernov, which embarrassed her, but Goldman's father saw it as a disgrace and a catastrophe and in the terrible days before and after the divorce his rage was murderous, and for this too he blamed her, although not quite so explicitly, and of course he blamed Goldman himself, and now she was left with Goldman and she would have been pleased if he had moved out of the apartment and left her all alone in the plain, yellow rooms, in which for the first time she did not feel lonely but on the contrary, she wanted to be alone in order to live her life without anyone to disturb her in the place of her heart's desire, a small town at the foot of the mountains, from which she made occasional excursions to Warsaw and Lublin, and twice to Cracow, once with Manfred, who walked beside her with his hands behind his back, and once, many years later, with Yanek, he was smoking a pipe and wearing a green hat and she told him that the green looked too raffish, but Goldman went on staying with her in the apartment, and when he walked past the living room, where she was sitting alone and reading a book, he glanced at her and once more he saw what he had first seen when he came back from the army and sat at the kitchen table eating his dinner—how much Stefana had come to resemble Naomi, as Naomi had remained engraved in his memory, and not only in her appearance, and he paused a moment and asked her how she was and then went into his room.

Now that he had learned to take no notice of her eccentricities Goldman felt a mild affection and sympathy for Stefana, and after a certain period, during which he had tried to ignore her completely and relate to her with total indifference, she no longer bothered him, and besides the "Bullworker" and his daily swim in the sea and his short conversations with Uncle Lazar during their chess games, and of course his work in the office, Goldman was utterly absorbed in the world of the stars and the immensity of the universe, and his only trouble was that he could not fall asleep, and although he took sleeping pills they didn't always help and he would lie awake for whole nights on end, sometimes in a kind of trance and sometimes in a whirling pool of thoughts, and sometimes tossing and turning and in the end getting up and switching on the light and opening his books—he read passionately but in an unsystematic and amateurish way—which dealt with descriptions of space and complex astronomical and astrophysical problems: the various stars, the solar system, the galaxies, the creation of the universe, its form and size and the various processes taking place in it. The infinite spaces, the mind-boggling multiplicity and dimensions, the abundance of possibilities, the many problems, and the imaginative and contradictory theories all filled him with enthusiasm and gave him a feeling of happiness and pleasure, and sometimes he would burst into admiring laughter, so amazing were the things he read, and at the same time he learned the names of stars and constellations and knew where they were located in the sky, although he never actually looked at them or followed their movements because it didn't interest him in the least to do so, and he familiarized himself with the history of astronomy and the biographies of some of the great astronomers, and for some reason the one who gave rise to the most sympathy and curiosity in him was Johannes Kepler, and he tried to read every bit of information he could get hold of about him and his life, including the "family horoscope" which Kepler himself had made up, a strange and fascinating document, which Goldman read over and over again, learning that Kepler was born in the village of Weil in Swabia to a family which had long been suffering from signs of degeneration. His father Heinrich, who had seven children, Kepler described in his family horoscope as follows: "My father Heinrich was born in 1547, 19th of January. A man vicious, inflexible, quarrelsome, and doomed to a bad end. Venus and Mars increased his malice. Jupiter combust in descension made him a pauper but gave him a rich wife. Saturn in VII made him study gunnery; many enemies, a quarrelsome marriage, a vain love of honors and vain hopes about them; a wanderer. In 1577 he ran the risk of hanging. He sold his house and started a tavern. In 1578 a hard jar of gunpowder burst and lacerated my father's face. In 1579 he treated my mother extremely ill. Finally he went into exile and died." Rumor had it that he enlisted in the Neapolitan fleet. At any rate, in 1588 he vanished from the sight of his family forever. As for his mother Katherine, an innkeeper's daughter, Kepler wrote in the family horoscope that she was "small, thin, swarthy, gossiping, and quarrelsome, of a bad disposition." She collected herbs and concocted potions in whose powers she believed and in this way she gained the reputation of being a witch and was almost burned at the stake for witchcraft and for consorting with the Devil, which was the fate that had met her aunt, by whom she had been brought up. In the year 1615 a witch craze seized hold of the village of Leonberg, where Katherine was now living, and six women were burned as witches in the course of a single summer. Katherine, who was by this time a hideous old crone, quarreled with another old hag, her former best friend, the wife of the glazier Jacob Reinhold, who accused her of having given her a witches' potion which had made her chronically ill—an illness which had in fact been brought about by complications following an abortion. It was now remembered among the villagers that a number of the inhabitants of Leonberg had been taken ill at various times after being offered a drink from a tin jug which Katherine always kept hospitably prepared for her visitors. The wife of Bastin Meyer had died of it, and the schoolmaster Beutelspacher was permanently paralyzed. It was also remembered that once upon a time Katherine had asked the sexton for the skull of her father in order to cast it in silver as a drinking goblet for her son, the court astrologer who was himself no better than his mother. She had also cast an evil eye on the children of the tailor Daniel Schmidt, who had promptly died. And she was known to have entered houses through locked doors and to have ridden a calf to death and afterward to have offered its meat to her other son, the vagrant Heinrich. The accusations were grave, and it was only after long, drawn-out proceedings which included interrogations, tests, all kinds of humiliations, and fourteen months of imprisonment, that she was eventually released, thanks largely to the efforts of Kepler himself, and saved from the stake. Kepler also described his own childhood and youth in this family horoscope, which he drew up when he was twenty-six, but in the same year he also wrote another document which fascinated Goldman far more, a self-analysis written mostly in the third person, mixing past and present tenses, and including a self-portrait that read as follows: "This man has in every way a dog-like nature. His appearance is that of a little lap dog. His body is agile, wiry, and well proportioned. Even his appetites were like a dog's: he liked gnawing bones and dry crusts of bread and was so greedy that whatever his eyes chanced on he grabbed; yet, like a dog, he drinks little and is content with the simplest food. His habits were similar. He continually sought the goodwill of others, was dependent on others for everything, ministered to their wishes, never got angry when they reproved him and was anxious to get back in their favor. He was constantly on the move, ferreting among the sciences, politics, and private affairs, including the lowest kind; always following someone else, and imitating his thoughts and actions. He is bored with conversation, but greets visitors just like a little dog; yet when the least thing is snatched away from him, he flares up and growls. He tenaciously persecutes wrong-doers—that is, he barks at them. He is malicious and bites people with his sarcasms. He hates many people exceedingly and they avoid him, but his masters are fond of him. He has a dog-like horror of baths, tinctures and lotions. His recklessness knows no limits, which is surely due to Mars in quadrature with Mercury, and in trine with the moon; yet he takes good care of his life. He has a vast appetite for the greatest things. His teachers praised him for his good dispositions, though morally he was the worst among his contemporaries. He was religious to the point of superstition. As a boy of ten years when he first read Holy Scripture he grieved that on account of the impurity of his life, the honor to be a prophet was denied him. When he committed a wrong, he performed an expiatory rite, hoping it would save him from punishment: This consisted in reciting his faults in public. In this man there are two opposite tendencies: always to regret any wasted time, and always to waste it willingly. For Mercury makes one inclined to amusements, games and other light pleasures. Since his caution with money kept him away from play, he often played by himself. It must be noted that his miserliness did not aim at acquiring riches, but at removing his fear of poverty—although perhaps avarice results from an excess of this fear." He died in Ratisbon after a serious illness, and according to an eyewitness report of his death he did not speak but kept pointing his finger alternately at his head and at the heavens above. On his gravestone they inscribed the epitaph he had composed for himself: "I measured the skies, now the shadows I measure/Skybound was the mind, earthbound the body rests," and Goldman later wrote this sentence at the top of the first page of his translation of the *Somnium*, about which he had at this time only read something in other books, and which was later, after he had obtained it and started translating it, to become his chief interest in life, but in the meantime he continued to display an unflagging fascination with the descriptions of the stars and the universe and the various theories of space, and also in the philosophical and theological problems connected with them and the controversies accompanying them, and from time to time he discussed all this with Uncle Lazar, briefly at first and then in greater detail, and Uncle Lazar listened to him and asked him questions, sometimes putting forward a suggestion of his own or casting a doubt, and afterward he started borrowing books from him, and Goldman lent them to him with a slightly heavy heart, because like his father he disliked lending books, even books he had no intention of ever reading again, but his enthusiasm had made him something of a missionary as far as cosmology and astrophysics were concerned, and in any case he could not refuse Uncle Lazar, whose conversation was such a pleasure to him and enabled him to unburden himself of his enthusiasm as well as stimulating him, but Uncle Lazar's visits grew less frequent because of the weather and especially because he was now spending much of his free time visiting Bracha, who ever since Shmuel's heart attack had been in a state of constant anxiety, which became intolerable and a burden to her and everyone around her, especially Shmuel, who wanted to forget his illness and return to his former way of life, but Bracha imposed a strict diet on him because he had to lose weight and cooked everything without salt because of his high blood pressure, and the food was so tasteless, and she dished it out in such tiny portions, that he started eating out in restaurants on the sly, and she also tried to stop him from overworking or getting tired or excited, and made him rest and go to bed early, and to this end she did away entirely with the Saturday night card games, which had been temporarily broken off during Shmuel's illness.

The truth was that in recent years these card games had in any case lost all the charm they had once held for her and had become a nuisance and a burden, because from one year to the next the circle of players had dwindled and shrunk as a result of all kinds of illnesses and deaths, and also quarrels, mostly very silly ones, but as the people grew older they became very touchy and obstinate and full of grievances and it became increasingly difficult to resolve these petty squabbles, while the players who remained and kept on appearing every Saturday night became increasingly boring and irritating as they grew older, and the jokes and laughter which had formerly accompanied the card games were replaced by interminable stories about their grand-children and great-grandchildren, who did not interest Bracha at all, and most of whom she didn't even know, in addition to stories repeated *ad nauseam,* in great detail and with stupid obstinacy, about illnesses and aches and pains and medicines and doctors and deaths and deprivations, which she hated more than anything, and although the Saturday night card evenings had become as much a part of the fabric of her life as the Saturday dinners and holiday and birthday celebrations, and what was more, an obligation, she put an end to them because of her anxiety about Shmuel, which was accompanied by an increasing anxiety about her children and grandchildren, on whom she came to rely less and less, and she was constantly afraid of accidents and catastrophes, and she kept calling them and inundating them with instructions and warnings until she became a nuisance, especially to Illana, who couldn't stand it any more and began treating her with irritation and impatience, sometimes bordering on rudeness, but Bracha, although she saw what was happening, could not help herself, she was ruled by her anxiety, and in addition to the telephone instructions she would bring her children, Illana and also Uri, gefilte fish and pickled herring, meat, and sometimes pots of *cholent* and carrots cooked with raisins, and also cakes which she baked especially for them, and at the same time, without at first noticing what she was doing, she began to devote a greater part of her time to the dead: She paid regular visits to her father's grave, Grandfather Baruch Chaim, and to the grave of Goldman's father, for whom she had felt a special affection, and Shmuel's parents' graves, and she saw to it that the graves were taken care of, and she also busied herself about the distribution of the clothes and household goods of Chaim-Leib, who had faded away and died only a few weeks after his wife, Mrs. Haya, succumbed to a bout of pneumonia which ended in sudden death, and altogether she spent a lot of time attending funerals and paying condolence visits and attending memorial services, and all this in spite of Shmuel and Uri and Illana and Zipporah and Uncle Lazar, who tried to make her desist, until in the end the dead enmeshed her life in so dense a web that one day, in an hour of repose, she said humorously to Uncle Lazar that with so many dead people and so many visits to graveyards it sometimes seemed to her that she herself was already dead, and Uncle Lazar said, "In that case perhaps you should cut it out for a while. None of the dead will hold it against you," and this happened not long before Uncle Lazar himself died one night together with Yehudit Tanfuss as the result of a senseless accident—the owners of the apartment next door had sold it and the new occupants had called someone in to fumigate the rooms and then seal them up for a few days to allow the chemicals to do their work, but that same night the poisonous fumes penetrated the tiny holes and cracks in the wall and spread through Uncle Lazar's and Yehudit Tanfuss' apartment, where the doors and windows were all shut to keep out the cold, and the two of them breathed in the poison and died together in their sleep.

The bodies were discovered the next afternoon by one of Uncle Lazar's coworkers, and the funeral took place two days later, after the police had completed their investigation into the circumstances of their death. Shmuel informed Goldman, who left the office immediately and hurried over to their apartment, where he found Bracha and Shmuel and Joel and Meir and Yehudit Tanfuss' brother with his wife and two policemen and a few people he didn't know, neighbors perhaps, or colleagues of the dead, some of them sitting in the small, clean kitchen and others in the room overlooking the street, because in the bedroom, on the broad bed, their two bodies were still lying side by side, the bodies of Uncle Lazar and Yehudit Tanfuss covered by sheets. Goldman went into this room and stood there silently for a moment, and then he went into the other room and exchanged a few words with Shmuel and Bracha—whose eyes were red and swollen with weeping—who were busy conferring with Joel and Meir about Grandmother Hava, and they decided that Bracha would have to tell her, and on the day of the funeral Bracha told Grandmother Hava, who was already deaf and whose mind was quite gone, about the death of her son Uncle Lazar, which did not upset

Goldman to the extent that he would have expected, and even before he went into the bedroom his first agitation had already died down and it seemed to him that he felt no shock or surprise, which made him feel uneasy and puzzled with himself, and afterward he stood in the corner of the other room and leaned against the sideboard, withdrawn and silent, alienated from everything around him, and listened without any interest to the conversation, and only when they removed the bodies in order to take them to the mortuary did he feel something again, and afterward, when the people started leaving, he hesitated for a moment and stealthily took *The Nature of the Universe* by Fred Hoyle which he had lent Uncle Lazar and noticed among the books lying on the bedside table the moment he came into the room, and he hid it quickly in the inner pocket of his coat and then he followed the others out.

During the funeral service too Goldman felt empty and apathetic, but this indifference was gradually replaced by a great, although detached, interest which awoke in him as he stood and surveyed, at first out of boredom and almost unthinkingly, the people who had gathered around the grave, noticing as he did so the faces, and they were rather numerous, which were missing because their owners were already dead, and his interest was especially awakened when he suddenly, and vividly, perceived the terrible changes which time had wrought in the appearance of the survivors, both old and young—only a very few were exempt: Temima and David Kostomolski and Aviezer and Ruth, who had even gained a certain delicacy—how it had dried their skin and flesh and distorted them and made them ugly, their bodies and their faces too, not to speak of their weariness and their dull, bitter, and despairing expressions, and all this repelled and frightened him, and he hoped that he did not resemble them and that his fate would not resemble theirs, but at the same time he knew that this was a vain hope, and he looked at Bracha and Shmuel and Meir, who had grown so old and bald, and at Yoel and Jeremiah and Jonah Kotchinski and Esther, who had grown very fat and whose belly was so big you could hardly see her breasts, and at Moishe Tzellermaier, who stood next to his wife, weeping heartbrokenly, and at Illana and her husband and Uri and Avraham Shechter, who had come to the funeral without Rachel, who ever since her brief meeting with Uncle Lazar on his return from his exile in Yakut had never seen him again, and neither had his son or his daughter, who did not attend his funeral either, or invite him to their weddings, and ostracized him completely, and nevertheless Uncle Lazar had sent them both presents when they married, without receiving a note of thanks or any kind of acknowledgment in reply.

After they had filled up the graves and the ceremony was over the people dispersed and walked toward the gates in the damp gray air of the winter dusk, and Goldman, his face cold from the long wait in the winter chill, walked among them with his hands in his coat pockets—for a moment he thought of going to visit his father's grave but he didn't do so—and the farther he retreated from the graves the more the sense of Uncle Lazar's death spread through him, at first as an almost pleasurable sensation of ending and loneliness, which turned into a depressing awareness of irredeemable loss and of longing, and afterward into a feeling that his life was already behind him and he was being thrust toward his death and parting from everything, and when he sat down in the crowded bus he wanted to cover himself up and cry without stopping—he felt that tears would bring him relief—but he couldn't do it, he had not cried since he was a boy, and when he came home he immediately absorbed himself in cosmology but the wish to weep, oppressive and frustrated, was still in him, but something hard was blocking the tears, and this barren desire, filling his chest and his head, did not leave him the following day and it came back from time to time in all the days that followed, right until his death. These were days in which the sense of Uncle Lazar's loss grew deeper and deeper, a sense of parting which kept on bringing the sense of someone else's absence to mind—Naomi's, his father's, Chaim-Leib's, or Dita's, or Sonia's, Sonia still as young and beautiful as ever rolling about on a bed somewhere with all kinds of different men—and this sense of loss kept making itself felt in all kinds of little details: the hint of a smell, the sight of a face, different objects, and the utter emptiness of the house, where Stefana's haughty, but somehow no longer ridiculous, eccentricity now ruled supreme. Sunk into a wintry silence and an obscure happiness, proudly and punctiliously observing certain airs and graces, dressed in spendid clothes, delicately made up—a Polish noblewoman, a little dusty and faded—Stefana turned her back on forty-five years of life in Eretz Yisrael and returned to the days of her youth in a Poland which she re-created in her imagination, and at the same time she detached herself from all the ties which bound her to family and friends, except for Yehudit Maizler, and she didn't even bother to reply to Manfred's letter, which arrived at the beginning of winter and to which she gave no more than a passing glance, and thus, the deeper they went into the winter and the colder it grew outside, her remoteness increased and her silence grew more profound, everything happened effortlessly, of its own accord, until she hardly troubled herself to greet Moishe Tzellermaier, who came dutifully to visit her at least once a month, or Israel, who asked her how she was whenever he came to visit Goldman, who because of the insomnia and sleeping pills veered, frequently for no evident reason, from depression and apathy to elation, and sometimes hilarity, which was distasteful to Israel, who had discovered by chance on the day of Caesar's wedding that Ella had left Tel Aviv and gone to live in Jerusalem.

On his way home from the solitary stroll he had taken along the seashore that evening he had bumped into a certain young man who worked as a laboratory assistant in the natural sciences department of the university, the same department for which Ella had made her sketches of animals and plants, and it was this young man who had, almost casually, given Israel this piece of information, which awoke new longings in him for Ella, quiet but persistent, and sometimes on the winter days which came and filled the dim rooms of the studio with cold and emptiness he thought of going to look for her, but he restrained himself out of pride and anger and devoted himself to his music, especially to playing the organ, and when Goldman asked him from time to time about Ella he replied curtly and sullenly, and he responded in the same way to Caesar's questions, which in any case were never as interested as Goldman's, because Caesar, in the last analysis, was interested only in himself and his own concerns, which at this time were focused chiefly on his son's illness, but also on his relations with Tehilla and with Eliezra, which had apparently resolved themselves after Caesar had gradually, by running frantically after women and throwing himself into work and pleasure and all kinds of other distractions, and especially as a consequence of the deterioration in his son's condition, become somewhat resigned to his married state and succeeded in exhausting his hostility toward Tehilla and his hatred for Eliezra, whom he had tried unsuccessfully to meet two or three times even after his own marriage, and this hostility and hate had frozen on some middle ground and turned into a dull, monotonous sense of oppression, which although it never left him did not break his heart either, and only once did Caesar's hatred erupt and tear him out of this routine oppression, which was when he heard that Eliezra was pregnant, because he still missed her and believed that only she could make him happy, and thanks to his boundless egotism and self-indulgence he was still capable of entertaining, beneath the façade of his apparent resignation, the belief that Eliezra's marriage was nothing but a passing illusion, or a mistake, which she would not be able to continue, and that the whole affair would soon come to an inevitable end, and everything would return to the beginning again in the way best suited to his own needs, and now that reality stared him in the face, and in such a cruel and unambiguous way, he cursed Eliezra and her husband and the child in her belly and he prayed that she would have a miscarriage, and he also cursed Tehilla, who was completely unaware of what was happening and was struggling with her own problems, worried and longing for a little support, or at least a little warmth, and at the same time being careful to hide what was happening inside her, not because she was ashamed or because she saw it as a sign of weakness, but because she did not want to be a burden to Caesar.

All day Caesar's hatred seethed, and as usual he dashed restlessly and aimlessly about the town in his battered Plymouth, went to see a woman he had slept with once but did not find her in— Vicky was in Europe with her husband; she had sent him a book of photographs from London—bought himself two new pairs of pants he did not need, and went up to the studio, but there was no one there and so he went to the movies, and afterward he went into Portofino and ordered a beer and cheese and sat in a corner and ate and drank and exchanged a few words with the bar owner, hoping that someone he knew would come in, and in the end—it was already nearly four—he got up and paid and went back to the studio and sat down opposite Israel, who had just returned from St. Antonio's and was lying on the couch, and looked at him expectantly, for he badly needed someone to restore his confidence and hope, never mind how groundless his negative feelings were, or at least say a soothing word, but Israel said nothing and there wasn't a drop of sympathy in his light blue eyes, because he considered the whole thing boring and idiotic and because his stubborn repudiation of his own longings had hardened his heart from day to day until it was as hard as a rock, and he was not prepared to say one single word to Caesar, he was hardly prepared to listen to him and look at him with his frozen look, and Caesar got up and began pacing around the room and complaining angrily about Goldman, who a couple of days before, when he had alluded to his son's illness, had tried to encourage him by saying that there was no reason to panic and even the best doctors sometimes made mistakes and he was sure that everything would be all right in the end, and in the middle of all this had suddenly changed the drift of his words a little and said that life was nothing but a journey toward death, as the ancients had known, and that this was the one certain thing in life, and not only that but also death was actually the very essence of life, growing inside it hour by hour until it enclosed and embodied it completely—like the larva forming itself inevitably into the chrysalis from which the butterfly will eventually emerge—and thus man had to train himself to accept death, which never came too early, and even when it seemed to come too early there was no point in rebelling against it, and Caesar, who listened impatiently to Goldman's words of encouragement, was filled with rage, because all he knew was that his son was fatally ill and all the rest was nothing to him but "impotent intellectual bullshit," and he repeated this in various ways a number of times, until in the end he fell silent and stood next to the window and glanced out at the street, where the sky was a little clouded and a rather strong wind was blowing from the sea and moving the treetops, and then he turned to face Israel and said, "If only I'd married her everything would have been different. But now it's hopeless," and a moment later he said, "I'm damned if I know why I didn't marry her. I could easily have married her," and he fell silent again, but not because he expected an answer, and afterward he picked up his camera and almost without thinking, as part of the same movement, he said goodbye to Israel and left the studio and went to visit his sick son, but he had gone to play with a classmate, and the second, younger son had gone to the movies with Tirza's parents, and Tirza herself welcomed him gladly, but as always during this period she was withdrawn into herself and spoke very little, thus giving the impression of a certain aloofness and reserve, although she was really full of dread and despair, sometimes she felt that everything inside her was on the point of collapsing, and she was very tired, and totally absorbed in the illness of her son, which liberated her from superficial obligations and the need to keep up a façade, and also from the sense of futility and loneliness which sometimes attacked her, while at the same time awakening in her strengths she never knew she possessed and giving her the power to struggle and to rely primarily on herself, and except for a brief period at the beginning she did not expect any help from Caesar, only a little consideration, and Caesar, who was, as always, preoccupied almost entirely with himself, surprised her by his helpfulness and his attentions, which she appreciated far more than she showed, and on the whole her feelings for him were those of friendship, the friendship of people who find themselves facing a common trouble.

She asked him to come into the kitchen and have a cup of coffee and he took off his coat and sat down at the table and asked her how she was and how the boy was and Tirza said there was no change in his condition and she asked Caesar, who was very tired and depressed, if he wanted anything to eat, and Caesar said, "No thanks, I'm not hungry," and then he said, "Well, maybe a sandwich," and Tirza gave him three slices of bread and cheese and pickled cucumbers and tomatoes and a saucer of olives with his coffee and she asked him how he was—she never asked him why he seemed troubled or depressed and she never asked him about Eliezra or Tehilla, not because she wasn't curious—and Caesar said, "Keeping alive somehow," and after that there was a silence which neither of them felt the need to break, and Tirza went into the bathroom to do something to the washing machine, and when he had finished eating and drinking she took the dishes and went to the sink and washed them, and Caesar lit a cigarette and stood next to her and looked at her face, which worry and suffering had closed up and made hard, and Tirza, who was a little embarrassed by his unprovocative but persistent stare, said, "Is anything wrong?" and Caesar said, "I'm tired," and he put his hand on her head and stroked her hair slowly and softly, and she went on washing the dishes without moving her head so as not to spoil the moment, and Caesar went on stroking her hair and as he did so he noticed the delicate lines on her forehead and around her eyes, and he let his hand travel down the nape of her neck and then he slipped it underneath her sweater and stroked her breasts, and when she had finished washing the dishes—her hands were still wet—he embraced her and kissed her throat and lips and tried to lead her into the bedroom, but Tirza resisted him, not too firmly, and said, "Not today, Caesar. Today I can't. In two days' time," but Caesar paid no attention and she went with him as if she were doing it against her will, and they went into the bedroom and she repeated, "Not today, Caesar; in two days' time," and they got undressed and lay down together on the big, cool bed and embraced each other slowly, with the conciliatory and compassionate gestures of two people momentarily brought together again by sorrow and misfortune, and they found a release for their grief and anxiety in each other's arms and for an hour they were consoled and felt a sense of closeness, and Tirza wept almost soundlessly, and when it was all over Caesar went on lying on the bed with his eyes closed, abandoning himself to the pleasant tiredness, and Tirza went out and came back with a damp towel to wipe away the blood, and he went on lying there peacefully, without realizing what was happening to him, as if it were happening to somebody else, and he wished he could go on lying there in the same detachment and tranquillity forever, but a little later he got up and dressed himself and without waiting for his son, who was due back home at any minute, he went away after kissing Tirza and promising to return the next day.

The sky was overcast and the day had grown dark, and although the wind had dropped there was a feeling that at any moment something would suddenly snap and the rain would come pouring down, and indeed the wind blew up again, stronger than before, and the trees swayed and rustled, and a cold rain started falling, blown by the wind against the walls of the houses and the cars and the road, and Caesar, who hurried into his car, hesitated for a moment and then unwillingly started it and went to visit his mother, who with the last of her strength was clinging to Erwin's death and continuing to celebrate it as a festive, or at least a moving and meaningful, experience—only apart from Yaffa she had no one with whom to share this experience, since Besh was dead and Caesar was impatient and irritable and Zvi and

Beatrice, whose relations with her had always been tenuous, were busy working and had little time for visits, while Max Spillman and Ruhama, who was due to give birth soon, had broken off relations with her almost entirely immediately after Erwin's death, since it was only through him and because of him that they related to her at all, and this estrangement was harder for Zina to bear than almost anything else, because it was precisely Ruhama whom she wished to draw to her and to possess—this was what she had wanted when Erwin was alive and what she continued to want now that he was dead—and to her disappointment even Yaffa, for all her efforts to participate and sympathize, did not really succeed because she was lost in the labyrinth of her own troubles, which drained her energies and sucked out the marrow of her life and which stemmed from her relations with Tikva, which were irredeemably spoiled and grew more poisoned from year to year, until in the end Tikva's hostility was so great that she could not bear the sight of her mother's face and almost every word that Yaffa said provoked instant rudeness, and even viciousness on her part, as if she wanted not only to humiliate her but also to obliterate her entirely, and with as much cruelty as possible, and this had turned Yaffa into a fearful and helpless creature, who never knew how to behave or what to say because whatever she did, however well meant, and whatever she said, was liable to bring a catastrophe down on her head, and she was so desperate that she wanted to lie down and die—sometimes she said this to Zina and once she even went so far as to say it to Tikva, who looked at her indifferently and said, "Go ahead, the sooner the better. You're not scaring anyone"—because death was her only way out of the vicious circle of humiliation and hatred, which she has never succeeded in understanding, for even if she had made mistakes here and there she had never deliberately withheld anything from Tikva, who ever since her divorce had lived in her elegant apartment which was full of beautiful furniture, for she had excellent taste, changing or adding pieces every now and then as the fancy took her, leading a life of luxury and wastefulness—she came to Erwin's funeral in a pair of new boots which she liked so much that the very next day she went and bought another pair—free of all responsibility or the need to make any effort at all. She had a maid to look after her children and cook and wash the dishes and do the housework and all she did was give them a goodnight kiss before they went to bed, and sometimes not even that, or an occasional rebuke, and once in a while she took them on various excursions, and sometimes she made coffee for her visitors or washed a couple of cups, and apart from that she did nothing at all, she didn't go out to work or even think of doing so, and so she was free to occupy herself solely with her own desires and amusements, an occupation which turned out in the end to be vacuous and disappointing, and all this had left its mark on her face, which in addition to the signs of aging and emptiness was set in a mean and bitter mold, and Besh, who met her at Erwin's funeral, gave her a slight nod and turned to Chemda and said, "At the age of forty everyone gets the face he deserves," and he stole another look at Tikva, but she didn't care and managed to distract herself, mainly by means of sex with the many men who came and went in her life, sometimes after very short and casual acquaintances and no more than a single night in bed, which was quite often enough for Tikva to develop far-fetched fantasies of love and marriage, because in the last analysis she longed to be attached to someone, but these relationships, full of artificial tensions, all ended in nothing, just like her relationship with the young man called Eli who accompanied her to Erwin's funeral—Caesar couldn't stand him at first sight, Tikva herself he had never liked—and lived with her for a few weeks in her apartment, during which time she conducted a short affair with another, married man, which Eli, who was almost ten years younger than she was, did not know anything about, although even if he had known it probably wouldn't have made any difference, he was so stupid and lazy, but even if he had left her she wouldn't have been particularly sorry about it, because she didn't love him, except maybe for the first three or four days, but somehow she grew accustomed to him and during this time in her life, he met her needs, first of all by the mere fact of his presence in the midst of her loneliness and by his complete integration into the emptiness of her life: He would wake up with her at about noon, make love to her, and then go into the shower, where he would linger pleasantly—when they met he had been working as a tourist guide but then he stopped working altogether—and after his shower he would have coffee and do exercises on the living room carpet, and if it was a sunny day he would stand half naked in front of the French windows (he had a nice body) soaking up the sunshine in indolent enjoyment and waiting patiently for Tikva to complete her toilette, and then, sometimes at four or five in the afternoon, they would go to a restaurant for lunch, they ate without a thought about the cost and usually without even noticing what they were eating, and after their meal, which could take up to two hours, they would go to a movie, and after that, unless they had been invited out, they would go to a night club in Jaffa or somewhere else, to eat and dance or chat and laugh in the company of various acquaintances, who also knew no other way of life, and after that, sometimes at dawn, they would go home and make love again—they hardly spoke to each other, neither about love nor about anything else— and sleep again until noon the next day, sometimes until the children came home from school. They spent Saturdays and a few other days every week with Yaffa, who wished that Tikva would get married and contemplated her way of life with a heavy heart, and also with shame, but said nothing, partly because she knew it would do no good and partly because she was afraid of Tikva's reaction, and from the moment she opened her eyes in the morning she would despairingly review the troubles which had befallen her, raking through everything again and again, going over all the mistakes, even the tiniest and most insignificant, which she thought she had made in relation to her dead husband, and her son Ariyeh, who had committed suicide, and her daughter Tikva, and they came falling down on her like an endless rain of ashes, and in her self-reproach she tried to go back and unravel the reasons for her mistakes and find justifications for herself in the difficulties of the circumstances and in her own lack of understanding, but she never succeeded in forgiving herself for anything and she took all the blame on herself for the bad things that had happened, and at the same time, with laborious persistence, she kept on thinking of all the things she might have done, most of them very small and insignificant, to make everything turn out differently, but now it was too late to do anything and Yaffa grew more and more enslaved to a past beyond redemption, which weighed on her like a gravestone, and on a couple of occasions she said to Zina that if only she could free herself from the past maybe she might still be able to get a little enjoyment out of the present, but all this remained a vain wish and she sank ever deeper into depression and a casual remark or a sight or smell which reminded her of something would suddenly set off silent and prolonged bouts of weeping, which drove Caesar crazy, and Zina too, but Zina controlled her annoyance and tried to ignore her sister's tears or calm her down, mainly so that she could go on telling her own stories about Erwin and her life with him, and although all that really remained to her of this life was a handful of happy memories as opposed to a great deal of pain and humiliation she refused to resign herself to this sad fact and her stories were a mixture of wishes and fantasies and plain lies combined with a few real facts, and after she had repeated them innumerable times she couldn't have separated the facts from the fantasies even if she had wanted to, because in the end everything merged in her mind into one reality which was the only one she acknowledged and of whose truth she had no doubt, and thus, in the wake of her own stories, she believed that for years after Erwin had stopped going to bed with Chemda she had refused to let him go and clung to him by means of emotional blackmail and pleading and threats, and he had never loved her, just as he had never loved his first wife, Elisheva, who had forced her to marry him by saying she was pregnant, and he had gone to bed with her only a few times, and unwillingly at that, and if only she could have she would have obliterated the physical relations between them completely, but the existence of their daughter Ruhama was a fact which could not be ignored, and she also believed, or at any rate she was close to believing, that Erwin had called her when he felt that he was dying, for the fact that she had not been there gave her no peace and she was prepared to go to any lengths to deny it, and she believed that she had hurried to him—fortunately she had come home just in time—and tried to help him, but all in vain, and he had died in her arms.

When Caesar came into the living room, which seemed to have grown bigger and emptier and more formal since the deaths of Erwin and Besh, he found Zina and Yaffa sitting and drinking coffee and Zina, who was distracted by his appearance, greeted him with her usual shriek of joy, while Yaffa greeted him with a brief nod, which in itself was enough to arouse his anger, but he replied with a cordial "Good evening" and exchanged a few words with her and with his mother, who did not try to make him change his mind when he refused to sit down with them and have a cup of coffee because she was in the middle of talking and impatient for him to be gone, and he went to call Tehilla on a momentary impulse to talk to her and tell her that he was on his way home, but he regretted it before he had finished dialing the number and called the studio instead, and when there was no reply he called Goldman and asked him if he wanted to go to a movie. Goldman hesitated for a moment, for by now movies had ceased to hold any interest for him, as had all other forms of entertainment, but in the end he gave in and said, "OK, let's go," and Caesar said, "I'll come and pick you up in a few minutes," and then he started calling Tehilla again and once more he stopped before he had finished dialing her number and put the phone down and said goodbye to Yaffa and to Zina, who asked him how the children were, and Caesar said, "Fine," and went out of the front door and got into his car and went to fetch Goldman, who closed the *Somnium,* which a friend had obtained for him in an English translation and which for two weeks now he had been busy translating into Hebrew, and put on his coat and went down to the lobby to wait for Caesar.

They went to see a movie with Marcello Mastroianni, but not long after it began Caesar got up and said that he was tired, and without another word he left the theater and drove home, where Tehilla had been waiting for him with his supper for over an hour, but she did not complain about his lateness. Caesar washed his hands and sat down at the table without giving her an affectionate look or word, and although she needed some sign of affection from him desperately now that she had discovered how slim her chances of becoming pregnant were after the abortion she did not say anything to him because she did not want to burden him pointlessly with something which she regarded as her own affair, and she made up her mind that if she did become pregnant she would have the baby, even if it meant a separation from Caesar, since she knew that he did not want another child, at any rate not now, but she was ready to take all the responsibility on herself and even before their marriage she said as much to Caesar, who slowly softened toward her and said, "It's quite cold outside," and after she gave him his omelet he asked her how she was and Tehilla said, "I'm all right, just a little tired," and Caesar said, "I went to the movies with Goldman but I left in the middle of the film. I couldn't concentrate," and for the first time since coming in he looked at her without hostility, and Goldman went on sitting in the theater and looking at the screen, but without taking anything in because the film aroused no interest in him and because his mind was on Elinore, who had arrived in the country ten days before with Manfred and with her brother Raphael, who was a doctor of physics, for a three-week visit, and after spending a week in Haifa with Manfred's brother they had come to spend a week in Tel Aviv, and the day after arriving in town Manfred had paid a visit to Stefana, faultlessly dressed as usual but showing unmistakable signs of old age: His face, which was less open and more skeptical than ever, had grown very haggard and his skin was flabby and faded, there were bags under his eyes and veins standing out on his temples; even his hands and fingers, which were still so sensitive, had grown old and had brown spots on them, and he sat on the sofa opposite Stefana, who was sitting on the heavy armchair as usual, and drank his tea and spoke without raising his voice and with very long pauses between his words, occasionally wiping away the delicate layer of perspiration covering his brow with his handkerchief, the room was too hot for comfort, or passing his hand over his mouth in his characteristic gesture, and Stefana looked at him and listened in silence, nodding slightly from time to time as a sign of life or lowering her eyes. There was a feeling of estrangement between them, and especially one of ending, since Goldman's father's death had all at once put an end to the exaggerated hopes and boundless expectations which for so many years had sustained them both and given content and meaning to their lives, only neither of them found the courage to express this in so many words, although they both knew they had nothing more to hope for and their love affair was over, and Manfred spoke of the cold and rainy autumn in Europe that year and said something about his work, and after a short pause for reflection he mentioned a conversation he had had during a train journey with a certain priest about the possibilities of religious development and the role which religion was capable of performing in the world today. He spoke quietly and his voice merged with the sound of the rain falling incessantly outside the window, and as usual there was something skeptical and unassuming, although not self-effacing, in his tone, and this time there was also a note of relinquishment, as if he had gone very far away, and afterward he repeated something he had read in a Catholic journal which said that now perhaps more than ever it was the vocation of the Jews to be dispersed among the nations in order to maintain the unity of the world, and this vocation was in accordance with the nature of Judaism, whose mode of existence was not territorial but historical, in other words not in space but in time, and without trying to make any connections he said something about the danger of mass regimes which were an expression not.only of what was most irrational but also of what was most opportunistic and irresponsible in man, and afterward he mentioned America and said that lately he had felt a desire to visit there, and as he spoke he felt that the time for this meeting was already past and he began to feel a great sense of relief because in a few moments they would part and everything would be over, and suddenly he was overcome by a feeling of discomfort, and also shame, and he fell silent for a minute and then he offered to marry Stefana, and she looked at him, at his lean and ugly face, and without any hesitation or the least hint of irony she said in Polish, "Thank you, Manfred, but I don't think we should be in too much of a hurry. Let's give ourselves time to think it over," and by so saying she deliberately snapped the last threads, however tenuous, which still connected her to life and this world and the future, and from now on, in the absence of any expectations or obligations, she was as free as a bird in possession of the worlds of eternity, and Manfred said, "I think you're making a mistake," but he didn't say it with any conviction, and afterward he said, "As you wish," and went on sitting a few more minutes in silence, as if he were thinking about something, and Stefana said, "It's going to rain all night," and after a short pause she asked him how his wife was, which she had never done before, and Manfred said, "All right. She likes the winter, although she suffers from it a little," and Stefana asked him if he wanted another cup of tea, but in spite of her question it was clear that she wanted him to bring his visit to an end and go, and Manfred, who wanted the same thing, said, "No thank you, I think it's getting late," and he rose and said goodbye to her, but in the same way as he always did, as if he would be coming back tomorrow or the next day, and before he left the house, with Stefana's permission, he knocked carefully on the door of Goldman's room, where Goldman was busy translating the *Somnium,* and went in to say goodbye to him too—he did everything quietly and as a matter of routine—and they exchanged a few words about the *Somnium* and about astronomy, and Manfred remarked that in his opinion it was necessary to acknowledge the existence of a meaningful cosmic order to make it possible to maintain the world and civilization and for it to be possible to understand happiness, and also the opposite of happiness, and to strive for it and seek it and, in short, to make it possible to sustain life as something more than a combination of vegetative processes, although he himself had unfortunately never succeeded in getting any further than the acknowledgment of this necessity, which was a consequence of rationalism, or rationalism which admitted its limitations, and as he said these things, standing facing Goldman in the doorway, he smiled with the hint of a twinkle in his eye and blushed, and a moment later he grew grave and said that he did not believe in the absolute autonomy of man who created himself or a world which created itself, and that the denial of the existence of God could be understood only in conjunction with the affirmation of the unrestrained rule of instinct, without any values, and after a short pause he added, "And we've already seen where that leads," and Goldman said, "Yes, maybe you're right," and Manfred, who realized the inconsistency of his views, said that this belief too stemmed, as far as he was concerned, from logic and experience of the world and had never transcended the bounds of a "faith due to necessity," if he could put it that way, and he passed his hand over his mouth and said that he had come to the conclusion that a rational morality was impossible and that the achievements of reason were mainly in the area of destruction, including its own self-destruction, of course, by the admission of its own limitations, and that this was its strength, but in the area of construction reason had not achieved much, because in the last analysis life was a purposeless chaos and therefore in order to build anything you needed something which transcended pure reason, and although it was hard for him to accept this it was apparently the truth, but at the same time he did not negate the value of reason, since he had great respect for the destructive element, with all its danger of nihilism, because it contained within itself the utopian hope of understanding and reform, and Goldman, who listened attentively but at the same time longed to ask him about Elinore, said that all this destroyed the basis for any kind of certainty, and Manfred nodded his head and said calmly and unprovocatively that there was no certainty, nor was there any need for certainty in order to live, and Goldman, who had lost all his old embarrassment in Manfred's presence, said, "That's frightening. I, at any rate, need it very much," and he accompanied Manfred to the front door, and only then, when he was about to leave, did he ask him about Elinore, and Manfred said, "She's hardly changed at all," and they shook hands and Manfred invited him to come and see them at the hotel where they were staying and he said that Elinore and Raphael would be very glad to see him, and Goldman thanked him for the invitation and promised that he would come, and he intended to go, but something stopped him, and while he was vacillating and trying to distract himself from thoughts of Elinore and at the same time resolving to go and see them the very next day, or the day after that, come what may, the time passed and they left the country and never came back again, except for Manfred, who during the following years came a few times to pay short visits to his brother, and Goldman, who with increasing disquiet saw the approaching end, slowly turned to stone inside, as if an infinite calm had descended on him and nothing disturbed him any more, and he withdrew into himself and continued working on his translation of the *Somnium,* which without his admitting it began to give rise in him to a feeling of uneasiness, and from day to day he lost interest in it, and in cosmology in general, which began to oppress him more and more, although he still went on devoting all his spare time to it—but all this came later, and as he sat and watched the movie by himself he was still interested in the *Somnium* and cosmology, and of course in Elinore, and he thought about her as he had thought about her almost ceaselessly ever since hearing that she was in the country, and he tried to remember what she looked like and imagine their meeting, but however hard he tried to behave naturally and easily in his imagination the meeting remained cold and forced, and he wondered if he shouldn't go and see her right away, even before the end of the movie—the hotel where they were staying was quite close to the theater—and he continued wondering after the film was over and he rose and put on his coat and went out into the street, where a strong wind was blowing and whirling branches and leaves and pieces of paper and sand about, and he wandered aimlessly around in the winter wind and found himself standing in front of Dita's apartment and he raised his eyes and saw the light in the kitchen window and for a moment he thought of going up to see her (he already knew that he would never go to visit Elinore), but he did not do so and he went on walking through the streets, and afterward he went home and sat down to work on the *Somnium* but he couldn't make any progress because he was tired and unable to concentrate, and in the end he stopped working and looked at the papers piled up in front of him, and listened to the wind raging outside the window, and afterward he glanced at the picture of his sister and brooded about what Manfred had said, and the next day Caesar called him at the office to apologize for leaving in the middle of the movie and Goldman said, "Nonsense, it's perfectly all right," and Caesar apologized again and asked if he could come over that evening for a short visit and Goldman said, "Of course, whenever you like. I'll be home," and Caesar said, "See you later, then," but he didn't go to visit Goldman that evening because when he went up to see his son on the way to Goldman's place he found him in bed with a high temperature and Tirza told him that he had to be taken to the hospital the following morning and Caesar stayed with the child until late that night, and he tried to amuse him and read him a story, although most of the time he kept quiet, and the next morning he took him to the hospital, and then he took Tirza home, and after that he called the studio and asked Israel to have lunch with him and Israel said, "OK. Call me from downstairs"—something in Caesar's voice made it impossible for him to refuse—and about an hour later Caesar came and took him to a restaurant outside the town for lunch.

It was a cold, clear winter's day, the sky was blue and clean and the sun shone as if it were summer, and when they got out of the car the cold wind ruffled Caesar's thinning hair and he held it down with his hand and cursed Jochem's Hormoon and all the other treatments and ointments which up to now had not saved a single hair on his head, and he went on cursing them, and also the weather, until they entered the restaurant and sat down, and the proprietor, who was wearing white shoes and white pants and a black lace shirt and had a dark red silk kerchief tied around his neck, approached them and greeted them with a slight bow and asked them what they wanted to eat, he was tanned as brown as a crust and had a thin mustache and a melting smile, and they ordered eggplant salad with nuts and stuffed eggplant with mushroom sauce and a bottle of wine, and the proprietor disappeared into the kitchen—in the meantime Caesar broke bits off the little rolls in the basket on the table and ate them—and a few minutes later the man came back and set their orders and the bottle of wine before them with a flourish, and Caesar began eating and drinking and as he did so he spoke about a client for whom he had prepared a series of photographs and abused him, and afterward he spoke about his parents: about his father, who all his life long had thought only about himself, and about his pathetic and irritating mother; he spoke about them contemptuously and obscenely, and about Max Spillman and Ruhama too he spoke with contempt, and the only one he had a good word for was Besh, and afterward he spoke about all kinds of women, married and unmarried, with whom he had gone to bed, and he burst out laughing and said they were a pack of whores and it was a good thing they were whores, and the proprietor came up to see if everything was all right, and Caesar said "Everything's quite all right," and afterward he spoke about Eliezra, who was going to have a baby in a few months' time, and he said that maybe the baby was his, and he burst out laughing again and broke off a piece of roll and said, "In any case I fucked her more than that engineer of hers will fuck her in the rest of her life," and afterward he said, "Don't worry. I'll get Tehilla pregnant, I'll show her, that bitch," and then he fell silent for a moment and drank a little wine and in a reflective and far from happy tone he said that you should never despair because nothing in life was the end and everything always turned out all right, and the proprietor came and took away the empty dishes and Caesar praised the eggplant and he and Israel ordered their second course, and Caesar ordered another bottle of wine, and when the man went away he looked after him and said, "Look how sunburnt he is in the middle of winter. I envy him. He's got no problems," and afterward he said that he would like to eat in restaurants for the rest of his life, only never the same one; he would like to go from one restaurant to the other just as he would like to go from one woman to the other, and he laughed, and Israel said, "Yes, that's right," and he drew up the plate that the proprietor had set before him, and Caesar filled his wine glass and praised Besh again and said, "What a shame he's gone. I'd give a lot to have him here now," and after a short silence he said, "The truth is that I'm sick and tired of all this crap," but he didn't explain what crap he meant and Israel didn't ask him, and Caesar took a sip of wine and looked at Israel and said, "It's all just words. You can never really know anything," and he grabbed the joint of chicken lying on his plate in both hands and tore off a piece of flesh with his teeth and started chewing it, and Israel saw his face changing, clouding over and coming apart, and he wanted to do something to stop it, but he did nothing and went on looking at Caesar, who went on eating fiercely and suddenly said, "Today I took my boy to the hospital. He's got leukemia," and the tears started streaming out of his eyes and they flowed slowly down his big face because he didn't try to stop them and they slid into his mouth and fell onto the plate and onto his hands and onto the chicken, which he bit into again and again, and he went on chewing, and repeated, "I took him to the hospital today. He's got leukemia," and Israel, who felt that he had to do something, said nothing, but he held the glass of wine out to Caesar and Caesar took another gulp and went on eating and crying, and gradually his tears subsided and he wiped his face with the table napkin, and they finished eating in silence, and Caesar paid the proprietor, who asked them to come again and saw them to the door, and as they were going to the car a group of people who looked like tourists came toward them, and Caesar stopped and stared at a woman with a big body and a broad face and gray hair and when she had passed them he said, "Grandma Clara—to a T," and afterward they got into the car and drove off without exchanging a word, but when they stopped at a traffic light Caesar, who was sitting withdrawn and sunk in thought, turned to Israel and said that he simply could not understand how a healthy body could suddenly become sick and how no power on earth could arrest the disease or cure it, and he hit the steering wheel furiously with his fist and said, "God damn it, that's what's killing me," and he started moving and cursed a driver who overtook him, and afterward, when they had passed the intersection, he hit the steering wheel again and said, "It's impossible. It can't happen. And if it does, then everything's a load of shit," and he fell silent and did not utter another word until he let Israel off at the studio, and Israel, who during the entire drive had sat with an expressionless face and who wanted more than anything to be alone and play the piano or lie down on the couch, put his hand on Caesar's shoulder and said, "I'll see you soon, Caesar. I'll call you," and he went upstairs, but the cold empty rooms oppressed him as they had never oppressed him before and made him feel terribly lonely, and he stood in the doorway for a moment and thought about Caesar, he was sorry that he had not offered to go on driving with him, and he looked at the piano and at the greenish-colored postcard and the table and the brown couch and the old reading lamp on the chair and the big wooden board with the picture of the old couple sitting on their little stools in front of their shop in the twilight calm. He had seen Caesar's son about twice in his life and that was a long time ago and he could on no account remember what he looked like, and he turned around and went downstairs and walked in the streets, he knew that he had seen the boy but that was all, and in the end he went up to visit Goldman, who was sitting and working on his translation in the growing darkness of his room.

It was already after five o'clock, and he welcomed Israel gladly because he was happy to put the *Somnium* aside and happy to have somebody to talk to, never mind about what: his problems and his plans and various cosmological questions and his translation and Caesar and women and something he had read in the newspaper and his sister Naomi, for whom his longings had increased ever since Uncle Lazar's death, and he missed her more than he missed anyone else and the sense of her absence made him restless and angry, since more than ever he refused to accept the fact that life was only lived once and death was final and however much he longed for her he would never see her again, not even for a single hour, and besides her death seemed to him somehow unjust and he began investigating her life and her love and the circumstances of her death—all they knew was that she had fallen from the open door of a car in motion—but his investigations had not yet produced any results because the person who was driving the car had been living in Brazil for three years now on some kind of government job, and Goldman hoped that when he returned he would be able to get some new and significant facts out of him, and as for the period of her service in the British army and her love affair with the Englishman, on which Goldman's father blamed her death, here too he made no progress because some of the people who had served with her and whom Goldman had succeeded in tracing had moved away and others remembered no more than her name and a few other unimportant details and there was only one man, whom Goldman met about two weeks later at Tzalik's wedding, who had met her a few times in Alexandria, where he was serving in a transport unit

and had apparently also tried to flirt with her, who had anything
to tell him, which was that she was in love with a British officer
in the tank corps or in the artillery called Aitcheson or Atkinson,
who was rumored to be a married man with two children, and
who had a big dog that accompanied him wherever he went, a
very frightening dog, and he had once seen them sailing on a
boat on the Nile in Cairo with this frightening dog, and these
were the only new facts which Goldman managed to discover in
the mist surrounding his sister's life, but in the meantime all he
had were a few old facts and a few old photographs, among them
the one which somebody, apparently his father, had torn in half,
in the remaining half of which she was standing in her army
uniform on some bridge or other with her head a little to one
side, and later on Goldman guessed that the missing half had
shown the British officer called Aitcheson or Atkinson, a little of
whose one shoulder could perhaps be discerned in the remaining half, which he now held out to Israel together with some
other photographs of Naomi, and Israel glanced through them
without any particular interest and gave them back to Goldman,
who hadn't been sleeping but was very alert, and he put them
back in the desk drawer and afterward he told Israel something
about the *Somnium* and the problems he was encountering in
its translation, and about Kepler's "family horoscope," and he said
that he himself would like to have his horoscope cast, although
he didn't believe in it, and in the meantime he had decided to
pay a visit to a certain palm reader, although he was skeptical
about this too, in order to obtain some assistance in clarifying his
situation and choosing a new profession—his present profession
had been one big mistake from the beginning, and even if it
hadn't he had reached the end of his rope at the office—and
maybe she would also be able to tell him something about his
future, and indeed, a few weeks later, after Manfred and Elinore
had already left the country, Goldman contacted this palm reader
and made an appointment, but a few days before it was to take
place he committed suicide and so the meeting never occurred.

At this time, however, he was still enthusiastic about the possibility, despite his doubts, and he enlarged upon it to Israel, who sat listening to him calmly and at the same time looked at his face and saw how eroded it had become lately and how deeply lined, as if something were corroding it from within, and about an hour later he stood up and said goodbye to Goldman and went back to the studio and wrapped himself in a blanket and sat down unwillingly at the piano and started playing with cold fingers, and Goldman lay on his bed and abandoned himself to his thoughts until the darkness in the room was almost complete, except for a little light from the living room filtering through the gap underneath the door, and the bookcase and armchair and standard lamp were no more than dim shapes barely discernible in the darkness, and then he rose and switched on the light and sat down at his desk and resumed his interrupted translation.

The next day Goldman and Stefana received an invitation from Jeremiah and Temima to their son Tzalik's wedding, which had been postponed because of Zipporah's illness and which now that she had been released from the hospital was to take place in two weeks' time, and Goldman gave the invitation to Stefana, who ignored it completely, and Goldman, who was not inclined to attend this wedding either, put the invitation away in the kitchen cupboard, but the day before the wedding he received a telephone call from Bracha, who asked him to come, if only for the sake of his father, and she also delicately suggested that he try to bring Stefana along, if only in honor of Zipporah, and Goldman, who couldn't say no, promised that he at any rate would come, and on the evening of the wedding he got dressed and took the bus to the modest reception hall, where quite a large number of people were already assembled, although there was still a long time to go before the ceremony, and Goldman, early as usual because of his wish to be punctual, was embarrassed, and he stopped just outside the door and thought of going away and coming back later, and cast his eyes over the guests, most of whom were strangers to him, and saw Moishe Tzellermaier and his wife and David Kostomolski and Jonah Kotchinski, who was beginning to shrink and shrivel with loneliness and old age, and Shmuel and Bracha, all dressed up and beaming with happiness, who were accompanied by Uri and his wife—Illana and her husband and children were coming later, and Avraham Shechter with Rachel, and a few other friends and relations and a number of his cousins and their children, some of whom he had not seen for years because they had not even come to Uncle Lazar's or his father's funerals—and while he was standing there he saw Joel, who had aged very greatly in recent months, and it seemed to him that Joel had seen him too, and it was too late for him to beat a retreat and he made his way through the people milling about him and shook Joel's hand and wished him "Mazel tov," and afterward he went over to Jeremiah and Temima and congratulated them and Meir and his wife, who were standing nearby, and exchanged a few words with them, and then he congratulated the bride and groom, whom he hadn't seen more than two or three times in his life, and that was a very long time ago, and if he hadn't known who the groom was he would never have recognized him, and then he shook hands with Avraham Shechter and Rachel, who despite her age was still pretty and feminine-looking, especially her smooth, tanned skin, and who ever since Akiva Weiner's death had been living with Avraham Shechter, who had been waiting for her for so many years, and leading the peaceful life of a couple in the twilight of their years, sometimes going to a movie or the theater and sometimes playing rummy for the money which they kept in an empty jam jar for this purpose, and Rachel asked Goldman how he was and how Stefana was, and he said, "All right," and Rachel said, "None of us are getting any younger," and before Goldman could say anything else, Shmuel and Bracha came up and shook hands with him, and they exchanged a few words, and afterward he shook hands with all kinds of relatives and aquaintances, who smiled broadly at him, and with cousins and their children, many of whom were already married with children of their own, and in the middle of all this he saw Aviezer, who came in and stood next to Joel and Ruth, wearing a pale blue sweater and dark blue pants, astonishingly handsome with his gray curls and his sad, closed face, and Goldman wanted to go up to him and shake hands with him and talk to him for a while, but at that moment there was a stir in the crowd and Zipporah appeared in the doorway to the hall. She was sitting in a wheelchair and Esther pushed her slowly among the guests, who came up to her one after the other and respectfully, admiringly, and also affectionately shook her hand and kissed her cheek and exchanged a few words with her, and Goldman remained standing where he was and he looked at her and saw her approaching him in her wheelchair—a small, erect woman in a dark woolen dress, with one foot shod in a white canvas shoe peeping out from under it, her short, curly gray hair tied in a black ribbon and her little face, as rosy and wrinkled as an old apple, shining with an intelligence and authority which were nothing but the expression of her own integrity and her confident and tireless affirmation of life with all its difficulties and suffering.

Goldman did not take his eyes off her and the closer she came toward him the more tense he grew, and then, when she was already very close, he took a few steps toward her and held out his hand and kissed her and she smiled at him and asked him how he was and how Stefana was, and then she said, "You have to go on and you have to forget. Look at me, I've already forgotten that I ever had another leg," and she smiled again and turned away from him to the other people who were clustering around and waiting to congratulate her, and Goldman, who was left standing alone, went on looking after her, but with a feeling of relief, and then he felt a light tap on his shoulder and when he turned around he saw a man smiling at him and holding out his hand and saying, "Shalom," and he tried to remember who he was and suddenly, as he stared at him and tried to remember, he called out "Avraham," and shook his hand again, but this time firmly and confidently, and they embraced and slapped each other on the shoulder and poured themselves glasses of wine and clinked their glasses and drank, and in the meantime the ceremony began and the noise in the hall died down and they stood on the outer edge of the circle crowding around the bridal canopy, a little apart from the others, and Goldman, who was still holding the wine glass in his hand, looked at Avraham out of the corner of his eye and saw how time had marked and changed him: He was completely bald and looked taller and thinner than before; his arms seemed too long for his body and his face, which looked as if it were made of paper, had also grown longer, and it was this which made his ears and mouth look so big, and as if they didn't belong to his face, but nevertheless it was Avraham, the son of Aharon, Shmuel's brother, who had been in the same class with him and with Avinoam Leviatan in school, and for a few years they had even been friends—he always had money in his pocket and he would buy them ice cream and treat them to the movies— but the War of Independence had separated them and as soon as it was over Avraham had gone to France to study economics, because his father wanted him to study abroad, and after he had completed his studies he had gone into business and become a consultant to a big stock company, and after that he had opened a big jewelry shop in Nice, where he lived alone in a luxurious five-room apartment, and now he had come home on a visit, mainly in order to see his mother, who was sick, and when the ceremony was over and the band began to play and the guests descended on the meat and fish and salads set out in large platters on the long table standing in the middle of the hall, Goldman and Avraham sat down together in a corner of the hall to talk, still beaming with the happiness of their meeting, but it soon became clear to Goldman that apart from a few unimportant memories which they had in common there was a gulf of strange-ness gaping between them, and the truth was that he had no interest at all in Avraham, who spoke about his parents and his dog and his business affairs in excruciatingly boring detail, which only emphasized the disagreeable sense of barrenness aroused by his appearance and his gestures and his elegant and spotless attire and manicured nails and perfumed smell; there was something miserly and oppressively lacking in feeling about him, as if everything inside him had withered up or shrunk, and he did not show any real interest in their boyhood memories or in the country, and his questions about Avinoam and Sonia and references to the landmarks of their youth were perfunctory, and Goldman, who was surprised to discover how little all these things interested him too, not even Avinoam and Sonia, promised him that he would take him for a walk the next day and that they would visit their old haunts together, but apart from the ritual purification building in the old Moslem cemetery and their old school and the workers' housing development and a few other places, which now seemed totally lacking in charm, and even pathetic, not a single building which Avraham had mentioned was still standing, since they had been destroyed during the course of the years and new buildings had gone up where they had once stood, and this was also the fate of the empty lots and gardens and parks and little woods and virgin fields where once, not so very many years ago, they had played their games and gone for walks, and which had now disappeared and given way to streets lined with apartment complexes and offices and commercial and industrial areas, and when they had completed their tour Avraham invited Goldman to have lunch with him, but Goldman said that he had to go back to his office to meet a client on a matter of urgency, and suggested that they contact each other toward the end of the week to arrange to go to the moshav on Saturday to visit Avinoam, but this plan too did not materialize because Goldman, who had already grown very detached and remote, did not contact Avraham or answer any telephone calls, including the ones from Avraham, who stayed in the country for about a month longer, during which his parents and his sister and Moishe Tzellermaier and all kinds of relations tried to fix him up with a wife, but all in vain, since he had grown used to his bachelorhood and solitary way of life and did not want to upset his arrangements and adjust himself to the wishes and habits of a stranger, and as far as he was concerned everyone was a stranger, just as he did not want to share his money with anyone else, and while they were sitting in the corner of the reception hall and dragging out their conversation Aharon approached them dressed in a dark suit, his clean-shaven face beaming with happiness, and he shook Goldman's hand with demonstrative warmth and said, "So you've met at last," and put his hand on Avraham's shoulder, and Avraham sat stiffly in his place trying to conquer his embarrassment and Goldman said, "Yes. It's been a long time," and Aharon patted Avraham's shoulder affectionately—he was proud of him and proud of his friendship with Goldman—and said, "Nu, so how are the two of you enjoying yourselves?" and Goldman said, "Very much," and Avraham, who was waiting for his father to take his hand off his shoulder, said, "Fine, everything's fine," and Aharon said, "This one will never get married. He won't give his parents the joy of grandchildren," and he laughed, and then he said, "Enjoy, enjoy," and patted Avraham on the shoulder again and joined one of the other guests and moved off with him and after a short, embarrassed pause they resumed their conversation, and in the meantime people started dancing, and Goldman, who was waiting for the moment when he could get up and go, jumped at this opportunity, and after arranging to meet Avraham the next day he slipped away without saying goodbye to anybody and walked toward the door, but just as he was about to leave he was accosted by a man a few years older than himself who begged his pardon and then asked if he was by any chance Naomi Goldman's brother, and Goldman said, "Yes, I'm her brother," and the man, who said that his name was Yizhak, told him that the moment he had set eyes on him he had felt that he must be her brother, because he knew that Naomi had had a brother and that her family was related to the family of the groom, and because of a certain resemblance he had detected between them, and Goldman asked the man where he had met her, and he said, "I knew her in the British army, in Alexandria," and he examined Goldman again and said, "You look like her, the way I remember her, but I can't really say why. Maybe it's something in your face. In any case I'm glad to have met you," and he was about to take his leave but Goldman detained him and asked him about his sister, and the man, who tried at first to evade his questions, although not rudely, told him in the end that he had met Naomi a few times in Alexandria, where he had been serving in a transport unit, and that he had liked her a lot, and maybe she had liked him too, once they had even gone dancing together and danced the whole night long, but nothing had come of it because Naomi was in love with an officer in the British tank corps or artillery called Aitcheson, or Atkinson, who was rumored to be a married man with two children, and who had a big dog that went everywhere with him, a very frightening dog, and once he had seen the two of them together in Cairo with this frightening dog sailing in a boat on the Nile, and that was all that he could tell him about her, and Goldman, who had hoped for more and went on questioning him without success, thanked him and shook his hand and went outside.

It was a beautiful winter's evening: The gray sky was pure and full of stars and the air was fresh and cool, and Goldman felt a great sense of relief which grew stronger the farther he walked from the hall and turned into a feeling of freedom which filled him with exultation and joy spreading through his body until he felt a desire to run down the street and dissolve in this pleasant air, whose very touch made him glad, as did the sight of the sky and the empty streets, whose strangeness or familiarity awoke no sensation of oppression or happiness in him, because he felt as if he were no longer connected to them, just as he was no longer connected to the people he had left behind him in the wedding hall, or to anyone else, perhaps only to the memory of his sister Naomi, and this was a tie which filled him with warmth and joy, and he thought especially of the farewell dinner they had given for her when she left home and went to join the army; he remembered every detail as if it had happened only the day before, exactly where everyone had sat around the table and the clothes they had worn and the china and the food and the taste of the food and the expressions on their faces and the shade of the light in the room, and he smiled to himself, or perhaps he only felt as if he were smiling, and for a moment it occurred to him to go to the Twenty-Nine and have something to drink, but he felt too happy for this, and so he went on walking through the streets and afterward he went home.

Stefana was sitting in her armchair in the living room and watching television, very calm and concentrating, and Goldman, who went in ostensibly to take the newspaper, but really to see Stefana, looked at her and suddenly she seemed to him beautiful even in her dereliction, and he stood there behind her, a little to one side, and he went on looking at her and the longer he looked the more she seemed to resemble his sister, and for a split second he had the feeling that she really was his sister, and he felt such a deep affection for her and it made him so happy that he wanted to embrace her and to be enveloped in her at one and the same time, but he didn't stir from his place and went on looking at her for a moment longer, and at the same time the thought crossed his mind that if she died everything would be over and life would become an empty movement, without meaning or purpose, and the world would become an accidental collection of houses and mountains and oceans and streets and people and cars and food, but of course she couldn't go on living forever, and he stirred himself and went into his room and threw the newspaper onto his bed and opened the window to let the fresh night air come into the room and fill it and sat down to translate the *Somnium,* and while he was reading the text and paging through the dictionary to look for a word his thoughts turned again in passing to his conversation with Manfred and to cosmology, which more and more, for some time now, had been filling him with a feeling of the nothingness and meaninglessness of the universe in the light of the infinite finiteness and the complete neutrality of time and of space, two facts which Goldman had at first accepted willingly and unquestioningly as part of the scientific approach, but which had gradually begun to undermine his soul, it was no longer even a question of certainty versus uncertainty, and thus he was obliged in the end to accept the fact that despite the existence of Stefana, so calm and childlike, together with Naomi his last remaining island of refuge, life was chaos, and he himself was lost, and he had to consent to being lost in order to be saved, but of this he was incapable, only now for the first time he was free of everything and Manfred's words and the problems of cosmology and the chaos of the world did not trouble him for more than a few moments, and he went on translating until dawn, and then he lay down on his bed and closed his eyes—he couldn't actually fall asleep—and felt a pleasant freshness and purity in his body, and an hour later he rose and had a cup of coffee and resumed his translation and he went on working on it for the next three days too, and with the same exhilaration and joyful feeling of freedom, bordering on a sensation of the dissolution of existence, which he had experienced that night, and these feelings accompanied him all the time, even during the boring hours he spent with Avraham, together with a sense of great closeness to Stefana, the question of whose existence or extinction had ceased to preoccupy him, and also toward the whole world, from which he was now about to depart. Besides working on the *Somnium* he spent a lot of time wandering about the streets, especially at night; he felt no need to sleep but on the contrary, the lack of sleep made him drunk with wakefulness, and at the same time he avoided meeting anyone he knew—even before this he had stopped swimming in the sea and abandoned the "Bullworker" and stopped answering the phone, and he didn't get in touch with anyone, not even Caesar or Israel, who came on the evening of the fourth day to see what had happened to him and found him lying dead on the bed in his room with an empty bottle of sleeping pills and an empty bottle of brandy beside him.

Israel went to call one of the neighbors and fetch a doctor and they told Stefana, who received the news without asking or saying anything. Something crossed her face for a moment which might have been interpreted as an expression of pain, but also as an expression of grief, and not at the deed itself, for the truth was that Stefana was a dead tree putting forth new blossoms, but it was an imaginary blossoming somewhere in another world, after life in this world, which had been an endless chain of errors and useless and pointless acts of submission, had drained her of every drop of vitality and capacity for compassion, and even if it hadn't it is doubtful whether she would have seen any need for grief, since for her, as for Goldman, it was by not doing rather than by doing that they were undone, and as a final expression of his will to live he had chosen death while she had chosen Poland, and like Goldman she no longer belonged to anyone and no one belonged to her, but that night she lay in bed for hours with her eyes open, and when Yehudit Maizler, who spent the night with her, offered her a sleeping pill she said, "No thank you, I don't need one," and she went on lying awake and open-eyed until morning.

The funeral took place two days later, and with the same resignation or indifference with which she had received the news of Goldman's death Stefana walked in his funeral procession, which included relatives and neighbors and acquaintances and a few of Goldman's friends, and they all crowded together in the courtyard of the funeral parlor and walked behind the stretcher in the mild winter sunshine, and right at the end, among those bringing up the rear, were Israel and Caesar, who had been restless and panic-stricken from the moment he heard the news, and as they walked out of the courtyard he looked distractedly at the mourners and at Israel and said, "Maybe he was right. He put an end to it and he's got nothing more to worry about," and Israel nodded, and Caesar glanced ahead and saw the bearers putting the stretcher into the black hearse and he said, "It's awful, the whole thing's awful. I want to vomit," and Israel said, "Yes," and Caesar, who did not accompany Goldman's body to the cemetery, kicked a little clod of earth and put his hands in his pockets and remained standing outside the funeral parlor until the convoy of cars set out, and then he hurried to the hospital to sit by the bedside of his son, whose condition was already beyond all hope.

After the funeral Israel went to Goldman's house and sat for a while drinking tea and eating the slice of cake offered him by Bracha, listening without interest to the listless conversation being conducted around the table by Yechiel Levankopf and Moishe Tzellermaier, whose face was yellow and lifeless, and Tzimmer's widow and Shmuel, whom Bracha had tried to dissuade from attending the funeral because of the excitement, and two or three other people who were sitting there; the atmosphere was gloomy but at the same time vapid, there was something dull and apathetic in the air, and as soon as Israel felt that he had done his duty he rose and took his leave of Stefana and of Matilda Leviatan and went home, and a few days later he returned to take the pornographic books which Goldman had borrowed from Caesar and which nobody had bothered to ask about and nobody needed any more. The apartment was empty but for Stefana and Yehudit Maizler, who were sitting and talking in the living room, and Israel, who felt out of place the moment he stepped over the threshold, was sorry he had come, but he sat down on a chair and exchanged a few words with Stefana and Yehudit Maizler, and soon afterward he rose and with Stefana's permission he went into Goldman's room, where nothing had changed and which looked as if Goldman had left it only a few minutes before and would be coming back in an hour or two: The "Bullworker" was in its usual place, and so were the weights and the old armchair and the standard lamp, the sole survivor of his marriage to the beautiful Jemimah Chernov, and the usual books and papers were lying scattered about the room, and there were books about astronomy and astrophysics and dictionaries on the desk, and also the *Somnium* and some sheets of paper covered with Goldman's unique handwriting bearing those parts of the book which he had already managed to translate, which he had frequently discussed with Israel, whom he had also told something about the contents of the work, which recounted the story of a boy called Duracotus who lived with his mother, Fiolxhilda, in Iceland.

The boy's father was a fisherman who died at the age of 150 when the child was only three. Fiolxhilda sold herbs in little bags of ramskin to the seamen and conversed with demons. At the age of fourteen the boy curiously opened one of the little bags, whereupon his mother, in a fit of temper, sold him to a seafaring captain. The captain left him on the Isle of Hveen, where for the next five years Duracotus studied the science of astronomy under Tycho de Brahe. When he returned home his repentant mother, as a treat, conjured up one of the friendly demons in whose company selected mortals might travel to the moon. The journey itself, the demon explains, is possible only during an eclipse of the moon, and must therefore be completed in four hours. The traveler is propelled by the spirits, but he is subject to the laws of physics. When the traveler reaches the moon he encounters the special conditions prevailing there. A lunar day, from sunrise to sunset, lasts approximately a fortnight, and so does a lunar night, for the moon takes a month to turn once around its axis, the same time it takes to complete a revolution around the earth. As a result it always turns the same face toward the earth, which the moon creatures call the Subvolvan half, while the other they call the Prevolvan half. Common to both halves is that their year consists of twelve days and nights, and the resulting dreadful contrasts of temperature—scorching days and freezing nights. Also common to both are the queer motions of the starry sky—the sun and planets scuttle incessantly back and forth, a result of the moon's gyrations around the earth. The worst off of the moon's inhabitants are the Prevolvans, for they never see the earth and their nights are filled with ice and raging snow storms. And the day that follows is no better, what with the burning sun and the unendurable heat. The lunar mountains are much higher than those on earth, and the plants and creatures are much bigger. These creatures for the most part resemble giant serpents, who lie in their caves or go in search of the receding waters and dive into them, all in order to find a refuge from the burning rays of the sun, for if any of them is taken unawares by the heat of the day its skin becomes hard and scorched and falls off in the evening. And yet these creatures have a strange love of basking in the sun at noon—but only close to their crevices, so that they can make a swift and safe retreat. At the end of the book the boy Duracotus is woken from his nightmare of giant reptiles and the terrible world of the moon by a sudden cloudburst—but Goldman still had a long way to go before reaching the end of his translation and he knew this only from reading on ahead.

Israel glanced through the pages which Goldman had already translated and read: "The inhabitants of Prevolva have no fixed abode: They wander in hordes from horizon to horizon in the space of a single day, following the receding waters on their long legs, longer than those of our camels, or fly on their wings, or sail in ships," and in another place he read, "Growth is rapid and life is short because all bodies grow to such enormous proportions. From growth to decay takes but a single day," and straining his eyes in the growing darkness of the room he read the following sentence: "The creatures that remain floating on the surface of the water are boiled in the midday sun and serve as nourishment for the approaching hordes of nomads," and in the end, as he was replacing the papers in the order in which he had found them, his eye fell on the passage describing the actual flight to the moon, which Goldman had translated thusly: "Worst of all is the initial shock of the acceleration, for he is flung and hurled upward as though in an explosion of gunpowder. He must therefore be prepared beforehand and dazed by the administration of narcotics. His arms and legs must be protected so that they will not be torn from his body. And then he will have to endure additional difficulties: dreadful cold and respiratory interferences. With the completion of the first part of the flight it will become easier, because on a journey of this nature the body no doubt escapes and transcends the magnetic force of the earth and enters that of the moon, which from now on gains the upper hand. At this point we set the travelers free and leave them to their own devices: They expand and contract like spiders and propel themselves forward by their own force, for, as the magnetic forces of the earth and the moon each attract the body toward themselves, the effect is as if neither of them were attracting it, so that in the end it will turn of itself toward the moon."

Outside the day had grown very dull, there was a sudden flash of lightning immediately followed by a long, loud roll of thunder, and Israel raised his eyes from the manuscript and looked out of the window at the heavy winter sky and the giant ficus tree and the bare branches of the lilac standing motionless in the deserted courtyard, and after that he tidied the pages of Goldman's manuscript, collected the pornographic books and wrapped them in a piece of newspaper, and went out of Goldman's room, which had grown very dark, as had the hallway and the living room, and once more there was a flash of lightning and a roll of thunder, and he took his leave of Stefana and Yehudit Maizler, who were sitting and talking in the dark, and as he descended the stairs he heard the sound of the rain, which suddenly came pouring down in torrents of big, crowded drops, and Israel remained standing in the entrance looking at the rain and the street, which had grown dark in the middle of the day and which was rapidly flooded with water, but his patience soon snapped and without waiting for the rain to die down he tucked the books under his coat and walked home in the pouring rain, and when he entered the lobby and went up the stairs to the studio he prayed that he would find Ella there, although he knew perfectly well that she would not be there, or Caesar, or someone who would break the silence and with whom he would be able to exchange a few words, never mind about what, but the studio, which was also dark and full of cold and dampness, was empty, and Israel put the books down in Caesar's room and removed his coat and went into the bathroom and dried his face and hair, and then he switched on the light and sat down to play the piano—outside it was still raining and it went on raining for three days and nights—although what he really wanted was to lie down on the couch and pull the blankets over his head and do nothing at all, not even read, because he was overcome by the feelings of loneliness and pointlessness which had taken root in him in the days following Goldman's death, in addition to the sense of loss which he had felt ever since Ella had left him, but he gritted his teeth and went on playing, mobilizing all the obduracy and forces of resistance at his command in order to turn his back on everything and everyone, including Caesar, who expected some attention and fellowfeeling, a sympathetic word or gesture; he didn't ask for much, preoccupied as he was with the sickness of his son, who was dying without anyone's being able to save him, and Tehilla's unexpected pregnancy, which had kept her confined to bed for the past few weeks. The doctors didn't hold out much hope for this pregnancy, but the very possibility, however faint, that Tehilla might have a child filled Caesar with panic and depressed him, not to mention the fact that it also made him furious, because it slammed the door shut and cut him off from his retreat, not that he had any idea of where to retreat to, and also because he did not on any account want children, including those he already had, although he loved them and was attached to them, and he said this frankly and repeatedly to Tehilla and also to Israel, who did not go with him even once to the hospital to visit his son, and who listened to him in silence and deliberate unconcern, and in the meantime the rain stopped and the day grew longer and milder and warmer, and one morning Israel got out of bed and went to Jerusalem to try to find work as an apprentice to an organist in one of the churches there—and thus cut himself off from Tel Aviv and his dependence on Caesar—and to turn over a new leaf in his life.

It was a beautiful day, fine and sunny, with something intoxicating and delightful in the blue air and the view from the bus window, which he contemplated serenely; he was very calm and relaxed, as if he had all the time in the world, and when he reached Jerusalem he strolled about the streets and as he was walking he suddenly caught sight of Ella among the people on the other side of the road, walking slowly with a big basket on her arm, and he quickly crossed the road and walked behind her for a little way until he caught up with her and touched her lightly on the shoulder, and she stopped and turned her head, startled, and when she saw him she let out a little cry of surprise, and her blue eyes filled with a shy happiness, which immediately died down without leaving a trace on her face, and Israel, who in the same split second saw that she was pregnant, felt something dark and confused welling up inside him and clouding his brain—the truth was that he had no idea what to do—but he controlled himself and asked her how she was and Ella said, "I'm all right," and she asked him how he was, and Israel said, "OK. As you see," and afterward there was a silence and they stood opposite each other in the mild sunshine, awkward and embarrassed, until Israel roused himself and asked her to have coffee with him and Ella agreed, although not very enthusiastically, and Israel put out his hand to take her basket, but she wouldn't let him, and they walked along the street a little way and went into a cafe and sat down at a table in the corner. Her fair hair had lost its luster and become hard and strawlike, and Israel wanted to ask her why she had suddenly run away and why she hadn't said anything to him, either at the time of her flight or in all the months that had passed since then, but he didn't ask, all he did was sip his coffee and glance from time to time at her face, which was stiff and completely unresponsive, and at the same time he struggled against a wild emotion, a savage feeling of despair and a desire to turn his back on her, and in the end, after a long silence, he asked her if she was married, and Ella shook her head, and then Israel gathered all his courage together and asked her if he were the father of the child, and Ella said nothing, and Israel asked her again, this time more aggressively and even angrily, but Ella still said nothing, as if she hadn't even heard his question, and Israel did not ask her again and he went on drinking his coffee without saying anything, and when they rose to leave he put out his hand and again offered to take her basket, but Ella refused again, and they went outside and stood in the street for a moment like two strangers, and Israel looked at her repudiating face and he knew that everything was lost, and he wondered what he should say to her, and while he was wondering Ella said, "Goodbye" and turned away, and he stood there for a moment looking after her, despairing and full of hostility, and afterward, even before she disappeared from view, he turned on his heel and walked away and he wandered for hours in the streets, which were so beautiful and so full of good and soothing sights and smells, and early in the evening, without having done anything about finding a job, he took the bus back to Tel Aviv and went home to the studio and after he had showered and changed his clothes a feeling of great peacefulness, and even happiness, descended on him, despite the loneliness yawning all around him, but the next day, in addition to the anger and the jealousy he began to be troubled by longings, as delicate as cobwebs, spreading and seeping through him, but it was she who had left him, and not only that but also she was pregnant, and he grew very gloomy and sullen and restless and played the piano for hours or wandered through the streets, or lay on the couch looking indifferently at his face reflected in the mirrors, and a month later he went back to Jerusalem, and without knowing exactly where to turn he began to look for her, first making inquiries at the university and then asking the few people he knew in the town, and the next day at about noon, tired and sweating and unshaven, he arrived at the apartment where she was staying with a girlfriend, but neither Ella nor her friend were in and Israel sat down on the steps and waited stubbornly, ignoring the passing of time and the suspicious looks of the passersby.

At about three o'clock in the afternoon the friend came home and when she saw him she gave him a startled look, and Israel introduced himself and asked her where Ella was and when she would be back, and the friend looked at him uneasily and Israel introduced himself again and pleaded with her to tell him where Ella was and when she would come home, and the friend, still hesitating, said, "She's in the hospital," and Israel said, "Has anything happened to her?" and the friend said, "Yes. She's had a son," and she opened the front door and asked him if he would like to come in and have something to drink, and Israel said, "No, thank you," and asked her which hospital Ella was in and when the visiting hours were and the friend told him, and he thanked her again and then he turned away and went down the steps and walked slowly to the hospital.

The hospital grounds were full of trees, pines and eucalyptus and cypresses, and the earth was covered with a brownish-green carpet of pungent-smelling eucalyptus leaves and pine needles, and Israel leaned against the wall and waited for the visiting hours to begin, full of a boundless calm, and even when the visiting hours began he waited a while before going inside and asking one of the nurses in the corridor for Ella, and the nurse gave him a hostile look and pointed and said, "She's over there," and Israel thanked her and walked down the corridor, which smelled of medicines and disinfectant and oil paint, until he reached a big hall full of white beds standing in rows where the women who had given birth were lying, surrounded by husbands and parents and friends, and Israel paused at the entrance to the ward and cast his eyes back and forth over the white beds until he saw Ella, who was lying in one of the farthest beds in the row next to the wall, and he started walking toward her between the rows of white beds, and as he walked he waved his hand at her, but she did not react, and he approached her, trying to control the wave of emotion which was surging through him, especially the repentance and the longing for closeness, and when he was standing next to her bed he smiled at her and said, "Hello," but she went on lying without moving, very pale and composed, looking straight ahead of her as if there were nobody standing there, until he was afraid that she couldn't see him, and he took another step forward and waved his hand again and said, "Ella," but now too she did not react, and she went on lying there with her eyes open, as if she were sleeping or in a trance, even when he re-

peated her name again and again and touched her, and then the head nurse clapped her hands as a signal that the visiting hours were over, and the visitors parted slowly from the patients, with kisses and hugs and waves, and started leaving the room, and in the meantime the nurses came in with the babies and started giving them to their mothers so that they could feed them, but Ella ignored her baby, whose head was covered with a fine black down, and the nurse held him helplessly in her hands and pleaded with Ella gently to take him, and then she asked her again, this time impatiently, to take him and feed him like all the other mothers, but Ella went on ignoring her baby, just as she went on ignoring Israel, who remained standing stubbornly by the bed and did not take his eyes off her as they slowly filled with tears and her face grew more and more blurred until it dissolved into the whiteness of the pillows, and behind him he heard the head nurse clapping her hands again, and finally she turned to him and asked him to leave—all the other visitors had already gone—and Israel took two or three steps backward and then he turned around and walked out of the room.

Yaakov Shabtai was born in Tel Aviv in 1934. He served in the Israel Defense Force from 1952 to 1954, and was a member of Kibbutz Merhavia until 1969. During his lifetime Shabtai was acclaimed as novelist, story writer, playwright, and translator. One of the "younger generation" of Israeli writers, he was awarded the Kinor David Prize for his plays and the Bernstein Prize for *Past Continuous*.

Yaakov Shabtai died in 1981, at the age of 47.

SCHOCKEN CLASSICS

THE TRIAL

by Franz Kafka, translated from the German by Willa and Edwin Muir

The terrifying story of Joseph K., his arrest and trial, is one of the great novels of the twentieth century.

"Here we are taken to the limits of human thought. Indeed everything in this work is, in the true sense, essential. It states the problem of the absurd in its entirety."
—Albert Camus

0-8052-0848-8 paper, $6.95

THE CASTLE

by Franz Kafka, translated from the German by Willa and Edwin Muir and with an Homage by Thomas Mann

Franz Kafka's final great novel, the haunting tale of a man known only as K. and his endless struggle against an inscrutable authority to gain admittance to a castle, is often cited as Kafka's most autobiographical work.

"One of the classics of twentieth-century literature."
—New York Times

0-8052-0872-0 paper, $8.95

THE METAMORPHOSIS, THE PENAL COLONY, AND OTHER STORIES

by Franz Kafka, translated from the German by Willa and Edwin Muir

This powerful collection brings together all the stories Franz Kafka published during his lifetime, including "The Judgment," "The Metamorphosis," "In the Penal Colony," "A Country Doctor," and "A Hunger Artist."

0-8052-0849-6 paper, $7.95

THE DIARIES OF FRANZ KAFKA

Edited by Max Brod

For the first time in this country, the complete diaries of Franz Kafka are available in one volume. Covering the period from 1910 to 1923, the year before Kafka's death, they reveal the essential Kafka behind the enigmatic artist.

"It is likely that these journals will be regarded as one of [Kafka's] major literary works; in these pages, he reveals what he customarily hid from the world."
—New Yorker

0-8052-0906-6 paper, $12.95

LETTERS TO FELICE

by Franz Kafka, edited by Erich Heller and Jürgen Born, translated by James Stern and Elizabeth Duckworth

Kafka's correspondence with Felice Bauer, to whom he was twice engaged, reveals the writer's complexities as a lover and as a friend.

"The letters are indispensable for anyone seeking a more intimate knowledge of Kafka and his fragmented world."   —*Library Journal*
0-8052-0851-8 paper, $13.95

THE FAMILY CARNOVSKY

by I. J. Singer, translated from the Yiddish by Joseph Singer

This family saga traces the lives of three generations of German Jews, up to the Nazis' rise to power.

"A titanic, overwhelming novel . . . filled with life, with people of every conceivable type, with suffering, and yet with an unbreakable optimism." —Joyce Carol Oates
0-8052-0859-3 paper, $11.95

YOSHE KALB

by I. J. Singer, translated from the Yiddish by Maurice Samuel, with an introduction by Irving Howe

A brilliant, haunting novel set in the world of competing hasidic dynasties in late nineteenth-century Galicia.

"This is a powerful novel, dashing and turbulent in style, and deeply interesting in its glimpses of Jewish customs."   —*Saturday Review*
0-8052-0860-7 paper, $8.95

A SCRAP OF TIME

by Ida Fink, translated from the Polish by Madeline Levine and Francine Prose

Winner of the first Anne Frank Prize for Literature and the PEN Translation Prize, a haunting collection of stories about life in Poland at the time of the Holocaust.

"Allows us powerful imaginative passage to an unimaginably infernal world."
—*New York Times Book Review*
0-8052-0869-0 paper, $6.95